Promise to
KEEP

A Novel

Elizabeth Byler Younts

HOWARD BOOKS
AN IMPRINT OF SIMON & SCHUSTER, INC.

NEW YORK   NASHVILLE   LONDON   TORONTO   SYDNEY   NEW DELHI

Howard Books
An Imprint of Simon & Schuster, Inc.
1230 Avenue of the Americas
New York, NY 10020

First Howard Books trade paperback edition October 2015

HOWARD and colophon are trademarks of Simon & Schuster, Inc.

For information about special discounts for bulk purchases, please contact Simon & Schuster Special Sales at 1-866-506-1949 or business@simonandschuster.com.

The Simon & Schuster Speakers Bureau can bring authors to your live event. For more information or to book an event, contact the Simon & Schuster Speakers Bureau at 1-866-248-3049 or visit our website at www.simonspeakers.com.

Manufactured in the United States of America

10 9 8 7 6 5 4 3 2 1

Library of Congress Cataloging-in-Publication Data
Younts, Elizabeth Byler.
   Promise to keep : a novel / Elizabeth Byler Younts.—First Howard Books trade paperback edition.
      pages ; cm
   I. Title.
   PS3625.O983P753 2015
   813'.6—dc23
                                                                2015012010

ISBN 978-1-4767-3505-4
ISBN 978-1-4767-3506-1 (ebook)

For Mom and Dad

Esther

1946
Sunrise, Delaware

A morning rain whispered a harmony of delicate drops against the second-story bedroom window. Esther Detweiler kept her eyes closed as she lengthened her legs and arms. Even as she stretched, dampness crawled through the cracks of the old house and wrapped around her like a shawl. A gentle nudging pushed her from the warped mattress, and she swung her feet onto the floor. The cool wooden planks were smooth and comforting. When she stood, the floorboard didn't creak as it usually did. The house was perfectly still.

Her gaze landed on Daisy Garrison, the seven-year-old deaf English girl, who slept peacefully in the cot against the opposite wall in the same room. Esther had been caring for her deceased cousin's child for four years. She was drawn to touch the girl's silken cheek, but a sudden chill drew her attention away from the sleeping child.

She turned and her eyes landed on the embroidered wall hanging her mother had given her decades earlier as a *Christtag* gift. *For God alone, O my soul, wait in silence, for my hope is from Him.* It was the last Christmas gift Esther received from her mother.

She shivered and pulled on her housecoat, then tiptoed down the staircase. At the bottom was *Mammie* Orpha's bedroom. The door was cracked open. Orpha always kept her door open at night, saying it was welcoming to the heavenly beings. But something was different this morning. Was it too open? Or too quiet? She leaned a shoulder against the wall next to the door frame, her eyes squeezed shut. She should hear her *mammie*'s easy snore through the small gap, but all she heard was the warm breath of summer wrapped in the scent of freshly turned soil. She reopened her eyes.

With her fingertips splayed, she gently pushed the door. Even the usual creak was silenced. Esther stood in the doorway. In front of her, Orpha lay as still as a painting. A faint smile was cast over her lips as if she was dreaming something pleasant behind her closed eyelids. She looked happy. Losing her husband decades ago had set the stage for many losses and hardships for the past forty years. She had been like an Israelite wandering, only she never found her promised land. Maybe now, in death, she would.

Orpha's hair, though disheveled the night before when Esther had bid her good night, was now perfectly combed and smooth, her night covering tied neatly around her soft-skinned chin. She'd taken the time to comb her long hair before she'd gone to bed. It occurred to Esther that Orpha had said *good-bye* last night instead of *goodnight*. Had she somehow known that she would pass into eternity while she slept?

The quilt neatly tucked around Orpha's chest had been on her bed for decades. Esther eyed the simple pattern, rows of triangles forming squares. Together, they'd repaired many of the pattern pieces, salvaging her mother's dresses to use as patches. She and Daisy had both learned to sew on the blanket.

A breath hiccupped in her throat and her hand clapped over her quivering mouth. She hated crying. Her heart drummed like the wooden mallet threshing harvested wheat, every beat aching more than the one before. Tears warmed her face and salted her lips. She heard a low groan just before she fell on this dearest of old women, a treasure that now was an empty vessel.

Orpha had been such a humble woman. A woman to follow after. Dedicated. Loyal. A *mammie* to everyone.

Esther wept, thankful to be alone. Loss burned within her, and her heart was heaped with ashes. Too many burdens to count. She'd faced death before, but when her *mem* and *dat* passed, the innocence of youth had cushioned her grief. Losing Orpha now was worse.

~

By lunchtime, the furniture in Esther's house had been pushed aside and the rooms filled with rows of backless benches and mourners whose presence provided comfort to Esther. Daisy remained glued to Esther's side, eyes wide, rosebud lips pursed, and hands mute. Orpha had never understood the little girl's deafness, but they still had had a special relationship.

Funerals weren't foreign to Esther. Life had come at her like an unbroken horse hitched to a buggy without a driver. Her father had left for the war in 1917 and had died as a conscientious objector in prison a year later. Her mother, Leah, gave up on living and died two years after that. Since Esther was only eight, the deacons had suggested that she go live with her other younger, healthier grandparents in Geauga County, Ohio. But that might as well have been another country, and Esther had refused. She would stay with Orpha. Stubbornness came as easily to her as pretending not to be hungry.

But those years had passed. A spinster at thirty-four, she and Orpha had made a life for themselves, and bringing Daisy into it had somehow completed their unusual family. It had been hard at times, and Daisy's deafness compounded the difficulties, but having three generations in a home had given hope and some peace that Esther hadn't realized she'd lost when her cousin Irene, Daisy's mother, had passed away. Before her death she had been lost to her community and shunned for her marriage to an Englisher.

The scales had tipped again with Orpha's death, and she knew what would happen next. Eventually Daisy's father would come home from war, though they hadn't received a letter from him in over a year when he explained he would be helping with reconstruction. A melancholy shadow in the shape of Joe Garrison hovered over her. While she never wanted harm to come to him, she didn't like to think about his homecoming and taking Daisy away, especially now that Orpha was gone. Orpha's death, however, made her consider when she may lose Daisy to Joe. And be alone.

"*Dangeh*," Esther said as she shook an offered hand and attempted to refocus on her thoughts. Since there was no church service on the in-between Sunday, many people had already visited her. Esther found sympathetic, lingering, and mournful eyes as she greeted her visitors, though their tight grips tired her hands. She thanked another sober-faced, bearded man as the line of visitors finally ended. Then she stood in the doorway alone and watched as the Peterscheim family walked down the drive in a black, single-file row, like worker ants always well ordered and never idle.

Beyond the families dressed entirely in black, shades of English brightness appeared, parting the small crowd. Mrs. Norma White walked with such an air about her. As she passed, the entire Peterscheim family turned their heads and stared. The skirt of her neighbor's peach-colored dress, tightly cinched about her waist with a belt, swished around her tan stockings. A small group of girls standing on the porch leaned their heads together, whispering.

"I brought a pie," Mrs. White said as she entered the house. She looked around, never meeting Esther's eyes, as she handed over a crumb-crusted apple pie. Esther had worked for Mrs. White at the neighboring farm since she was thirteen. Mrs. White was a strong-minded woman. She'd run the farm and raised her daughters after losing her husband in a farming accident. Mrs. White was a rigid and uncompromising employer, but she'd never used her husband's death as an excuse to forsake living, the way Esther's mother had. The woman's grit had stirred Esther over the years not to give in to loss. Mrs. White hadn't depended on anyone to rescue her from her circumstances and had risen to the occasion. She had run the farm on her own for many years, when many other women would have sold it and walked away.

When Esther had started working there, she'd seen Mrs. White in overalls doing men's work. That was why she needed a housekeeper in the big farmhouse. That had been years ago, however, and although she still ran the farm, she now wore stylish dresses instead of overalls. She no longer needed to do the hard work herself, but the earlier years had taken their toll. It was rare that the woman didn't wear dainty gloves. Esther understood why when she realized that the elegant woman had the hands of a hard-working man with gnarled knuckles and rough skin. Esther then understood why there was a bottle of skin cream in every room.

"Thank you." She accepted the pie with both hands and set it down on the wooden countertop, along with the array of other goods. Esther had baked the pie herself only the previous day in Mrs. White's modern oven, which she privately coveted. She gestured toward the small table in the center of the kitchen. "There's coffee and water."

"Oh, Esther. I'm so sorry, but I can't stay. I'm already running behind." Mrs. White smiled and slowly batted her eyelashes. "I have a prayer meeting at church tonight, and you know how

I dislike tardiness. I would have been over sooner, but I had so much cleaning to do after church and dinner." Mrs. White cleared her throat. "You understand, I'm sure."

Esther inhaled as gently as possible. Making dinner for one could not have been of any consequence, and the farmhands served themselves on Sundays with food Esther had prepared ahead of time. Mrs. White wouldn't have had to do more than perhaps sweep the kitchen or run a washcloth over her newly installed laminate countertops—in *Lillypad Pearl*, as Mrs. White called it. Esther considered it just plain green.

"Please accept my condolences," Mrs. White offered as she patted Esther's arm. Though her gloved hand was warm, a chill pressed through the thin black fabric of Esther's sleeve and onto her skin. Mrs. White turned to leave, but returned a moment later. "Oh, will I see you tomorrow?"

Esther's lips pinched, and a moment later she relaxed them, not wanting her employer to see her vexed.

"We have three-day wakes and then the funeral. I'm sorry, but I won't be there until the day after the funeral."

"And must you—" the English woman began.

"I can send a cousin's wife in my place. Dorothy," Esther suggested, keeping her voice steady. "Dorothy is one of the women on the food delivery route—she could use the extra money. You will be pleased with her."

One of Norma White's thin eyebrows pushed up toward her hairline. Several moments of silence passed between the two women before the elder nodded curtly.

"Send her over in the morning, and I'll handle it from there."

Esther watched through the kitchen window as her neighbor tiptoed across the road to keep her pumps from pressing through the damp gravel. In less than a minute, Mrs. White was behind her picket-fenced, colorful existence, leaving behind Esther's plain life in shades of black and white.

As Daisy slipped around behind Esther, her left arm curled around the little girl's shoulders. She squeezed three times, their special way of saying *I love you*. She couldn't remember the last time she'd been told the same sentiment by anyone but Daisy, and the gesture was as intimate as she'd ever been with another person.

"*Sellah hooheh frau realleh meint sie sahvet,*" Lucy, Esther's aunt and Daisy's grandmother, said in a low voice.

Esther wondered how long the older woman had been standing there. She nodded in agreement that *the English woman did think very highly of herself.* But hadn't Esther herself learned to stand taller and stronger because of the high-and-mighty woman?

"Are you sure you need to work for her?" Aunt Lucy whispered candidly.

Esther sighed. "Where else can I work?" She and Aunt Lucy stepped in front of the sink and washed out water cups to put out again. "Now that most of the men are back from the war, many of the factory women are out of their jobs. I know not all of them will keep working, but either way, housekeepers are a dime a dozen right now."

"You could teach. Our school needs a good teacher. If you don't do it, then it'll probably be that silly girl Matilda Miller from the district over. She's a fright."

"I am not a teacher." Esther raised an eyebrow at her aunt.

There would never be enough support or approval within the Amish leadership for that to happen anyway. Esther had far too many unusual circumstances to make her a good example to *kinnah*. Although she strived to follow the church's standards as laid out in the *Ordnung*, she was still an orphaned unmarried woman raising a deaf English child.

"Maybe not, but you sure have taught Daisy." Aunt Lucy patted her granddaughter's *kapp*. Daisy smiled at her *mammie* before burying her face in her guardian's long black skirt. Lucy sighed. "She looks so much like Irene did at that age. You've been very good for her." An expression of loss and hurt cascaded over the elderly woman's face. She swallowed hard and looked away from Esther and through the window.

Esther patted Lucy's hands. They both knew Lucy would have liked to have taken Daisy when Joe joined the Marines after Irene's death, but she didn't know—no one knew—how much additional work it would take to raise a child like Daisy.

What Esther had never told Lucy was that Irene had pleaded with her that if something ever were to happen to her, she wanted Esther to help Joe with Daisy. Irene made Esther promise. Joe admitted to Esther that Irene had made him make the same promise. *Somehow she sensed it*, he said. She could hear his words engraved in her memory. *She said you would love Daisy like your own and take care of her in a way that her parents never could. She made me promise.*

Lucy, however, insisted so passionately that she wanted to care for her granddaughter herself that Joe allowed his mother-in-law to keep her overnight before he shipped out. It didn't take long for Lucy to see that Daisy needed a great deal of attention—more than she could give—and finally agreed that Esther was a better match.

Esther gazed out the window, reminiscing. Her eyes landed on the harmonica that lay on the kitchen windowsill. It had been her father's. When he left, he told her to keep it and said that someday, when he came back, he'd teach her to play. He'd never returned. Orpha's death compounded on all the former ones.

Esther

The next two days of the wake continued the same as the first day. Esther's exhaustion had taken on a greater breadth than she had imagined. She was grateful when her aunts and uncles arrived from Pennsylvania, Iowa, and Ohio to carry some of the burdens and duties that had landed on her. Tears were shed, rhythmic prayers recited, and hymns sung. Through the wake, the dear deceased lady lay in her bedroom in the glow of a single candle that the Amish lit for their dead. Discussion of Esther's future plans without Orpha went unspoken during those early dark days. Light conversation about community happenings and the life that God had given Orpha were the only words on the mourners' lips.

Late at night, before Esther fell into sleep, or in the early morning, between her dreamlessness and wakefulness, she imagined the gossip over what seemed like a generational curse. Orpha's husband, Atlee, had died surrounded by rumors about having been a man few trusted, just like his father before him. People whispered that none of the Detweiler men would ever be chosen for church leadership, that there was a wild hair embedded in their hearts, leading them astray.

Some said that the devil chased Atlee back to the church after he had walked away for over a year. Although Esther's own father had died in prison, put away because he had maintained his loyalty to their community's nonresistant standards after he'd been drafted, people still said that the Detweilers were a tormented family. No one else they knew who had gone to prison during the war had died. They'd all returned. Although Orpha had the kind of peaceful passing that the elderly hope for, there was no doubt that there would still be lingering gossip through the district that Orpha's and Esther's lives were cursed.

Esther rose on the morning of Orpha's funeral with these thoughts wandering through her mind. A summer storm thundered above the roof of her home like a herd of cattle and continued as she filed into the Yutzys' barn, where the funeral would be held. The Yutzys were cousins to Orpha and had the largest farm in their district, which was needed for such a well-attended funeral. Although they would sit in the barn for the funeral, there would be dozens of women in the large farmhouse preparing the meal to serve after the burial.

Hours later the large red barn still creaked and groaned in the howling wind. The rows of backless benches were filled with hundreds of church members. Esther could feel the heat of every eye on her back and tried to focus on the steady stream of cool air that whistled through the broken window nearby.

The preachers, one local and two visiting, spoke about living humbly and always being prepared for death. Always being ready to be judged by the Lord. Never being caught off guard.

"What if our *schvester* Orpha had been in the midst of speaking poorly over a *bruder* or *schvester* when she passed from this world? What if she had cheated her neighbor or lived in dishonesty? Eternity will reflect her life. Oh, woe to the brother or sister who cannot live a life of purity and separation from this world." The old preacher inhaled quickly and continued with admonishment and a little encouragement.

Like Mrs. White's radio, Esther dialed back the volume of the traditional rhythmic High German preaching. While still looking straight ahead, she listened to how the rain had gone from thrashing about to a gentle shower. Though High German was always used for church services, the language sounded foreign and distant when all she wanted to hear was Orpha's contagious laughter and sweet treble voice.

With sweat at his receding hairline, the second visiting preacher finished, and Esther was suddenly lining up behind her aunts, uncles, and cousins. It was time to make her last good-bye to Orpha. Esther had been the closest to Orpha and would have the privilege of being the final person to bid farewell before the pallbearers closed the casket for burial. As Esther approached the casket, Daisy's small hand in her own, every eye was trained on her.

During the three-day wake, Esther had not visited Orpha's body. She was afraid if she saw her lying there in the candlelit room, she would not be able to control her emotions. But now her family created a wide half circle around her back as it was tradition to remain together at this point in the funeral. She took deep, long breaths to keep her composure. She finally looked down at Orpha; her heart pulled against her chest like a tree uprooted by a stiff wind.

She tasted blood from biting the insides of her cheeks and swallowed hard when she finally looked at Orpha's face. This was the woman who had cared for and loved Esther the most. While no one expected her eyes to remain dry, she couldn't release her burden. Her grief was her own, and she didn't want anyone's pity.

Esther looked down at Daisy. The little girl's eyes only grazed the top of the casket, and Esther wanted Daisy to take one last look at the still figure.

See, Esther signed. The mute communication helped her to briefly set aside her grief.

Daisy tucked her chin and shook her head *no*. Esther sighed and looked back at Orpha. Visions of the years gone by poured through her mind. Remembering Orpha's hair, which had not salted over until she was well into her sixties. Even today, through her *kapp*, she could see entire sections of hair that remained as black as Esther's own. The soft, round woman always had a way of looking at the bright side of things. Most people called Orpha *fahgesley*, a nice way of saying absent-minded. But the spirit of the woman she'd been was gone now. Orpha didn't even look like herself anymore. Esther closed her eyes, took a deep breath, and conjured the image of the old woman's smile, letting it penetrate her mind.

A pull on Esther's skirt caught her attention, and she looked down to find Daisy's round eyes. The little girl used her pointer finger and made a circle around her lips.

Who? Daisy signed. Then with the same finger she pointed to a man who had walked into a small gap in the line of family.

Esther's gaze moved over the man's face and a flash of a memory crossed over her vision. A memory from long ago— so long ago it was almost a dream. Somehow she knew that the man's hair had been black and thick and used to be cut in the traditional Amish style; now, what little remained of it was salt and pepper and smartly trimmed. The mustache wasn't just different from every other man's in the open space of the barn; it seemed out of place for the stranger himself.

The English suit reminded her of the ones farmer Bart White used to wear all those years ago before he died. He wasn't a large man in any way—almost small, really. He stood there with his hands stuffed in his pockets, shifting from one foot to the other. Who was he? He looked up into the rafters, making it impossible for her to see his eyes.

Then Uncle Reuben turned to the man, and after an expression of recognition passed over his face, he put out his hand to the stranger. The men shook hands.

The heat in the room seemed to heighten for Esther. Her ears burned with the din of whispers that filled every cracked floorboard and the gapped wooden slats of the walls.

The stranger stepped toward her, but then stopped as their eyes met. She recognized herself, and Orpha, in the man's eyes. She recognized a man she once knew. He inhaled and then gifted her with a weak, crooked smile, a smile etched deep into her memory.

She realized who he was.

This man was her dead father.

Esther

The next moments blurred in Esther's mind. She watched as Uncle Reuben whispered something behind his large carpenter's hand before gesturing toward Orpha's casket. Her eyes moved over the rest of the crowd as the murmuring began. There were hidden whispers and faces turned toward one another, but all eyes were on Esther and the return of Chester Detweiler. Esther's eyes went back to Orpha and then to the suited, balding man. Was this really her father? The man's strides were long for his stature, and he was in front of Esther and Daisy in a few ticks of the second hand.

"Essie," he whispered. He looked down at Daisy, who instantly hid behind Esther's black skirt. Up close Esther saw a scar on his chin. That had happened when she'd tried to hoe the garden like a grown-up and gotten him in the chin instead. He'd only laughed about it, not whipped her for her carelessness. Orpha had stitched him, since Esther's mother, Leah, wasn't good with blood.

Chester turned away from Esther. His hands gripped the side of the simple varnished casket, and she saw that he was missing a pointer finger. He hunched over his hands for several long seconds before standing upright. He sniffed loudly and pulled out a handkerchief. He blew his nose, and the sound bounced around in the hip roof of the barn, but he seemed not to notice or, if he did, care.

How was this possible? How could he be here? Her breathing quickened with shock.

"*Mem*," he croaked. "Oh, *Mem*. *Vee kan ich dich nah geh lessa?*" He pleaded several times, asking how he could now let his mother go.

Esther grimaced, sympathy mixing with her confusion. Where had he been all these years? She'd been told he was dead. If he wasn't a ghost and he wasn't dead, where had he been? Had it all been a mistake? Had he been sitting in a prison cell all these years?

When Esther was a little girl, after he'd gone to prison as a conscientious objector, some of the other children in her church used to torment her by saying that he'd never gone to prison but had become a soldier; they called him murderer. Others were convinced he had gone out west to become a real-life cowboy. These rumors ceased when her mother received a letter saying that he had died serving out his prison sentence. That news had killed her mother's will to live.

Memories now came back of the way he would race through the field bareback on his horse and pull her up to join him. The wind in her face would pull her *kapp* strings into ripples behind her. She remembered the way he winked at her after their silent mealtime prayers, and after her mother tucked her into bed, he would sneak up and give her a small piece of candy. He made one red-and-white-striped peppermint stick last for weeks this way. Then suddenly he was gone. Over the years, her memories had decayed, but now they were flooding back like spring warmth melting an icy stream. What started as a trickle was now gushing. There were so many unanswered questions.

Why did this have to happen in the middle of her *mammie's* funeral?

He wiped his tear-dampened face with his hankie and then stepped back. The pallbearers took this cue and moved in to pound nails into the lid of the casket, forever separating Orpha from the living.

As the sun peered from behind the storm clouds and dissolved into thick humid air, a line of buggies drove on gravel roads to the graveyard. A younger cousin held the reins of Esther's horse as she and Daisy stepped out of their buggy onto the wet gravel road. At the rumbling of a car engine that disturbed the peacefulness of the grassy graveyard, Esther turned to see Chester's car pull up behind the long line of buggies. She was ashamed of him. It would have been respectful for him to arrive in a buggy with a family member willing to take him.

Esther refocused her mind and took Daisy's hand and followed the other mourners through the path between gravestones. The ground was damp, and everyone's black shoes soon were caked with mud. Esther's stockings were wet as she stood still in front of the gap in the earth where Orpha would be laid to rest. Chester stood next to her. The scent of the passing rain and his aftershave teased her nose. She kept her eyes down. This wasn't the time or the place to ask her questions.

This also wasn't the time or place for him to return after twenty-nine years away. She hated him for it. Would her hate cause God to refuse her a place in heaven someday? That thought ushered in the next: How could she hate a man she didn't know?

She was glad when the preacher spoke only a few quiet words at the graveyard. There was little left to say after the hours of preaching in the Yutzys' barn. Relatives dropped handfuls of the moist soil onto the casket that was deeply planted into the earth—a seed that would never grow. Her hand plunged deeply into the mound of dirt and her finger-nails filled with the dewy blackness. Esther moved forward and tossed the handful of soil into the open chasm. She'd done the same at her mother's funeral—and her father's. Her eyes flitted over to the grave marker next to where Orpha's would eventually be placed.

Chester R. Detweiler was etched into the small stone, with the years 1893–1918. Esther's lungs tightened and she stepped away. She looked around and the tension among the small group at the gravesite was visible in the lines of the foreheads and in the eyes that diverted from her.

Chester was dead. But, yet, here he stood—only feet from her. Was he really the man he appeared to be? Reuben had shaken his hand as if he'd recognized his brother. The man had called Esther by her old nickname, Essie.

The drive back to the Yutzy farm for the prepared lunch was slow and monotonous. Through the front windshield of the buggy she could see that the meal had already begun for those who didn't go to the gravesite. Crowds of people were milling around everywhere from inside the house to the barn, where tables and chairs had been set up. The boys helped with the horses and buggies, and the younger girls offered help to mothers with babies. All the buzzing around reminded Esther of worker bees. It was nothing out of the ordinary for a funeral, but suddenly she couldn't bring herself to join in.

"Give me a few minutes?" Esther said to the boy who offered to take care of her horse and buggy.

The boy shrugged and moved on. Esther pulled the reins to the left, and when she stopped again, Daisy pulled at her sleeve. She put her hands up in question. Esther knotted the leather reins and dropped them from her hands.

"Aunt Lucy will get your food." Esther signed the letter *L* moving down from her left jaw for Lucy and then touched the tips of her fingers to her mouth to sign *eating*. The little girl smiled and nodded. She slid the door open and hopped out without a glance back. Esther reached across the buggy to close the door when a four-fingered hand grabbed it instead. Suddenly she was looking into the face of her *dat*.

She pulled back as if stung, and the buggy shifted under the weight of Chester Detweiler as he climbed inside. He slid the door shut and looked at her solemnly.

"What are you doing here?" The words fell out of her mouth before she could catch them.

"Hi, Esther. I thought we should talk." His eyes shifted back and forth.

Esther could suddenly think of nothing to say. Shouldn't she have a slew of questions? She did, only her tongue was paralyzed. After several long moments, Chester started talking again.

"Well, um, you look good." He paused and smiled at her, then leaned toward her and winked. "You're taller than I remember."

Esther remained placid as she willed her mind to gather her thoughts. It had been only an hour since he'd walked back into her life. How was she to navigate this, having no time to think or space to breathe?

Esther's gaze fell on his missing finger. There was something vaguely familiar about it, only she couldn't quite remember exactly why. The air became thick within the small confines of the black buggy walls.

"I am sure you have a lot of questions and I . . ." His Pennsylvania Dutch sounded awkward.

"How are you here?" Esther articulated each word with great care. She looked out through the windshield and watched her community gather in groups to socialize and eat and wished she could be just one of them. She looked back at him for an answer.

Chester stuttered and ran a hand over his face.

"*Mem* told me you were dead. We had a funeral for you. Were you in prison this whole time?" She became breathless. "Why didn't you write to me if you were in prison?"

"I can explain," Chester said in English.

"You can explain?" Esther responded in English. "How is that possible? Just answer one question. Were you in prison for all of these years?"

Chester inhaled and exhaled slowly. "No."

Esther's heart seemed to take on a new rhythm at his quiet answer.

"Could you have come back sooner?" Did she want to know the answer to this?

"Esther, I never meant to be gone for so long." He whispered with his eyes downcast. "I was just going to go for my medical exam and then everything went wrong and—"

"I have to go." This was too much for her. Esther grabbed her black vinyl purse and after fumbling with the door got out of the buggy.

"Esther, we need to talk." Chester grabbed Esther's arm.

She looked over her shoulder at him as she pulled her arm from his grip.

"Have you been away from the church for so long to forget that we don't put private family business out on the laundry line for everyone to see?" Esther spat every word. "This is not the time or the place to have this conversation. Besides, I just buried my *mammie*. She was the one who raised me and loved me. I won't do this here."

"Esther," Chester said. His eyes furrowed, and if Esther didn't know that he'd been lying about his death for decades, she would think he looked sincere. "Maybe we can talk at home? Tonight?"

"Maybe." It was all she could say, but as she imagined him

walking into her home, her stomach flopped from one side to another. "I have to go."

Sweat bloomed under her arms as she walked away from the buggy and looked for a place to gather her thoughts. Across the drive stood the large farmhouse, and she knew that by now every corner of the house was filled with young mothers finding a space for their young babies to rest. The girls who were dating, *rumspringa,* would be huddled together to gossip over the boys. There was no place for privacy.

She remembered there was an outhouse near the ball diamond, behind the barn—the one most people wouldn't use since it was out of sight. She began walking fast, past the barn and lined up buggies, past the boys who were watering the horses and toward the outhouse.

Esther couldn't turn over the wooden latch fast enough to lock herself inside the small wooden structure. The damp air hung around her, gluing her dress to her skin. She leaned her head against the door and took deep breaths. But the putrid air inside filled her lungs and she dry-heaved.

She needed fresh air, but her hands couldn't work the handle. It was stuck, and she pounded on the door. Sweat dripped from her face and her lungs tightened. Why couldn't she work the latch? Finally it opened, and she fell onto her knees outside the outhouse, her hands plunging into the warm, wet grass and soil. The dampness from the storm soaked through her dress and stockings at her knees.

"Esther?" Uncle Reuben said, several long strides away from the outhouse. He offered his hand to help her up. He'd always been a good man and was much younger than his brother, Chester. Reuben had been in his early *rumspringa* years when Chester left.

"I couldn't open the door," she said, breathing as heavily as if she had just run around the bases in the next field. She took his hand and mumbled an apology for her wet and dirty hands as she got to her feet.

"I saw you walking this way." Her uncle rubbed his hands together, brushing the dirt off. His eyes didn't meet hers. He paused for several beats before he began again, his eyes remaining off in the distance. "I know you have questions about your *dat* and I'll answer what I know."

Esther was tongue-tied. The shock of everything had suddenly rendered her as mute as Daisy. Esther wondered when the surprises would stop.

"I got a letter from Chester a few months ago. He was in Dover and wanted to meet. We did." He cleared his throat and returned his gaze to look at Esther.

"Why didn't you tell me?" Esther's voice sounded shrill in her own ears. He should have told her about the letter months ago. "He just tried to talk to me in my buggy and I know he wasn't in prison all these years. I couldn't talk about it with him yet. It's all happening—*tzu schnell.*"

It was going too fast, but the twenty-nine years without him had been long and slow.

"He made me promise not to say anything to anyone— I didn't know what I would say anyway. Who would ever have thought . . ." His voice faded away then he spoke again. "He said he wanted to talk to you himself. I didn't know what to do. I'm sorry, Esther."

Esther inhaled. She looked away from his stare and let her eyes linger over far away into the distant tree line.

"But then *Mem* died, so I got in touch with him. I—" Their eyes met again.

Reuben bit his lower lip and looked up at the blue-gray sky. When it appeared that he found no answers there, he looked back down at Esther.

"Why now?" she asked him.

"He was worried about our *Mem*. He said that he hadn't gotten a letter from her in years and wanted to know if she was still alive."

"*Vas? Mammie* knew?"

Reuben smoothed his beard before putting a heavy hand on Esther's shoulder.

"I haven't told anyone else about *Mem* knowing." His voice hushed. "Millie doesn't even know."

It surprised Esther that her uncle hadn't even told his wife. None of this seemed real. She was sure she would wake at any moment and her eyes would find the ceiling of her bedroom instead of the sky.

"I don't want anyone to know that my *mem* was a part of this—" He paused as if searching for the right word. "—part of this *lie*. I don't want her memory . . ." He didn't finish his thought.

Esther's nod was listless and faraway. She wouldn't want Orpha's memory to be dirtied either, or for anyone to question what a loyal and good woman she truly was.

"*Fahgep mich?*" Reuben's blue eyes drooped at the corners in burden over his secret.

Esther swallowed away her emotion. "*Ya.* I forgive you. I just don't understand why he didn't come home sooner."

"I'm sure we'll learn more now that he's home."

"Home?"

"He's planning to stay in Sunrise."

Esther

Esther and Uncle Reuben walked back from the outhouse to the Yutzys' house for their lunch. Reuben bore the guilt of his own part in the matter on his brow. Esther wouldn't hold a grudge against him—she had always found him to be a fair and kind man. But the reality was that Chester was back, and he was a complete stranger to her.

They were each given a tray of food, and both sat down at a table surrounded by aunts, uncles, and cousins. Chester was walking toward them, holding a tray heaped with food. He pulled out a chair almost directly across from Esther. She opened her mouth to speak, but nothing came out. Chester offered her a smile, but she was too taken aback by his presence for the gesture to warm her.

"Howdy, Chester," his *bruder* Ammon said with a mouthful of food. "Isn't every day I get to eat a meal with a dead man." Ammon didn't look at Chester as he spoke but lifted his chin, eyeing those around him. "You understand what I'm saying, *ya*? Or should I talk in English?"

Chester looked at Esther. She let his gaze linger for a long moment and in searching his eyes she was sure she saw as much discomfort in them as she felt herself. She looked away.

"*Bruder* Ammon, *vella spater schvetzah*," Chester said in dialect and sat down.

Esther was surprised that Chester suggested they talk later.

"*Spater?*" Ammon said and waved a hand at his words. He was an outspoken man and was clearly the voice for the group. "We all thought you were dead. Walked by your gravestone today. Where've you been? Esther, I bet you want the first crack at him, don't you?"

Chester shifted in his chair and cleared his throat. His eyes were trained on his plate. Esther's sympathy arose, but she shoved it away. He'd been nearby for months without a word. He *should* be uncomfortable.

"Esther," he said with a furrowed brow as he looked at Esther. "I can—"

"You can what?" Ammon pushed.

"Ammon," Reuben barked in interruption. "*Less es geh.* Esther doesn't deserve this."

Reuben was right. Ammon needed to let it go. No one wanted all of the family disappointments and burdens out for everyone to prattle and cackle over, though she knew well enough that Chester Detweiler's name would be whispered behind everyone's closed doors for weeks to come, and her name would be sewn alongside.

Now there were too many eyes on her, and the discomfort was too heavy. Esther picked up her tray and left the table. She couldn't do this now, not in front of a crowd of onlookers. As she entered the kitchen the women washing dishes stopped talking. Some averted their gazes, and some started talking loudly on another topic. Esther's appetite had spoiled.

"Esther." Aunt Lucy's voice came to her like an angel of mercy. "Come help me with the pies."

She joined Aunt Lucy on the cool back porch. Away from the crowd of people, she was finally able to breathe again.

"*Vie bish en du?*" Aunt Lucy asked Esther how she was doing. She turned a bucket over and sat, then gestured toward a small wooden stool.

Esther inhaled and then took the offered seat. She bit her lower lip hard enough to take the sting away from the tears in her eyes. They sat in silence, staring through the screened porch at the fading day. The tension in Esther's lungs was so full and tight she thought they would burst, and she exhaled deeply.

"I don't know what to think." She matched Lucy's quiet voice so no one could overhear them, then leaned toward her aunt. "Reuben said he was in Dover these past few months but didn't say where he'd been before then. And why would someone pretend to be dead?"

Lucy raised an eyebrow at Esther. "You need to ask him." Lucy had never held back from talking directly. She was one of the few women in the church with a bold tongue. "This isn't a conversation you can push off on someone else. He's *your* father. You lost the most with his absence. You're the one who needs to hold his feet to the fire."

"He tried to talk to me, but I don't know what to say." Esther's whisper rasped from her throat. "I don't have your backbone, Lucy. *Des ist tzu viel.*"

This was too much, but what was new about that? Her life had always been too much.

Lucy reached and held tightly to Esther's hand.

"Nah, Esther. You're full of vinegar, and you've got more pluck than any other woman I know. Look at all you've done for yourself—and without a husband to depend on. Leah would be so proud of you." Lucy offered a smile, then with creaking knees she stood. "Get the story for yourself. If you turn around and he's gone again, you will regret not knowing," she said with a wag of her finger.

Lucy's recognizing Esther's pluck encouraged her.

There was a pause in their talk, and the sounds of playing children drifted toward them. Esther looked up to see Daisy playing blind man's bluff with a handful of little girls. Blind. Deaf. Mute. That's how she felt right now.

As the day grew older, the sea of black buggies grew smaller. Esther focused her attention on the fading sunset in the distance and found Chester's silhouetted figure leaning over a wooden fence overlooking the field. A lump lodged in her throat. The fact that her anger was braided together with some strange sympathy toward him was unnerving.

Before Esther could unravel her feelings, Chester jogged over to his car and drove off. The echo of his engine was all that lingered of his presence. The thud in her chest reminded her of Lucy's words. What if he was gone for good, and she would never know where he'd been for most of her life?

～

Later that night when she and Daisy were finally tucked away in their little farmhouse, Chester's words echoed in her mind. *You look good.* She wished she'd never heard his voice. He'd changed so much. He was a different man, as far as she was concerned. Of course, after twenty-nine years, Esther had changed a lot also.

She set the oil lamp down on her dresser and picked up her mirror, studying her face as if looking at it for the first time since her childhood—as Chester had today. What would he see in her that was even recognizable? Had he noticed that she had Orpha's widow's peak that gave her face a heart-shaped appearance? Her thick black eyebrows and lashes matched her rich hair. These were characteristics of the Detweilers, as were her full lips. Her skin, however, was like her mother's—fair and like the porcelain dolls at Mrs. White's farmhouse. Esther was dark and light. Hard and soft.

Esther

As Esther and Daisy walked out onto her porch the following morning, Esther brought her hand up to her eyes to shield the still-rising sun. In the distance she could see her neighbor walking among his hayfields that lay between their homes, likely inspecting the growth and considering the timing for the next cutting.

As the Delaware countryside awoke around her it offered the deep inhale that she needed. Her gaze tiptoed down the road that curved in both directions and took in the scene. Sunrise View Road was true to its name. It gave those living in Sunrise, Delaware, a landscape to greet each new day. She'd lived on the long, twisty road her whole life. She knew everyone who lived from where it split from Bright Peach Road to where it made a T on Dutch Apple Road.

The countryside was dotted with farms. Green cornfields, yellow hayfields, and colorful orchards surrounded them. Some English, some Amish. Inside the Amish homes many of the women were clearing away the breakfast dishes so they could start their mending, since it was Wednesday. Stately surnames were painted on the silos: Borntrager, Yoder, King. The large red barns and the white farmhouses always looked immaculate.

Joe Garrison's red farmhouse and barn were just beyond the dip in the road—sitting silently out of sight.

Esther took Daisy's hand, and they walked down the three porch steps, only to tumble to the bottom. The second step had broken beneath their feet.

Esther and Daisy had both landed on their knees, and Daisy began to laugh. Esther couldn't help but smile, and she playfully shoved Daisy, who fell into the grass giggling. Esther tapped her and brought her pointer fingers close without touching. *Was Daisy hurt?*

"No," Daisy vocalized with her nasal, songlike voice. "You?"

Esther shook her head and stood. While dusting off her apron, she found a hole in the fabric and sighed deeply. She had no extra money to buy cloth for a new one. She'd have to patch it later and hope it didn't show too much. Mrs. White would consider a tear unseemly. Daisy was already up and running toward the large farmhouse across the gravel road. The Whites' farm had been in business for as long as anyone could remember, though they'd nearly lost it during the Depression but for Mrs. White's quick-witted business dealings and hard work. That had been about the same time that Esther left school to work for Mrs. White, once Orpha became unable.

Esther turned back toward the house. *Mammie* Orpha wasn't in there—she was gone. Hadn't it been only a few days ago that she'd touched Esther's face and told her not to work so hard? She'd told her to take a break now and then to enjoy life.

Several hours into Esther's cleaning at Mrs. White's house, three hard raps at the door forced her from her knees. She left the scrub brush and wiped her hands on her apron before she padded across the washed portion of the wide-slat wooden floor. Damp footprints followed her through the kitchen. A small stream of sunlight cascaded through the window and erased the fading footpath. Three more knocks came louder a second time.

Esther tapped Daisy's shoulder. The little girl looked up from her place at the kitchen table. She held a stump of chalk between her small fingers. Simple drawings of flowers and stars covered the green slate.

Esther mimicked someone knocking on a door and pointed toward the entrance. Daisy followed after her. Daisy rarely let her Amish guardian out of her sight when Esther cleaned Mrs. White's farmhouse. They passed through the mudroom and down one flight of stairs to reach the front door.

"Coming," Esther called as she stepped quickly down the wooden stairs.

Angelica Blunt, who looked nothing like her heavenly name, stood on the other side of the door. Esther inhaled at the sight of the woman's pointy features. Angelica was even more haggard than usual, though for several months she'd seen her only from a distance. Her hair was frizzy and out of control, and her housedress hung on her bony shoulders and wide hips. She was little more than skin on a skeleton.

Seeing her, Esther suddenly realized the state of her own appearance. She was barefoot and her apron was wet, wrinkled, and torn. She pushed a hand against her hair, damp with sweat, and in a threadbare *kopftuch* instead of her usual *kapp*. It would be pointless to stuff her stray curls back inside the old headscarf. The job of cleaning the big farmhouse all morning had left perspiration marks beneath her arms. Esther crossed her arms and the cut sleeves of her faded work dress tightened around her skin. When had the dress gotten so restrictive?

"Angelica," she finally said and stepped through the doorway with Daisy on her heels, letting the door slap shut behind them. Joe hadn't even asked his sister, Angelica, if she might take Daisy while he ran away to war after Irene's death. The woman had called Daisy an animal.

Esther's hand found Daisy's and squeezed it three times.

I love you.

Angelica's lips pinched together as she shoved a small wad of cash at Esther. "Here's the money from Joe." Without counting it, she knew it couldn't be more than six or seven dollars. Though she was thankful, she knew they were supposed to get more. Joe insisted on providing Esther with some money from the beginning, but Angelica seemed to resent the responsibility, wanting to keep the money to care for her own family.

"I went to your house first, but I didn't want to leave the money in the door. There's an old automobile in the drive and a man sitting on the porch swing smoking. That's where Orpha usually is this time of morning." She paused for a moment and jutted out her pointy jaw. "Where's that crazy ole Orpha? And who is that man?"

Esther quickly glanced through windy trees at the road's edge to see the old cream-colored automobile sitting in her drive. Chester was there. Passion rose in her chest, but she instantly sensed a blend of resentment and relief—she still wanted to know where he'd been for all of these years. This would give her the chance. She wouldn't, however, explain to Angelica the intricacies of the issues she faced because of Chester. Angelica didn't need anything more to gossip or write about to Joe.

She cleared her throat and refocused her eyes on Angelica.

"My grandmother passed," Esther said it quickly so she wouldn't be able to taste the words.

Angelica tucked her chin and her eyebrow went up at the same time.

"Well, I hadn't heard," Angelica said almost gently. "Who's the stranger?"

"He's my—" She couldn't say the word. "That's Chester Detweiler. Orpha's son."

"Your old man?" Angelica questioned.

"In a manner of speaking." Esther cleared her throat.

Daisy gripped a handful of Esther's plain gray dress and peeked around her. Esther hadn't signed any of the conversation. At times like these, Esther was glad Daisy was deaf and couldn't hear anything, though she intuitively picked up on tension quickly enough.

"Hmm," Angelica said. Her eyes wandered for a moment.

Esther's waterlogged fingers gripped the stiff paper more tightly as she recalled Joe's promise of a regular allowance. There hadn't been much, but the little bit did help. Orpha and Esther had never had anything extra. She tucked the bills into the waistband of her white apron. The stipend was so sporadic she'd taken odd jobs from Sunrise Dairy, milking alongside the crude Englisher farmhands when they needed the extra money.

Esther didn't blame Joe for the irregular income—he did the best he could. She'd learned from an early letter from him that he was paid monthly, but sending mail wasn't always convenient or possible. Mail sent from so far away wasn't always reliable either. What Esther did not accept was that Joe hadn't written to his daughter for years.

For the first year, he tucked short, curt letters to them both—merely stating that he was alive—next to several dollars. When months went by without any correspondence Esther was nervous that Joe may have been killed, but Angelica came and handed her a few crumpled bills. And this became their new routine. It was sometimes weeks or months between visits. Esther continued to write for another year, trying to keep him informed of Daisy's well-being, but when he kept silent, she eventually stopped writing.

"Esther?" Mrs. Norma White's high-pitched voice cut through the closed door and through Esther's thoughts. "Who's at the door?"

Esther cracked the door open to answer. She found Mrs.

White peeking through the kitchen door off of the mudroom. Her chestnut hair was styled in perfect waves and her lips were brighter than usual. She was in her sixties and tried desperately to appear younger.

"Angelica Blunt is just dropping off some money for Daisy." Esther tried to sound friendly to deter from the coolness she felt toward Angelica. Angelica and Mrs. White attended the same nearby community church, but Esther wasn't disillusioned enough to believe that they were friends. The Whites and the Blunts had more differences than similarities.

"Make it brief."

"Yes, Mrs. White," she responded.

Esther waited for Mrs. White to retreat before she closed the front door and turned back to Angelica to resume their conversation.

"Joe wants to know how the girl's doing." Angelica nodded her head toward Daisy. She always spoke of her niece like she wasn't there.

"So Joe's alive?" Esther's insensitive words rattled around in her conscience. She could almost see *Mammie* Orpha waving her pointer finger, scolding Esther. But Orpha was gone. She didn't have anyone to admonish her to be more feminine or to encourage her to think before she spoke.

Esther had mixed feelings about Joe Garrison. He had already stolen Esther's dearest cousin from her, Irene's family, and the entire church. It had started innocently. Irene had been the newly elected teacher for their Amish church district, and since Joe was a teacher in a nearby rural school, she said she wanted to ask him questions. But Esther knew it was more than that. Their marriage had caused Irene to be shunned, and it was difficult not to hold this against the man who wooed her away.

It wasn't lost on Esther, however, that if Irene had never left the church to marry Joe, Daisy would never have been born. Esther was willing to turn a blind eye to her cousin's sin in marrying outside of the church if it meant that she could have Daisy. And deep down in the reserves of Esther's heart, she knew that Irene had been happiest in the four years before her death when she was married to Joe. This was why Esther couldn't completely despise Joe.

Esther had never had the kind of happiness Joe brought Irene. Her own few dates as a young woman had never become anything more than sharing a few pieces of pie. As an old maid, the only time the topic of marriage arose was when there was a new widower looking for a wife. Esther was willing to do whatever it took to take care of her district, but she was not interested in marrying a widower who merely needed a mother for his children. She'd grown used to the invisibility and the responsibility of her singlehood.

"Of course he's alive." Spittle flew from Angelica's mouth. Her lips were pale and stretched.

"Well, I haven't heard from him in many months, maybe as much as a year—and we haven't seen any money in at least four months. What was I to think?"

"And wouldn't you just love that. You could just go on playing house with this simpleton and pretend she belongs to you. You and your sweet little Amish community. You think your people are just so perfect, but I see your young people carrying on in the fields behind me. They don't think anyone knows they are there, but I know and—"

"Pardon me," Esther interrupted. Her eyes closed, trying to tuck away her frustration. She opened them and continued. "Of course, I don't want Joe to die. But you know that I'll care for Daisy for as long as needed. Even if that's forever."

"She's costing him money when she could be in one of those institutions and he wouldn't have to pay a dime. You know she's *simple*."

"She's not going anywhere, and she's not costing Joe much because I've covered the majority of her expenses." Esther's words were spoken roughly as she put an arm around Daisy and pulled her tightly to her hip. Her nerves winced at her audacity. She shouldn't be speaking to anyone like this—even if it was Angelica Blunt. She should learn from her fellow church members and be more passive and patient.

"Joe told me about the doctor you wanted the girl to see." Saliva crept into the corners of Angelica's cracked lips. "He didn't want you spending his money like that. She doesn't need a doctor. She needs strict rules and to be with other—simpletons."

"What? Is that why the money has been so sparse? And why he stopped sending it directly? He thought I would take her to a doctor against his wishes?" She half laughed at the new information.

"Listen, I saw her wearing new shoes. My six young'uns ain't never had new shoes and I figured we needed the money more."

"Those shoes were given to Daisy. They were used and two sizes too large. And that was two years ago, and she still wears them when it is cold; otherwise she's barefoot."

"And what about her dress?" Angelica gestured toward Daisy, who was wearing a blue dress. Anyone who took a moment to look closely would see that the top half was a different blue from the bottom.

"It's made from Mrs. White's old fabric scraps."

"Well, it's more than what we got, and I got a hungry bunch of young'uns and Daisy's only one mouth. Donald can't work and . . ." Angelica's eyes were glassy as she looked away.

Donald and Angelica Blunt had struggled to survive since before they were married. Irene told Esther all the gossip when she'd started sneaking off to see Joe.

Esther and Irene had watched Joe grow up. He had always been handsome, with his royal-blue eyes and sandy hair and a world-by-the-tail smile. Angelica never had Joe's good looks, so she married the first man who showed interest. She and Donald were married by sixteen and having babies by seventeen. Now she had six and her husband struggled with holding a job since his leg was permanently withered by polio.

Esther let go of Daisy and fingered the cash in her waistband. She left three dollars tucked away and handed Angelica the rest. Esther would manage.

"Here." The wind caught the bills and made them wave in her hand.

Angelica swallowed hard, her eyes fast on the bills. The hunger in the woman's gaze for the few bills squeezed Esther's heart. If there was one thing she couldn't stand, it was hungry children. This was one of the reasons she'd taken it on herself to drive donated food around to the less fortunate families along Sunrise View Road. Most of it came from the pantries and cellars of the Sunrise Community Church that Mrs. White attended. Unfortunately the Blunts were not included in the donations since the proud Angelica refused charity from anyone but Joe.

"I mean it, Angelica. You have more mouths to feed." It was true. Esther only had Daisy now that Orpha was gone.

Angelica's hand reluctantly lifted, quickly took the cash, and stuffed it into her handbag.

"I need to get back to work." Esther grabbed the handle of the screen door behind her and started turning to go inside. But Angelica suddenly spoke, startling Esther.

"Joe's coming back, you know." Her voice was raspy.

"Yes, he will come back. I know it's been—difficult for you." Esther's tongue stumbled over her words. She was trying to be kind, but Angelica's defensiveness and hatefulness toward Daisy made her efforts tiring.

"No, I don't just mean *sometime*. I mean soon." She pushed

her chin out. "You ain't heard from him, but I have. He'll be back for Daisy in a week—maybe two. He wants Daisy at the train station. I'll send over Edwina or Roberta with a message when I know the day and time."

With that, Angelica turned and left. It was as if she'd left that information as the final twist of the knife in Esther's gut. For several long moments Esther stood still, taking in the news. The June breeze picked up and a rain shower slowly began. The large summer-warmed drops shined iridescent in the sun, their beauty a stark contrast to Esther's situation.

Esther stepped inside with Daisy and watched as Angelica climbed into her rusted stake truck. The engine revved louder and black exhaust flew into the air before she was finally able to pull out. The wooden fence around the edge of the flatbed rattled as she drove off. Esther expected that several stakes might even fall off before she made it to her house only a mile down the road.

Daisy tugged her arm. She vocalized in a way only Esther understood. Her voice, like an off-pitch tune, was soft and nasal. Esther knelt down to her level. She swallowed a lump in her throat that felt like gravel. Once she gathered herself, she pulled Daisy's covering ties to the front and tied them into a small bow, then tucked the little girl's hair back into the edges of the *kapp*. Her hair was the same deep blond as Joe's and her eyes were his blue, but they were wide-set, like Irene's. Smart.

"What will I do without you?" Esther was glad Daisy couldn't read lips.

Daisy spread her left hand out, shrugging, then with her right hand in the shape of a *Y* touched her chin. "What's wrong?"

Esther repeated the little girl's sign. Would Esther be able to tell her? After Daisy's first year with Esther, the little girl asked about the red clapboard house where she'd lived with her parents. Her little brow was furrowed as if she was trying to place the memory of the home. When Esther reminded the little girl that it was her home and that someday she would live there again with her father, Daisy flew into a rage and declared she'd never leave Esther. To keep peace with her charge, Joe had become an unmentionable ghost between the two.

Esther looked into Daisy's wide eyes. The fresh scent of summer surrounded them, but all Esther could smell was the vinegar she had used earlier to clean the windows. The bitter smell infiltrated her lungs, and she held it for several long moments before exhaling.

Her right hand made the shape of a zero.

"Nothing," Esther lied.

Esther

S everal hours later, Esther and Daisy made their way back to their small house across the street. Cleaning Mrs. White's house had never gone more slowly. All Esther could think about was that the man who had broken every promise he'd ever made was at her home. There would be no running away this time and no excuses about the funeral crowd.

As they walked up to the house, Chester stood from the porch swing. He wore older denim pants with a plaid shirt. After his eyes shifted for several moments, he lifted them to Esther's.

"Who's this little sweetheart?" His head nodded toward Daisy.

"This is Daisy." Esther put a smile on her face and signed her name—pretending to pluck petals from the letter *D*. The little girl waved at Chester but kept close to Esther's side.

"Why did you name your *maetleh* 'Daisy'?" His pronunciation of *little girl* was laughable, and Chester cleared his throat as if embarrassed. "It's not much of an Amish name, last I knew."

"Daisy is my cousin's daughter. Her father is over in the Pacific."

"Oh, her daddy's a soldier. And her mother, she's . . ." His voice trailed off.

"Irene, Roy and Lucy's *maedel*, died when Daisy was three.

That's when Joe left for the war. I've been caring for her ever since." Esther realized she was having a conversation with her dead father. She shouldn't be talking to him about anything but where he'd been for twenty-nine years.

He nodded. "I remember Roy and Lucy, but they had a brood. I don't remember which one . . . And you use your hands to speak to her?" He squinted at her.

Esther ignored his question and knelt down to Daisy's level. She signed for her to wash the potatoes for supper. The little girl nodded and obeyed instantly.

Esther walked up to the porch and stepped over the broken stair. She took these few moments to gather her thoughts, she remembered that the evening before Orpha's death, she spoke of her son and called him *such a good boy*. Esther stood in front of the open door and faced Chester.

"Essie. *Meh missah schvetzah?*"

Esther agreed, "Yes, we do need to talk."

Chester gestured toward the house.

"The house looks nice. I remembered it being bigger. Know what I mean?" His words were laced with a nervous chuckle. He spoke in a mixture of English and their Dutch dialect. "Nothing's really changed. Same couch and table. Even the dent in the wall. Happened when your uncles and I played too hard and my heel dented the plaster." He shook his head, then smiled at her.

Esther couldn't find her voice, but his—his voice—took her back to being a little girl. The little girl he left behind. He shrugged when she didn't respond.

"Can we sit down inside?" he asked.

Esther didn't answer but instead just walked inside. Chester followed her into the house. This had been their home together; they'd both been raised within its walls. The house floorboards creaked as if complaining at the betrayal of Chester's presence after his abandonment.

"I didn't want to barge in like this," he said to Esther's back. He paused for a moment, and Esther put down her basket of old cloth rags she used to clean when he began again. "Well, lookie here, I didn't see this earlier. My harmonica."

Chester walked toward the kitchen window.

"Don't pick that up." Esther's heart drummed.

Chester's hand stilled and after several beats put his hand in his pocket.

"*Mammie* cleaned that every week since you've been away. Every week. I thought she was just being sentimental, but she was keeping it clean for you." Esther's shock made her skin numb and the house suddenly felt like a teeter-totter beneath her feet, making her feel unsteady. She closed her eyes for several long moments. Daisy patted Esther's hand, bringing her back.

"I have no place to go." He spoke in English. "This is the only home I've ever had."

"The only home *you've* ever had? I think you have that backward. This is the only home *I've* ever had. You've been living somewhere for almost thirty years, so you can't say—" Esther's heart bloomed with courage. She finally blurted out, "Why are you here, Chester?"

Chester looked surprised, and his eyes got larger. "*Mah mem ist schtavah.*" His Pennsylvania Dutch had an accent, and it sounded odd as he spoke.

Yes, Esther knew his mother had died—but that hadn't answered her question.

"You didn't come when *Mem* died—*dah frau.*" He hadn't taken the time to return when his own wife died.

Chester's nod affirmed what she said. Though it was subtle, the pain of the truth broke the facade of strength in her face.

"There's so much you don't know." His voice was raspy, like a strong wind forced through a missing slat in a barn.

"So much that *I* don't know? I could say the same about you.

Do you know how *Mammie* Orpha still grieved for you even the night before she died? She talked about you. She wasted some of her last words on you. I thought her mention of you was because of her forgetfulness, not because of this secret. And *mem*, *auhm mem*. How could— Why would—" She shook her head in consideration of her poor mother and all she'd gone through. She bit her tongue and winced at the pain. Her anger needed to be abated. It was not the Amish way to lose one's temper. But as Lucy had told her, she had a right to know.

"I won't ever forget that day. I was almost seven. *Mem* ran to the mailbox as soon as the mailman came. It was almost like she knew." Esther could see her now. Her mother wore a drab brown dress, and even though Amish dresses were made to accommodate many waist sizes, this dress was at its smallest and still hung around her skeletal frame. On her head was worn-out fabric, tied at the nape of her neck. They'd been working outdoors all day. "She opened the letter and read it and her face went white. Her hands shook." Esther's breathing heightened. "She dropped the letter and collapsed on top of it."

"Oh, Esther." Chester took a step toward her. His brow furrowed like a wrinkled seam.

Esther stepped back. "No, I'm not finished." Her harsh whisper rasped against the soft humid air in the small house. "I called for *Mammie* Orpha to come. We couldn't wake *Mem* up. I ran to get Mrs. White and she had smelling salts. When *Mem* woke, she looked at *Mammie* and said—I'll never forget it—she said, *he's gone*."

"But—" He extended a hand toward her. He swallowed hard and cleared his throat. Esther decided to ignore his eyes, which had begun to shine in the late afternoon's waning light. She would not mirror his emotion. She would not cry.

"I'm not through," she said, an open palm against him. "We put *Mem* in bed that day, and she didn't get out for weeks—not even for your funeral. She didn't die for another two years, but

I lost her the day that letter came. I lost *both* of my parents with that letter. What did it say? I was told you were dead."

The clip-clop of several horses and buggies passing by filled the silence between them. The horse hooves branded their shape on the road and beat down and hardened the gravel. Her heart felt no different.

Chester cleared his throat and pulled Esther from her un-bridled thoughts. "Now listen. You don't know the whole story. I never meant to be gone for so long. I just—" He paused, and his Adam's apple moved up and down. His eyes shifted away from hers. "Please, sit down. I'll tell you all about where I've been—and—don't you—"

"*Mem* died longing for you, and now so did *Mammie*." Her chest rose and fell heavily and quickly. Her hands shook. She'd never spoken to anyone in this manner before. "What did that letter say?" she asked again.

"That letter told your *mem* I was dead." He cleared his throat. "I done some bad things in prison, things I couldn't accept, and I had a guard send a letter telling her I was dead. *Mem* didn't know I was alive." He looked down, and the toe of his boot poked at a too-large groove in the wooden slat floor.

"About two years later, when I finally got out of prison, Leah was dead. I grieved her death, Esther, I promise you I did. My grief over it all turned me into a different person. I lost myself. I couldn't come back."

"Then how was it that *Mammie* knew the truth? Reuben said the two of you wrote each other."

"I sent her a letter," Chester whispered. "I ain't proud of my actions."

Esther eyed him with soundless suspicion. He shifted his weight, and the floor creaked beneath him.

"And what about all the other years?" Her palms were sweating. She'd made such a point her whole life to remain in the shadows and to be as invisible as possible. If avoiding talking to the father who had abandoned her for nearly thirty years was possible, she would've done it. This was not a conversation she wanted to have.

"Mission work overseas. Oil in Texas. Ranching in Colorado." He waved a hand. "I've gotten around."

"And you continued to write to *Mammie*? And she wrote you back?"

"For a few years. Then we lost touch." He looked down at his feet. "You would've loved it out west, Essie. They call it *big sky country* and I don't think I would've quite known what that meant until I lived it. I would've loved for all of you to see it."

Esther shook her head and waved a hand at him.

"I still just don't understand why. Texas, Colorado, or wherever—it's all the same to me. You weren't with your family who needed you."

Chester looked up at the ceiling. But Esther didn't look away from him, hoping he felt as uncomfortable as she did.

"I never meant for it to be so long." His gaze returned to her. "I wanted to forget about how much it hurt for a little while, and then a few months turned into years. Then it was just too hard and everyone thought I was dead. It was easier to just—stay dead."

"Easier for who?" Esther shook her head.

"I'm sorry, Esther. I want to make things right." He paused for a moment and looked at his feet before looking back at Esther. "Let me stay, will ya?"

She wasn't sure how she could let that happen, but Orpha's influence over Esther had been strong. So much of the old woman still filled the quiet spaces of the house. All the times she spoke so highly of Chester came back to Esther like wind washing over a golden wheat field. Rippling over her mind, moving her. She closed her eyes. Inhaled. Exhaled.

"I'll let you stay for a few nights—for *Mammie*'s sake—not because you can make things right. You can't. Not ever."

Esther

Go back to bed, Esther," Detteh said. "It's still dark out."

"Dah hant?" Esther pointed to her dad's hand, and her head tilted to the side. "Bloot."

"Just a little blood." He winced, and his face grew whiter. "I'm leaving the Bivel for you and Mem. Read it every day." He laid the thick black book on the table in front of him.

"What about you? Don't you need to read the Bible?"

He hesitated for several long moments, his lower lip tight between his teeth. His dark hair was waxy on his forehead beneath his black hat, the good one that he wore to church. He was wearing his nice suit too, she noticed.

"Esther, why are you out of bed?" Her mother walked into the house. Her face was white and shiny. Ghostly. Why was she outside with Detteh? The old dishrag she held was bloody.

Her parents looked at each other, but neither spoke. Her dat grabbed the suitcase that was on the floor and turned toward the door. Her mother inhaled deeply, then her fast footfalls went up the stairs without even giving Esther a second glance.

"Where are you going, Detteh?" Esther asked.

"Listen, Mem will explain it all to you—later. I'll be back soon."

"But you said you would teach me to play the harmonica." Esther pointed at the small mouth harp on the kitchen windowsill.

"I'll teach you when I come home."

"Promise?" Esther raised her eyebrows.

"I promise."

"And you promise you'll be back soon?"

"I promise, Essie." He stepped forward and his hand reached out to her but never touched her. He pulled it back, rubbed his black beard, and was out the door a moment later. Her nightgown flapped as a cool draft pushed through the doorway. He was gone.

Esther's eyes startled open. This wasn't the first time she'd dreamed about the morning her *dat* left. It was the first time, however, that the memory of his bloody hand had infiltrated the dream. She'd called him *Detteh* back then—just the way little English children used *Daddy*. Not all Amish children did this, but she had always loved the affectionate term.

She tried the word in the dim morning light.

"Detteh." The soft-spoken word floated around the room but she privately vowed that it would never land on her lips again. Instead, the word brushed against the glass panels of the windows and the embroidered scripture wall hanging with its reminder to be silent and patient.

~

A June breeze danced through the open crack of the window and carried with it the scent of rich soil, dew, and freshly cut grass. The field behind the house had perfect rows of rounded stacks of hay. The serene and orderly view brought Esther comfort and peace, but there was Chester, taking up residence in her mind. She didn't want to think about him. Her time with Daisy was diminishing fast and Chester's presense was a constant disruption to her.

Was this the last time she and Daisy would make peanut

brittle for Mrs. White? Had this spring been the last time her little pointer finger would poke deep into the moist soil to drop in a seed for Esther? Time with Daisy was what she wanted to focus on, not stewing over what to do about her father who had returned from the dead.

This was Chester's third morning in their home, and he was like overripened fruit—he was past his usefulness to her. She didn't need a father now. Hadn't she told him only two nights? He didn't socialize with the community, except for meeting with Reuben once, as far as Esther knew. The rest of his siblings lived out of state and had left soon after Orpha's funeral. During the days, he had left in his Oldsmobile for hours, only to return with the smell of brew trailing in the air behind him. This was the first morning he'd stayed for breakfast.

"How'd you learn to do all of that signing stuff?" Chester wiggled his fingers and hands around as he sat waiting for the fried eggs Esther had reluctantly offered him.

Did she really want to share with him the journey she'd taken with Daisy? He made easy conversation that led to him acting more at home and less like a guest. She didn't like it, nor did she want to accept him. She would have to ask him what his future plans were since he could not continue to stay here. The meek and humble Amish women her church had bred would continue to allow him to stay indefinitely, but she would not.

"A church in Washington, DC, worked with the deaf." She flipped the egg onto a plate and put it in front of Chester. She wanted to enact shunning rules with him, which would mean she couldn't eat at the same table with him, but the church had not officially shunned him yet. Though for a man who had abandoned his family, then returned and planned to stay, a shunning was anticipated. The church leaders would visit him soon, and then it would be brought before the church. A shunning for his lifestyle and actions was inescapable. "An Episcopal church."

He chuckled. "An Episcopal church? How'd that happen?"

Esther sat at the table, waiting for his questioning to end so that they could pray for their food with a silent blessing. She clasped her hands in her lap.

"A librarian in Dover gave me the church's address. She knew of them through a friend or a cousin or someone." Esther exhaled. "I wrote to them and they sent me a book—for free."

Chester rubbed his shaved chin and nodded his head.

"And you've learned it all just from a book?" His voice and eyebrows rose.

"We don't use that many signs, and we come up with some of our own." She didn't really answer his question.

Daisy's early months with Esther had been a nightmare. When she recognized that the little girl's problem was that she couldn't hear, things began to get easier. Esther had started creating her own signs before she received the sign language book. Although Orpha never grasped all that Esther had done for Daisy to learn to communicate, Chester understood the enormity of the undertaking after having observed for only a few days.

"You're a smart one, Esther. I venture to guess that there aren't a whole lot of men around here who could handle a smart woman like you." He smiled at her, then took a large bite of his buttered toast. His Pennsylvania Dutch was coming back to him, but his accent still sounded off.

Esther couldn't explain the contradictory feelings that played tug-of-war inside her. He ate without praying and had said that she wasn't the type of wife a man was looking for. But he'd also said it with the kind of pride and admiration that Esther had never received from anyone else.

Esther's feelings betrayed her. She could hear the awe in his voice and sensed his pride in her. She imagined herself signing *take away*, where the right hand scratches something away from the left hand, only this time she would scratch away the feelings from her heart.

She caught Daisy's eye, and they bowed their heads together. Her usual silent breakfast prayer was less about appreciation for the food and more about asking God for the answers she needed. What was she to do with her back-from-the-dead father living with her? Most of all, how was she to handle Joe's return?

"Amen," her father piped up when she raised her head. His mouth was full of bread and he smiled at her.

Daisy instantly began eating while Esther slowly gathered a bite on her fork, debating how she would bring up the uncomfortable topic of him finding a different home.

"Looks like you have a load of somethin' on your mind," he said in English without any apologies.

His glibness gave her confidence to just say what she was thinking.

"I said you could stay for two days. You've stayed for three."

Chester didn't answer but bobbed his head up and down in agreement. He chewed his bite slowly and looked out through the open back door toward the fields.

"Yep, you're right. I've overstayed my welcome," he said in agreement. "I was hoping you'd change your mind."

"Well," Esther hesitated, "I haven't."

"I see." He pushed back his empty plate and leaned back in his chair, rubbing his belly. "I figured that's what you'd say, so I'm moving across the road to the Whites' farm. I'll be working around the farm for a spell too. I've got a few bills to make good on."

"So you're staying?" Esther's eyes diverted away from his. "In Sunrise?"

Chester leaned forward and looked out of the tops of his eyes at Esther, raising his eyebrows. "I came home for *Mem's* funeral, but I'm staying for you. I want to make it up to you."

Any response to this that Esther had thought of over the last few days vanished from her mind. She couldn't help but pause at this, but she was as mute as Daisy and couldn't think of anything to say. Silence was the answer Chester received.

"I'll be out by lunch."

"Well—I mean," she stammered. What could she say to his quick willingness?

"When's the girl's daddy coming back?" Chester changed the subject. Unfortunately, this topic was as uncomfortable as the former.

The food in Esther's mouth became like sand—dry and impossible to chew. She gulped a mouthful of water and swallowed the food, feeling it move down her throat.

He was always full of questions that she didn't want to answer.

A crow screeched as it flew by the window next to the kitchen table. He moved back and forth, back and forth, squawking loudly each time.

"A few days."

The crow's racket grew louder.

Esther

On the day of Joe's arrival, things happened in the Detweiler home like any other morning. Esther sat at the rickety kitchen table with the *Bivel* that she and her *mammie* had shared. She hadn't opened it since Orpha's death. She touched the aged leather and picked at the corner that had once been chewed by an uninvited mouse. She flipped open the front cover, revealing the name written in scrolled penmanship inside: *Chester R. Detweiler.* She remembered her father taking the Bible out of his bag and leaving it on the same kitchen table. It had been the same morning his hand was bloodied, and he had been pale and shaken. Then he was gone.

Chester had kept his word and moved into Mrs. White's farmhand boardinghouse. Esther still saw him daily when she went to work. Her small farmhouse was especially quiet now. Even the few days with Chester, though unwelcome, had brought life into the home. Now it was just Esther and Daisy.

She ran a finger over her mother's name beneath Chester's: *Leah D. Detweiler.* She'd been a Bender before she married Esther's father. The final name in the book was Esther's: *Esther C. Detweiler.* The *C* stood for Chester in the Amish tradition that the father's initial would be used as their daughter's middle name. The rest of the page remained blank.

The bookmark, a piece of white fabric, flopped out from the top of the old black book. Her *mammie* had given her a swatch of Leah's burial dress, telling Esther she'd want to keep something from her. She fingered the old piece of cloth before opening the Bible further.

The heavy pages were familiar in her work-worn fingers. The black and white lines were filled with such wisdom, though she rarely knew where to turn. The best she could do was read a few verses daily and hope that whatever was meant for that day was what she needed.

Daisy tapped Esther's arm. Esther smiled at the little girl as she gestured to the open page and tried to vocalize the word *read*.

Esther looked back at the passage.

For which cause we faint not; but though our outward man perish, yet the inward man renewed day by day. For our light affliction, which is but for a moment, worketh for us a far more exceeding and eternal weight of glory; While we look not at the things which are seen, but the things which are not seen: for the things which are seen are temporal; but the things which are not seen are eternal.

She knew the passage should be an encouragement to her; these ancient, holy words promised that her pain was only a vapor in comparison to eternal glory in heaven. But the way she saw it was that her pain was not temporal. Losing Daisy wouldn't be a passing wound, and it was not light. Esther could not unite the biblical encouragement with her pain, and she didn't experience the daily newness of which it spoke. There was in fact a great piercing ache in her chest. Was her heart formed out of quills? As ill-equipped as she had been to take on Daisy four years ago as a misunderstood three-year-old, she was even less prepared for Joe's return. Nothing could make her ready for this journey—regardless of what was right.

When she first started signing, Esther finger-signed her name or just patted her chest when referring to herself, but Daisy had quickly begun using the sign for *mother* instead. *Mother Esther*. Esther had learned from the sign language book that only the deaf could assign signed names to another, and while Esther knew she should've resisted the tender acknowledgment, she didn't. She loved Daisy the way a mother would.

Esther tried to take a deep breath to manage her emotions, but she couldn't get enough air into her lungs.

If only Mem or Orpha were here.

Esther thought this only briefly, though, then decided it wouldn't have mattered. Orpha was often lost in her own world and wouldn't have understood how she felt. Her mother would also have been little help; she never appeared to be strong enough for much. Leah was always pale and weak and almost invisible. When she died, Esther, even at the young age of seven, vowed never to be that way. She would never be weak or let anyone make her feel as if she couldn't take care of herself. And she was thankful for that decision now, when all she had was her own nerve and the love for a little girl. Her devotion to the church and serving God didn't waver, though she rarely understood how He was working in her life. What she couldn't understand was whether it was God who brought Chester back or the devil. Confronting her father had strengthened her will, but it was all a facade. On the inside she was a frightened girl.

Daisy nudged her again, bringing her thoughts back to the verses in I Corinthians.

How could she translate a passage that she couldn't see in her life? Daisy was going to see her dad today, and Esther, the woman she trusted most in the world, hadn't even told her yet. She knew it was wrong not to prepare the little girl.

She signed slowly. "Mother Esther has to tell you something."

Usually she would vocalize *and* sign the words to Daisy. Now, Esther barely mouthed them as she used her hands. A callus grew over the lump deep in her throat. She winced as she swallowed it down.

Today, she signed.

Esther gently touched Daisy's chest. *Your.*

Daisy's eyes looked at Esther with such hope. Round and innocent. Blue and perfect. Rare.

Esther's thumb touched her forehead with an open palm. *Dad.*

Then her pointer fingers pointed out and then back toward her chest. *Is coming.*

She hesitated signing the final word, though she sensed that Daisy could have finished it for herself with her brow, which had evolved into a deep furrow. Daisy's head tilted. Esther's fingers and thumb on her right hand came together and touched her mouth then slowly moved to her right cheek.

Home.

Sergeant Joe Garrison wiped the sweat from his forehead with the back of his arm. The buttons of his uniform shirt were open in an effort to catch a breeze. His finger ticked against his M1 rifle next to him on the hot sandy ground, the Philippine Sea ahead of him. A large bug crawled on his canvas-top jungle boot. He kicked it, sending it several feet, hitting a squad buddy, Corporal Toby Fielding. Fielding hollered and hopped up trying to get it off. Everyone laughed.

"Dumb walking cigar." Fielding hated the insects in the Pacific worse than anyone else. He usually called the long, black, shiny insect something other than a walking cigar.

Garrison stopped laughing when he heard buzzing above him and grabbed his M1. The muscles in his back tightened against the mound of sand as he leaned into it, preparing himself. It wasn't an attack but a sudden swarm of insects that flew at him, pelting him relentlessly.

They were larger than normal and were dive-bombing him, as if he was the only one on this death trap of a beach. He started swatting at the bugs as they landed on his arms and chest and sucked up every bit of sweat on his sunburned skin. He fell back, and the damp sand stuck to him. The more he swatted, the more they came. They pinched his skin, and the buzz in his ears got louder and louder. They didn't relent.

What began as the familiar clamor of mortar rounds became the sound of a train whistle. Why was there a train whistle in the small lump of sand and jungle that the general called Saipan?

Joe startled awake.

Where was he?

He blinked rapidly to force his eyes into focus, and a row of train seats brought him back to reality. He was on the train to Dover. The woman in black who sat across the aisle looked at him cautiously. He glanced down and found he'd made a mess of the sandwich he'd been eating as he'd fallen asleep. As he stood, bits of the bologna sandwich fell around his feet and into the aisle.

When he brushed away the lingering crumbs, he realized that his uniform wasn't as stiff as it should be. His shoes needed polishing too. With a huff he sat back down.

He needed a drink. A quick shot of scotch to help clear his mind.

But it was too late for a scotch: the train was screeching into the station. His hands went over his ears when the engine released a long scream. A tap on his back startled him, causing him to drop his arms to his sides and turn around.

"After the first war, my husband had a hard time with loud noises too," the woman wearing black said. "Welcome back."

She smiled warmly at Joe, like a grandmother would to a naughty grandchild she can't help but love.

Was he that pitiful?

"Ma'am," he said and touched the woman's arm ahead of him. "How is he now? Your husband."

The woman's head tilted and she looked out through the window. "He killed himself." Her tone of polite affection made the words all the more eerie, especially when her hand reached out to Joe. She patted his arm then walked away. He watched as she walked the length of the rail car. She didn't turn around before she exited.

Heat crept between his clothing and his skin. He needed a scotch.

Joe wished that he could be anywhere but his *home of record*. That's what the military called it. It was impersonal to be sure, but it sounded more official than just calling Sunrise home. He wasn't sure the small town was home anymore. Hadn't it been only weeks ago that he'd buried Irene? Hadn't it only been days ago that he'd gone to tell Esther that he was going off to war? He'd found her standing in the garden with newly turned soil. But that hadn't been only days ago. It had been four years.

Joe could close his eyes and put himself back at the Whites' dairy farm. Daisy was at his side, Esther kneeling in the garden. When she stood, dirty knee marks soiled her gray dress, and she crossed her arms over her chest and tucked her fingertips out of view. Her face was wet with sweat, and a spray of damp curls framed her forehead.

Esther, his wife's dearest cousin, was the most unusual Amish woman he'd ever known—not just because she was unmarried at her age—over thirty—but also because Irene often spoke of how Esther was too strong-minded for a husband and unwilling to even consider dating in order to find one. Still, she did follow the Amish church's lofty rules, the *Ordnung*, without question.

Everyone was off the car now except him. The few other servicemen who had been on the train with him were greeting their families. He'd intentionally sat far from them. He didn't want to reminisce about his Marine days, which often happened when a few servicemen were gathered. Even when you'd accomplished good things for your country, you'd sooner forget it all than relive it again and again. The memories would revive in his nightmares. He felt no shame about his work as a soldier, but they had been painful days. He was ashamed of some of the missteps he made, especially because those mistakes had cost lives. In his wildest ideas of war, in all of the history books he'd taught his students, he never could've imagined the reality.

He shook his head and leaned against the seat, trying to forget the way the shrapnel scraped against his heavy helmet and ripped his uniform. He never again wanted to see another irate Jap running at him, dagger in hand. His eyes squeezed shut, remembering the sound of a cracking neck and the gurgling of his fellow Marines as they tried to breathe but couldn't.

"Oh, I thought the car was empty. This ain't your stop?"

Joe's eyes snapped open. A man in a conductor's hat approached Joe. A cigarette bounced up and down when he spoke. His name tag read *Roger*. Roger pulled the cigarette from his mouth and looked around for a place to extinguish it. "Not supposed to smoke in front of passengers."

"I'll take it," Joe said. He extended his hand toward Roger's cigarette.

"I'll do better than that," the man said and pulled out a new cigarette.

Joe took it and put it between his lips. Roger popped his smoke back into place and promptly lit Joe's. "Welcome home, Sarge."

"It's 'corporal,' actually." Joe mumbled the correction then nodded as Roger walked past him and left him standing in the aisle. He took a long pull from the cigarette. It tasted good. The burn in his lungs reminded him that he was alive. He blew out slowly, then walked through his own smoke toward the exit. It was time.

He stood on the bottom step of the train car for several long moments. The sun was bright. Was it really the same sun that had poured over him and his fellow Marines in the Mariana Islands? There was no comparison, however, about the heat and humidity. The train station looked permanent and American to him. After living in temporary buildings, tents, and foxholes for four years, he'd forgotten how American America looked.

Against the wall were wooden benches for people tired of standing. Not even minuscule specs of dirt remained on the swept sidewalks. The awning above protected people from the rain, snow, and even heat. America suddenly appeared the picture of protection.

So why did he feel more vulnerable than ever before? The pain of losing Irene and the baby, of effectively abandoning Daisy, poured into his heart like the sunshine that fell between the train and the station. The pain was too raw even after four years away.

It hadn't taken long for him to realize that he never should have left his daughter. Irene would never have approved. But the idea of parenting Daisy on his own had been too much in his state of mind. He couldn't understand her behavior and had no way of knowing how to help her. Joe left thinking he'd leave the pain behind as well and that he would return healed and ready to rise to the challenge. But the pain he was running from was made worse by the burden and intensity of war.

The fact that he'd abandoned Daisy was perhaps the deepest pain because it was the one thing within his control. Now that he was back, he would do everything to make it up to Irene's memory. He would do all that it took to make Daisy happy.

He checked his hat out of habit and stepped down on the sidewalk. The light glared in his eyes and he squinted into the brightness. He went farther into the shadow of the canopy over him to let his eyes adjust. A woman stood just ahead of him. She seemed familiar—her height and the way she leaned on one leg. Irene had stood like that. He stepped toward her almost frantically and grabbed her arm. She turned toward Joe. Her face wasn't familiar. He wished she'd never turned around. Of course she wasn't Irene. Irene was dead.

"Sorry, ma'am," Joe said. He nervously took a drag from his smoke.

The blond woman's husband, an army officer also just returning home, glared at Joe. His chest puffed, and protectiveness was written across his brow and the tightness of his jaw. He put an arm around his wife.

Joe lifted his palms in surrender, and he offered a halfhearted casual salute as he backed away. He hadn't meant any harm.

The stares of those around him invaded the personal space he coveted. He didn't like the attention—having learned deep in the jungles that any attention was dangerous. Joe refocused and went to retrieve his sea bag, which was waiting next to the bench behind him. With the cigarette held loose between his lips, he scanned the train platform.

The two figures who stood ahead of him nearly blended into the darkness of the platform wall. He pulled out the cigarette, and the vision of Esther and Daisy in front of him turned cloudy behind his exhaled smoke. A thin breeze pushed the haziness away, and Joe settled his eyes on the pair. Outside of the fact that Esther had black hair and eyes and Daisy's hair was a sandy color like his own, they appeared like two sides of the same coin. Esther had her hands on Daisy's shoulders. Even from his distant view, he could see Esther's skin was stretched white over her knuckles. Both of them were tight-lipped. He pulled out his cigarette and inhaled the clean air deeply, refreshing his mind, and moved toward them.

"Esther," Joe said. He returned the cigarette to his lips so he could put his hand out to shake hers. He'd seen her often enough before Irene's death that he was comfortable around her. Irene's death, however, had changed all that. He was lost and ashamed of his actions. The last time he saw Esther, he couldn't even look her in the eyes. But now as he looked at her, he was reminded of how lost he felt four years ago and how bold her eyes were, so different from Irene's playful blue eyes. The magnetism in their gaze brought an intensity he wasn't prepared for.

Esther's eyes diverted, and she looked at the smoke blowing from his mouth, then raised an eyebrow. She did not take Joe's extended hand. His eyes went to her unresponsive hands. They were well worked, dried, and cracked—so different from the exotic women he'd met in the bars and clubs that he'd gone to during his R&Rs. Almond-eyed women with skin like silk and soft slender hands who had offered themselves to him. If it weren't for the aging picture of his ghostly wife tucked deep in his uniform, he was sure he would have dishonored more than one woman during his four years away. Esther's hands didn't have the beauty he'd been tempted by, but the intimidating strength they declared intrigued him.

When she recognized where Joe's gaze landed, Esther curled her fingers into her palms. He looked up at her. She looked down and her long black eyelashes rested against her cheeks. Feminine yet mysterious. Joe's insides turned over.

Irene had once said that while Esther was as pretty as the next girl, she was as adept and capable as a man. Joe had believed that, but he had never recognized that she was still fully woman. This secret acknowledgment provoked his frustration and his curiosity.

This silent and uncomfortable homecoming was not what Joe had imagined. Of course, he had imagined his homecoming with Irene, even though she had been dead and buried before he'd enlisted. When the imaginings of Irene came at first, he quickly stopped himself, but after barely surviving the first year overseas, those visions of coming home to Irene became the only way he survived. His dreamed-up visions were so vivid that he sometimes forgot they would never happen.

"Joe," Esther spoke quietly and in the deep tone he remembered from before. Her voice was cool with an edge of nervousness. She nodded toward his smoke and eyed the nearby trash.

Joe pulled his hand back and took the cigarette from his lips. He looked at it and then at Esther again.

"Just a few more drags?"

Esther pursed her lips.

Joe sighed and threw the cigarette onto the sidewalk. When he let it smolder, Esther twisted her shoe over it. A man came around only seconds later and swept up the extinguished cigarette into a long-handled dustpan. He eyed Joe, who realized he should have thrown it in the trash.

"Sorry." He didn't mean to say it so lamely, but with his heart hammering in his chest and the shock it was to be home, he wasn't sure he could muster more than that.

Joe turned back to Esther to see her tap Daisy on the shoulder. The little girl turned to look at Esther. Esther knelt down to Daisy's level. She fixed his daughter's hair, smoothing it back behind the white covering she wore. He couldn't believe how Amish she looked. Esther's eyes glistened, but her face did not dampen with tears as she blinked them away.

"Daisy. This is your dad."

Joe

Esther didn't just speak out loud. She also used her hands. Daisy whipped her face toward Joe and met his eyes. Though she had grown so much, changed so much, he recognized the spirit behind her eyes. His own mother had always called him spirited, though everyone else called him wild. He wanted to believe the same was true of Daisy, but she hadn't started talking by the time she was three. Most children were talking at that age, but she was making only loud and confused noises. The sounds took Joe back to his childhood, when his brother Jason had been sent away to an institution for the simpleminded because he'd been too hard to handle. His chest tightened. He would never do that to a child of his.

In one of her early letters, Esther had written that Daisy wasn't simpleminded at all; in fact, she was a deaf-mute. Joe at first considered this as a possibility, but then remembered that his brother had been similar to how Daisy was, and he didn't believe Esther was right. If she was, that meant that his parents had likely been wrong about Jason. Irene had been convinced that Daisy was just special and would grow out of her simple ways.

Esther never wrote much in her letters, just a few quick lines telling him of Daisy's well-being. Once she'd asked if she could have the child evaluated by a doctor who dealt with deafness. Joe had refused, perhaps out of fear of the truth or disbelief. He didn't know.

In another letter, months later, she briefly mentioned sign language, which he knew nothing about. He had honestly expected to hear back at some point saying that Esther's non-expert opinion about deafness was merely a rabbit trail. When he never heard more, he put his mind on more pressing things— like staying alive or at least dying well.

Even now, as he watched them communicate with their hands, he wasn't sure that it was really because Daisy was deaf. Esther attracted far too much attention, waving her hands about and making shapes with her fingers. People watched them from the corners of their eyes and admonished their children not to stare. It didn't look any more like a language than if he started drawing pictures in the sand with his finger and called it art. Esther's and Daisy's faces contorted into a variety of expressions as odd as the signing.

Then Daisy's eyes burrowed into his and brought him back to reality. His chest was still constricted. He was holding in a bitter breath that hurt to release. He squatted down to his daughter's level. He wanted to take her in his arms and croon to her, as he'd done when she was an angelfaced tot. He also wanted to get back on the train and pretend he wasn't a father at all. His little girl's resemblance to Irene was startling, but at the same time, he could see himself in the blueness of her watery eyes. He dug through his pocket and pulled out a small lollipop.

"Hi, Daisy. I know you don't remember me, but I'm your dad." He handed her the lollipop. He raised his eyebrows and tried on a smile.

"It doesn't matter how loudly you talk, Joe, she can't hear

you." Esther's voice was first cutting before it faded, sounding anxious.

Joe's neck muscles tightened, and he inhaled deeply, his eyes staying on his daughter. He hadn't realized that he'd spoken loudly. He moved the lollipop a bit closer to Daisy. When Daisy didn't respond or take it, he exhaled and pressed his lips together. He stood again and considered throwing the candy into the trash, but stuffed it back into his pocket instead.

Daisy instantly hopped up and down and pulled at Joe's uniform. The sound she made startled and even embarrassed him. He looked around and saw that several small groups of people had turned and were watching. One woman even had the audacity to talk behind her hand as she watched.

Esther calmly put her hand on Daisy's shoulder and squeezed gently, and Daisy turned to look at her. Esther then brought her right hand down on her left like a blade and mouthed a word.

Daisy nodded and turned back toward Joe. She opened her hand and rotated it in a circle over her chest.

Joe looked at Esther, who opened her mouth, but before she had a chance to speak, he said to Daisy, "Here, here." He quickly pulled out the lollipop and handed it to her. Daisy's eyes softened by degrees and she grabbed the candy from his hand.

Esther's eyes caught his, and he watched her face wash clean of color. What did that expression mean? It wasn't anger—though she had every right to be angry at him for leaving Daisy the way he had. He knew Esther hadn't thought much of him—he had romanced Irene away from the church—but she had accepted their marriage, and she and Irene had built a new friendship behind closed doors after the shunning. But it was something more than that, deeper than anger, that was troubling her now.

Esther took Daisy's chin gently into the palm of her hand, seemingly to get her attention. When she had that, she let go of her chin, and words flew silently from her mouth and hands. Daisy signed back, breathy words falling from her lips. When they were done, Daisy handed Esther the lollipop, who then stuffed it in her black vinyl purse, which instantly reminded Joe of something his Amish mother-in-law, Lucy Bender, would use. For several moments, their eyes connected, and Joe saw the woman who had loved Irene. Those dark eyes had seen Daisy's birth and Irene's death. She'd heard the whisper of Irene's last breath. They'd been together in the upstairs bedroom with the doctor and his dead infant son.

"Your travels went well?" Esther asked. "I—"

"Travels?" He half laughed. "Not sure I'd call what I did *traveling.*"

Esther bristled. "Well, I didn't—"

"Where's Angelica?" Joe interrupted. She didn't need to correct her insinuation; he would pocket the offense and coat his heart with it.

He could see Daisy was not the same child he left behind. Esther had helped her, that was clear, but had she also embittered the little girl against him? She used to reach for him and wrap herself around his legs. She used to try to tickle him so that he would tickle her back. Where was that girl? Had she forgotten him?

"I don't know. Edwina said they would be coming." Esther looked around the station.

"Maybe they'll just meet us at the house." His eyes darted between Esther and Daisy.

"We're—Daisy—is not going home with you," Esther said. Her words were clipped and clearly reflected her discomfort and nervousness.

"What?"

Joe blamed himself for imagining his homecoming differently, but he hadn't expected this. Of course, Daisy would be shy and maybe hesitant, but he hadn't predicted the anger and resentment he saw in her eyes. It was clear that his four years away had dimmed any memories of him.

The time away hadn't been the salve he'd expected either. Esther appeared tougher than he'd remembered. He'd expected her to be sympathetic because of everything she knew about his burden, but her protectiveness toward Daisy infuriated him.

"Daisy isn't ready to go home with you yet," Esther said quickly and cleared her throat. "And I agree with her." Her eyes diverted from his.

"If you'd stayed in my house when I was gone, this wouldn't be a problem," he whispered through clenched teeth.

Esther narrowed her gaze. "I couldn't have lived in an electricity wired English house for four years. That never would have worked."

Joe didn't release the tightness in his jaw for several moments, considering this. There was no use arguing over it now.

"I have a car waiting for Daisy and me. I paid a driver to bring us here."

"Well, he can drive us all to my house." Joe started to walk away, expecting them to follow.

"We will walk over tomorrow and every day until Daisy is— ready." Esther didn't budge from her spot on the sidewalk. Her nerve ruffled Joe. He could see her clench and unclench her jaw.

Esther's dark eyes didn't flinch or resist meeting his. She swallowed hard, however, and a shadow of dread passed over her unyielding eyes. Joe looked down at Daisy's round eyes. They were confused or afraid—or both.

Joe knelt down in front of Daisy again and recalled the feeling of her in his arms. The warmth of those early hours after her birth and the instant unconditional love he'd felt comforted him now. She'd looked right into his eyes the night she was born. Irene was weak and ill for weeks to follow, and he had managed to care for mother and baby better than anyone had expected him to.

Now Daisy looked at him with contempt, and it took all his strength not to take her by the shoulders and shake his warm, sweet memories into her, to compel her to love him again. Could she somehow see that he was a terrible father because he'd gone through terrible things—done terrible things?

Joe hesitantly touched Daisy's arm. She inhaled and pulled back—slowly, and only a little—and Joe's heart stopped for a few beats. He took his hand away. His jaw clamped several times as she looked up at Esther, catching her gaze.

"I know you don't understand me and I don't think you re-member me, but I just want you to know that I'm glad to see you."

Was he? he asked himself honestly. *Yes, he was.* But in the moment, it would've been easier for him to protect his fellow Marine with gun in hand than to be there with his heart unpro-tected in front of his seven-year-old daughter.

"Joey." His eyes followed a familiar voice, but when he found it, he barely recognized the woman in front of him. His sister had aged in the years since his absence. He stood and opened his arms to her.

"Angelica." He held her skeletal frame for a long minute and then pulled away from her to look at her. Her hair was in a tight bun at the nape of her neck. It reminded him of their mother. Her dress was thin and threadbare; she wore a belt around the middle, as if to spruce it up. With no rouge on her cheeks or kohl on her eyes and with pale lips, she appeared ashen and ill. Esther didn't wear her face made up either, but she looked healthy and rosy.

"Is everything okay?"

"It will be now that you're home." She cried in his chest and Joe soothed her. His brother-in-law, Donald, limped as he walked toward them, leaning heavily on a cane. He'd grown heavier than Joe could've imagined possible. "Donald." He nodded toward him.

They shook hands while Angelica clung tightly to Joe's other arm.

"The pickup broke down on the way in," Angelica said with a nervous giggle. "I was plain frantic."

"Well, you're here now. Take me home?"

"Just you?" Angelica looked over at Esther and Daisy. The silence between the two spoke loudly to Joe.

"For now. Daisy's a little nervous, is all."

"We'll see you tomorrow," Esther said and walked away with Daisy's hand in hers.

After a few steps, Daisy turned and looked at Joe. He waved at her and the unresponsiveness in her expression was disappointing. But what could he expect? He was a stranger to his daughter.

"That Esther. You're going to have to explain a few things to her, Joey," Angelica said as soon as Esther was far enough away.

"We can talk about that later." Joe had no energy to discuss Angelica's feelings about Esther. He'd put the woman in a precarious position and knew he could never make it up to her. When her eyes landed on him, there was a magnetic pull toward her depths that he didn't understand. But it had been four years since he had been a man to a woman—his wife. The tug toward Esther was not real attraction, but the war's bewitchment on him. It was only temptation.

All he wanted now was to get home.

After a little roadside work on the pickup's motor, they made a quick stop for a few grocery items. Joe used the rest of his cash on hand to put gas in Donald and Angelica's truck. When they finally made it to their childhood home, Angelica hugged Joe tightly again before inviting him to supper then leaving with

Donald. For how thin she was, her strength surprised Joe. Joe and Angelica only had each other. Their parents were dead, and their brother had been lost to their family long before he was dead and buried.

Angelica had still had enough spunk to insist on renting out the house while he was away. It wasn't what he wanted, but the rent money had helped, though it wasn't much. But now it was empty, and it was strange to see the house he'd spent his whole life in.

The freshly mown grass filled Joe's senses. He'd never given it much thought until now. One would think that after years in the Pacific, he would have come to love the smell of the salty ocean air, but it was difficult to smell it over the odor of exploded shells, the spent bullets, and the stench of too many living and dead bodies in one place. Joe breathed in deeply, reminding himself that he wasn't in hell anymore. He was home, though he realized at the train station that home was a different kind of hell—one he'd created all on his own.

He went around to the back door and stopped in his tracks at the flowers blooming in the old tire. Irene's shadow hovered close by.

The memory of finding Irene at this door one day asking for advice on how to be a good teacher broke into his thoughts. She had offered to clean his house in return. He remembered thinking how pretty she looked when he invited her in. Before he knew it, they were sitting at his table over tea that Irene had made and talking about everything but teaching.

He had been twenty-eight, a messy bachelor, and had selfishly wanted help with his housekeeping. Since he wasn't sure being alone with an unmarried woman was appropriate, she would come and clean when he was at work. Her excitement and friendliness made him curious about this beautiful Amish woman. Joe could always tell the days she'd been there. He would come home from teaching school to find the house spotless and supper made. One day she had moved one of the old tires from the barn and planted flowers in it.

There it was still, next to the back door. He blinked away his emotions and went in the door, through the small mudroom, then into the kitchen. The sight of the small space where his wife had made so many meals for him flooded his mind. He closed his eyes and could almost smell his favorite meal, venison roast. The vision—the way she looked over her shoulder at him and slapped his hand if he picked at the food before supper—was so clear. An old familiar smile found his mouth, but he wiped it clean before the haunting completely seduced him. He needed to resist indulging in these sentimental memories. He shook his head and forced the images to fall around him like autumn leaves from a wind-blown tree.

When he cleared his throat, the empty house swallowed up the bit of sound. The counters were clean and appeared recently washed. Hadn't it just been the night before that Irene bustled with a stew on the stove? He smiled at the thought of the stinky cabbage soup. How he'd hated that soup, but what he wouldn't give . . .

Joe left the food he'd bought on the counter and stuffed the beer into the icebox before he walked out of the kitchen. He made his way through the dining room and to the staircase. As he looked up the stairs, the window at the top dared him to jump through, pressing for physical pain to cover his melancholy. Leaving Sunrise had only created a scab over his wounds. He hadn't healed. Returning home had opened the wound wider than ever before, and it was bleeding into his life all over again.

The bed was draped with the quilt Irene had sewn for their wedding. He tossed his green sea bag onto the wooden floor and turned his back to the bed. The doorknob of the closet rattled in his hand a few times before he was able to pull it open. He pushed the duffel into the closet with his feet. His eyes traveled to the high shelf. The small box called to him, taunted him. He pulled it out, sat on the bed, and cautiously opened it. The framed photo of Irene, Daisy, and himself inside forced his breath to quicken. He placed it on the nightstand. There were a few other items inside, but he took out only one other item— the first gift he'd purchased for Irene, just before he'd asked her to marry him. It had been a partially used tester perfume from Woolworths, all he could afford at the time. Teachers, especially in rural schools, weren't paid well. It was the only perfume she'd ever had.

With care, he pulled off the cap and put the nozzle to his nose. Irene. In the next moment he pulled out a small piece of barely white fabric from his pocket. The wedding dress swatch was dirty from the years he'd carried it with him. He carefully sprayed only one spritz on the fabric and breathed in the scent.

Although it smelled like home, home didn't give him the sense of protection and comfort he desired.

Irene was dead. His baby son was dead. Daisy hated him and didn't need him.

Why hadn't he just let himself die far away in the Pacific? Why had he fought so hard? Why had God chosen to spare him? No, God had not spared his life—the devil had.

Esther

Seeing Joe Garrison step onto the platform and move toward them took Esther back to the time he'd walked down Norma White's gravel drive to tell her of his plans. She had been in the garden, dirty and sweaty, her toes curled in the moist soil as he spoke. The last time she'd seen him had been at Irene's burial weeks earlier, where her toes had bowed around the cool grass at the graveyard. Esther hadn't any shoes then. He hadn't even looked at her that day as they lowered Irene into the damp ground. He hadn't shared his grief with her as she expected. He had isolated himself, and then he was gone. She wondered how or if he'd explained this to Daisy. Did he tell her that she would be okay? When she'd tried to explain things to Daisy herself, she'd become inconsolable, and hadn't understood anything Esther said.

At the train depot, when she saw Joe again, her toes ached at the memory, making her yearn for the cool garden earth and the warm sun against her face. Instead, she was restricted with too-small shoes and her only pair of black knee stockings. Her toes were squeezing out of a hole in the stocking, making her even more uncomfortable.

It was a mild pain, however, in comparison to the thought of losing Daisy. She tried to soften her fear and panic, but she was sure it was written along every line of her face. The anger she'd felt over Joe's abandonment of Daisy had diminished in contrast to the growing fear she had over losing her. The anger was still along the edges of her heart, but she'd gotten over the worst of it. Yes, he had wooed Irene away, but she had gone willingly. All of the pain and sorrow, from her leaving to her death, had still brought Esther's greatest joy—Daisy. Daisy was as much Esther's as anyone else's, but no one, including Joe, saw her as anything more than a spinster nanny. Maybe that was all she was, but Daisy saw Esther as her mother. And with Joe's return, everything would change.

When Esther's life had fallen apart, no one fought for her. Everyone had grieved with her, but Esther had had to fight for herself. Even Orpha just accepted a natural responsibility for her but was lost in so much grief that it wasn't long before Esther was taking care of her *mammie* instead of the other way around. She didn't want to move away to live with anyone who hadn't been willing to take care of her without prodding from the church. She wanted to be wanted.

She would not let Daisy be put in the same position. Daisy deserved to be with someone who loved and wanted her. Joe was her father, but he needed to prove he wouldn't walk out on her again. He needed to be ready to take care of her, love her, and keep her safe before Esther would let her go.

When morning came, Esther startled awake. Her entire body was still weary from tension. She'd slept only fitfully, and her disheveled bed confirmed it.

She could hear the sizzle of the eggs through the floor register. Then Chester's loud voice singing an unfamiliar song came through as well. What was he doing there? The smell of breakfast and awareness of his presence roused her senses into wakefulness. She untangled her legs from the coverlet and slipped onto the floor. She sat near the iron floor register with her knees pulled up beneath her nightgown, recalling times when he would sing her songs that didn't come out of the church's hymn book.

The hedge she'd built around herself was being torn down with Chester's rich twang, and she closed her eyes to the burn of tears. She heard words like *San Antone, enchantment*, and *Alamo* before she closed the grate, leaving her to hear only muffled sounds of his singing as she got dressed.

When the sound of the harmonica drifted through the floor register, Esther readied herself in a hurry. When she reached the kitchen, she was surprised at Daisy's cheerfulness. Chester was stomping his foot to the beat while he played "Oh! Susanna" on the harmonica. His face was red as he puffed, and Daisy mimicked his movements while giggling uncontrollably. The smile they shared reminded Esther of her five-year-old self. When Chester caught sight of her, he stopped and withdrew the mouth harp.

"I just—" he began, and returned the instrument to the sill.

Esther continued into the kitchen, and when she met Daisy's eyes, the little girl crossed her arms and turned away. Clearly Daisy was still angry with her for taking her to meet Joe at the train station. She decided to let Daisy sulk for the time being.

"Fried up some eggs," Chester said before she could ask why he was there at all. His smile was soft and kind, like warm milk. His head tilted, and their eyes locked as understanding flowed between them. It appeared to her that he'd come to see how she was doing with Joe's return. Like he understood how difficult it would be.

Esther's heart plunged into her gut.

"*Dangeh*," Esther said in a whisper as he handed her a plate of food. But her stomach swirled, and she wasn't sure she would be able to eat.

Esther took the plate of twin eggs and a thin slice of bread.

A portion of her heart was pocketed deeply in her soul, and she needed a kind gesture like this. Maybe she needed someone to take care of her—even love her. When it was offered so sincerely, as it seemed Chester had done, she didn't want the moment to pass.

Esther sat and then tapped Daisy's shoulder. The little girl turned just enough for Esther to see that her eyes were puffy. Daisy had slept as restlessly as Esther. She hadn't noticed this when Chester was amusing her. Esther tilted Daisy's chin toward her, only to watch as the little girl's gaze darted away. A heavy sigh escaped Esther's chest that deflated the very edges of her lungs. Daisy was not as angry with Joe as she was with Esther. The last time her young charge had acted this way was during the first few months she lived with the Detweilers. She'd been an angry and frightened little girl then, and now she was again. For their time together to end like this brought hot, bitter tears to Esther's eyes. But she swallowed them down as she ate her breakfast quickly.

Esther signed to Daisy to sit at the table so her hair could be done. Daisy's eyes sharpened, and with the loudest voice Esther had ever heard Daisy use, she yelled "No!" And then she ran out of the house.

Through the window, Esther saw her run down the road toward the Sunrise Dairy farm. She was likely running to Mrs. White's library, the only place the little girl was comfortable alone in the big house. It was the last place Esther wanted her to flee. She watched through the window as Daisy looked both ways as she crossed the road and bounded up the hill toward the large white farmhouse that dwarfed their own.

Esther leaned against the small table in the middle of the kitchen. How should she handle this? How could she give Daisy up to Joe? She had never intentionally embittered Daisy against her father. It had come as a natural consequence of their circumstances.

A sigh that began in her soul escaped through her mouth.

"Just give her a little time." Chester offered his advice in English. Then changed it to their dialect. "She'll come around."

"Maybe," Esther said softly. Then her shoulders stiffened. "But I wouldn't count on it."

He nodded his head, his lips pursed and eyes downcast.

"Esther," he said, extending his hand. "I'll tell you anything you want to know when you're ready."

"Why are you here this morning?" Esther asked coldly.

"I wanted to see how yesterday went. Wanted to check in on you." His Texas twang filtered through his mixed English and Pennsylvania Dutch words. "I know you love that little girl, and with her daddy coming home—well, I can understand why that would be a mite tough."

Esther looked away and kept her eyes trained on the farmhouse in the distance as she bit her lower lip. He had come because he cared.

"I'm fine," she whispered. She got up from the chair and stood at the kitchen counter to begin cleaning the mess Chester had made.

She could count on one hand the times she'd cried since she was a child, and now, in a matter of a few weeks she'd had to fight the urge more than she'd ever known possible. What was wrong with her? She didn't want Chester to see her break. She heard his footsteps behind her, heard the door open and close, and saw him jog to the barns across the road. Mrs. White emerged from the farmhouse and stood on the porch facing Esther's home, her arms crossed over her chest.

Daisy.

Since it was Friday and Esther would be picking up food to distribute, she had to go over there anyway. After she briskly walked toward the big house, she arrived more out of breath than she should have. Her nerves suddenly stretched too far.

Having Daisy upset with her shallowed her breathing and made her blood rush through her veins like feed through a chute.

"Esther, over here," Mrs. White called from the screened-in porch on the side of the house. Her voice carried the usual timbre, patronizing, like she was talking to a four-year-old. In Esther's dismay she hadn't noticed Mrs. White sitting there with Daisy on her lap.

Esther filled her lungs and tried to slow her breathing as she opened the door and walked slowly toward her employer. Daisy looked off toward the barns, her jaw clenched in stubborness. Mrs. White held the child in her arms as if she were her own. She had rarely paid Daisy any mind, apart from being a heroine several times with hand-me-down fabric or some canned goods in the dead of winter. Esther was thankful, to be sure, but usually Mrs. White treated Daisy like a germ in her home.

"I'm sorry, Mrs. White." Esther could hardly look at her. She was ashamed to have such a private dilemma spill over onto her employer. "I don't know what came over her."

"Nor do I, for that matter. I can't speak—well, that *hand language*." Mrs. White patted Daisy on the back and encouraged her to walk to Esther by gesturing wildly like one would when shooing away an unwanted animal. Daisy did look wild with her long hair blowing wickedly in the wind. Her face was covered in red blotches and she was barefoot. "Go on. Go on."

Daisy finally looked up at Esther but didn't meet her eyes. Esther signed the word *please*. The little girl lifted her chin slightly before she slowly walked over to her. Daisy's lips pursed but didn't pout; she was stubborn, not spoiled. She stood next to Esther with her hands clasped tightly, declaring her desire to remain untouched and, more important, silent. Her hands would not be talking.

Mrs. White had spoken in an easy manner, her words dancing up and down like the notes of a song. She was, however, unfailingly strict, and when she was not obeyed to the letter, her kind-sounding words were laced with reprimands. Esther knew that with every gift and donation came obligation.

Mrs. White had given her old curtains, books she didn't need anymore, old buttons, pieces of yarn, and sometimes hair ribbons her young grandchildren had grown tired of. Once she'd even given Daisy well-used hand-me-down shoes from a granddaughter. They were cute saddle shoes, but Mrs. White was vexed when she saw that Esther had painted the white sections black. When Esther tried to explain to her that the church didn't allow white shoes, Mrs. White scolded her on two fronts. One, generous gifts were not to be mutilated and ruined. She would think twice before she gave so generously again. And, two, Daisy wasn't Amish. The latter was a fact; the problem was that Esther had no idea how to raise an English girl. She hardened herself against the ridicule and nodded in agreement, knowing she should choose her responses carefully. The job with Mrs. White was the only way she could survive.

Mrs. White stood and took a step toward the door before she turned and cleared her throat as she caught Esther's attention.

"The girl is—*disturbed*. I'm sure you can see, Esther. Don't you think it's time she get *professional* help? You've done a better job than I really thought you could do, but she's far from *normal* and she still has these fits and outbursts. I have heard that her father has returned. Can he handle her?"

Professional help? She'd tried to get help for the girl, but Joe had refused to pay for it, and the Amish church did not believe Daisy was their responsibility and reserved their funds for members of the church. There was no malice in their decision, but their district was large and had many other needs that took priority. The community was spread out farther than some of the other districts and had fewer profitable farms also. Nonetheless,

Esther had been chided over Daisy's problems before and had an answer poised on the tip of her tongue.

"You're right in saying that Daisy is not normal. Her outbursts are because she is deaf and confused about her father's return after four years. *Normal* children have tantrums about gum, candy, or going to bed when told." Esther knew she sounded harsher than she should. She held her breath and her nerves rattled, making it difficult to exhale. Her lungs burned. Mrs. White's eyes sharpened as her attention trained on Esther. She lifted her chin and began again. "As for Daisy's father, no, I don't think he can *handle* her. But I can handle him—" She paused. How terrible that must sound. She stuttered through her words as she continued and made an effort to soften her tone. "I can teach him how to take care of Daisy."

At this, both of Mrs. White's eyebrows rose. Then a smile crossed her lips. "I believe you can handle Joe Garrison. How are you handling your own father's return?"

Esther's ears rang at those words. Sweat burned the skin under her arms and the beating of her heart raced against her thoughts. *How was she handling her father's return?* Up until his return, she'd nearly forgotten what he looked like. Only an occasional dream whispered to her the reminder of his dark hair and underbite—and, recently, of his bloodied hand the morning he left. Now his stature was slight and his brow deeply lined, giving the impression his twenty-nine years away had not been easy. His dancing eyes and his ready grin both pleased and peeved her—she had lost her own years earlier. Or had she never had dancing eyes or a ready grin?

"I'll be over to get the food as soon as I hitch up," Esther said, and walked away without answering Mrs. White's question.

"Come along, Daisy." She gently took Daisy's hand in hers and they walked back to the house in silence. Esther was relieved that Daisy had submitted with ease. She even rubbed

Esther's arm with her other hand once they were across the road.

"What is it?" Esther held her hand out in question.

Daisy rubbed a fist around her chest in apology. Her eyes glassed over. Esther knelt and pulled Daisy into her arms but hadn't the ability to speak. Tears wrapped tightly around her eyes. A hard swallow revived her doggedness. She stood, and they continued to walk to their shabby house.

Once inside, Esther sat on the woven rag rug and gestured for Daisy to join her. Her face had returned to its normal sweet pink, the redness gone, and her tawny blond hair twirled in ringlets that Esther rarely saw since she usually pulled her hair back into her *kapp*. She fingered the tresses, suddenly feeling sad that she'd concealed such beautiful hair beneath a covering for four years. Covering her own thick black hair was no great sadness. It was frizzy and unruly. The only time she could comb through its blackness was when it was wet. Daisy's eyes met Esther's and the little girl's lips turned down. Esther's insides grew less rigid, softening for the pain she saw in the little girl's eyes.

"I'm sorry also." Esther rubbed her fist in a circle on her chest. "I know you're angry." Her clawed hands moved up her torso and her face mimicked the anger. The sign was always so vivid and had been an easy one to remember.

When Daisy got excited or upset, she often tried to vocalize as she signed, as if to better express her feelings.

"Hate him." As Daisy attempted to speak the words, she threw her hands away from her body like a dirty rag, her face filled with disgust. She signed that she never wanted to see him again. Her breathing became heavy again, and her eyes pierced Esther's. But a moment later her face softened, and she signed that she loved Esther and wanted her to be her mother forever.

"Please trust me," Esther said, her fists tightened. She meant the words more than just about anything she'd ever signed. All of Daisy's trust, however, couldn't change the fact that their lives were being torn apart. The reality was that Daisy was Joe's daughter, and Esther knew she couldn't stand in the way of what was proper. It was proper for Daisy and Joe to be together. The pain of this truth was enough to make her second-guess the rightness of it. She vowed silently to do everything she could to ensure Daisy's happiness. That was what was right. That was all she could do.

Esther pulled the little girl into her arms, folding Daisy's smallness into her lap. Esther gently put Daisy's ear against her chest and began humming. Although Daisy couldn't hear the sound of her tune, she could feel the vibration. This had become a source of comfort to them both. Was this the last time they would do this?

Esther

Esther and Daisy went through their visits quickly, not in the mood for gossip—but she usually wasn't. No one asked about how she was doing after Orpha's death. No one asked after Chester. Many of them had no idea that Joe was back and wouldn't understand why losing Daisy would affect her so deeply. She wasn't a mother, after all. No one meant to be insensitive, only practical. It boiled down to the choice of accepting God's will in their lives without murmuring.

As Esther pulled the buggy into the short drive of Alvin and Dorothy Bender's small Amish home, their two young children with summer feet greeted them. Alvin and Dorothy had a small white farmhouse, typical of the area, that was nearly as run-down as Esther's. Its chipped wooden siding and sagging porch had been the result of the Depression and the previous owners' neglect. Alvin had slow but steady work as a horse trainer, but had to go to his parents' farm to do that work since he had only a small shed for his buggy horse.

"Candy-*frau*, candy-*frau*," the young children chanted as Esther stepped from the buggy. This was the nickname that many of the children had given to *Mammie* Orpha, who had

been known as the candy lady for as long as Esther could remember. How she missed her smile and calming ways. A sudden rush of warm air brushed against her face but was gone a
moment later. It comforted Esther, but as she leaned against the
side of the buggy, she was reminded that Orpha was dead—she
wasn't in the wind. So was it God? Or simply a breeze?

"Ich hap ken candy, kinnah. Sorry." Esther walked around to
the children and showed her empty hands.

"Kinnah," Dorothy called for her children. "Leave Esther
alone. The candy-*frau* isn't here anymore."

For a moment, the faces of the children drooped until Daisy
hopped from the buggy and pointed to their swing set and sandbox. They all simultaneously signed the word for *play* and ran
off together. This happened every week—every Friday when
Esther came visiting.

"I wasn't sure if you'd make it today." Dorothy stepped
off the porch steps and looked up into the sun, as if checking
the time of day. The little Amish woman seemed as small as a
child though she had two children, and a third would likely not
be far behind. She was married to Irene's youngest brother,
Alvin.

"I got held up at Mariellen's." Esther walked toward the
small house after peeking over at Daisy playing with the Bender
children. Junior was only four and Rebekah barely two, and they
loved Daisy. "Their baby, Rachel, has the croup still. Mariellen
is in a fit of worry."

"Oh, she always is. That baby would be *goot* if she stopped
fussing over her so much. My Junior and Rebekah had it last
summer. They were *goot* and were only three and about a year.
They are as *tsunt* and busy as can be now. See how healthy they
are?" She pointed out the window at the children playing. "Have
you already been up to see Marty?"

Dorothy winked at Esther.

"I have. Why do you ask?" Esther knew it was because Marty's widowed son was visiting from Ohio.

Conversations about the widowers of the community were old news to Esther. She was always one of the first to hear that she might be the man's next choice for a wife—after all, his children needed a mother, right? She'd also always been told that a man couldn't take care of himself after first having a mother's care and then a wife's. In part, she resented this, having had to do much for herself when her mother died and even more when her *mammie* was unable to work any longer. Weren't men supposed to be the stronger sex? And here she had never had a consistent man in her life to prove this or provide any strength. She'd done a lot with little help.

My strength is made perfect in weakness.

Esther didn't have time to be weak.

"Well, I heard her son Harvey specifically asked about you." Dorothy raised an eyebrow. "You were in your *rumspringa* at the same time as Harvey, right?"

Esther never could understand the desperate craving some women had for gossip. It was certainly emphasized enough in the Bible that women should refrain from talking about their neighbor, but believing and doing were two different things. She'd learned this about her community since she'd grown up hearing them whisper about her poor circumstances.

"New curtains?" Esther changed the subject and pointed at the curtains that the breeze pulled out the window. She winked back at Dorothy. Esther would not humor her friend by prattling on about a widower that she had no interest in.

"*Ya,*" Dorothy said, playfully jabbing Esther's ribs. "*Mem* gave me some fabric."

Dorothy's parents, who lived in a neighboring district, often helped Dorothy and Alvin, who had come on hard times after Alvin's sickness last winter. He'd been so ill with pneumonia that the doctors said he would always be weak. They had significant hospital bills as well.

A lull settled between the two. Dorothy would never have asked what Esther was bringing her that day, but the woman stood all too patiently, making Esther nervous. She wanted to get the food to her before the waiting woman brought up any more embarrassing topics.

"Mrs. White gave me milk for you today." Esther handed her several quarts.

Dorothy's dark brown eyes glassed every week when Esther handed her the donations. Mrs. White considered the milk as part of Esther's pay but she knew that Esther kept only what they needed and distributed the rest.

"Oh, this will be fine, just fine," Dorothy said. "You know, Esther, I was telling Alvin this morning that we needed milk. I can water it down for soup and make some butter with the cream and—well, I don't need to tell you all the things milk is good for, do I?"

The grateful woman took the milk and kept chatting as she set it in the kitchen.

"I think what you do is so nice. I've thought long and hard about all you do for us and I am mighty thankful that you're able to have this job since you're unmarried."

"I also brought some beans. Can I trade you for some canned corn?" Esther offered with a smile. They often swapped canned goods and considered this another way to serve one another.

Dorothy led her down to the cellar through the square hole in the floor of the kitchen. It was cool and comfortable.

"Careful of the latch. It's broken," Dorothy said, then continued to chatter about news from her family in Ohio.

As they made their way back up the cellar stairs, a wild cry came from outside. It was Daisy. The little girl barreled into the house and waved at Esther to hurry. She put the jars of corn on the table and began to sign.

"What's wrong?"

Junior's and Rebekah's cries came next.

"Junior? Rebekah?" Dorothy ran out of the house.

Daisy and Esther followed to the shed behind the house where she saw a small glow. Daisy looked up at her and made the gesture for striking a match.

"Junior," Dorothy yelled.

Though the fire was small, Dorothy hastily grabbed her daughter and pushed her out of the small barn and ordered Junior to follow her. Then Esther stomped out the bits of flames with her shoes. It was put out in a few moments. The women both sighed with relief.

Esther picked a box up from the ground. "Where did they get this box of matches?"

"I told Alvin to put them out of Junior's reach," Dorothy said, breathy with anger and fear. "They could've burned the shed down."

Esther signed to Daisy, asking if she'd participated. She insisted she hadn't, and Esther believed her. The young girl had never been one to take risks or be mischievous. Junior, on the other hand, had been a rascal from the moment he could sit up. Even at Orpha's funeral, he'd put his thumb in the center of half a dozen pies before he was caught.

"Junior's going to catch it when Alvin gets home." Dorothy's complexion was ashen.

Before they left, Dorothy gave Esther a small bag of scrap yarn she'd saved. Many of the ladies would do this as a thank-you on Esther's visiting day. Esther had been crocheting a small blanket for Daisy for some time, but without the money for yarn, she was dependent on the scraps from friends and neighbors.

Esther and Daisy moved on and went to visit the old widow

Matilda Yoder and the even older widower Marlin Miller. Their houses were so close you couldn't whistle in the kitchen without someone in the other kitchen joining in harmony. The two had married brother and sister and the couples were the best of friends. After brother and sister, Matilda's husband and Marlin's wife, both succumbed to the heart disease that ran in the family, the remaining two only had each other. They visited each other daily, just as they had in the decades before the deaths of their spouses. Esther had heard that they ate many of their meals together and it was often suggested by their children that they marry, but they seemed content enough without remarriage. The older woman wasn't in need of donated food, but she enjoyed Esther's company and appreciated the help with tidying up her small home. After this final stop, as she drove the buggy toward home, she passed by Angelica Blunt's house.

Daisy waved her hand out Esther's side of the buggy at her aunt Angelica's house. Even from a distance, Esther could see Angelica shake a finger and hear her yelling at her two younger daughters. When Angelica saw Daisy's gesture, her aunt shooed the little girl away rather than wave back. The yelling had stopped, however.

Play? Play? Daisy formed a *Y* with her hands and shook them back and forth several times. A bright smile crossed over her fair-skinned face as she asked.

"Sorry, *gleah maetleh*." Esther apologized to the little girl by rubbing her right fist over her chest as she held the reins with her left. Mixing English and her first language, Pennsylvania Dutch, and sign language had become second nature, even when driving a buggy. "Not now."

The last place Esther wanted to go visiting was Angelica's house. After another quarter mile, on the other side of the road, was Joe's red clapboard house, one of the prettier houses on Sunrise View Road.

Esther and Daisy drove into the gravel drive. Joe was nowhere to be seen. Daisy didn't move from her place in the
buggy. She wore a placid expression having collected and
stowed away the anger from earlier. The little girl was giving
her best effort. Esther didn't unhitch Deano, but tethered him
to a small tree on the front lawn. Joe didn't have any buggy ac-
commodations. When she turned back toward the house, she
saw him in the doorway. He stood in the slouched way she'd
always remembered, wearing a white undershirt and denim
trousers. Memories of his former life traced pictures in her
mind—before Irene died, before he was a soldier, when his life
was happy.

Should she wave? She wasn't sure how to be around him
anymore. He took a drink from a can, then walked back into the
house. When the screen door slapped shut, Esther winced. She
looked at Daisy, who widened her eyes. This was not the kind
of father she needed.

Daisy let Esther help her from the buggy, though usually she
hopped out on her own. They turned toward the house and took
in the view. In rural Delaware, with the fields and country roads
dotted with white houses, the red clapboard stood out like electric lights on a dark night. It had been maintained impeccably,
though the white barn in the back needed some work. The white
porch looked pristine in the late-morning sun, and despite the
comfortable wear on the path leading to the door, there wasn't
even a creak from the rustic wood beneath their feet. Her own
house had not been painted since her father left and every plank
of the wooden floor sang an off-pitch tune.

Esther raised her hand to knock when Joe's voice sounded.

"Come on in."

When she touched the door handle, a warm breeze circled
around them and whisked away her courage.

Esther

Esther pushed open the door and led Daisy through. Joe, sitting on the couch with a can of beer in his hand, looked them both up and down. What was he doing, and why was he drinking? Irene never had to disallow alcohol because Joe never drank. Esther was shaken by this change in him. His clothing was the same as before Irene died, but his face was different. Lined and weathered. He'd grown up.

He smiled at Daisy and leaned forward on his knees. But Daisy just gripped Esther's hand tighter and pushed into her side. Esther rubbed her thumb over the small hand inside hers. Joe inhaled deeply, making his chest grow thicker, and he exhaled slowly.

"We would've been here earlier, but we do our visiting on Friday," Esther said simply. "And I thought you might like the extra sleep after . . ."

Esther realized when she couldn't finish the sentence that she was shaking. She looked away from Joe and took in the living room instead. She had been to the house often enough when Irene was cleaning for Joe. Irene had insisted Esther come with her when she was able. It was this room where Irene admitted to Esther her feelings for Joe, which came as no surprise. The fact that Joe returned Irene's love had surprised Esther, however. He'd asked her to leave the Amish and marry him. Esther had never thought that in a world filled with bright colors, long wavy hair, and red lips a man could still be interested in someone who lived within the black and white of the Amish.

As Esther looked around, she desperately wanted to feel Irene in the room, and she did, but it was more haunting than comforting. Her ghost was everywhere. The room looked just as it had the day Irene died. Esther recognized photographs that Irene had been so proud of and a few rag rugs on the floor that they'd made together. Irene had told Esther that she and Joe didn't have much money for anything special, but the house was comfortable. The couch was nicer than Esther's own threadbare one, and there was a fireplace. Beyond the living room, dirty plates littered the small table.

"Hello, my girl," he said, unnaturally loud. He put his beer on the wooden floor at the foot of the couch and knelt near Daisy. He took her hand gently in his.

Daisy did not respond.

"Your blue eyes are like your mama's." He spoke these words pleasantly and in his natural rhythm, without trying to yell or go slowly. His voice was like velvet and brushed softly against the burlap that wound tightly around her heart. Esther had found kinship with the old Joe in their mutual love for Irene. But so far this Joe had been like a different version of the same man. His face was worn and weathered, and his voice at the train station had sounded disconnected from any emotion. As she waded through her memories, the only one she could conjure of his voice was in the last moments of Irene's life, with his ragged pleadings for her not to leave him.

The nostalgia in his expression diminished when he realized that his daughter would not respond to him. He dropped her hand and stood. She could have offered to sign for him. He could have asked. The moment had passed by them both.

Joe may have been right that Irene did have beautiful blue eyes, but Esther never saw her in Daisy's. She saw Joe. Against his reddish tan, which only grew richer in the summer, his eyes were as blue as she'd ever seen. Irene had always talked about how handsome he was, and Esther couldn't deny or argue this truth. Today his eyes were just as blue, only there was something more within them she could not resist seeking. Had it been Irene's death or the war that changed him?

"Why do you have her dressed like this?" He touched Daisy's *kapp* string, letting it loop and fall over a single finger. Daisy carefully watched every move he made.

"What did you expect?" She worked carefully to pull the resentment from her voice, but only partially succeeded. She could've said it in a nicer way, but something about this circumstance brought out the worst in her—as if she needed to defend and protect herself and Daisy. The commitment to making sure Daisy was happy with Joe was going to be far more difficult than she'd imagined.

"She's not Amish, Esther," he said. "You could've gotten other clothes."

"I wouldn't know the first thing about what to buy for an English girl. Besides, after she grew out of the few dresses you left for her, she wanted to fit in with the other girls at church." Esther readjusted her black purse strap, nervous.

Esther tapped Daisy on the shoulder to get her attention, then signed to her to go take a look around. If she hadn't already picked up on the fact that the two adults were arguing, she would likely soon.

"Angelica could've helped you. What do you think the money was for?"

Esther had just opened her mouth to rebut his suggestion when the screen door screeched open and slapped shut.

"That's what I said." Angelica's voice was like a cat's claw. Her appearance was only slightly improved from a normal day. She'd done her hair at least. Instead of the frizz circling her face, every strand was smooth, and the waves at the side of her head were under control. Esther had seen Mrs. White's daughters wear their hair in a similar fashion. Irene had also done her hair in these English rolls and always giggled about them with Esther.

Daisy ran between them and pulled Esther's arm. The little girl signed that the outhouse was indoors, just like at Mrs. White's farm. Her smile stretched wide across her small face. She looked about her, and her brow furrowed as she took in the adults' expressions. Her lips returned to the small heart shape they usually took, eyebrows up and eyes round.

"Here we go," Angelica spat out. "It ain't right, Joe. Making all these signs when we don't know what they are saying."

"Then I suggest you learn." Esther matched Angelica's venom.

Angelica's eyes shot to Joe's and she huffed, "Do you see how she treats me?"

Joe inhaled and his gaze shifted from his sister's to Esther. "What is she saying?"

Esther didn't want to tell them the truth. The fact that Daisy had the option of a perfectly fine modern home with indoor plumbing and even refrigeration made the run-down Detweiler home with an outhouse and a pump outside and a small icebox seem meager. Comparing the two would only prove concretely that Daisy was truly *better off* with Joe. As Esther took a moment to consider, the sting of reality penetrated deeply. There was no real option but to be truthful. No matter how anyone looked at it, Joe was Daisy's father, and unless he handed her over to

Esther for good, she would be hers no longer. Esther's duties as the little girl's temporary guardian were coming to a close.

Her inhale was weighted with the truth and the air of defeat filled her lungs.

"She is asking about the bathroom."

"The bathroom?" Joe asked, chuckling.

"She likes using Mrs. White's indoor bathroom, since we have outhouses. She didn't know you had an indoor one as well." Esther diverted her gaze from Joe, to Daisy, then to her own well-worn shoes.

Angelica stayed for several hours. She suggested that Esther leave but was reminded that no one else could communicate with Daisy. This sedated Angelica for the time being. Esther prepared a simple meal of buttered bread, from her own pantry, and some canned tomato soup that the renters had left behind.

A too-large bite of bread stuck dry in Esther's throat as she watched Joe's eyes linger on Daisy. She and Joe had experienced birth and death together. All of this should be easier—so why wasn't it? Was it her or him? Was it Irene?

Esther and Daisy didn't stay long after the meal, since Esther had promised Mrs. White she would weed the garden before the weekend. By the time they were out of the house and down the porch steps, Esther wanted to run. If they hadn't had the buggy, she would've put Daisy on her back and galloped home like a horse heading for the barn. In the early months after Daisy came to live with Esther, these were the only times she'd laughed like any other child.

Not like the other children who could hear—like the other children who had mothers.

Joe

Joe had slept soundly the first few nights at home. He'd opened the windows and enjoyed the chorus of sounds. The scent of summer rain, the heat against the grass, and the earth bursting with life brought peace. No sulfur. No gunpowder.

Esther brought Daisy over each day, and they had at least one meal together. He still had no indication as to whether Daisy would find her way back to him. He was as nervous as his daughter looked.

"Has she started school yet?" Joe asked Esther as she cleared their lunch plates to clean.

"The children in our communities start at seven. She could start this fall. Isn't that the same at the school where you taught?"

"Yes," Joe agreed. He was failing in his effort at conversation.

"No one knows how to sign well enough, though. I wasn't sure if I would send her if I . . ." Esther's eyes grazed his face, then diverted quickly. "I don't know—"

"Then how will she learn to read and do arithmetic?" Joe interrupted. Panic rose in his chest because he was lost when it came to how to teach a child who couldn't hear.

Esther set down the stack of plates she was about to carry to the kitchen.

"She has actually learned quite a few words by sight in order to finger-spell," she offered. "I've done my best, Joe."

"That's not reading." Joe knew he was picking a fight, and bit back his frustrations, which had nothing to do with Esther herself but his own insecurities. "I didn't mean—I just . . ."

"I know what you meant. No, I can't teach her all those things. I don't know what's next for her." Esther picked up the plates and left Joe sitting alone at the table while she cleaned his kitchen. Daisy played with the paper dolls that Esther had brought for her—and likely made herself as well. Joe was, as usual, expendable.

～

Angelica insisted again that Joe go to her house for supper. All Angelica could talk about was Joe getting a job and getting a new wife. His sister was right that he needed a job, but he didn't want to remarry. After supper with Angelica's family, he took a drive up to the graveyard where his wife lay in her eternal sleep, but he couldn't bring himself to visit her grave. The gate at the entrance of the cemetery looked the same, but that was where the similarities ceased. This time the moon spread its glow across the overgrown grass. Four years ago, there had been new spring grass with morning fog hanging in the air—exactly the kind of day that Irene loved.

He sat in his truck and didn't return home until after dark. He went through the front door and into the blackness of the living room. When he reached to turn on the lamp, he kicked a beer can from earlier across the room. The unexpected sound from the ricochet startled him, and a surge of adrenaline shot through his chest. He began to sweat instantly, reminding him of the heat on the Pacific Islands. He grappled toward the lamp again and twisted the small knob, but after a flash and pop, the bulb died.

Death followed him.

It was too real and too palpable in the house. He stood in the dark for several more moments and made an effort to slow his breathing. His hands shook. He knew he wasn't at war. He was at home. It frightened him, however, how quickly his mind returned to war even when it was so far from his new life. He wouldn't let those memories win. He moved quickly through the house and out the back door to the barn where there were extra bulbs stored.

He pulled a long string that was just inside the tall sliding barn doors, exactly where he remembered it. The hanging bulb above him turned yellow and bright. The light glared in his eyes and he quickly looked away. He pulled another string, shining two bulbs in the barn.

Joe took in his dim surroundings. His father, also Joe Garrison, though he'd gone by *Garry*, had used the old barn as a repair shop and woodworking garage after the Great War. Joe used to love to watch his dad work on a variety of items, from radios to farm equipment to cabinets and chairs. Before Joe started his own schooling, his dad had added repairing automobiles to his roster. This was where Joe learned the difference between a wrench and pliers, how to change a tire, and how to drive a nail with one blow.

Old lumber and tires were piled high in a small mountain on the right of the barn. A heavy wooden table on the left was littered with old tools covered in cobwebs. A 1917 Stephens Touring auto was in the back. The black roof was ragged and the green paint nearly all peeled off. His dad had taken it as payment from a customer in the 1920s and had always planned to fix it up. Garry died before that could happen. Looking at it now, Joe realized it was little more than a step up from a horse and buggy.

He sighed aloud. He couldn't do fine work like woodworking or work with cars. But he also knew he couldn't go back to teaching at the small country school either. His pupils had always been ready to learn, even when their stomachs were empty. Angelica said that the school district was planning on asking him to teach again in the fall. It wouldn't work. No one would want a man like him teaching their children. Too broken. Too weary. Haunted. Was he even safe to be around children? What about Daisy?

He pushed the thought away and looked on the shelf near the entrance only to find that the box of bulbs was empty. He tossed the box into the garbage barrel with frustration. Why had he assumed that his cousin who had rented the house would've continued to keep a stock of bulbs waiting for Joe's return?

Suddenly, large menacing shapes played over the old wooden slats of the barn. The dark and light flickered, moving quickly. His heart pumped, and his hand went over his head, feeling for his helmet. It wasn't there. Where was his helmet? Where was his M1? When he swatted against the moths that dive-bombed him, he realized he was in his barn. The moths that fluttered around the hanging bulbs had been the foreboding threat? Though it was only a momentary adrenaline rush, his breathing quickened, forcing his hand to his chest. His hand found the long light string again and he ran from the barn as if a consuming darkness chased him.

~

As the sun peeked over the tree line, Joe startled awake and found he was still in his clothes from the night before. He'd spooked himself in the barn and hadn't been able to shake the feeling that someone was after him. Now he quickly showered and changed. With the first swallow of his coffee, he decided to leave the house. The coffee was worse than normal and the house was too big and empty.

A twinge of guilt settled into his gut when he passed the Det-weiler house and saw Esther cutting her lawn. Her mower, of course, lacked the engine to make it efficient. Daisy appeared to be weeding their small flower garden. Neither looked up as he passed, even though he slowed. It shouldn't bother him that she didn't have a better mower. The Amish, as well as anyone else, could make a choice to buy a powered one. It wasn't his fault that she followed their rules to the letter.

But when he got to the corner of Sunrise View Road, he made a U-turn, spraying gravel as he did. He was frustrated with himself for not letting things be, but there was something about Esther. While Esther's melancholy eyes lingered in his mind, Irene's bright smile and melodious giggle trumpeted in. The view of Esther struggling through the same plot of grass she'd been working on when he passed the first time tore the image of his pretty wife from his mind's eye.

This was the woman who had been so loyal to Irene and wouldn't leave her side no matter what the doctor said. She had suffered almost as much as he had. But she'd stayed. He'd left.

He pulled into the drive and got out of the car. Esther turned to look at him and then returned to the mower. A quiet grunt escaped her lips with every other push, and sweat had accumu-lated at the back of her neck. Her skin glistened. He'd never met a harder-working woman.

"What are you doing here?" Esther asked him as she kept mowing. The dress she wore was clearly meant for working but it fit her too snugly, and he had to divert his gaze to her face. She was shapely, but she was his daughter's caretaker and his deceased wife's cousin. He should not see her as anything but that. She wasn't wearing her ususal white covering either, but a thin blue headscarf tied at the nape of her neck beneath a thick mound of hair. Though she didn't turn around to look at him, he could see wisps of black curls around her hairline that gave her an almost childlike, innocent appearance.

"I want to help." He said it hesitantly, then cleared his throat and tried again. If only he could get his own motored mower, but he didn't want to cause any further issues at this point. "Let me help."

"I don't need help," Esther said between grunts. There was a stubborn patch of grass with weeds that didn't want to budge, even after the blades ran over it several times. When Esther took a brief pause to run the back of her hand over her forehead, Joe stole the moment and put his arms around the back of her and his hands on the handle. Esther's hands tried to peel his away to keep control of the mower.

"Joe," Esther scolded when he wouldn't budge.

Joe didn't let go of the grass cutter. He tried to push it against the weeds and grass while she still hung on, forcing their bodies to move together.

"Let me do this." He could hear that she spoke through gritted teeth. He paused. The back of her body was against him. How long had it been since he'd had a warm body against his own? The pleasure he had in the closeness of a woman suddenly made him release his hands and back away. He could not relish it. His change of heart made her turn around and look at him. Their eyes connected.

"Please, let me," he whispered. "I just want to help."

Esther bit her lower lip and turned to look at the grass ahead of her. She stepped aside and held one side of the grass cutter out to him.

"Okay," she said breathlessly.

He inhaled deeply and took the handles into his hands. Esther turned to leave.

"Esther," he said, and she turned. "See, maybe we can work together."

She held his gaze for several moments before she gave him a soft nod and went to her next task.

The strenuous labor of cutting the grass brought new energy to Joe. By the time Sunday had come around a few days later, he had worked on every home repair that he could do without buying more material. Staying busy was all that kept him from finding Irene's ghost in every corner of the house and the muddle of war memories that cluttered his mind. How far back did he have to go to find memories worth reminiscing over? His sleep had become plagued with a heavy darkness, and many nights he woke to find himself out of bed and standing or crouching somewhere in the house. He would wake when he tripped over a rumpled rug or after the crash of a vase or a dinner plate that had been left out. Though he had no memory of throwing the object himself, how else could it have flown across the room and shattered into pieces?

The nightmares and terrors made him want to stay busy and out of the house. He was repainting the barn when he saw Esther and Daisy walking up. The evening was fair and he imagined what a nice walk it must be. Esther's head was covered with the large black bonnet she always wore, though she removed it when she entered the house. He understood it as a practice of modesty. Daisy skipped near her until the little girl's eyes caught Joe's, then she stopped and, like a magnet, attached herself to Esther's side.

This was the tenuous routine they'd settled into. It was often made more stressful by the abrupt appearance of Angelica. Almost regularly, before he and Esther could even greet each other, his sister would knock loudly at the door or pop into the drive. And today was no different, except that Angelica seemed ready to burst with excitement and he felt his head begin to pound.

"Angelica, what brings you around?" He hugged his sister and kissed her sunken cheek.

Angelica looked around, and the two of them watched as Esther and Daisy passed them in the drive and went into the house. Her smile drifted from her face, and a frown cut in. Her pointy jaw jutting out reminded him of an aunt he'd been afraid of as a child. As soon as Angelica refocused on Joe, her smile returned.

"I have news." Angelica grabbed his arms.

"News?"

"I got another job, and I think I found one for you. I interviewed with Mrs. Wayne Good about the housekeeping job at the apartments her husband builds, and I got the job. What do you think about that?" Her smile grew toothy, and Joe smiled back. "She even has a pretty housekeeping uniform for me, and it pays more than double what I'm making now."

"That's great." Joe smiled, meaning it. Angelica cleaned a few houses now, but with Donald unable to work and requiring expensive medicine, they were struggling more than usual, especially since Joe wasn't sending money anymore.

"And," she held the word out long as she winked at him, "she said she thinks that her husband would hire you on one of his carpentry crews. You heard about all those houses going up on this side of town? Well, Mr. Good is the one putting them up. If you're not going to go back to teaching, this would be a great new start." She patted his cheek like his mother used to do. "Think about it."

He watched Angelica leave and stood in the drive until her truck lumbered out onto the road. Would it even make it as far as her new job? He walked toward the house wondering if Angelica was onto something. A construction job could be perfect. Working with his hands kept him as busy as he liked.

When he entered the house, he could see Esther looking over the broken pieces of china on the table. He watched as she pulled the small trash can over and began pushing the pieces into it.

"What are you doing?" Joe walked in long strides across the living room and into the kitchen.

"I'm cleaning up." Esther stood, her brow laced with confusion. "There are several broken plates and beer cans laying around. Really, Joe."

"Don't throw them away." Joe grabbed the trash and began picking the pieces of the rosebud china out. "We didn't have enough for a set of china so I bought her two plates. One for her and one for me."

Joe placed pieces on the table, some of them dripping with the beer that had leaked from the cans Esther had thrown away.

"How'd they break?" Esther asked, and while her tone wasn't laced with suspicion, her eyes narrowed as he stood and caught her gaze.

His face grew warm. He didn't want her to know how the plate had broken. She could not know that when darkness fell, his demons came out.

"I dropped it," he lied.

"Both of them? They were all over the living room, Joe. I think I know how it happened." She inhaled deeply then tossed another empty beer can into the trash.

She was wrong. It had nothing to do with the alcohol.

"Listen, you came to help me with my lawn. It was good of you. I want to help you too. If you even think you want to be a father to Daisy," she said without looking at Joe, "then you can't drink."

"That's not how the dishes were broken," he blurted out.

"Then how?"

His heart was pounding, but he had to keep his secret. He hated that she assumed the worst of him, but he had to let her believe the lie. It was better than the truth. It made him angrier than it should. The speed of his heart heated his blood.

"I'm just thinking about Daisy." Her voice was firm, yet she spoke quietly. She threw another empty can into the trash.

"You don't understand," he started. How could he begin to convey to her how desperately dark he was on the inside and how he didn't like the man he was either. He didn't want to be the kind of man who needed a beer to numb the visions in his head and help him fall asleep. He wasn't getting drunk, but the beer did have a calming effect on his sleep.

He held her gaze, and the strength it bore enticed him. What was it like to be so self-assured? He suddenly wanted to touch her again, not just because he had mowed her lawn, but because he wanted to be a part of whatever made her so confident. His hand reached to her, and she flinched. He put his hand back at his side.

"I don't need you to take care of me." He matched her quietude. This was true. Esther did not need to mother him. But he was drawn to her caring ways.

Esther looked away and down at the broken pieces of the plate.

"Someone has to. You've been home for a week and a half and the house is already a mess—and these plates. Irene would—"

Why, even when speaking softly, was she such a force?

"Do not bring up Irene." He meant it. She shouldn't bring up Irene. It wasn't as if he wasn't reminded at every moment how he had failed her years earlier and every day since her death.

"Do you think this is what she would've wanted for you? For Daisy?" She picked up a piece of the plate, using it as evidence against him. "You weren't like this—before."

He could feel the resistance in her words.

"That man isn't here anymore. He's gone." He leaned toward her when he spoke. There was anger laced in his words, but he meant what he said. Their bodies were close as they faced each other. She didn't quake at his nearness, but traces of the clean scent of homemade soap and the outdoors moved around him. His focus returned when she spoke.

"But you're still Joe. Irene's Joe. And you abandoned your daughter." She was so close that he felt her breath on his face. "You just left her. I had to put the pieces back together. I was the one who figured out that she was deaf and fought against everyone who told me I was wrong." She stopped briefly, and her breathing was heavy. "I was just as scared as you were, Joe. But I stayed and you left. Irene would be so disappointed."

"What?" He stepped back.

Her eyes grew rounder and larger than he'd ever seen them.

"I didn't mean—" Esther shook her head but didn't finish her thought. She moved to return the trash can to its place.

Daisy walked into the kitchen. Esther signed something to her, then promptly left the room and gathered her things. The two of them left Joe standing in the kitchen, and once the hammering of his heart slowed down, he surrendered to Esther's opinion. She was right about everything. He had turned and walked away from his child and Irene would be disappointed.

Joe knew that he'd never be a good enough father. He was sure Daisy could forgive him for leaving her, but she would never forgive him for returning.

Esther

Esther's heart pounded. Would it fall out on the very gravel road they walked? Why had she spoken to Joe that way? And why did she have such conflicting feelings about him? She found him so changed from before he left. She'd witnessed such kindness when he'd come to mow her lawn. She'd never been that close to a man's body and was glad he couldn't see her face, for it burned from the inside out. Joe's body so near to hers had started a furnace inside her, and now his presence alone brought back the fire. But that did not negate the fact that he was getting drunk, breaking plates, and proving himself unfit as a father. His light blue eyes swirled with passions that she didn't recognize and were so different from any other set of eyes that she'd looked into.

She couldn't tolerate the drink, and she'd seen bottles in Chester's car, which was parked in her drive at the moment— Mrs. White had no space for him to park it. She didn't want the same for Daisy. She didn't deserve a father like Esther's.

Just as Esther returned from Joe's, a knock came on her door. She found Chester and two church leaders standing on the small porch. Chester's eyebrows were raised, and he was dirty and dusty from his work at the dairy farm. She hadn't seen him in several days. The two preachers had matching melancholy faces, frizzy gray beards, and black hats, but one was tall and the other stocky. They stood on either side of Chester like bookends.

Esther stepped back and gestured for the three men to come inside. The quiet among them was uncomfortable.

"*Vie gehts*, Willie?" Esther's greeting sounded a little too cheerful under the circumstances, even in her own ears. He was always known for his staunch stance on the *Ordnung*, often exceeding any standard it had. He was the bishop, after all. Even though he was strict, he was not intimidating or unapproachable, unlike many bishops she'd met over the years. He could even be a bit of a jokester when given the notion.

Willie nodded his head, and his mouth barely moved when he spoke. "*Sis goot*, Esther. Berthy wanted me to bring this to you." He handed Esther a small paper sack. He had kind, light blue eyes and a gentle smile. She was glad that he was doing well.

Esther opened it to find several small balls of scrap yarn. It didn't matter that the colors were duller than many of her other scraps.

"*Dangeh*." Esther smiled.

"She also said that if you want her help on your visits and deliveries on Fridays to let her know."

Esther nodded. Visiting was the easy work—she didn't need help with that. But if someone wanted to take the responsibility of gaining a father and losing a daughter, they would be welcome to remove that painful burden from her.

She turned her attention to the shorter of the two visitors. Ray was one of their district's preachers. His eyes were like small round marbles, and he had a hollow, gaunt look, having had a slow recovery after being quite ill.

"Ray. You are looking stronger." Esther smiled at him. *"Hock anah.* I'll get some coffee." She gestured for the men to sit in the living room.

The two church leaders walked through the small kitchen and moved toward the couch in the living room. Chester didn't follow them. Esther's gaze landed only for a moment on his face. His complexion went pastier than normal. He jiggled a loose floorboard over and over with his foot. His knuckles lost their color as he gripped the back of the kitchen chair.

"Coffee?" Esther asked. When he looked up at her, she realized that she might sound disingenuous, like she delighted in his shame. Truthfully, she could think of nothing else to say to fill the uncomfortable silence, but there was a part of her that had wanted this meeting to happen. Chester Detweiler could not return after being away for so long without consequence.

Several silent and long minutes later, the three men and Esther sat in the living room with coffee and buttered bread. She'd anticipated this conversation for a few weeks, but now that it was here, she suddenly longed to be the faceless doll that Daisy was playing with. But she wasn't. Her face had always been known throughout the district, first for her unfortunate circumstances, then for her spinster status, and then because of Daisy. She'd had to speak for herself and Orpha when no man was there to do it for them. She'd had to handle Orpha's health needs over the years with little money. When they'd sold the land and farm to pay back taxes owed since her mother's death, they didn't burden the church over it. If they had, the church might have tried to intervene and send both Esther and Orpha away to other family members who could care for them. Esther had done this on her own, making many of these decisions from the age of thirteen.

"Chester, we are glad to see you've come home. I have to say, it was quite a shock to us all." The bishop, Willie, chuckled shyly. "We were told years ago that you died. Leah told us about a letter she got from the War Office telling her that you died of dysentery in prison."

Esther didn't speak. She had believed this story as the truth for most of her life. Hearing it a second time brought on feelings of disbelief and anger as if it was the first she was learning of his years away.

There was a long pause before Willie spoke again.

"You know that usually with church issues the *aumah deanah* would come to the house and have this talk. It is one of his chief responsibilities as the head deacon. In this case, however, the preachers and deacons and I spoke and prayed for several weeks to find the best way to go about this. We would've liked to have come to you sooner, only this situation was so unusual. But we decided that as the bishop, I should come, and I brought Ray with me since he had no background with you, whereas everyone else had—many were your grade school friends. I wanted this visit to be as fair as possible."

"I moved here with my *frau* and *kinnah* about ten years ago from Lancaster County." Ray's voice was nasal but direct and unapologetic. "I agree with Willie that these circumstances are highly uncommon, but we will do our best to follow the *Hah* and His wisdom in how to best handle—all of this. I am confident that God will show us the answers we need."

A cloud of stillness hovered over the room. The uncomfortable silence made Esther's heart drum against her chest.

"Well, fellas, I was twenty-four when I left for my army physical. It seems like a lifetime ago. I don't think I ever had a visit from the preachers in those twenty-four years either." He paused as if suddenly realizing he was speaking in English. "Sorry, habit. *Is dess bassah?*"

She wasn't sure that it *was better* since the mixture of the Amish words and his Texas twang sounded unusual. He sipped

his coffee, and the subtle shake in his hand drew Esther's attention. The charisma he'd carried so confidently in the almost
month he'd been home had shifted. He cleared his throat and
put down his coffee on the small stand near his chair and folded
his hands in his lap.

Chester had told her about his years away, but this conversation still put her heart into her stomach. His explanation hadn't
been wholly convincing, but Esther wasn't sure what part of
his story to question. As the weeks passed, however, she'd had
little time to consider the reality that Chester was living across
the road. Joe was back. Daisy was upset. Nothing had gone
smoothly for so long there was part of her that was afraid of
hearing more.

"What do you want to know?" He took equal time to look at
each of the men. "I really had no intention of staying away. But
when I heard about Leah's death, I just—"

"We hardly had any money, especially after *Mem* died, and
Mammie was often ill—to think that all the while you were
alive." Esther wasn't planning to talk at all, but suddenly she
spoke with the rush of water from a pump. She caught herself before she spoke about the land taxes, nervous that Willie
would feel she'd lied to the church by not revealing their desperate need years ago.

Her breathing was rapid, and when she met Willie's eyes, she
could see his dedication to her. He wanted answers too.

"We've heard talk about Texas and working in oil," Willie
spoke up.

"You've spoken with Reuben?" Chester's pinched face registered nervousness.

Willie nodded. "We have."

"And what did he tell you?" Chester cleared his throat.

"That's between Reuben and the church," Ray answered.

"Reuben is right. I was in Texas, but not the whole time," he said in English, and then shook his head and returned to their dialect, occasionally using English words among his Dutch. "Prison was terrible. For several years I sat there and dreamed of getting out. But when I did, Leah was dead." He ran a hand down his face instead. "After that, I went to Canada to help with some relief missions work with the Mennonites. It was a good couple of years. I worked on a sheep farm in Colorado and on the railroad in Washington State. Then I started hearing about all this oil in Texas and I needed a job. I worked odd jobs to get myself down there, even worked on an offshore rig in the Gulf as a roustabout. I stayed in Texas until the last few months. I knew I needed to come back—to make things right."

He'd been places that the listeners had only ever heard of—real places that were faraway dreams to Esther. Could the frailty of her home and her guarded heart handle this bold life he spoke of?

No one spoke for several moments. Daisy's sounds as she played laced the edges of the prickly silence. A breeze rippled the simple blue curtains in the open window. Esther's own skin was drawn toward the window, wanting to flee. She looked around at the men. Were her eyes as round as Willie's and Ray's?

"Listen, I ain't proud of it." Chester spoke in English and shook his head again then looked out the window for a long moment, his eyes growing glassy. "I'm not proud of how I've lived. I want to make it right. Just tell me how." The rest of his words were in their dialect, and his eyes landed on all three of them as they stared at him.

"It's against *da Hah*'s will for you to leave your daughter and your *mem*. They thought you were dead. God would never approve of such behavior." Willie's melancholy tone bottled up the breeze and gave the room a sudden staleness. The curtains stopped waving and everyone was still.

"Why did *Mem* say you were dead?"

Esther's cheek twitched as she spoke, and she forced herself to wait a beat before looking at Chester. Though she didn't want to admit it, his words wrote upon her heart like a sharp feather quill on thick parchment. His words mattered to her, and the truth as he shared it hurt to hear. Chester was biting his lower lip in obvious nervousness. He leaned forward, putting his elbows on his knees. He pulled out a white cotton *schnup-duch*. Without warning, his tears spilled over and he covered his face with the handkerchief in his hand. Mournful sobs filled the small house and the May breeze began again, as if triggered by his clamor. He blew his nose into his hanky and no one made a move to console his grief.

"*Ich wah en schlecta mahn,*" he said between hiccups, not answering her question.

He admitted that he'd been a bad man. Esther's face contorted, not out of sympathy but because she found herself questioning his sincerity. Were his tears contrived?

"I am ashamed to say that they only let me out because I agreed to put on an army uniform. Then they cut my finger off—like the sign of a coward. I can't even hunt without this finger." He held his hand up, displaying the gap between his thumb and middle finger on his right hand. His eyes were red-rimmed, and his mouth curved down at the edges. "After that I begged them to send a letter to Leah telling her that I'd died. I felt dead inside for what I'd done by then. When they let me out, Leah was dead instead of me. I had nothing but the clothes on my back, and I just ran. I couldn't come back here. I was too ashamed."

The image in her memory suddenly became more vivid than ever before: the bloody hand and cloth. He'd just lied to them about his missing finger. Esther's memory of that morning sharpened. He hadn't lost his finger in prison but before he'd gone to his army physical. If he was dishonest about this, what other deceptions had he told?

"But why? Why couldn't you come back for me?" Esther's voice in her own ears sounded hollow, and it wavered up and down with emotion.

"I came back once, but I couldn't stay. I saw you, Esther, outside, taking the laundry off the line. You were already a foot taller, it seemed, since I left. Your *mammie* called for you to come inside, and I barely recognized her." He broke down and sobbed. "She looked like a skeleton, and I knew I'd done that to her. I couldn't stay."

He hadn't shared this with Esther previously. Was it true?

The silence built a wall like cinder blocks, thick and heavy. The mortar ran from a range of emotions, holding the blocks in place. Disbelief. Anger. Hurt. Shock. None of them brought on the sympathy that Chester seemed to desire. None of them lessened her distrust and distaste for the man but heightened them instead. The anger in her heart wanted to call it hate, but the little girl who still resided deep beneath the layers of her dresses, pins, and coverings couldn't resist the desire to have a father. This connection was the only reason she wouldn't tell Willie and Ray about the lie about his finger. She reckoned with herself, however, that she would learn the truth. The depth of her confusion was suffocating.

"But I'm back now," he finally said, looking at the two other men and wiping his eyes. "I want to make it right, and I want to return to the church. I've lived a life I'm not proud of, but come hell or high water, I'm ready to change my ways."

The two church leaders looked stunned at his use of the word *hell*, but they said nothing. They encouraged him to be at the next church service to make his confession and said that at that point they would provide him with their decision on how long he would be in the *bann*. Chester nodded.

Even after the men showed themselves out, the silence continued and squeezed the air out of every corner of the house. It seemed like hours later when Chester turned to face Esther.

"Esther, *kange du meehk fagevah?*" He sniffled and blew his nose again, then his eyes landed back on her. She wanted to be absorbed into the floor beneath her.

He wanted her to forgive him?

Her body betrayed her and she shook her head *no*. She remained quiet, but the silent response spoke loudly.

"I know you lied about your finger. I remember your bloody hand the morning you left," she said with a shaky voice.

He looked at her, and then to the floor. He absently nodded his head in agreement.

"What else do you remember about that morning?"

"You were sweating. *Mem* was so pale. You gave me the Bible." She glanced at the place on the table where he'd laid it all those years ago. "You left your harmonica and told me you'd be back to teach me. But it was a lie—just like your finger."

Chester looked into her eyes. "Why didn't you tell Willie and Ray?"

She held his stare for several long beats before she turned away. She couldn't answer him. She didn't know why she didn't expose this lie. How many more lies were folded within his story?

Chester cleared his throat and got up from where he sat and left her alone. Her father was gone.

Esther

Esther sat on the back porch and watched as distant clouds washed over the moon, a sliver of gold. Light and dark were so close. One did not exist without the other. Her eyes glanced above her toward her bedroom window on the second floor, where Daisy had been asleep for several hours. Esther had gone through the motions for the rest of the evening. When Chester left the first time, it was because of the war; this time he left because of her.

Since Daisy was sleeping soundly, Esther rose to her feet to take a short walk. She removed her covering and hung it on a nail on the porch. It was late and her hair was mussed, but a summer breeze pushing through her escaped curls would feel nice. Her bare feet found an old friend—a footpath that had grown wild since Irene's death. A path they'd walked in secret after her shunning. Only the scar of the trail remained, but it felt familiar as soon as she began to walk. The hay in the field to her left smelled sweet in the breeze, and everything was quiet the way she liked it.

"Esther?" Joe's voice startled her. He was standing right before her. Lightning bugs flew around, pouring light into the darkness. He was wearing worn denims and a white undershirt. His hair matched the moon, and his eyes lighted the space around him. His presence sparked heat inside her again.

"Joe?" The memory of her hateful words toward him brought the drum of her heart. "Daisy's sleeping—she usually—she should be okay for a short walk."

Joe waved away her words.

"You would know better than I." His voice was soft and luxurious, but his brow still looked beaten down from her earlier words.

"Joe, about before—" Her hand went to her forehead, pushing away a stray curl. Her embarrassment that she wasn't wearing a covering was only diminished by the prevailing darkness. Maybe he wouldn't notice.

"I don't want to talk about that right now," Joe interrupted. Esther couldn't read his level of anger. "I came out here to get away from—*everything*."

"Then I should leave you to your solitude." Esther turned to go, but Joe's warm hand wrapped around her arm. She turned to look at him. He was closer now and she could smell the faint scent of a shower. He slowly released her arm and she instantly felt cold and disappointed. She pushed away those feelings by clearing her throat.

"Walk with me?" he asked.

Shyness was braided into his words. A pull radiated through her chest, and Esther fell in step with him as they walked toward his home.

What was he after? Surely it wasn't simply her company after how she'd treated him.

"Irene and I used to meet on this path." As soon as she spoke her dead cousin's name, she regretted it. Irene's very spirit pressed against Esther, proclaiming how different everyone always said they were. She was light, and Esther was dark.

Everyone always spoke of Irene's beauty and of Esther's hard work.

"I know." He looked over at her. There was something behind his eyes that made Esther curious. Maybe something close to reminiscent happiness, and the softness was comforting to her. "She loved you very much." An old Joe smile flourished then wilted in a single moment.

"Hmm," Esther responded simply, not knowing what else to say. The Amish didn't often talk of feelings openly.

"She told me once, soon after she was shunned, that losing you was the most difficult part of leaving the church. I didn't understand then, but I do now."

Esther looked up at Joe, and their eyes connected. Joe stopped walking and after another step so did she. Nervous from his intensity, she turned away and saw Joe's white barn silhouetted in the distance.

"I've never seen you without your *kapp*." She couldn't see his face but could hear the smile in his words.

Usually Englishers called it a bonnet, and the fact that he'd called it the proper name caused her to reconsider his motives. Her stomach swirled and brought on a wave of confusion. She squeezed her eyes shut. Joe had been Irene's husband—yet he was so changed from that man. When he'd mowed her lawn and invited her to walk with him, there was something different in the way he looked at her than other men did. His eyes saw *her*. It was confusing. Frightening, even.

There was a burn of heat behind her for a moment when she realized that Joe was close. Too close. She didn't move a muscle when he spun one of the curls at her temple around his finger. The slight pull of the strand spread a sensation that radiated through her whole scalp and down her neck.

"Joe," she started to say, and turned to look at him. He was so close. She'd been given a sloppy kiss from a boy when she was only sixteen, but never since. He moved closer by measures. One of Joe's hands pressed against the side of her neck, and the feeling of his calluses against her skin stirred her senses. His gentleness was nothing like the shameful groping when she was a youth during her *rumspringa*. That years-ago kiss had made her feel foolish.

Joe's touch was electric, forbidden. But the current couldn't be broken. When Esther smelled beer on Joe's breath, she woke up.

She pushed him away. "You've been drinking. Why would you—?"

A desperate ache grew like a weed from her stomach to her throat. He wasn't quite himself since she found him on her path. His calm and even conversation wasn't anything like the Joe who had walked off the train. The mockery of the drink that flowed through his veins was all this was. She was a fool. She'd almost let him kiss her. She'd even wanted him to. Why? She didn't know.

Joe stepped toward her, reaching for her.

"Esther, I—"

He was interrupted by a loud cry from Esther's house, still visible in the waning moonlight. There was no question who was screaming.

"Daisy. I need to go." She turned to leave but he grabbed her arm.

"What? That's Daisy? Why is she screaming? I'm coming with you."

Esther looked down at his hand around her forearm. He didn't let go.

"You're not coming with me," she said forcefully and pulled her arm from his grip.

"If she's in trouble, I need to be there." He started walking toward Esther's house, and then she took his arm and pulled him back.

"Dreams, Joe. She has bad dreams." Her skin was taut around her jaw.

"Dreams?" He turned around and came within inches of her, his hands on both of her forearms this time. Their breathing mingled together with the evening chorus of nature. "Esther, tell me."

"She had a lot of them when you first left. Almost every night for months. Then they were gone."

He let go of her arms and his chest deflated.

"They came back?" he asked. "When did they come back?"

She was breathless and wasn't sure she wanted to answer him.

"They came back when you came home."

Without another word she turned and left him standing there alone.

Joe

1944
Mariana Bay, Saipan

I t was the squad leader's job to do an ammo check and distribution just before dusk. Sergeant Joe Garrison grabbed
an ammo can and slung an M1 rifle over his shoulders, and
Corporal Fielding and Private Crane both did the same. Garrison sent up a silent prayer that they wouldn't have to use them
as they ran from foxhole to foxhole. Not that he expected God
to listen to a word he said.

The dry, sandy terrain was tough to walk on, with uprooted
trees, holes, and earthly wounds from gunfire and mortar
rounds. The distant sunset was teasing to come early. Scraggly
tree carcasses split the coming orange and purples. It could almost be pretty.

Garrison looked at his men. "You ready?"

Fielding always had the look of fear in his eyes. It was a
flaw, in Garrison's mind. Crane, on the other hand, was a beefy
hothead.

The three men crouched as they ran, and they made it to
the first and second foxholes without issue. They continued to
the third, and just before they reached it, Joe sensed the whir
of a nearby bullet. As he hit the ground with a loud grunt,

the ammo from the unlocked can he was carrying scattered everywhere.

Garrison had only enough time to get up from the ground before the bullets rained down. He jumped into the nearest foxhole, and the first thought on his mind was that he should have locked up the ammo can. This kind of mistake would cost lives if they ran out of ammo before getting to the other side of the secured area.

"You'd think a sergeant would know how to square away an ammo can," Sergeant Barker said from across the foxhole. The only thing more impressive than Barker's ability to fire fatal shots at the enemy was his capacity to lob numerous cuss words at Garrison for his mistakes. As they continued suppressive fire, Barker took a moment between shots to glare at Garrison. "Not only did you draw their fire, but Marines are going to die without that ammo."

Joe

When Joe had gone out to walk, it had been to escape the demons that consumed his sleep. The whisper on the summer breeze had called him to the old moonlit path. Walking through the tall grass made him think of Irene, and he remembered how the moon used to glisten on her hair.

When he saw Esther in the distance walking toward him, he became anxious. Her earlier words had hurt, but she'd been right. It should've made him angry with her, but instead it pulled him more toward her. Her surety. Her boldness. There was something in her that he'd never seen in another woman—not even Irene. Irene had been beautiful and kind, a breath of fresh air. He shouldn't so easily forget his grief. Even though she'd been gone for four years, he'd been home only for a little over a week, and it seemed too soon for him to be drawn toward Esther or any woman for that matter.

When he touched her hair, he knew he wanted to kiss her. He hadn't kissed a woman since Irene despite the opportunity and temptation while overseas. He'd never before been so ravenous for touch and warmth. It was an unexpected sensation that got stronger the nearer Esther was to him. Was it because he wanted to feel more alive? He didn't think so. He didn't feel more alive now than at war, where death was so entwined with life. His body had reacted as a man's would to the nearness of a woman. Had hers also responded to his touch? The guilt of it brought him to his knees once he got back to his house.

"Stop, Garrison. Just stop," he scolded himself. Did he want Esther, or just a woman? Either way, how could he be so disloyal to Irene? He shook his head and stood.

Learning that Daisy was having nightmares had only heightened the moment between them. He and his daughter did have something in common: they both had nightmares. Knowing he was the cause of them, however, struck him like a bullet in the darkness. The unexpected blow broke his resilience. He wept that night as he fell asleep for everything he'd lost and for what he'd caused.

Joe awoke hours later. His feet were in moonlight that streamed through the window, and he was standing in his living room. The quiet, mixed with his heavy breathing, reminded him of a ghost story from long ago. It was a warm night and his undershirt clung with sweat to his chest and back. Why was he standing there?

His hand went to wipe away the dampness from his brow, but the movement came with a clanging sound on the wood floor. His reaction was quick and animalistic, and he found himself crouched on the floor like a wildcat. The fireplace poker was next to him. He'd dropped it. He had made the clanging noise. Why did he have the poker in his hand? Why was he standing in the middle of the living room? Why wasn't he asleep in his bed?

He sat on the couch and rested his head in his hands. The last thing he remembered was falling asleep to the thudding of distant mortars that he couldn't push from his mind. The cold gun held in his moist hands. Heavy breathing with sweat dripping down his face and onto his lips. Drinking a beer with his buddies on a ship between battles. Watching the enemy flying through the air, their bodies mangled. Death. Visions of Irene. Esther's eyes. Then he was here—standing in his living room in the glow of the moon.

His breathing slowed, and instead of returning to his bed, he lay in the dark on the couch. What if Daisy had been there? What if he had hurt her in his sleep? He needed to stay awake to keep the haunting at bay.

But he did fall asleep and was startled awake when the sound of crashing metal and gravel burst through his fitful sleep. He bolted upright. The sun had risen. Where was he? Were the Japs close? No, they weren't, but his breathing still quickened. He was in his house. In Sunrise.

Without thinking, he stood and walked through the front door and began running toward the sound. His heart slowed to a normal pace when he found that a cream-colored Ford had crashed into his mailbox. He ran toward the car, and a balding man with a mustache came stumbling out. He stumbled over his feet and rubbed his beer gut.

The man looked at the mailbox that tilted against the automobile. Joe was close enough now to hear the man swear.

"Are you okay?" Joe asked.

The man looked up at Joe. His eyes, round and startled, didn't seem to focus well. There were empty beer cans inside the automobile. The man was drunk.

"I think I'm all right." The man's voice had an unusual twang to it. Where was he from, and who was he? The vehicle looked familiar, but Joe couldn't place where he'd seen it.

"Looks like I might owe you a new mailbox." The man rubbed his chin, looking over the damage.

"I can fix it easily enough." Joe bent over and moved the mailbox off from the vehicle's hood, revealing a long black scrape against the cream-colored Ford. "This a '34 Victoria?"

"1932." The man looked back over the damage. "I'm sorry 'bout this, son. I'm Chester Detweiler, but my friends call me Chet."

"Detweiler?" Joe asked.

"That's what I said."

"You know Esther Detweiler?"

Chet inhaled and exhaled deeply before nodding yes. "I do. She's my daughter."

"I'm Joe Garrison. Daisy's father." Joe stood and walked over to Chet and put his hand out to him.

Chet reached out, but then the hand went to his head and the other arm went to steady himself on the car. Then he waved Joe's hand away.

"Not much for formalities." Chet laughed. "So you're Joe. I think between the two of us, we've done a number on our little Essie, haven't we?"

"Well, you've thrown me for a loop. I thought you were dead."

Chet flipped his hands this way and that way as he looked them over.

"Nope. I'm alive." He laughed.

Joe didn't ask for clarification. All he could think of in the moment was that he'd almost kissed the man's daughter in the moonlight only the night before. What would Chet have to say about that?

"Chester and Esther," Joe said. "I suppose I never knew what your first name was."

"Leah, Esther's mother, insisted on the rhyming names since Esther wasn't a boy." Chet winked. "Kinda made me proud."

"Is your Ford still going to run?" Joe gestured toward the vehicle.

"I think so. Only I can't keep driving this baby around."

"Why's that?"

"You see, son, I've been gone for a while—from the Amish church. Came back when my old lady passed. I'm trying to get back into the church's good graces, and I can't have myself a car."

"Then why were you heading home with the car just now?" Joe asked. This man wasn't making much sense. Esther didn't mention anything about her father living with her either. "Why didn't Esther tell me you were back? Are you staying there?"

"You sure have a host of questions, son. Not sure I can follow them all." Chet blinked rapidly. "Might've had a few too many. I guess I have to kick that ole habit also. But to answer at least one of your questions: No, I'm not living with Esther right now. I'm living at the dairy where I'm working, or at least I was, but I missed a milking last night and this morning. Pretty sure that Norma isn't going to keep me on." He rubbed the whiskers on his jaw with his hand that was missing the finger.

Joe sized up the other man. The Amish didn't allow any recreational alcohol. He remembered Irene telling him that they used wine for communion, but that usually was their only exposure to alcohol. Joe had been curious about the goings on of the younger crowd in the church during what Irene called *rumspringa*. Irene hadn't admitted to anything unsavory during these dating and running-around years, but he'd heard stories about some of the youth.

"You're probably wondering why I'm drunk," Chester suggested.

"Well, I did wonder. You shouldn't be driving like that." He gestured toward the beer cans in the car. "I don't know a whole lot of Amish men who would be drinking that many cans of beer—or who own a car for that matter."

"You're right about that. I'm not so good of an Amish man, been gone so long. Hardly know how to be." He wiped his forehead with a hanky that had the initials C.D. in the corner.

"I understand more than you know."

"But I had a good reason for the drinking. I got whipped like a snot-nosed kid by the preachers yesterday and just had to get outta there—outta that house. But I had it comin'. I know I did. I felt the fire of hell on my backside one night in a dream and knew it was time to make a change." He shook his head. "Gotta put this English life behind me, starting today, and start living the straight and narrow." He sliced his hand in the air in front of him.

Joe didn't respond. Why would a man like him come back anyway? Why not just stay away? Why give his English life up? It didn't seem as if he wanted to anyway. Why give Esther the grief of his return after believing he was dead?

"You play poker?" Chet changed the subject. "Pretty sure I don't have a job anymore, so I'm going to have to pay for my boarding room and some debts." He mumbled the last few words. "Spent all my money last night at the local watering hole."

"Never been much for poker. Do the Amish play poker?" He squinted his eyes at Chet.

"Oh, it's just a little sin. They'll never find out. Even the straight and narrow has a few dips in the road." Chet clicked his tongue at Joe and winked.

Joe opened his mouth to respond, but Chet started talking again.

"You know, son, I think that this little accident might have been pure providence. I am looking to park my good ole Ford somewhere. Can't have things like this if I mean to get on the good side of the church—you know, that *straight and narrow*."

Joe and Chet said the last three words together and laughed as they both threaded a flat hand through the morning air.

"Besides, I owe a man some money and hiding my car away might not be a bad idea—you know, until I clear things up." The older man cleared his throat and dug his toes into the gravel road. Then he looked up at Joe with sudden brightness. "I see you've got a big barn back behind your house. What would you say to parking it in your barn?"

Joe wondered what Esther would think about this. He didn't know a lot about Chet or why he had suddenly come back after decades away. Chet must have noticed his trepidation and added, "You know, just until I can sell it. How 'bout it?"

"Sure. I think that would be fine."

The two men rigged up the mailbox so that it would stay up until it could be fixed properly. The car started fine, and Joe had it in the barn in no time.

"Why don't you come in for a cup of coffee and some breakfast?" Joe offered. "I'm checking on a job this morning. Maybe you'd like to ride along. I heard they are looking."

"What kind of job?"

"Carpentry. There are some housing developments going up just outside town. It'll be steady work."

Chet's head bounced up and down as he thought. "I think that might be just the ticket. I can still hold a hammer. Even with this." He showed Joe the gap where his finger should be then clapped his hands. "Now, about that breakfast."

Joe fixed both of them some eggs and coffee, and between the two, they ate nearly a dozen. Chet cleaned himself up with some cold water, and they were off in Joe's truck.

"I have to make a quick stop at Esther's before we go." Joe pulled up to Esther's house.

"You gonna squeal on me, are ya?" Chet raised his eyebrows. "She can't know about the Ford."

"No, sir," Joe said, laughing. "I'll only be a few minutes."

At first Joe stepped carefully as he walked toward the run-down house. He took in the wilted porch floor and the broken middle step. The house was somewhat dilapidated, but the small garden was planted in perfect rows without a single weed.

If he'd not insisted, she would've cut all the grass herself. Across the road the same work waited for her, and on a larger scale. And for how much in wages? No wonder her house was in disrepair. Irene had told him that Esther was as good with a hammer and nails as a man, but with her job, caring for Orpha for years and then also Daisy, it was still too much for one woman. He hopped over the broken step onto the wilted porch and walked to the door.

He bit his lower lip as he lifted a closed hand to rap on the door but before his fist hit the door, it opened. Esther's dark eyes were bigger than he remembered.

"Joe?" Her fingertips grazed over her lips for a beat before she looked around him toward his truck. Her eyes squinted. "Why is *he* in your truck?"

"I wanted to see you." Joe leaned against the door frame, wanting to get closer to her. "Can I come in?"

"No." Esther shook her head, and he could see her swallow as her eyes glanced around them. What was she worried about? "We can talk out here."

She closed the door behind her and leaned against the opposite side of the door frame from Joe.

"I ran into your dad this morning—or he ran into me . . ." Joe tried to make light conversation.

"Don't call him that," Esther said.

"What?"

"Dad. He hasn't been a dad to me since I was five. But that's not why you are here. What do you want?" Her voice was breathy yet deep. Soft and hard. Light and dark. It was Esther.

"I wanted to talk about what happened last night." Their closeness, their near kiss, had warmed his insides.

Esther's eyes looked away. "Nothing happened."

He shook his head at her dismissal.

"I know you thought I was drunk. But I wasn't—not even

close." His hand went out to her, then remembering Chet in the truck behind him, it retreated back to his hip.

"I could smell—" she began then stopped, her face turning a bright blush. "I could smell—it—on your breath."

"I had a few swallows before I left the house. Then I thought about what you said and I poured it out." Joe felt an urgency in making her understand this. It had been a battle, since on the nights he had a beer his night terrors weren't as destructive. Or maybe it was that he felt numb toward them. He couldn't tell her that he was so plagued with horrifying memories that all he really wanted to do was get drunk and stay drunk until the memories faded. But what if they didn't?

Esther crossed her arms and looked out toward the road. She didn't believe him. He could prove it to her now by kissing her to show her that his desire to kiss her had nothing to do with a few sips of beer but rather a plaguing draw to her that he couldn't explain. But he wasn't prepared for the guilt he would feel. Besides, at the moment, they were standing on the front porch of her home. Anyone could see. Daisy was inside. And Irene was everywhere.

"I'm sorry." Her eyes snapped to his and then softened as she turned away, biting her lower lip. "I just wanted you to know that I wasn't drunk. And you weren't either."

"I don't find that funny, Joe."

"I'm not trying to be funny. My point is that neither of us was drunk, but we almost kissed each other. You can't deny it."

He stopped himself before he admitted that she was like a magnet to him. Was it because she'd been the closest person to Irene? Or was it because she was nothing like Irene? Was it simply because he'd deprived himself of the body and touch of a woman for too many years? He didn't know. What he did know was that having her so close had awakened something that had been dormant since Irene's death.

Esther

It was the first church Sunday since the church leaders had visited. The ready memory that wouldn't let her rest, however, was that Joe had almost kissed her. Esther replayed how it felt to be so close to him too often to be prudent. It was sinful and hedonistic, and it made her heady and warm. She couldn't understand why a man like Joe would want to kiss an old spinster like her—until she remembered it was only because of the alcohol, despite his denial.

Joe was not the only person consuming her thoughts; Chester remained rooted in her mind as well. Both of them had gotten jobs building homes for Wayne Good. Somehow this made Esther worry less. Perhaps knowing that she and Chester weren't working on the same dairy farm all day was a relief. She hadn't seen his car since the evening the church leaders came either. She saw him only from a distance as Joe picked him up in the mornings for work. She and Daisy began visiting Joe after he returned in the late afternoon.

There was some comfort in the routine that had begun to form. A routine that would've seemed foreign only a month ago, when Orpha was still alive, Joe was across the ocean, and Chester was dead. How had life changed so quickly?

With her handheld mirror, she inspected her hair, ensuring that every curl was pulled into submission. It had become a habit since she'd been baptized into the church. No hair out of place. She had gained more than enough attention due to her circumstances; she didn't want to be approached by a preacher or deacon over an issue of modesty.

The hand mirror reflected her warm pink lips. She traced them with a finger and unintentionally wetted them with her tongue. She thought of what it might have felt like to kiss Joe. She dropped the mirror, and the reflective glass scattered about the wooden floor. But there was no time to sweep it up now. Daisy was downstairs waiting for breakfast and it was nearly time to go to church. It was an important Sunday. Chester would make his confession today.

She turned toward the bed where her black dress lay. It was common for the family of a confessing member to wear black. Chester didn't feel like family, however. And she knew that at least part of the story he gave to the preachers was a lie. She hadn't the courage to tell anyone, though. She took the black dress and hung it back in her closet again and pulled out a navy dress. Wearing navy would prove to everyone that she didn't see Chester's sin as an embarrassment to her. She wanted him to know that she wasn't taken in by his circumstances. It was a lie, she was ashamed, and his sin blanketed her, but she would hide this deep inside.

Esther pinned her white covering onto her black hair. While all the rest of the unmarried women wore black on Sundays, she wore white. At some point in an unmarried woman's life, it became assumed she would never marry and the white *kapp* was appropriate. For her, it had happened around her thirtieth birthday. Orpha made her a white covering one day and left it on Esther's bed. Nothing was ever said about it, but Esther understood the message. It wasn't that she couldn't get married, but after thirty the chances were slim.

The late June morning sun embraced Esther as she hitched up Deano. She lifted her face to greet the orange and yellow warmth and breathed in the summer air. The sun's rays made the light sprinkling early that morning look like crystals sitting atop blades of grass. It had been a slow transition into summer, with late spring showers. When she arrived at the stable, she found Chester brushing down the old bay horse. Deano whinnied when Esther drew closer.

Chester looked up at her with sober eyes and offered a quiet smile. He was nervous. His jaw boasted what appeared to be several days of growth. His upper lip, on the other hand, looked odd and naked—his mustache had been sheared off. He looked more Amish than she'd expected, with the suit that a cousin had sewn for him since Esther had made no move to help in this way. His old Amish clothes had been given away years ago.

"Thought I'd start being of some help around here. Mucked out the stall for you too. I'll take care of ole Dean from now on."

"I've managed just fine." Esther was curt on purpose.

Chester released a soft chuckle. It rolled around in the humid air and into her ears. She wouldn't admit that the familiar sound brought back the memories that were worth remembering.

"I see that." He pushed his jaw out and caught her gaze before replacing the curry comb in the small barrel at the side of the stall. "You've done a right good job. Better'n any man could've done. I'm proud of you, Esther."

"If you're saying this to butter me up, it's not working. I know you lied to the preachers about how you lost your finger, and I'm wondering what else it is that you lied about." Her emboldened heart pounded.

Chester inspected his hand twice over and pursed his lips. He nodded and looked back to Esther.

"You're right." Chester's eyes looked past Esther. Her head turned to find where his gaze landed and found the ax that lay next to the stump used for cutting wood. Another job Esther had taken on at a young age.

"The ax?" Esther's voice was barely audible.

Chester swallowed hard. He didn't answer but continued to stare at the old tool.

"But who? You couldn't have done that yourself." Esther blocked Chester's gaze from the ax to force his eyes on hers. The moment that passed between them startled her with realization. *Mem* had come inside holding a bloodied rag on that morning so long ago. "*Mem? Mem* cut your finger off?"

Esther's eyes filled. All the pieces had been there all along, only she had continued to view it all through the mind of a five-year-old, not wanting to put the puzzle together. Her mother had been pasty white that morning, and it was because she'd just cut the finger off her husband so that he could forgo his conscription. How could this have been worth it, since he'd gone to prison regardless?

Chester wiped his face with his hands.

"Was it worth it?" she asked.

"I was a coward, Esther." The old man turned away from Esther, and she watched for another minute as he pulled the buggy up behind Deano. When she knew he wasn't going to say anything more—and she wasn't prepared to hear anything more—she returned to the house. When it was time to leave, the buggy was ready, but Chester was nowhere to be found.

David Coblentz's home, where church was held that week, had a section of benches for the women. The first row was reserved for the old maids and widows. Women with young children and babies filled the middle benches. This left the back benches of unmarried young women to wink at, tease, or shrewdly ignore the unmarried young men on the other side of the living room. Daisy sat with Esther, the only little girl on her bench. From Esther's vantage point, she could see Chester. He didn't quite blend in with the men around him with their long graying beards. When their eyes met, he snapped his away. Now that she had the truth to one of his lies on the tip of her tongue, he knew she could tell the preachers. She wasn't sure what she would do with what she'd just learned, or if it was all that he was hiding. The morning conversation stirred in her mind like a brewing storm.

By the time the preaching service was nearly over, Daisy had fallen asleep, her head on Esther's lap. Esther tucked a blond tendril back inside Daisy's covering. How many more Sundays would Daisy come to church with her? Everyone around her began kneeling at the benches for prayer at the end of the service. Esther gently repositioned Daisy and knelt with everyone else, but she found it hard to follow the prayer. All she could think about was that after this, Chester would be brought forward.

At the end of the bishop's prayer, he announced that it was time for nonmembers to leave. All those who weren't baptized left the house without question. This included Chester; he would be brought in at the appointed time. All knew that this request usually meant the bishop had a matter to discuss with the members who were in good standing. This wasn't unusual. With a district of several hundred, it was not uncommon to deal with a confession every few months. Two months ago, there had been a newly married man who had confessed to having lingered near the radio at a farming supply store, wanting to hear more of the music that he left behind in his *rumspringa* years. In that instance, he'd come forward himself to confess his guilt. In the late winter, there had been a young mother who had accepted a birthday gift from a shunned sister.

Esther, however, had never had to confess anything in front of the church. Besides some gray areas with Irene, she practiced the *Ordnung* in all the ways that really mattered. She had no desire to stray. After seeing what it led to with Irene and her father,

her heart was framed even more concretely within the boundaries and protection of the church. Her friendship with Irene had been her greatest weakness. But they hadn't exchanged gifts or shared a meal. Those things were strictly forbidden, and she hadn't crossed that line. They took walks, talked, and Esther was present for the deliveries of her children—and her death.

Sins and confessions were always handled with clarity and forthrightness when a member was in need of cleansing. Just as with Chester, the guilty member was visited first. Generally it was the *aumah deanah*, the head deacon, who was in charge of such visits. In Chester's case, it had required more than the deacon alone.

Daisy leaned into Esther's arm and smiled sleepily. Esther was glad that Daisy's deafness allowed her the chance to stay.

"*Vit en schnupduch boppleh?*" Esther whispered, asking her if she wanted a hanky doll, showing her the special Sunday handkerchief. Daisy nodded, smiling. She began rolling and twisting it into a doll. Her hands shook fiercely, nervous about Chester's confession. Daisy began rocking back and forth with impatience. Esther had to unroll the hanky to start again. She lowered her head and squeezed her eyes shut.

A moment later the white-haired widow next to her, Alberta Yoder, took the hanky from Esther's hands and within a minute had it rolled and tucked into a doll shape. She handed it to a happy Daisy, who instantly began playing the part of a little mother.

Esther looked at Alberta for a brief moment. Her mouth trembled as she tried to smile.

"*Bisht alraiht?*" She asked with a hand on Esther's arm.

Was she okay? Esther nodded, a lie, and tried a smile again. Alberta's arm returned to her own lap and Esther looked back toward the front where the bishop was ready to speak. She tightened her jaw to restrain her emotions. Chester would not continue humiliating her.

"Chester Detweiler is coming forward today to confess his

sin," Bishop Willie Zook began. "He was thought to be dead, but instead he left the church and lived as an Englisher. Ray and I went to him this week, and we talked over how he was living. He owned a car and went to bars where he drank beer and smoked—cigarettes, not pipes. He wore an Englisher haircut and mustache and clothes. If one had seen him at a store or on the street, he would've looked like all the other Englishers of the world. He has been in the *bann* since our talk and comes today to make his issues right *mit da gmay und de Got.*"

Esther considered his words. His issues were *with the church and with God.* But were the Amish so entangled with the will of God that if you offended one, you offended the other as well? Or was there a distinction? Was God offended by sharing a meal with a shunned member more than He was offended by the shunning and rejection itself? These questions had plagued her since Irene's shunning.

What she couldn't reconcile to herself was that Irene had become more settled, peaceful, and happy after her shunning. She hadn't left the church because of any downfalls with it or because she desired the world. She left because she loved Joe and desired a life with him. She had never turned her back on God or left Him behind. In Esther's observation, Irene had grown more faithful and devout in her English life than she'd ever been before.

Esther had never let herself answer these questions fully, afraid they would confuse her loyalty to the black-and-white law of the church. At least in this situation with Chester there was no confusion as to the sin.

When Chester was escorted back into the house by a preacher, the walls closed in on Esther. The cloudless sky through the windows grew brighter, but a tangible blackness crept inside her heart, darkening her mood even further. The widows and spinsters around her simply watched and listened. Their knuckles

weren't white with clenching, their hearts weren't racing, and
their underarms weren't burning with new sweat. Her instinct
was to look down at her feet, the floor, anything but watch this
happen in front of her eyes, anything but show her emotions.
She couldn't let anyone else see how ashamed she was, how
vulnerable she was to Chester.

Chester's face grimaced in what looked like pain and anguish
as he knelt in front of the congregation. Usually the guilty member would sit in the front row with downcast eyes, but Chester
had knelt. This revealed that his sin was considered greater and
worse than possibly even what was stated. Adultery was likely
among his sins. Her face grew warm, and her very bones trembled inside her skin.

Chester's eyes roamed the room for a brief moment. Was he
looking for her? She was glad he hadn't found her.

When his voice rang out, she wanted to cover her ears. He
spoke much louder than the typical confessor's mumblings.

*"Ich bekan es ich kfeld happ. Fashpaht Got und de gmay, hatslich
geduld aw, fanna hee bessah sige drah."*

Several muffled sobs followed his words, and he slumped
over weeping. Had he meant those words? The phrase rumbled
around in her gut, making her feel ill as she replayed the confession. *I confess that I have failed. I promise God and the church, in
humbleness, from here on out to make better choices.*

A tug wrenched painfully in her chest. No. Esther would not
feel this way about a man who had abandoned her and her *mem*
and *mammie* twenty-nine years ago. His story was questionable and
bound together with at least one lie. She didn't respect him. Her jaw
tightened. Tears burned her eyes, but she would not cry for him.

She squeezed her eyes together and found herself silently
pleading with God that Chester would make better choices.
That whatever his life was like in the Englisher's world, he
would turn from it and become the kind of man he should be.

She had no confidence that he could actually be a father to her, but it might not be too late for him to become a good man.

She opened her eyes when she heard other members give their *ein vaht*, the *one-word* response to Chester's confession. Each member would have three options: say *ya* that they agreed that he was remorseful, say *nay* that they did not stand in agreement with his confession, or choose to not have any part of it and say *ivah lessah*. She heard many *ya* responses from the members on the benches nearby. She suddenly heard a quiet *nay*. Esther's eyes snapped to find the voice belonging to her mother's closest friend and cousin, Anna May. Anna May looked from the corner of her eye to Esther, then quickly lowered her head. She'd known that Anna May had been devastated at Leah's death and had been bedridden herself for several weeks following it.

If three people said *nay*, they could not overlook his sin despite the confession, his *bann* would continue, and he would have to confess again in another few weeks. A strong male voice rang out *nay* from the other side of the room. Esther knew it to be Anna May's husband. One more no and the church would not accept Chester's confession.

An elbow nudged her arm. It was Alberta. Esther looked over to the older woman and found sympathy in her eyes. She nodded to Esther.

"*Deh ein vaht?*" she whispered and raised her eyebrows with a nod toward the man who stood in front of them.

Esther turned and found one of the preachers standing in front of her waiting for her *ein vaht*. The preacher's black eyebrows knit together in question and concern. He was younger than Chester and probably hadn't known anything about him. And now he stood in front of her, waiting for a response.

Her tongue went to the roof of her mouth to give her negative response. She had every right to say *nay*. She'd lost everything because of him: her father, her mother, Orpha, security, music, and her childhood. And now, as an adult, she realized she'd also lost the good character and reputation she thought her family had. All the adults in her life who should've protected her through everything had lied to her. Had lost themselves in protecting their mistakes. There was nothing more she wanted to do in the moment than to say *nay* and not accept Chester's confession. She inhaled, ready to speak, but in the last twinkling of the moment, she bowed her head and closed her eyes.

"*Ivah lessah.*" Her voice was barely a whisper. She couldn't say no to Chester, she couldn't say no to her *dat*. She put a hand up to her forehead to shield her face from view. Hot tears streamed down and dropped on her navy blue dress. From the corner of her eye, she saw Daisy unroll her hanky doll and try to wipe away Esther's tears. The gesture almost forced her weeping to deepen, but with a deep breath, she gently took the hanky and wiped away any evidence of her burden.

"Now hear me, brothers and sisters. *Des bruder*'s confession has been accepted. He will be in the *bann* for six months as penance. In the meantime we should be on our guard for Satan's attacks within our folds. Let us follow the *Ordnung* and not gossip over the faults of another. This brother is sorry and he is forgiven by us and by the *Hah*. In six months, we will give him the right hand of grace, and from here on we need to leave it behind us. Then it will be finished."

Finished. The word repeated itself again and again as she and Chester fled the scene, as often happened in the shame of these circumstances. Esther had never imagined that she would flee along with her *dat*, who was in the fold of protection again despite his *bann*. By this very occurrence, she felt more unprotected and lost than ever.

Joe

1944
Mariana Bay, Saipan

The foxhole was crowded with five people. Garrison knew that Japs were crawling through the brush ahead of them, but they were hard to see in the dimming light. He had to get to the remaining foxholes and get ammo to the men. Since he'd lost a significant amount when he'd fallen, he'd have to distribute what he had left.

The shots on their side slowed down and then stopped. He used the short reprieve to regroup with his men to get on to the next foxhole. His squad was on the other side of the secured area, and when the firing began again, Garrison knew exactly where it was coming from.

He, Fielding, and Crane moved on to several more foxholes. Now that it was dark, he called out the word *Christmas* to answer the challenge word, *Wombat,* to alert those in the foxholes that they weren't the enemy. They made sure everyone had enough ammo and moved on quickly. They were nearing the foxholes under fire and the blanket of night had fallen. All Garrison could hear when they jumped into the next foxhole was Private Rix yelling out in pain. Garrison went to him first and instantly saw he needed medical attention.

He had Crane take Rix to the corpsman at HQ. A Japanese soldier's body was flung across the foxhole, with blood dripping from his mouth. Another Japanese soldier lay a few feet away with his face down and his leg at an awkward angle.

He needed to get the ammo to his men, the final of the three platoon squads. It was time to move on. Garrison grabbed his can and Fielding picked up his own and Crane's and ran ahead.

Garrison quickly pushed himself up and out of the foxhole and his boots dug deep into the ground. He was halfway to the next foxhole when the thought-to-be-dead Japanese soldier grabbed his ankle. As Garrison fell, he saw the enemy bare his teeth and lift his knife.

Joe

J oe enjoyed working for Wayne Good. He was a good boss, and direct. No one had to wonder what the man wanted or needed. Both he and Chester were given a job on the spot over a week ago and put to work immediately. Joe was on the framing crew, and Chet worked on the concrete foundations.

The physical exhaustion and heat satisfied Joe's need to wear himself out. Maybe with hard enough work, he wouldn't wake up with nightmares. He couldn't have Daisy stay with him, he couldn't be a real father to her, until he was free from his night wanderings and destruction. He had put breakables away and secured the dinner plates and cups behind the kitchen cupboards with a broomstick through the handles. He'd still found the bathroom mirror cracked and cuts and bruises on his knuckles.

"You ever take breaks, Garrison?" Wayne Good asked as he checked in with Joe one afternoon.

"Don't need any," Joe replied, out of breath from just having put up another wall. If it weren't that the crew took a lunch, Joe would work while eating. Exhausted muscles surely could not do as much damage, right?

"You've been working hard. I haven't heard you complain,

and you ate your lunch fast. And you must know something I don't because I'm not even sure I saw you hit the head all day."

Wayne spoke like a military man, with evenly cut syllables and his arms crossed over a wide chest. He was completely bald, as if he'd shaved his head. He rarely smiled. "If you keep it up, you'll be a crew leader in no time."

"Thank you, sir," Joe nodded.

"But your buddy over there—man, I don't mean to bust your chops about him, but he took enough breaks for the both of you." Wayne eyed Chet.

"He's not my buddy." It wasn't that Joe didn't like Chet; he simply didn't understand him. He didn't seem to have any pride in a job well done or care what his coworkers thought of his lack of work ethic.

"There aren't any pennies from heaven around here. He has to work for his wage. If he doesn't step it up, I'll send him packing. There are plenty of men willing to work."

"I hear you loud and clear." Joe gave a half wave, half salute to his new boss. He decided that he'd have to say something to the older man on their drive home.

"Garrison, one more thing," Wayne said, and waved him over to the trailer on the job site that he used as an office.

"I'll be at the truck in a minute," Joe called to Chet, who shrugged and walked wearily to Joe's truck. Joe turned back to Wayne. "Yeah?"

"You got a wife or daughters?" the boss asked.

What was he getting at? Joe felt a rush of heaviness move over his heart. Could he say that he legitimately had a daughter when she didn't live with him?

"I have a daughter." That was safe enough to admit.

Wayne glanced up at him, his brow closing into the center of his forehead.

"Widower?" he asked gruffly.

Joe nodded.

"Me too." Wayne opened the door to the trailer and pulled out a can of paint. "Remarried?"

"No," he said too quickly.

Joe was sure he'd heard Wayne talk about his wife as if she was still alive.

"I remarried when I came back from over there."

Joe felt his face adjust to the news. He didn't want to be that transparent, but he couldn't help it. Yes, he'd wanted to kiss Esther and would have had she not stopped him. But he hadn't breathed the word *remarriage*. The gentleman inside him reminded him that there was no point in kissing any woman if there wasn't a chance of marriage in the future. Or had he desired her only to fulfill his physical desires? Perhaps it had been nothing but a weak moment. Esther's mortified expression when she pulled away from him had been all he needed to know that it should never happen again.

"Don't look so shocked, Garrison. It's not so bad."

"No, I didn't mean . . ." He couldn't finish his thoughts.

Wayne mumbled under his breath as he waved off Joe's words.

"I ordered some paint for my Watercrest site. The paint store insisted that it was a tan rose—a dusty rose—but not pink." Joe waited as Wayne opened the can and flipped over the lid. "What would you call this?"

"Pink," Joe said with a chuckle behind his smile.

"Doggone it." He pushed the lid back onto the can and grabbed a rubber mallet sitting inside the trailer door to close it. "Here. Maybe your daughter will like it."

Wayne pushed the can of paint into Joe's arms. A smile stretched over Joe's face. Yes, Daisy would love a pink room, and it would be perfect for her bedroom if she ever moved back home with him again.

Joe was alone with his thoughts as they drove back to Sunrise. Chet had fallen asleep before Joe had even climbed into the truck. As he neared Esther's house, his stomach flopped back and forth as he looked forward to seeing Daisy—or was it because of Esther?

Joe pulled into the drive of the small farmhouse, turned off the engine, and looked around through the truck windows.

The engine cutting off roused Chet. He looked around.

"Must've fallen asleep." He stretched and yawned. "Thanks for bringing me home," Chet said as he rubbed his face. "Oh, wait, I'm not home. I guess I can walk over to the boardinghouse. Esther won't even talk to me since Sunday. She's hellbent on hating me. She's a tough one, that girl. I'm in a heap o' trouble with the church, and I really do want to make sure I can keep my hands clean. Oh, and don't think I've forgotten about the mailbox. I'll get it fixed as soon as I got some money in my back pocket."

Joe battled with sensing sincerity in the man and an ulterior motive. What was he after?

"Well, don't worry about the mailbox. I'm sure I've got everything I need in the barn."

"Well, that's good because I don't know when that workhorse Wayne is going to pay us. He's a bit of a Nazi, don't you think?" His words clipped as he got out of the truck.

Joe didn't like the reference but let it go. Wayne Good was nothing like that. Calling him a Nazi was insulting.

"I think he's all right. Just wants the job to get done. Might want to watch how many breaks you take, though." Joe climbed out of the driver's seat. "Usually Esther comes over with Daisy, but I noticed the other day that there are a few projects that need tending to. I thought maybe I could help after all she's done for me."

"Good luck, buddy. Esther's just about the strongest-minded

woman I've ever met. Can't say I blame her." The older man paused briefly and leaned on the truck. "Hoping she'll give me a chance to make things up to her, though. Or at least try. I guess I can muck out the stall before I go over to the dairy for some grub."

He didn't know where Chet had been all these years, but either way, he didn't like the idea of the hurt it must have brought to Esther. Chet went over to the one-horse stall to start working. Joe walked toward the front porch, he bent over to inspect the tread and broken riser. Maybe he would run home to grab his tools and fix it before someone got hurt. He moved to the porch to survey the structure further. The wood slats on the porch creaked under his weight. He knelt to inspect them and found that several were unattached from the joists.

"What are you doing here?" Esther's sharp voice cut in like an unwanted dance partner.

He turned to find that Esther was not wearing her usual white covering, but instead had tied a scarf around the back of her neck. Her dress wasn't the usual brown one, but a faded blue-gray with the sleeves cut off at the elbow. Her face was shiny, likely from hard work, and she looked uncomfortable. She pulled a basket of yarn closer to her and wrapped the other arm around Daisy. The little girl was dressed in her usual Amish attire that Joe had begun getting used to. After having thought about it, he realized it had made sense.

Joe stood and cleared his throat. He looked from Esther's confused brow to Daisy, who looked up at him. He smiled at Daisy, and for the first time it actually bloomed from his face naturally.

"Hi, Daisy." His hand waved and he began making the sign, like pulling flower petals, but then stopped, feeling uncomfortable. Esther's face twitched at his effort to sign. It wasn't negative, more like surprised.

Daisy buried her face in Esther's side, leaving only one eye visible. But her hand waved slightly at her side. Joe winked at her. Esther's eyes looked down at Daisy's hand that waved and then back at Joe. Her deep breath couldn't go unnoticed, and in her eyes he saw something—fear, relief, sadness.

"I was planning to bring Daisy over later, like I—" Esther said it simply but there was a breathiness in her voice. Was she nervous?

"I thought maybe I could fix a few things," he interrupted.

"Fix a few things?"

"Just some little things. Like the step there, and these floorboards are loose here." He bent down to show her.

Daisy pulled at Esther's arm and signed—as if she was bringing something to her mouth. Was she hungry?

"Yes, we will eat supper soon," Esther spoke the words aloud and gestured several signs.

Daisy whined and signed again, then pointed to Joe. Esther signed something back, this time without speaking. This went back and forth for a minute before she looked at Joe.

"Daisy would like to invite you to dinner—here with us."

A tremor ran through him. An invitation. Daisy wanted him to stay. His mouth spread into a smile that pulled his skin tightly. Since his job had begun, he saw Daisy only after supper for a few hours in the evening at his house. She usually didn't communicate with him much, and Esther stayed busy cleaning and making him nervous.

"How do I say *yes* to her?" he asked, flipping his hands this way and that. "Can I just nod my head, or what should I do?"

Esther tilted her head when she looked at him. Her lips opened slightly.

"Like this," she said with the softest voice he'd heard from her. She took her right fist and bobbed it up and down. Their eyes were focused only on each other, and for several long moments Joe wondered if even Esther forgot that Daisy was standing next to her.

He mimicked the gesture and looked at Esther. "Like this?"

Esther nodded. Her face remained soft.

Joe looked at Daisy and did the sign for *yes*. "Yes."

Daisy smiled at him, then looked at Esther and repeated the *yes* sign. She vocalized something that he couldn't understand, and Esther waved her into the house. When she passed Joe, she looked at him with a slight smile on her face but still kept her distance. He smiled back at her.

"I don't mean any offense by offering to help repair the porch or barge in on your meal." He turned back to Esther, who was at the bottom of the porch now.

Her eyes roamed over to the horse stall where Chet was busy working. He was whistling and didn't notice he had an audience until she spoke. She turned back to Joe.

"Just don't hurt her." Her voice was soft, but threaded with sadness and maybe regret. He knew she could've told Daisy *no* and he would be walking to his truck right now and eating at his house without his daughter or the woman who was a better parent than he was. But she hadn't said no. She saw the value of having him join them. Did this mean she was ready to let go of Daisy? Her eyes were dark against her fair face, and when he met them with his own, the same stirring spread through his body that he'd experienced the night of their moonlit walk.

"I don't want to hurt anyone." He meant it.

Esther stood near enough for him to detect the lingering scent of vinegar and soap before she moved past him.

"I'll start supper."

"I'll work on the porch." He didn't say it as a question, but he did raise his eyebrows. "I have scrap wood and nails back in my barn."

"Can you tell—" Her gaze landed on Chet again, and then she looked back to Joe. "He can join us tonight also."

"Okay," Joe said simply.

She nodded with her lips pursed. He could see that this turn of events was one measure closer to Daisy's return to him. He didn't like the hurt in her eyes.

"Esther," he said, keeping his voice quiet, desiring the intimacy with her. "I know that this isn't—"

Esther shook her head and just before she looked away he was sure he saw her eyes glisten. "She's your daughter. I'll be fine."

She walked into the house.

Joe

While the outside of the house was worn down, the inside had been well taken care of and was very clean and simple. Joe enjoyed sitting around the small table like a family. He took in the pleasure of it and his surroundings. Daisy was next to him. Chet sat in the chair in the living room, but turned it to face the kitchen. Esther placed a kettle of potato soup in the middle of the table.

"I can smell bacon." Chet rubbed his hands together. He stood up from the chair and peered over the side of the kettle.

"Bacon is over forty cents a pound right now. I can't afford it." Esther spoke with a nonchalance that Joe knew had to be false. She cleared her throat then continued. "Mrs. White gives me the bacon grease she doesn't need. I fried the potatoes in it."

Chet looked at Joe with raised brows.

"Well, next time I see Mrs. White, I'll have to thank her," Chet said.

Joe wasn't sure if Chet meant it sincerely or mockingly. His eyes flipped over to Esther, who had turned her back to slice the loaf of bread. She placed the plate of bread on the table and pulled the ladder-back chair out and sat.

"I'm sure she'd appreciate your gratefulness," Esther said with a measured tone that Joe didn't find believable. She didn't look at her father when she spoke but placed her hands in her lap. The silence after her words rested heavy between Esther and everything else in the room.

"Well," Chet said with a clap of his hands as he stood next to the table, "shall we eat?"

Daisy pulled Chet's arm then signed several words. She vocalized a word he couldn't understand. Chet tilted his head at her and squinted.

"What's she sayin'? I can't understand all of that gobbledy-gook." He waggled his hands around as he winked at the little girl, making her giggle.

Joe spoke up and nodded over to Esther. "I think she wants us to pray over the food."

Esther's face twitched when she found his eyes.

"Of course," Chet said and nodded to Esther. "Since I'm not sitting, I'll let you lead."

Esther gestured to Daisy to put her hands on her lap, and Joe followed her example. Then Chet lowered his chin and eyes and everyone followed his lead. The quiet of the house wrapped around him as he waited for the next step. He knew from Irene that this was how the Amish prayed before and after meals, but he'd never practiced this type of prayer. He hadn't been praying much before meals at all lately, and he hadn't while at war. Since he'd been home, he hadn't found his way back to prayer—or his Bible and church for that matter.

Esther cleared her throat, and Joe lifted his head. Now it was time to eat. Esther served Joe first, giving him several ladles of the soup. She gave Daisy one ladle and herself the same. Then she served Chet, giving him the most of all. After a slice of buttered bread and the first bowl of soup, Chet stood and leaned over Daisy and dipped the ladle back into the pot. Esther's shoulders sagged, and Joe wondered why.

"Looks like we could've used a little more soup," Chet suggested. "You know, when I worked as a hand on a sheep farm in the foothills of the Rocky Mountains in Colorado, I ate better than any other place I ever lived. And I've lived in a lot of different places."

Joe watched Esther. She had eaten slowly, and after Chet spooned seconds into his bowl, she set her own spoon down and used her bread to clean her bowl. Daisy was still eating, but looked at Esther with a sweet expression as she pointed at the butter. Esther smiled and buttered the little girl's bread with another layer, then filled Daisy's bowl with a half-ladle of soup.

"Would you like more?" Esther asked Joe, her tone friendly and kind.

"Thank you," Joe said, looking her in the eyes. He saw that there was a story behind her black eyes and found himself looking deeper in search of it. "But only after you take more."

"I'm finished. I'm fine." Esther's eyes glanced down and before Joe could say no, she gave him the rest of the soup.

Joe ate every bite with a swallow of regret. Something was wrong in that household and he didn't know what. Esther was not full, and she was not fine.

"Oh, the cook on that farm. *Hoo-wee!* What was her name again?" Chet returned to his previous conversation. He leaned back in his chair, making it creak. "Miss Ronda Sue—but she let me call her 'Sweetie.' Now, Joe, that woman could cook. Nothing was watered down, and we had meat. Lots of meat."

Joe wasn't sure if Chester was just sharing his experiences, but his words could easily be taken as insulting to Esther. He looked at her and found her eyes on him.

"I'm almost done with the porch," Joe said quickly, changing the subject.

Daisy tapped Esther's arm and signed several words. Esther

signed back and repeated what Joe had said. It appeared Daisy asked what he'd said—but she hadn't done the same when Chester spoke. His stomach flipped. Daisy was beginning to pay some attention to him.

Daisy signed several more words.

"Daisy says she's glad because it was hard for her to skip over the middle step." Esther continued to sign the conversation for Daisy. She smiled as she signed back.

Joe smiled at his daughter. She signed more, with added expression and liveliness. He was noticing that when she signed with such energy, sounds—not quite words—escaped from her mouth as if she was trying to vocalize her words.

"What's she saying?" Joe asked.

"She said that she's glad you're a carpenter like Jesus." Esther appeared to resist Joe's eyes until she finished the statement. She paused for a moment. "I'm grateful to you."

"Did she say that, or did you?"

"I did." Their eyes met, and he softened his by degrees.

Chet chuckled. "You two trying to be nice to each other is like rubbing two pieces of sandpaper together."

Esther kept the end-of-the-meal prayer short then she cleared the table, and Daisy helped her without a word or a sign. He thought that maybe he should leave, but the family atmosphere in the home impelled him to stay.

"Mighty glad you asked me to stay, Esther." Chet patted his belly. "That was delicious. I'd venture to say it was at least as good as your *mammie* used to make." He winked.

"Thank you." Esther let a small smile play over her lips.

Then Chet leaned forward and spoke quietly to Esther. Joe couldn't hear him. She only nodded when he was finished, and then Chet left for his room across the road.

"It's time for Daisy to go to bed." Esther got Daisy's attention and signed to her. The little girl stood and hugged Esther, who kissed the child's forehead. Daisy turned and looked at Joe. A small smile crept up on her face, and she signed.

"She said she'll see you tomorrow."

Joe nodded at her and returned her smile before Daisy ran upstairs. Esther followed her with a lit kerosene lamp and returned a minute later.

"Thank you for letting me stay," Joe said. His voice was almost swallowed up by the quiet in the home.

Esther paused. "It meant a lot to Daisy."

Joe nodded. What did it mean to Esther? He wanted to know but couldn't bring himself to ask.

"I'll be working until around five each day except for Sundays. Can we do this again? I would be happy to bring some food here, or you could come to my house. Maybe that will help Daisy get used to being there." As soon as he spoke, he wanted to take his words back. He couldn't have Daisy living with him until he was sleeping soundly. He couldn't trust himself not to be destructive during the nights.

Esther's eyes diverted from his.

After several beats she answered simply: "I think that would be nice for Daisy."

He nodded.

The flickering of the kerosene lamps moved their shadows around the walls. The clock ticked in time with the katydids song that came through the open window. Esther wiped down the counter again, but it was already clean.

"You know, Chet might be right about the sandpaper." Joe chuckled a little.

"What do you mean by that?" Esther challenged. She set down the washcloth to cross her arms.

"But it's my fault." Joe defused the comment. "I didn't think it would be this hard—to come home."

He wasn't sure how to finish the sentence as his eyes lingered on Esther's. Their darkness and depth did not give an inch, but her eyes called to him, lulled him. He shook his head slightly and brought his thoughts dead center on Irene.

"Sometimes it feels like she died last week instead of four years ago," he muttered, not doubting she'd understand.

"That's what happens when you run away, Joe. You can't run away this time, though."

His guard went up. "That's rich, coming from you. You're not making it very easy for me—keeping my own daughter from me." He regretted his words as soon as he said them. He could see she was making an effort, even though it pained her to lose Daisy. It was Daisy who clearly resisted, but Esther was the easy target.

"I've cared for Daisy for four years. I've put her needs ahead of my own, and it hasn't always gone as smoothly as tonight. You left when it got too hard."

"When are you going to stop throwing that in my face? I didn't know I was going to be gone for four years. You make it sound as if it would've been better if I'd never come back, like Chet. What do you want? You want Daisy to grow up just like you? Without a father? Not able to trust anyone and push everyone away?"

Esther's eyes caught the flame from the kerosene lamp. They burned into his.

"I've never belonged to anyone since I was just a little girl. I never want Daisy to feel that way. You knew you could be killed, and you were prepared to make your daughter an orphan. Since I know a little about that, I find that wretched. And as for pushing people away—" He saw a break in her exterior for a split second. "Everyone has pushed *me* away, not the other way around. Including you, Joe. Did you ever stop and think that when you took . . ." Her eyes sparkled with tears.

She was wrong. She was also right.

"What were you going to say?" But he knew. He knew what she meant with the dull realization of a shot to the gut. Esther was thinking about Irene as much as he was. Irene was always there, between them. When he took Daisy back, Esther would be alone. He was standing close to her, though he hadn't remembered moving toward her.

"It doesn't matter. We can't go back. And I hate that I can't even regret that Irene married you because of Daisy." Esther turned away from Joe, but he didn't let her get far.

Joe reached out a hand and brushed his fingertips over the torn sleeve of her dress. She stiffened, but he didn't return his hand to his side until *he* was ready to. Until his return, he hadn't thought of Esther as much more than Irene's cousin, Daisy's caretaker, and maybe even an old maid. But she was more than that. She was a flesh-and-blood woman with a heart that was hurting. The realization of the hurt he would cause her by taking Daisy away made him as nervous as his night terrors. The fact that he was drawn to her like any red-blooded man would be to a beautiful woman frightened him even more.

Esther

J oe's touch had been too much for Esther in the moment.
In her years of being a spinster, she'd never felt more temptation than she had when he was near. His closeness was
like a struck match that had caught fire in a hay field. The flames
ran wild. She ran up the stairs, hoping to hide her sudden desire
for him that was muddled up with her resistance to his return.
It was confusing and frightening. She leaned against the wall at
the top of the staircase. Her heart beat so fiercely that her hand
went to her chest, as if to extinguish the fire, but it only continued. Her eyes closed as she hung her head.

When she heard his quiet footfalls against the floor and then
the door open and shut, she sank down onto the floor. He was
gone—for now. But how would she do this every day? How
would she be able to ignore the electricity between them? What
if he touched her again? What if he tried to kiss her again?

Her abdomen stirred as she imagined what that might be
like. He'd brought her body so close to his that night and she'd
never felt more alive than in those moments. She fell asleep trying to avoid the constant echo of memories, but she dreamed
of him and in the morning, when his truck came into view to

pick up Chet, her heart hammered until he drove away. She was ashamed of herself for thinking of Joe as much as she did.

Joe had picked up on Chet's awkwardness and the fact that he didn't sit at the table. She'd seen it in the sensitivity of his eyes and heard it in his voice. She wanted to be able to explain to him that Chester was in the *bann*, and one of their rules was that Esther, as a member of the church, was not allowed to eat at the same table as a person under these restrictions. Once Chet had dipped soup out of the pot, Esther could not eat any more. This was why she'd given him an extra helping to start with. She needed to live by the church-ordained standard, even though she had still been hungry.

As she cleaned Mrs. White's home and pulled weeds from the garden, her mind was thinking about seeing Joe that evening at his house. Perhaps that would diffuse the spark, since his house was filled with Irene's ghost. The thought of it made her feel guilty. She shouldn't think in this way toward the dead, and she shouldn't call Irene a ghost. But there seemed to be no other word to describe the feelings of her presence. It had grown to the point of being palpable in the very air she breathed.

Irene had talked about how kind and handsome Joe was and what a good teacher he was to his students. These words were a constant recording that ran through her ears. It forced Esther to notice even more Joe's handsomeness when wearing his work clothing, with his skin tanning more deeply every day. When he ran a wet hand through his growing hair, it took away his military appearance, displaying a head of blond waves that perfectly framed his sky-blue eyes. She had to remind herself that this was Joe, Irene's husband, and she was Esther.

Her anger toward him was her salvation. Esther had, however, begun to see glimpses of the man Irene said Joe was and whom she'd seen before Irene's death. A young man with a cigarette hanging from his smile, tousled hair, book stuffed in his back pocket, and his arm around Irene. He was carefree and in love with her.

With the Joe she remembered finally coming to the surface, Esther had a sense of gladness, but defeat came in sequence. How she loved Daisy, but how bitter it was to know that eventually she would lose her. Joe would never understand what it was like to be rejected the way he'd turned away from his daughter. Esther did understand this, since her entire life had been one rejection after another—even more so now that she knew the truth about Chester. But her anger toward Joe was waning and losing steam as he continued to try to reconnect with Daisy.

~

The hot July air beat down on Esther as she and Daisy approached Joe's red clapboard house the following evening just as his truck pulled to a stop. Chester was lumbering slowly into the house. Why was he there? Joe remained on the driver's side as she and Daisy walked up the drive. She wasn't sure how to respond to him after the tension from the night before. Their eyes caught each other's through the mirror on the side of the truck.

Joe held her gaze for several moments too long and Esther diverted her eyes. He got out of the truck, jogged over to them, and knelt down in front of Daisy.

"Daisy?" Joe did the sign for her name and offered his daughter a wide smile. "There's a swing on the big oak out behind the house."

He did an unusual swinging action that made no sense to Daisy. The little girl looked up at Esther and shrugged.

"How do I sign it?" Joe looked at Esther, flustered.

"I don't know the sign for swing," she admitted. Even if she did, she wasn't sure she would've been able to focus enough to recall it for the hammering in her heart and drumming in her ears. She cleared her throat. "I came up with using a sign like you're cradling a baby and then doing the sign for tree." She put her right elbow into her left hand and made her hand wave back and forth.

He did the signs and pointed toward the oak.

Daisy tilted her head, and as he did it again, the meaning registered. She smiled and looked at Esther and signed *please*. Esther smiled back and bobbed her fist up and down. Daisy ran down the drive with her feet kicking up gravel behind her. Esther couldn't help but chuckle at her enthusiasm.

The silence that followed was filled with expectation.

"So you never told me that your dad was so full of jokes." Joe smiled and dug the toe of his boot into the gravel. "He had his whole crew laughing today."

"I don't know him, so how would I know that he's—funny?" Esther shielded her eyes from the sun as she looked at Joe.

"I'm sorry," he said quickly, "for what I said to you yesterday."

Was he sorry because he was wrong or just wrong for saying it? She wasn't sure.

"It seems like we're always apologizing to each other for things we say." Her eyes looked past him to the line of wind-spun trees.

"Chet did call us sandpaper." Joe winked, but Esther didn't find it amusing.

Esther started toward the house. She wanted to get supper started and not spend her entire night there. Not only did she have some of her own chores to do at her house, but the more quickly she could perfect this routine, the better. Though she knew that meant that Daisy would soon be leaving her home and moving in with Joe.

"I invited your dad—I mean, Chester—to eat with us." Joe eyed her as he spoke. "I hope that's okay."

"Fine." She continued on toward the house.

"What was with Chet not sitting at the table yesterday?" Joe stepped in front of Esther.

"He's in the *bann* right now. For six months." She tried to move around him, but he moved in front of her again. "Because he left for so long. Lied to us. Pretended to be dead. And probably plenty of other things that I don't care to talk about."

"The *bann*? Is that like being shunned?"

She exhaled an audible sigh. "Yes, it's the same, but since he wants to return to the church, it will eventually be lifted." She stepped around him.

"Irene's was never lifted though, was it?" He stepped in front of her again.

There she was again. Irene. She was never far away from either of them. She took a few moments before deciding to nod her head in agreement rather than saying anything. Sadness and anger crossed over his blue eyes at the mention of Irene. It pained her to see, though she felt it deeply inside her own heart too.

"So he's in the *bann*," he repeated. "And that means he can't eat at your table?"

Esther nodded.

"And that's why you didn't eat more soup—because he'd eaten out of the pot?"

Esther pursed her lips. Irene had explained a lot to him.

"No one would've tattled on you. Who would I have told?"

"It's not about who would have *tattled*. It's that I know better. I know it's against our ways, and I don't want to go against them."

"Even for such a little thing? It's just soup and you were hungry."

Esther looked past him. Living a pure lifestyle according to the *Ordnung* was what she desired, and that meant following the standards that kept everything in order. Why was this so difficult for him to understand? Why was he badgering her? Yesterday he had looked at her the way a man looked at a woman—she had no other word but to say that there had been desire in his gaze—and now today he was challenging her at every turn.

"Sin is sin, right?" She hoped he would leave her alone, and she stepped around him and walked again, this time faster.

"Just because something is against your Amish rules doesn't make it a sin—it just makes it against the church." He walked next to her, keeping pace.

"What makes you so sure about that? And why do you feel the need to argue with me?" She stopped and leaned into the words that just flew from her mouth.

"Do you really think that it's a sin to eat from the pot after him?"

Esther swallowed down a disapproving groan.

"Do you believe Irene was sinful for marrying me?" The tension in their stare tightened like a knot.

Hadn't she been considering this question in the reserves of her mind since Irene left? Hadn't she also decided not to answer it, but to keep living the life that she felt was most pleasing to God? His blue eyes were trained on her as if they could see right into her soul. She turned away from him and walked toward the house. She had to start supper.

"It's not a sin, Esther, and you know it." He let her pass him, but then came from behind her, his mouth close to her ear and she stopped walking. "You're pushing Chet away because he hurt you. Irene wouldn't let you push her away. Remember? And I'm not going to let you push me away either."

"But we're sandpaper, remember?" she said as she walked away.

An hour later, Esther had finished preparing supper and set the table. She retrieved Daisy, and the men came into the dining room. Joe had cleaned up and changed his clothing. The sun lit Joe's skin in a way that made him glow. Esther turned away from him and looked at Chester, who was still wearing his work clothing but had washed his arms and face.

"I put your plate right there," she said to Chet, pointing at the plate on the end table next to the couch.

Daughter and father met eyes and Esther turned away before he did. She was just following the rules.

"I'm not Amish, so I don't have to follow those silly rules, Esther. Come on, Chet, sit at the table."

Daisy tapped Esther's arm. Esther placated her, simply telling her that it was nothing but the men talking.

"I hate to put Esther in a difficult position." Chester nodded toward Esther. "She's the one doing the right thing here."

The next several days were no different. Esther worked harder for Mrs. White than she ever remembered in an effort to push away her thoughts of Joe. She managed to wash every window in a matter of hours and sighed with accomplishment before she left for the day.

"Esther, dear," Mrs. White spoke with a drippy smile as she walked toward her. "I have some clothing that you might like to give to Joe."

"Clothing?"

"I would take them over myself, but I'm so busy with the Ladies Aid. I simply don't have a moment. Would you mind? I'm sure you'll find the clothing to be in excellent condition."

Esther fought her desire to remind Mrs. White of all the time she had to sip tea on her front porch and how she slept in until past eight in the mornings. What was she so busy doing when Esther cleaned her house and made the farmhands their meals?

"I put all the dresses in this bag." She set the bag down in front of Esther's feet. "I'm sure Joe is ready to see Daisy in some pretty little dresses."

"I'm sure you're right." Esther's response grated against her pride. "I'm sure he'll be grateful."

Mrs. White patted Esther's hand and turned away.

Pretty dress. Daisy signed and then pulled out a dress with a ruffled pinafore. The little girl began bouncing up and down and signed that it reminded her of the little girls in storybooks.

"Do you want to wear these dresses?" Esther asked reluctantly.

Daisy looked at her own dress and then back to the pretty English dress, then back again. The little girl's eyes then landed on Esther's dress. She touched it and then looked up at her guardian.

She shook her head and signed. *No, I want to look just like you.* Then she stuffed the ruffled dress back into the bag.

The dresses altered Daisy's mood, and Esther decided it was best to put the bag away until the time was right. When they got back to the house, Daisy went upstairs and curled up with her doll in her small cot. Her nightmares had improved, but the energy it took to accept her dad into her life had exhausted the little girl and she was asleep within minutes. Esther understood it better than she expected. But instead of bringing sleep, her turmoil cursed her with restlessness and sleepless nights.

Esther focused on cleaning out Orpha's wardrobe cabinet, which she'd avoided for over a month. It was well into July now.

Esther hadn't entered the room often since Orpha's death. Her *kapp* strings blew over her shoulders from the breeze that washed through the two windows in the room. The blue curtains Orpha had made decades earlier flew out toward her.

Esther closed her eyes, letting the warm breath of sun envelop her. *Orpha.* When she opened them she only briefly took in the quilt on the bed that was filled with memories then turned away toward the wardrobe cabinet.

As she took each dress from the hanger, she folded it maticulously, just as Orpha had taught her to do when she was a child. Folding them gave her the sense that just a moment later, the *ault mammie* would be walking into the room behind her. A whistled tune would be on her lips, and she would pat Esther's arm and then wander off again.

When she opened the bottom drawer in the attached chest of drawers, she found old stockings folded inside each other and chuckled because she had always known that Orpha didn't throw anything away. And then, underneath the stockings, at the bottom of the drawer, were yellowed envelopes and folded-up stationery.

Esther picked them up and stood. They whispered to her—called to her—to be opened. She pulled one end of the twine that was tied around everything.

She first took the stationery.

Dear Esther,

Please, forgive me.

Love,
Mammie

She laid the three envelopes on the mattress next to the newly folded dresses. The top one was from the War Office from 1917, only weeks after her father's medical exam. As she leaned against her mattress, she inspected the envelope's ragged edges that declared it had been opened and read. She opened the brittle paper, and pulled out the letter—only one page. It listed Chester's name and his serial number and briefly stated that he did not pass the physical examination due to a heart murmur and missing finger. This made him ineligible for military service and released him from any form of duty now and in the future.

Esther wondered if her *mem*'s and *mammie*'s fingers had held this paper just as she was doing now. They would have learned that he had received an exemption from service. He'd been turned away due to a heart murmur. He'd cut his finger off for no reason at all. He'd lied about being in prison and this letter proved it.

What else had he been dishonest about? It was disturbing and ugly. Maybe their lies had spared her years of knowing she had been abandoned, but at what cost?

She returned the letter into the old envelope and then opened the letter that had been addressed to her *mem*:

June 2, 1918

Dear Leah,

Today is Esther's birthday. I've been thinking about her all day.

I got out of the county jail yesterday but I still have to pay my gambling debts that got me thrown in there to start with. I have to say that the Englishers aren't as forgiving about owed money like the Amish.

I reckon all of this is punishment for my sins, Leah. If only when I'd gone to my physical a year ago I'd just trusted it would all work out somehow. Isn't that what the preachers say? That if we trust God, He will work things out for our good? Or something like that. I didn't know I had a heart murmur. The army doctor spoke slurs to me about my cowardice the whole time he tended to my missing finger. I thought going north to Canada to do mission work with the Mennonites would make me feel that I've paid my dues, but it hasn't. I just got myself into more trouble.

I am sorry about the back taxes. With that and my gambling debts, I know if I don't do something soon, I'll end up back in jail. So, I'm heading to Colorado to make it big in ranching. I'll send you money when I can.

I'm so ashamed. So ashamed I don't know how I can return to you and our old life. You'll be better off without a misfit like

me for a husband. It would've been better if the army had just
thrown me in prison and let me die. Just tell everyone that I
died in prison. Someday, when I come back to you, my riches
from the west will make up for the lie. I promise.

Chester

Esther couldn't believe what she was reading. He had
known about the taxes. He had known how much they needed
him and had taken no responsibility. She sniffed, suddenly realizing that she was crying. Tears fell from her eyes onto the
letter.

He had gone to jail for his debts, and it sounded as if trouble
had continued to follow him.

She replaced the letter and picked up the third one. Orpha
had written this one to Chester, with an address in Corsi-
cana, Texas. It had been stamped "return to sender" back in
1935. Esther looked at the open bedroom door, as if she was
nervous about being caught with the letter. But who would
look in on her? There was no one. The first brittle tear in the
paper sounded loudly in the empty room. She slid out the
letter and relished the look of her *mammie*'s handwriting. It
looked so neat in comparison to her penmanship before she
passed.

September 5, 1935

My dear son, Chester,

In the name of our Lord and Savior, may we serve Him
with humbleness and fear.
I haven't heard from you in years. This is the last address I
have for you. I hope it reaches you.
I'm sick, Chester. The doctors tell me that my heart is

weakened. They've been telling me that since I was a young wife having babies, and it didn't stop me then, but it is stopping me now. It's not just my heart. Sometimes I get confused, and I'm not sure where I am or what I'm doing. I'm not always sure of your story—our lies.

I've almost spoken of our hidden sins out loud in my confusion. Esther's still working for Norma but we have had to sell everything except for the house. She's twenty-three and unmarried and won't even go to the Singings anymore. She repaired a hole in the shed roof a few days ago, along with the buggy wheel. She works harder than any man I know and then still cooks every meal for us. She's afraid I'll burn the house down if I cook. I'm useless to her.

We never meant to keep this secret from Esther for so long, but now that she's a grown woman we'll never be able to make it right with her. What have we done, my son? What have we done?

Come home, Chester. We need you. Esther needs you and she doesn't even know it. I don't know how to fix the lie, but together we can figure it out. I'm ready to make a confession for it if you are. I'm afraid without a confession I'll never make it to heaven and neither will you.

Come home,
Your mom

Esther's hands shook, and the letter fell silently onto the bed. There was too much to take in. Through blurry eyes she read the last paragraph again. Her *mammie* believed she would not make it to heaven with this lie staining her heart. If that would keep her from heaven, then surely Esther herself would never reach this celestial home. In heaven there was no hate, but she hated Chester for what he'd done and forgiving was just too difficult.

Joe

1944
Mariana Bay, Saipan

When Garrison woke, he was back in the foxhole he'd just run from. There was water on his face, and his surroundings were spinning in circles. He could hear the familiar sounds of a battle—gunfire, English-spoken commands, Japanese words in the distance. His head ached, and when he touched his temple he found warm, sticky blood.

Fielding had blood splattered across his face too, and Garrison was able to focus enough to see that his fellow Marine was wiping blood off his knife.

"You all right, Sarge? Took care of the Nip after he tried to stick ya. Wasn't as dead as you thought he was, eh?"

"I gotta get this ammo out to the rest of my men." Garrison tried to crawl toward the ammo can, but when everything turned in circles again, he fell back and held his head in his hands.

Japanese gunfire increased, but Garrison could hear that the American fire was coming less frequently. It was so sporadic it was clear that his men were holding back to make every shot count more than the previous one, a clear sign that they were almost out of ammo.

"I'll go," Fielding said and grabbed two ammo cans. "I'll come back for you when I'm through."

Garrison didn't want him to go, but the rest of his men needed ammo. As Fielding ran off, Garrison's men, nearly out of ammo, were barely firing anymore. Fielding needed to get to them right away.

Joe

A vibrating yell rang in Joe's ears. He pulled his leg and it wouldn't move. He pulled harder and when it still wasn't free, he began to sweat. There was heat and pain in his ankle. He struggled and was jarred awake when he landed on the floor of his room. When he sat up, he realized that the rope he'd used to tether himself to the bed had worked. Now it wouldn't be too dangerous for Daisy to come home.

After work that day Joe pulled into Esther's drive. Chet remained asleep in the passenger seat. Before he went inside, Joe patted the buggy horse that was hitched and ready. He knew that Esther had an invitation to supper at his mother-in-law's house. They had family visiting from out of state, so he would not be eating with her or Daisy that evening. He went from the horse to go inside to say hello to Daisy. A moment after he walked into the house, he saw Esther walk out from a bedroom with a stack of clothing that looked like Amish dresses in her arms.

"Oh, you're here." Her eyes were red and her face was pale.

He and Esther had kept each other at a safe distance as they developed a routine with their puzzle-pieced family. Esther continued walking past him, and he heard her feet move briskly up the staircase and come back down less than a minute later. She was wearing one of her nicer dresses, one that he'd seen her wear on Sundays for church.

"Daisy and I will be leaving soon to go to Lucy's." Esther didn't meet Joe's eyes but she did what she was good at—keeping her hands busy even when there was nothing to do. She moved a freshly baked pie from the counter to the table, then back again after a few moments. Then she grabbed the broom from its hook on the wall and began sweeping the clean floor.

"I thought I'd say hello to Daisy." Joe wanted to take Esther by the shoulders and make her look into his eyes so that he could see what was plaguing her.

"On the back porch playing." Esther spoke with labored distraction.

Joe moved closer to Esther and took the broom from her and leaned it against the table. His brow furrowed in concern as he took her forearms in his hands. Her muscles tightened beneath his touch, but she looked up at him. The corners of her mouth fought to remain composed and she pursed them.

"What is it?" he asked in a whisper as he searched her eyes. She gave him little through them.

Just then, Chet walked into the house. Esther pulled away from Joe's hold. He let her walk away.

"Smells like pie in here." Chet's lips pulled into a crooked smile. Then he leaned in toward Joe. "I've been laying it on pretty thick that I've been craving some peach pie. Maybe she took pity on me." He elbowed Joe.

Esther pulled yellowed envelopes from the kitchen cabinet and set them on the table. "I found these." The mood in the house changed in a moment.

"I want you gone by morning." Esther spoke boldly to her

father. "I want you out of Sunrise. I want you to leave and never come back."

"What? Gone?" Chet waved her words away, then walked to the kitchen table to see what she was talking about.

Esther walked past Joe to the back porch. A few moments later, she came back through with Daisy at her side. She didn't look left or right but grabbed her black purse and the pie and walked out the door. Joe and Chet were left in Esther's wake.

Chet stared at the envelopes then released a groan. Joe walked over to him and, without asking permission, picked up the envelopes. A new blanket of silence rested over the two men in the room as Joe took his time reading each letter. He'd seen the weight of them on Esther's shoulders and now understood why. These letters proved that Chester had never gone to a military prison. He'd abandoned Esther and the rest of his family, and both Esther's mother and grandmother knew. They'd all kept it hidden from Esther.

"I think she's right, Chet," Joe said. All of his instincts told him to protect Esther. "I think you'd better leave."

Chet pulled out a kitchen chair and collapsed into it. "You don't understand. I have to stay."

"It doesn't even seem like you want to be here. Why stay?" Joe pushed for answers. "Look at how you've hurt Esther."

"I've got nowhere else to go. I'm supposed to be here. I'll respect Esther and steer clear, but I'm not leaving Sunrise. I felt the devil's fire one night in a dream and knew ever since that one way or another, I was supposed to come back and make things right."

"And conveniently hide away from your debts?" Joe eyed the older man suspiciously.

"Don't judge me, Joe Garrison. Yes, I do owe some money, and I'm paying my debtor as much as I can, but that's not why I'm here. I'm here for Esther. I just need time to prove it." He paused for a moment and ran a hand over his face. "I've been here for well over a month now, and I want to be the man Esther deserves. I don't want to be a burden to her."

"But why not just tell her the truth from the start?"

Chet's jaw clenched shut.

"I was afraid. You don't think I know what happens when you make plans without consulting the Big Fella? Look at my hand." He had started out yelling, then softened. "I couldn't face what I'd done—and what I'd let Leah be a part of—and I started drinking and gambling my life away. I made a big mess of everything."

"But you're still hiding behind your lies." Even as Joe was judging him, he found himself sympathizing with the older man, who now sat with his head in his hands. "These letters are proof that when you take things into your own hands, you're fighting against God. But still you keep doing it with your lies."

There was a long pause, and Joe repeated his words to himself in his mind. He could probably do well to take his own advice.

"Where will you go?" Joe finally asked.

"I already said I ain't leaving. I'll stay at Norma's farm and do what I can to win Esther back."

Joe didn't have the outstanding debts that Chet had or the lies, yet his heart squeezed in his chest over their parallel circumstances. He left the man to his burdens and walked out with his own.

Esther

Esther saw Joe pick up Chester from the dairy the next morning. While she wasn't sure he was going to listen to her and leave Sunrise, she did want to make sure she wouldn't run into him at the farm. She wanted him to keep his distance. She knew that much. What she didn't know was what to do about the new information she had about his lies.

She had her garden weeded before the sun was completely up, and after breakfast, she and Daisy went to gather what Mrs. White had for donations. The woman stood out on the porch as Esther loaded the goods onto the open buggy. Esther breathed heavily after loading everything up. Many of the goods had come from Esther's cooking, baking, canning, or gardening, and the milk came from Mrs. White's cows. Today the open buggy was fuller than usual.

"Your father left the same year that Mr. White died." Mrs. White puffed on a long cigarette. When had she started smoking again? Esther remembered that years earlier, when the Whites had young children, that the elegant woman occasionally smoked, but it had been a long time. "Your mother and I lost our husbands within months of each other."

Esther stopped and turned toward Mrs. White. In all the years that she'd been working for the woman, she had never once talked about Mr. White or Leah Detweiler. Any insinuation to her circumstances were never personal.

"You probably don't remember Mr. White, do you?" Mrs. White walked closer to Esther and leaned against the buggy. At this, Esther signed to Daisy to go play on the swing and sandbox. She ran off without a glance back.

Esther shook her head. "No, I don't. I'm sorry."

"He was a wonderful man," she said with a smile and let her eyes graze over the expansive field across the road. "He and your father were friends."

Mrs. White's eyes twinkled when she caught Esther's gaze. "They were so much alike."

Esther's brows knitted together, and she tilted her head. That was the last thing she'd expected Mrs. White to say.

"How is that?"

Mrs. White mused over the question for several moments. "Well, they were hard workers, and they loved to joke and laugh. They both loved their cigars too much and playing cards. When you were a baby and Orpha would watch you, your parents would come over and we'd play cards together every Friday evening."

Hearing all of this made Esther's heart heavier. If Chester had told her these stories, she would've thought he was lying. But Mrs. White wasn't a liar—she was honest to a fault—and Esther believed every word she said.

"I had no idea." Esther leaned against the open end of the buggy and stared out at the same open land as her employer. They'd never shared such quiet and easy moments together.

"When Chester was drafted, Leah was petrified."

Esther turned toward her.

"Tell me more, Mrs. White. All of this has been—" Esther shook her head, trying to find the right words. "It's all been so—"

"Confusing? Shocking?"

"Yes," Esther whispered.

"Leah ran over the day before Chester was to leave. She had always been a fitful woman—easily thrown in a tizzy, you understand. You're not like her. You're far more your father's daughter."

She wanted to interrupt at this comment, but Mrs. White continued.

"I remember making her some tea, and we sat right there on the front porch." She pointed. "Of course, that was before I screened it in. She told me that she was expecting a baby. It was still very early."

"A baby?"

"She just knew that if Chester left, they'd make him go as a noncombatant and he'd die somewhere far away. I could barely calm her down from the mere thought of it. But I did."

"How's that?" Esther put her hands on her hips, trying to catch all the cool air she could.

"I told her that he wouldn't be sent anywhere if he didn't have a trigger finger." Her voice was almost dreamlike, almost as if she didn't mean to say it aloud.

"It was your idea? You're the reason . . ." Esther couldn't finish.

"Now, Esther. Leah was my best friend, and when I said what I did, I never thought she'd take me seriously. I never thought she'd—"

"But she did go through with it." Esther couldn't bring herself to imagine the horrifying scene of her mother and Chester, the ax . . .

Mrs. White shrugged. "I never did hear exactly what happened. Leah didn't confide in me anymore after that day."

There was a long lapse in the conversation. What was Esther supposed to say to that? She watched as Daisy picked tiger lilies that grew around the mailbox.

"Why are you telling me all this, Mrs. White?" Esther asked quietly.

"I guess seeing Chester again after all these years brought back a lot of memories. Nothing happened the way it was supposed to. I always felt that I was punished for giving her such a terrible idea. I tried to visit with her, but she wouldn't look me in the eye. Maybe because I knew what she'd done. Maybe she was ashamed of it or angry with me. I wished for months that I could turn back the clock and never have breathed those words to her. But it was too late. God punished Leah and me over and over. It was less than six months, and Bart was dead. Leah lost the baby and then faded away into nothing." Mrs. White took a long pull of her cigarette and shook her head before she blew the smoke out into the summer breeze. "Oh, Esther, how do our lives become a mess so quickly because of one bad decision?"

"You were my mom's best friend. I never knew that till now," Esther said.

"And she was mine. I was so sad to lose her." Her words were spoken within a long sigh.

"I lost my best friend too—four years ago."

The two looked at each other, and what passed between them comforted Esther. Who knew that Chester's return would lead to such a conversation with her employer?

"Thank you, Mrs. White, for telling me all of this. Can we talk again sometime?"

Mrs. White smiled and nodded. "Call me Norma." Then she smiled again and walked away.

～

By the time Esther made all of her regular stops several hours later, she realized she'd estimated wrongly and still had milk, canned stew, and bread left. She could already taste the stew in her mouth. It was in fact *her* stew; she'd canned it last summer from Mrs. White's harvest. It had just about every vegetable in it, along with some beef broth and even a little meat. It was savory. Delicious.

Daisy's loud rounded sounds called Esther from her day-dreaming. The little girl was pointing and signing *play* as they passed Angelica Blunt's house. Daisy continued bouncing up and down and sounding the word *please* as best as she could.

Esther looked at the box of food left. She knew the Blunts could really use the food. This would be the right thing to do, no matter that she didn't want to and even if Angelica always refused charity.

Esther turned into the drive before she could decide otherwise.

"Whoa," she told the horse.

Angelica's second daughter waved at her. "Hi, there, Esther. Hi, Daisy." Edwina's voice was always cheerful despite her circumstances. She waved sweetly at Daisy. The cousins didn't know each other well because of the age difference, but Edwina was always helpful. "Can I water your horse?"

"Thank you, Edwina." Esther smiled at her. "Is your mom home?"

"She's inside. Be careful, though. She's been feelin' awful sick. It's been going 'round the house. Daddy and Geraldina still got it. Mama won't even sit down for a minute to rest, but she's not looking so well today."

She tapped the little girl on the shoulder. "Daisy, stay outside and play."

She did not want the little girl to catch whatever was going around in the house. She climbed down from the buggy and Edwina helped Daisy down and patted her smooth hair as if she was some type of rare pet. Then the two youngest, Jonna and Paulina, waved Daisy over to the teeter-totter. Daisy was calling loudly *hi* and waving as she ran.

"I have some food here," Esther said as she pulled the wooden crate out from the back. "I'll take it inside."

"Oh, Esther," Edwina said as she peeked into the box. "Is all that for us?"

Esther could almost see Edwina lick her lips as she looked at the canned goods. Esther reminded herself that she was only feeding one small child and the Blunts had many mouths. An ache ran through her heart as she walked toward the front door.

Edwina opened the door for Esther. "Come on in." She called into the house: "Mama, Esther's here and she brought a whole crate full of food."

A crackling voice stirred in the soiled air. "What did you say?"

Esther wished she could cover her nose and mouth. Angelica turned the corner and stood face-to-face with Esther. "What'er you doing here?"

"I have food." Esther spoke quietly as she took in the woman's poor health. "It's from Mrs. White."

"We don't need no charity. You can—" Angelica interrupted herself with a hacking cough.

"I'm not asking your permission," Esther said and pushed past Angelica's bony shoulder. "When was the last time you've eaten a real meal—any of you?"

Angelica's shuffling walk came slowly behind her. Esther imagined the air she coughed grabbing the back of her dress and holding on tightly.

"You can't make food for us." Esther could barely make out the words over the cough and Angelica's shortness of breath.

"Mama, leave her be. She's a nice lady," Edwina scolded. "I'm going to water her horse. Roberta, come here."

The third daughter, Roberta, ambled over. She was a bit like her father in that she seemed both overgrown and oversized somehow. Esther hated thinking such thoughts, but it was just so. She was only fourteen, but her oaflike appearance made her seem older.

"Roberta, you help Esther here," Edwina ordered with a smile. "Mama, you go sit down."

Edwina marched off and threw a wink over her shoulder to Esther, who couldn't help but smile.

"She's right, Angelica, you need to sit. You look terrible."

"Well, you've just been dyin' for the chance to say that now, haven't you?" The statement was punctuated with a long stream of coughs.

Esther knew she would get nothing done if this woman wouldn't leave her alone. The house was a disaster and smelled. She took Angelica gently over the shoulders and led her through the kitchen and past the table, then through the small living room and up the closed staircase, where she suspected were the bedrooms.

"You are going to bed," Esther said.

"But—" Angelica began to resist but didn't appear to have the energy for it.

"Donald," Esther yelled loudly to wake the huge man. "Donald."

"What, what?" The man sounded drunk, but he was just sick. "What are you doing here?"

"Move over. Your wife's sick, and she needs to lie down." Esther made sure not to use any tone that would insinuate a question. The large man obeyed with raised eyebrows and watched as Esther helped Angelica lie down. "Now, you sleep. I'll get some food ready and help the girls clean up a bit."

"Geraldina is still sick too." Angelica pointed out the bedroom door and toward the girl's bedroom.

"I'll look in on her."

Over the next few hours, Esther did exactly what she'd said she would do. By the time she was ready to leave, the house was clean and filled with the mouth-watering scent of beef stew.

"Now, Edwina," Esther said as she walked to the door. "Don't let the stew burn. Just keep it on a low simmer. When you've eaten tonight, add some water and some more vegetables and keep it going for at least another meal. And remember, there's a bone in the icebox. Get that out tomorrow and follow the directions I wrote out for you to make some bone broth. After the stew is gone, that will help them get well. Can you do that?"

"Yes, I can. Thank you, Esther," Edwina said, walking out with her. The girl hugged her, and Esther returned the sentiment. "I can't tell you how much I 'preciate your help."

Exhaustion hit Esther while she sat to have supper with Joe and Daisy. She didn't say anything to him about Angelica but found the two siblings so vastly different. It made her consider Jason, the child whom Joe's parents had sent to an institution at age ten. The same parents brought up Joe, Angelica, and Jason. How could those siblings be so different? Jason had been considered simpleminded, though now Esther wondered if he'd been deaf like Daisy. Angelica usually handled life in a bitter and mean-spirited way. Then there was Joe.

Since the first time he'd mowed her lawn, Esther had realized that the good man she had known was still inside the war-torn exterior. He'd fixed the porch, and then fixed the shed door that had needed repairing for some time. He'd brought them butter, flour, and several bags of potatoes. He insisted it wasn't charity, since Daisy was his daughter. With Chester not eating there, dinners had become easier to stretch, and for the first time in years, Esther wasn't struggling to pay for everything they needed. But now she realized that what she really needed were things that couldn't be bought.

Esther

Daisy pulled at her sleeve and asked to go to the swing as soon as they walked into Joe's drive.

"Come in for water when you get too hot." Esther mimicked drinking from a cup and then wiping the back of her hand across her brow. The July evening was hotter than usual, and the air ahead of them blurred in the haze of humidity.

Daisy bobbed her fist up and down. *Yes.* And she ran off.

Esther set tomato soup on the stove on a low simmer and went about the house to see what needed cleaning since Joe wasn't back yet. The bathroom window was shattered. After picking the pieces up from the floor and out of the tub, she washed the floor and then moved on to the rugs. She pulled the rugs outside, and when she caught Daisy's eye, they waved at each other. The little girl smiled and jumped from the swing into the tall grass.

Daisy did Esther's *too hot* gesture and pointed toward the house. Esther watched as she jogged around the back of the house to go in through the mudroom and kitchen.

Esther returned to her work and noticed that with the first hit of the broom, the dust on the rug flew everywhere and almost glittered in the hazy, damp air. Again and again, she beat the rug. After she was satisfied with the results, she took the rugs back inside and found Daisy had pulled out a small basket that Joe had shown her with his old toys. She was holding a small wind-up bird that hopped about. Still inside the basket was a small faded wooden horse on wheels with a pull-string. A small pouch with either buttons or marbles inside, a tin spinning top, and a small string-hinged doll with only half her hair remaining. Daisy had been given some blocks when she came to live with Esther, but she never had as many toys as were in that basket.

Esther returned all the rugs to their places and then checked on the soup. She looked out the front window and didn't see Joe yet. He must have been delayed. She went upstairs. She knew she should wash Joe's sheets, but she had such reluctance to walk into that room again where so much had happened. She'd been up there only a few times. The first time was just after Irene had gotten married, and then again when Daisy was born. The last time Esther had been upstairs was when Irene and the baby boy died.

The bedroom was hotter than downstairs, so she opened a window to let in a breeze. The bed had the white-and-peach double wedding ring quilt Irene had been so proud of, but today it lay crumpled on top. Irene usually had had it perfectly tucked around the bed. Esther could see that the sheets and the quilt could use a good washing. A picture on the bedside table caught her eye, and she moved to it like a magnet.

It was Irene wearing a white wedding dress with her hair flowing down over her shoulders. She had been so beautiful. It wasn't that she hadn't been beautiful when she wore her Amish dress and covering, but there was something so free about her smile in the photo.

Esther put down the frame and stood. She found herself

looking up at a small dresser with an oval mirror and an elegant wood frame around it. It was hinged on the sides, giving it movement. Her hand went to her own face and she looked back at Irene. No. She would never have Irene's kind of beauty. She turned back toward the bed and pulled off the quilt. She would have to wash it.

Esther walked over to the small closet and opened the door before realizing what she was doing. What had gotten into her? There was a basket on the floor and a small heap of clothing inside. Above the basket Esther's eyes landed on the colors. Teal, yellow, peach, green. Nothing resembling the familiar navy, black, or brown she wore. Her hands grazed the peach dress, and she pulled it out and held it against herself.

"What are you doing up here?" Joe's voice startled Esther. He walked over to the bed and stood there like a soldier.

"I was cleaning," Esther said and returned the dress to its place in the closet. Her eyes shot to Joe's. His brow was creased.

"What are you doing with Irene's dress? And our bed. Where's Irene's quilt?" A cigarette hung out of his mouth as he spoke.

"I was just cleaning up and—I wanted to wash your sheets and quilt." She stuttered through her words. "I was just in there to look for your dirty clothes. I didn't know Irene's clothes were still in there."

"Where else would they be?"

Joe's fast breathing filled her ears. That was all that Esther could hear. She didn't say anything. What could she say? She pushed past him and walked down the stairs, only to hear his footsteps behind her. Why was he so angry? Esther reached the bottom of the stairs and turned to face him.

"Where else would Irene's dresses be?" Esther repeated his words. "Joe, she's been gone for four years. Why are they still hanging in there?"

"If she could hear you say that."

"If she could hear *you* right now, Joe. You know I loved Irene. Loved her more than anyone else before Daisy, and I know she wouldn't want you to live like this—holding onto all of the sadness."

"But I just got back. And who are you to talk of being happy when you—"

"Where's Daisy?" Esther looked at the basket of toys strewn about the floor.

"What?"

"Daisy—she was here playing when I went upstairs and now she's gone." Esther went to the window.

"She's probably outside playing."

"No. Something's not right."

Esther threw open the front door and ran toward the tree swing. When she didn't find Daisy, she ran past the swing and when Joe checked the barn she ran behind it and toward the field behind the property line. The humidity cloaked her instantly.

Esther's underarms stung with sweat. Joe ran from the barn toward her and their eyes met, and she could see that he recognized her fear right away. He squashed his cigarette and repositioned his hat nervously. She went back to the swing, as if looking for clues.

"Daisy," Joe started yelling. "Daisy."

"She can't hear you," Esther said, breathless. She suddenly realized how hot she was and held onto the rope of the swing to steady herself.

"Over there," she yelled and pointed at the thin blue *kopftuch* on the ground that Daisy had been wearing.

Esther and Joe looked at each other and they ran over.

"Is it her headscarf?"

Esther nodded when he picked up the small cotton hanky

that Daisy wore as a covering when they cleaned at the dairy—so her *kapp* wouldn't get dirty. Her bitter prickles toward Joe melted into tears inside her eyes, but she didn't cry. This was no time for tears. Where was Daisy? Where could she have gone?

She looked up and found the sun deeper in the sky than she thought possible—it barely peeked over the horizon now. When had it gotten so late? She'd taken much longer beating the rugs than she realized. Joe began surveying the property line. Green cornfields stretched out nearly to the horizon. The other side was wooded before the fields began again.

"What if she went on the road, Joe?" Esther ran to him. "She won't hear an automobile coming. Maybe she went home."

"This is her home." Joe's voice was like icy daggers in the midst of the humid day.

"You know what I mean," Esther responded roughly. "Home to her is my house. You know that."

Joe's only response was to run to his truck. Esther followed quickly. She glued her eyes to the side of the road, looking for any signs of the girl. Her mind wrestled with wild ideas of what could happen to a deaf girl. As the sky ahead began to shade itself with the day's end, panic arose in Esther's heart.

"She'll be okay," Joe said and nodded to her twisting hands.

Esther looked over at him. His hair waved around his sweaty forehead, reminding her of the young boy she'd watched grow up. His bright blue eyes probed her. Why was she thinking about how handsome he looked in the middle of this?

"I just want to find her."

Esther jumped out of the truck before it was completely stopped in the drive of her house. She jumped over the three porch stairs and opened the door and looked around. The rugs hadn't been moved, and Daisy always shuffled the rugs as she walked. It had been the one thing she could not get the girl to quit doing. Her blocks sat just where she'd left them on the floor by the rocking chair. Nothing was out of place.

"Daisy," Esther called before realizing what she'd done. How would they find her if they couldn't call out to her? She ran up the stairs and found their bedroom also untouched.

"Esther?" Joe's voice filled the house.

She returned downstairs and her panic grew.

"She's not here and she hasn't been here."

"Is there anyplace you can think of?"

They checked with Mrs. White, who said that if she saw Daisy, she'd keep her safely with her. Chet jogged out from the room he rented and Esther was surprised at the relief she felt in seeing him. He would help too. He offered to keep an eye on both Esther's and Joe's houses while they searched.

They searched for over an hour and the remaining light was vanquishing into the night. It was now past eight o'clock, and Esther was out of ideas as to where she could be. They'd checked with the nearby Amish farms and families she was familiar with. The King farm was behind her, the Yoders' around the corner. They sat in the truck at the end of a road. It stretched out ahead of them and no other vehicles were coming or going.

"What's next?" Joe asked, his eyes round and filled with alarm.

"I don't think she would go as far as her grandparents, but we could check." The two of them climbed back into Joe's truck. On the other side of the Amish graveyard was the Bender farm—Daisy's grandparents.

The silence in the truck was magnified by the hollowness of Daisy's absence. The blanket of night was beginning to settle around them with heavy stillness. Slow drops of rain plunked down on the windshield and dark clouds made the waning night darker than it should've been. Esther instinctively reached her hand through the open window to her right, and the warm drops dotted her skin. She had always loved the rain, but it seemed tonight that Daisy would wash away with it.

Joe's hand found Esther's, folded it into his own, and gently pulled her toward him. Esther followed his lead, comforted by his touch. Their shoulders were close and their breathing almost in sync. Joe's hand squeezed hers, making it hard for her to concentrate on anything but his touch. His skin was hot, like everything around them.

"Irene," Joe finally whispered.

Esther pulled her hand out of his and slowly scooted her body away.

"Does Daisy know where she's buried? Irene, I mean." Joe looked over at her. His eyes desperate and his lips pursed, as if buttoning up any emotion that might slip through.

"Of course. We pass the graveyard every month or two. Several families in our district live down the road from it."

"Would she go to Irene?" Joe's suggestion was laced with fear.

"To the grave?"

"Haven't you taken her while I was away?" His chest rose and fell deeply.

Esther looked down. Esther didn't want to tell him the truth. She had taken her once in those first few weeks. Even with the little girl's deafness, she had been able to say what sounded like *mama,* and would call for her over and over. Esther took her to the graveyard and the already wild Daisy became not just inconsolable but so out of control that Esther was frightened.

Daisy hadn't ever again asked to go see Irene or called out for her mama. After nearly a year, Esther encouraged Daisy again to visit Irene's grave, but Daisy refused. She said that Esther was her mother.

She couldn't tell Joe this. He would despise Esther's influence and maybe blame her and refuse to let Daisy be around her anymore. But the girl knew where her mother was buried, and every time they walked past it, the little girl's gaze would linger over the small hill of gravestones.

"You haven't, have you?" When she didn't say anything, he continued, "How could you, Esther? I trusted you. I thought you, of all people, would—" Joe hit the steering wheel with the heel of his hand.

"I tried, Joe." She spoke loudly at first and then whispered. "I tried."

The deep quiet in the truck was filled with regret, reluctance, and fear. Distant lightning punctuated their frustrations. The night was a murky gray because of the rain, and the moon wasn't bright or high. Where was she?

"Has she ever run away before?"

Esther shook her head. "Almost."

"Almost?"

"She was angry with me. We weren't able to communicate well until I got the signing book. Even that took some time. She didn't want anything to do with me."

That was putting it mildly. It had taken Daisy months before she even smiled at Esther. During this time, Esther had been sure Daisy was deaf. Everyone else told her that she was wrong and the girl was simple and defiant. But Esther wouldn't believe them.

"Might she be at Irene's grave?" He didn't look at her when he spoke, but his eyes were trained on the road ahead. "You would know better than I would."

"I don't know. Maybe with your return, she's become curious about her mother," Esther said, defeated. She had no sense of what the little girl would do at the moment. "Let's go and see."

Joe didn't waste any more time. The tires squealed, and Esther's hold on the handle inside the door tightened. The tail of the truck moved side to side for a stretch, and she moved along with it. The feeling of insecurity worked over her nerves, and she was glad that she didn't have to ride in a vehicle often. Joe righted the truck and put his foot down hard on the gas. His jaw was tight and his knuckles were white as he gripped the steering wheel.

"I can't lose her." His voice was quiet but clear.

"You won't." Esther's voice reflected his, but with the statement, she realized that she was losing pieces of Daisy daily, like plucked petals, and soon all she would have were memories. After Daisy returned to Joe for good, would she even remember their years together? Would Joe allow them to have visits, or would that make it difficult for Daisy to move on? It seemed her life was always directed and designed by those around her.

The drive seemed eternal, and the flood of raindrops doused for several long minutes and then suddenly vanished, leaving dewdrops hanging in the air like clothes on a line. She closed her eyes and imagined the landscape between Joe's backyard and the graveyard. To get to the graveyard, Daisy would have had to cross through a small wooded area and then a number of cornfields and gravel roads. Her heart plummeted and her hand moved to her chest.

"What?" Joe pressed.

Esther shook her head then opened her eyes.

"Just get there."

Joe's foot pushed down the gas pedal even more, and he scooted closer to the steering wheel, a distressed jaw jutting out. Esther wasn't altogether sure that he even breathed or if he had held his breath for the next few minutes. His focus was completely fixed on finding Daisy.

"There," Esther said and pointed. "There's the graveyard."

The truck skidded on the loose gravel and into a shallow ditch. Esther jumped out before Joe had completely stopped.

All she could hear was the sound of their breathing as they ran up the slope of the hill.

Under normal circumstances the incline was inconsequential, but with the wet grass, it had become another obstacle. Joe made it to the top faster. Esther's black shoes had been worn smooth on the bottom, so she struggled. He looked back and after a moment's hesitation put a hand out to Esther, who had toppled down onto a knee. She took his hand and was glad for the help.

Joe's brow was furrowed, and he appeared disoriented as both stood under the archway at the entrance of the graveyard. The darkness was heavy and hung from the trees like moss. How would they find Irene's grave?

Joe

"There's hardly even a moon." Joe's voice was depressing even to himself. "How will we find her even if she's here?"

"We'll find her."

Joe's heart drummed against his chest. He hated graveyards at night. Every ghost story from his youth resurfaced, and every midnight patrol plagued his mind. He knew he was in a graveyard, but all he could think of was that at any moment, there would be mortar rounds coming from the darkness. He looked around and no one in his squad was with him. Where were they? They were nowhere to be found. Joe's hands were empty—no gun. He checked his belt and then squatted down to check his boot and found no knife either.

"Joe?" Esther's voice ratcheted him back to reality. "Is everything all right?"

He stood again. In the time it took him to realize he wasn't back in Mariana Bay, his vision had adjusted to the darkness. Gravestones stood like a parade of soldiers in front of him. Were they the ones who had died because of his carelessness? Gray with small wet streams moving down from the rain, reminding him of blood. Irene's plot was near the far corner, diagonal from where they stood. They would have to walk through the entire grave-yard. There would be no foxholes to jump in. No gun on his back.

"Come on," Joe said, deciding not to explain his strange behavior. He found her hand in his as he led her through the winding path between gravestones. Had he grabbed Esther's hand again?

Esther's presence had once been awkward, but now came as his greatest comfort. At first he thought it was because she could communicate with Daisy for him, but it didn't take long for him to know that it was because of her strength. She was nothing like Irene, but she brought him something different that he had never expected to find in a woman. He respected her enough to keep his distance, as it appeared she wanted him to, but the closeness they'd had as they searched for Daisy brought his feelings to the surface once again.

"Look," Esther whispered, and pulled her hand free.

It was Daisy's doll. Esther picked it up and tucked it tightly under her arm.

"Where is she?" Joe asked quietly. "She was here, but where is she now?"

The moon reflected in Esther's widened eyes. Joe watched as she stepped around a graveyard angel and behind Irene's gravestone. Her hand went to her chest and she exhaled. She looked up at Joe and their eyes met, and he was drawn into the moment. Before he got over to them, Esther had bent down in the overgrown July grass.

"Daisy?" Esther took the little girl by the shoulders.

Daisy looked at Esther and then at Joe and back at Esther. Her jaw was hardened and set. She didn't seem to care that she was in a dark graveyard.

"Why did you run away?" Esther's hands moved slowly. "We were afraid."

The palms of Esther's hands were up and she shrank behind them. Joe wanted to tell her that she couldn't ever do that again. That she could've been hurt or worse. He wanted her to know that she was all he had left.

Daisy tried to speak while she signed. Joe watched as she tore clawed hands down through the air and bared her teeth, conveying anger. Her hands signed fast, and she was shouting. "What's she saying?" Joe asked.

Esther looked up at Joe and then down at his daughter. Esther signed again, and this time without speaking out loud. The feeling of being left out intensified. Didn't he have a right to know what they were saying to each other? Daisy's voice was getting louder and he couldn't stand it any longer. He moved in front of Daisy and sat down in the wet grass.

"Daisy, you can't run away like that. Do you know how afraid I was?" He couldn't help but speak loudly and clearly, hoping somehow his passion would speak to her.

Daisy lifted her nose at him and closed her eyes.

"She's angry with us." Esther sighed and sat. "She followed you up the stairs when you came home and saw us arguing. She said she hates when we argue. Apparently arguing doesn't need sign language."

This was his fault. He'd picked a fight with Esther when he knew he was being overly sensitive. He had been afraid she would find the rope he used to keep himself in bed at night. He could not explain that to her. It did bother him that Esther had gone into his room and touched Irene's things. But why was that so offensive to him? How could he explain to her, or anyone else, that when he was at war, it was as if he'd hit pause on his real life, and returning brought all the grief back? It hadn't been four years since Irene's death to him, only weeks or months. How would Esther have understood that? And why was she so easy to argue with? Joe tapped Daisy's shoulder, and she opened her eyes. Her stare, icy and chilled, was in contrast to their muggy surroundings.

"How do I say that she can't run away again? That she could've been hurt or even killed." He looked at Esther with his hands ready to try some signs.

"You can't tell her that. She already knows that." She paused for a long moment. "Tell her something she doesn't already know."

His sigh reached through the overgrown graveyard grass and pulled up dirt below him.

"How do I tell her that I'm sorry and that I love her?" He bit the side of his cheek to confine his emotions. He was a Marine, after all.

"This means *sorry*," Esther said, and she moved a fist in a circle around her chest.

Joe mimicked her movements, then looked at Daisy, who wasn't looking at either of them but into the distant darkness. He tapped her shoulder, and she turned and glared at him.

"I'm sorry," he said and repeated the sign. Then he looked at Esther. "How do I say *I love you?*"

Esther's eyes were full, and she pinched the corners of her mouth together. She cleared her throat, but didn't speak when she signed. She pointed to herself, then crossed her arms over her chest, then pointed toward Daisy. He nodded his head.

"Okay," he said.

He looked at Daisy. Her blond hair was damp and small waves clung, matted, to her face and neck. Her nose and cheeks were red, and white streaks lined her face—she'd been crying. Her knees were pulled up inside her dress, and her black shoes peeked out from beneath the skirt. Joe tapped his daughter's knee, and she looked at him.

"I love you." He spoke the words slowly as he made the three signs.

The corners of Daisy's mouth turned down in snatches, then she sniffed and turned her face away from Joe. He looked between Daisy and Esther, stuttering words that didn't make sense. He closed his eyes and hung his head.

Irene, please, help me with our daughter.

As soon as his heart breathed these words, a voice broke into his thoughts.

Irene is not the one you should be speaking to. I am.

His hand wiped down his face. Hadn't God been completely silent all these years? Or had Joe merely chosen not to hear Him? He heard Him now.

"Daisy, I need you to hear me," he spoke, then stopped to look at his hands, then at Esther. "Will you?"

Esther nodded.

"Daisy, I need you to hear what I'm saying. I'm sorry that you're angry with me. I shouldn't have argued with Esther." He stopped, making sure that Esther had gotten it all. When her hands paused, she looked at Joe, and in a moment he could see why she'd resisted him so greatly. He wasn't a good dad and didn't deserve Daisy. "I have been so sad about your mama and your baby brother all these years I haven't been able to find anything else to be happy about."

Esther looked at Joe, then to Daisy, signing the words precisely.

"Things are going to change. I want to be a good dad."

He waited for the signs. This time Daisy looked over at him instead of keeping her eyes trained on Esther. Her fingers uncurled, and signs flew from her hands.

"When Mama died, you acted like I died too." Esther spoke what Daisy signed. Her voice was quiet but the words spoke loudly.

Daisy continued to sign, and her hand flipped from back to front.

"What did she say?" he asked.

"She said: I'm not dead," Esther said quietly.

Joe looked at Daisy, and for the first time he realized that she wasn't just leftovers of his happy life with Irene. Daisy was her own person, not just a piece of someone else. She was his daughter, his family. Warm tears fell from his eyes and he sniffed, then wiped them away. He'd been wrong for so long. Daisy wasn't just all he had left—she was everything. She wasn't just a piece of his past—she was his future.

"Come here?" He opened his arms, and when he spoke the words, he could see that for the first time she understood him without needing sign language. She stood quickly and fell into his arms crying. Daisy cried for several long minutes. He stood and held her in his arms, relishing the feeling of her weight against his chest. He could mourn no longer. It was time to live again.

With Daisy in his arms, he and Esther wandered back along the path they'd made to return to the truck. He put Daisy down on the seat between himself and Esther. Daisy's eyes were heavy by then, and when he climbed in and started the engine, his heart swelled when she rested her head against his arm. He looked over at Esther, sharing the moment, but finding sadness in her eyes—though she still smiled at him.

When they arrived back at his house, Daisy was already asleep. Chester waved at them from a distance, and they saw him jog off. Joe carried his daughter inside and heard Esther's steps close behind. He opened the door to the first-floor bedroom where he had set up Daisy's bed and mattress. He'd cleaned up an old chest of drawers from his own childhood bedroom, and though it was empty, he was ready to fill it with new clothes. He'd painted the room with the rosy pink that Wayne Good had given him.

"You did all of this?" Esther said as he laid his daughter on the bed. Daisy instantly curled up.

He looked at Esther, embarrassed by the awe in her voice,

and nodded. She walked around and touched the photo on the small nightstand. It was of Irene. She touched the patchwork-knotted comforter on the bed. Her fingers followed the line of the stitching that pieced the patches together.

"These are Irene's Amish dresses, aren't they?" Esther looked at Joe.

Joe nodded. "She wanted to make a comforter for Daisy but we didn't have any extra money, so she used her dresses. It was the last thing she made for her. She wanted Daisy to have something special for her new bed when the baby came. This was the bed from my boyhood, but she never slept in it."

His whole body warmed at the bittersweet memory.

"May I undress her and tuck her in?" she asked.

It was the first time Esther had asked permission to do something with Daisy. He nodded and turned to leave.

"What about a nightgown? Could she wear one of your undershirts? Or maybe Irene had something small that I could pin up?" Esther's voice was gentle and calming.

Joe went through Irene's drawers in the dresser upstairs and found a nightgown. He pulled it out. It was a powder-blue cotton gown with buttons up the front with a collar and long sleeves. It would be far too big, but better than sleeping in a wet dress. He went back downstairs and quietly opened the door. He found Daisy sitting up in bed still in her damp clothes and Esther singing to her quietly, her hands moving slowly. He didn't recognize the pretty lullaby in her Amish tongue. Neither Esther nor Daisy noticed him, so he cleared his throat. Esther turned to look; then Daisy's eyes followed.

"Here," he said, and handed Esther the nightgown. "It's going to be way too big, but it'll be okay for the night."

Esther took it and looked it over.

"This will work. Thank you." A sad smile traced Esther's lips. "Tomorrow I'll bring over the rest of her—"

"We don't need to talk about that right now," he interrupted her, sensing her melancholy.

Esther nodded and then turned back to Daisy. She took off her shoes and rolled down her socks. Daisy signed something to Esther, then got out of the bed. She ran over to Joe and tugged at his shirt. He knelt down and Daisy threw her arms around him. A smile broke across his face. Joe wrapped his arms around his daughter in response and kissed her forehead.

Once Daisy pulled away from Joe she vocalized something as she signed, folding one arm over the other. When he didn't understand, she giggled and repeated the sign. She then took his arms and helped him do the sign as well. Joe looked over Daisy's shoulder to catch Esther's tear-filled eyes.

"She's saying *good night*," Esther explained.

"Oh. Good night." He mimicked the sign again, and Daisy hopped up and down at his success. "Good night, Daisy."

As he walked out of the bedroom so that Esther could help Daisy change into the oversized nightgown, everything around him carried a new note. He heard a new song in the air as the night passed through the open windows. The rain water that dripped from the eaves fell like percussion against the harmony of insects and night creatures that filled in all the empty spaces. He had finally come home.

Esther

Esther helped Daisy get ready for bed, tucked her in, and sat on the side of the small bed.

"Are you going to be okay to sleep here?" She spoke the words quietly as she signed. "Your dad kept this bed for you, and your mother made this blanket out of her Amish dresses."

Daisy smiled and nodded. Then she finger-spelled P-I-N-K. Esther smiled as she took in the painted walls. It was luxurious in contrast to what she could provide for the little girl.

Esther took in the room around her and recognized the small hope chest beneath the windowsill. Daisy would be so pleased when she learned that the chest had been her mother's. Esther had been given her mother's small hope chest after Leah's death, but she'd used it only for the few books she owned. What was hope anyway? She'd hoped her mother wouldn't die and that her grandmother wouldn't be sick. When she was a little girl, she had often hoped her father hadn't really died and that he would come home and rescue them from their burdens. None of that had come true, no matter how much she'd hoped. She had nothing to put in a hope chest anyway, and shouldn't the first item to place inside be hope itself?

Daisy tapped Esther's arm, bringing her out of her melancholy.

Is Mama Esther sad? She signed.

Esther kissed the little girl's hands before tucking them inside her own. She decided not to answer Daisy's question.

"Are you okay here?" Esther said and signed, swallowing down the emotion. This was the moment that she'd dreaded for years, but she knew it was exactly what Daisy needed.

Daisy's head cocked to one side, then signed, *I'm still Mama Esther's girl, right?*

Esther smiled and caressed the little girl's cheek with the back of her finger. In this moment, more than any other, she knew that Daisy had never been hers and never would be.

Sleep well, my girl. I'll see you tomorrow, Esther signed, unable to speak above a whisper.

She rose from the bed and walked quietly across the small room. When her hand touched the doorknob, she wanted to look back but couldn't. She turned off the lamp and eased herself through the doorway. Once out in the short hallway, she leaned her back against the door, closed her eyes, and breathed deeply for several long moments.

"Are you okay?" Joe's deep resonant voice caught her attention.

His voice was like rich coffee. The sometimes bitter voice she had grown accustomed to was instead strong.

She couldn't answer him.

"Esther?"

Again, Joe's voice was different. It was as soft as she'd ever heard it. Like new milk pouring from a silver bucket. The house was dim—the single lamp that was lit reminded her of her own kerosene lamps, but the glow was less ornamental. The house was quiet save for the clock on the mantel that ticked softly in cadence to the strain of night sounds.

With no reserve strength, she began to weep. Her hands covered her face. Joe's arms were suddenly around her, and she let herself weep in relief at finding Daisy—and then in grief at losing her.

Joe's soft shushing filled her ears and washed over her heart. She gripped his shirt and cried into his chest. She could not recall letting herself cry in front of anyone since the early days after her mother's death. But he was warm, and his scent comforted and filled her.

But in only a few minutes she would walk alone to her house in the path of the solitary moon. The damp air already coaxed her to suffocate.

"Come," Joe said and led her away from Daisy's door.

Was he taking her to the front door? Was he going to lock it behind her? No. He helped her sit on the sofa in front of a cold fireplace that she suddenly wished was filled with a crackling fire.

"I'm sorry," Esther said, stuttering. Her voice was still thick with emotion, and she pulled her hanky from the waist of her dress and wiped her face. "I don't usually—"

"I'm the one who should say sorry." His voice lit with concern. "It wasn't until tonight that I realized what I've been doing. How I've been living. How I haven't been living."

Esther looked up at him; her memory of a grown-up boy with a cigarette hanging from his mouth was replaced by a war-worn man whose once playful eyes had seen too much. He tilted his head to look at her, and a soft smile quietly wrapped around his words. She could see the former man through the latter.

"I don't know what I would've done if I'd lost Daisy—if *we'd* lost her." His eyes rested on the black fireplace as if imagining time gone by. "Irene would never have forgiven me."

"She wouldn't have forgiven *us*." Esther changed the last

word. "I've been as guilty, if not more. I've never been very good with change—with moving on."

"You love her as your own. That's nothing to apologize for. Irene would be proud."

The last word lingered in the room, and the quiet enveloped them like a blanket of morning dew. Esther still shivered, even in the warmth of the night. She felt guilty for resisting the mention of Irene. She was her cousin. Why did she feel jealous of her? She was gone and Esther wasn't. But her shadow was too great, and Esther could never live up to it.

"I'm sorry for touching her things. Part of me isn't sure who I miss. She lived two different lives. The happier of the two was as your wife."

When Joe didn't respond and the silence grew thicker, Esther resumed her thoughts of Irene. With regards to Joe, why did it matter that the spirit of her cousins was always around? It wasn't as if Esther had any reason to compete with Irene.

"I should go," she said in a whisper.

When Joe's head turned to look at her, his face was close to hers. Before she thought about it, her hand went to his face and she traced along his jawline. The stubble against her hand heightened her senses. He closed his eyes and leaned into her touch. He wanted her touch. He wanted her nearness. She could sense it in the electricity between them. The realization sped her heart and brought a rush through her body.

He opened his eyes, and they drew her toward him. When her lips touched his, heat like embers filled her body. One of his hands gently held the back of her neck, then moved down around her shoulders, pulling her closer. Her hands found the front of his chest, and she could feel his heart beating beneath her touch and his skin. The kiss deepened, and it surprised her when he pulled away. Their eyes connected, and their breathing was quick and heavy. He took her hand and kissed it, and kept it to his lips for several long moments. She pulled from his hold, embarrassed.

Her skin chilled. She stood and looked around for her purse. How would she ever be able to look at him again? With her purse under her arm, she went to the door and Joe pulled her back to him before she could turn the knob.

"Esther, don't go." Joe turned her toward him and put his hands on her face. He bent down and gently kissed her twice, then pulled her close and held her like she'd never been held before—their bodies so close and his head in the hollow of her neck.

"Stay here tonight," he whispered.

Esther's heart sped faster. What was he saying?

"Joe?" She let him go and eyed him warily.

If they spent the night in the same house and someone in her community found out, she would surely be reprimanded for it and be required to confess. It wouldn't be proper, since Joe was neither a relative nor her husband. Surely he understood this?

Joe smiled. "I meant *you* stay. I'll go to Angelica's."

She nodded in agreement and relief.

"I'll be over in the morning. And—I'm sure—I know—Irene would be proud for you to wear something of hers to sleep in."

He was out the door in the next moment, and Esther watched through a rain-dappled window as his truck lights turned on and he drove away.

Joe

While finding Daisy had lifted a heavy burden from Joe, a new one joined him as he assumed his role as a father. She was sleeping in her bedroom and not at Esther's house. Daisy had hugged him and said she loved him. He was finally ready to look past his grief and the horrors of war and be a real father. But what about his nightmares? What about Daisy's?

"Joe?" Angelica came out onto the porch as he walked up. "I heard your truck pull up."

"I'm sorry I'm just showing up like this," he said and kissed her offered cheek. "Can I stay for the night?"

"Come on inside out of the rain. Blasted rainy summer," his sister said, and pulled his arm as she looked at the clouds overhead. They were darker than the navy sky. Once inside, he noticed how thin she continued to get. She wore a housecoat, and her hair, parted in the middle, covered her face to the edges of her eyes. Her skin was ashen and her eyes drawn.

"Are you feeling well?" he asked her and looked around at the disheveled home. There was a smell he couldn't place.

"We've all been sick for weeks. Started with Jonna and

Paulina, and it ran through just about all of us. We were miserable."

The sudden recollection that he hadn't done so much as stop by in that same time frame brought on a wave of guilt.

"I'm sorry. I didn't know. I'm not sure how I could've helped, but—"

"I thought Esther would've mentioned it." Angelica pulled a kitchen chair out for him and gestured for him to sit. She grabbed her corn pipe from the small bowl on the tabletop and puffed on it.

"Esther?" Joe questioned. "Why would she have?"

"She came over and cleaned the house and fed us one Friday afternoon." Angelica's voice cracked, and she stuffed the pipe back between her lips and kept her eyes from Joe's.

Joe wasn't sure how to respond. Esther hadn't said anything about it, but that was like her. Heat moved from his gut to his face at the thought of Esther. He could almost feel her lips on his in that moment, and he pulled at the collar of his shirt.

Angelica tilted her head, then pointed her pipe in his direction. "Don't tell me you're falling for that woman."

Joe had never been a good liar, so saying nothing was all he could do.

"Joseph Garrison, what do you think you're doing?" She leaned forward in her chair. "What is it with you and Amish women?"

"Don't say that, sis." Joe ran a hand through his hair and couldn't meet her eyes.

"But it is true. You and Esther?" Angelica slapped the table.

Joe thought about her question. Yes, they'd kissed, but at this point it didn't give him any ideas of what the future held for them—or if there was a future at all. Adrenaline rushed to his heart and he cleared his throat.

"I don't know," he said truthfully.

Angelica took a pull from her pipe and nodded her head.

"So, why ain't you sleeping at your own place?"

Joe debated on how much he should tell her. She already thought that his daughter was a wild animal. Telling her that Daisy had run away would only heighten her opinion. His thought moved to Esther. Where would she choose to sleep? Surely she would sleep on the floor near Daisy or on the couch.

"Joe? Why are you here?" The pipe bobbed up and down in her mouth.

"Daisy's sleeping at my house tonight, and I thought it would be best if Esther stayed with her for the first night. I can't do sign language. Well, I know a few signs."

"So you're buying her claim that the girl is a deaf-mute? She's just like our brother Jason. She's simpleminded. When Mama sent Jason to that home, remember how much better everything was at home?"

Joe wished he'd not brought it up at all. Making up some sort of lie would've been better than this. His brother *had* been simple, but looking back, he wondered now if he'd been deaf. Without a real way of communicating or learning, had he become more simpleminded every year? Their mother had given up. Jason gave up too after that, and he was sent away. He was dead a few years later.

"It wasn't a home. It was an institution. I'm not sending Daisy anywhere." Joe dismissed his sister. "Besides, Jason couldn't manage to do anything for himself, and he was ten when he was sent away. Daisy is rather self-sufficient, and it's all because of Esther teaching her sign language."

The uncomfortable pause in the conversation brought a heavy silence between the two.

"Go to bed, Angelica. You're exhausted."

Angelica nodded and set her pipe on the table. Black ash painted the laminate, and she didn't seem to mind or care.

"You're welcome to the couch." She gestured toward the living room, where several makeshift clotheslines bowed under the weight of damp laundry.

Angelica hugged him goodnight, and when his hands touched her back, his heart sunk at her boniness. She went up the stairs slowly only for him to hear one of the little girls calling *Mama* urgently and a series of coughs came next. Nothing came easily for Angelica.

He sat on the edge of the couch, unlaced his shoes, and pushed them aside. He wiped a hand down his face and rubbed his eyes until he saw stars. His tired body ached, and after a deep sigh, he fluffed a dingy pillow and lay his head down, only to smell the odor of sickness even more fully. He pulled off his shirt, leaving on his undershirt, and wrapped it around the pillow, hoping he wouldn't get sick himself. He fell asleep with a prayer, pleading with God for a night's reprieve from his terrors, since he didn't have the rope tethering him to the bed. His eyelids were so heavy. He exhaled and let them fall.

~

"Uncle Joe. Wake up, Uncle Joe."

The happy girl's voice prodded him awake. The sun was gleaming through the window nearby. It hadn't seemed as if he'd slept at all, but he had remained on the couch and his night had been free from his demons. Paulina was the youngest of Angelica and Donald's six daughters and close in age to Daisy. How different she was from his daughter. Her hoarse cough resounded against the dull painted walls in the living room as she bounded around in a circle and pretended to be galloping with a broom horse.

Angelica had already left for work, having to be at her job by five o'clock. Donella, his eldest niece, came down the stairs shortly after Paulina had woken him. She was a miniature version of Angelica, with drawn eyes and ashen skin. The fifteen-year-old meekly asked Joe to stay for breakfast, but he said he needed to get home. When he knew that they had so little, he didn't want to worry her with feeding him.

All he could think about was getting home to Daisy and Esther. He was equally excited to see them both, but he was more nervous to see Esther. How would she respond to him in the light of day? When he'd pulled away from her, it wasn't in rejection. It was for himself. His intense feelings and desires frightened him. And why did the possibility of love have to be with his deceased wife's cousin? The reality had pinched his heart and pulled him from her lips.

He left Angelica's house, but before he went back to his own, he drove a little further down, past Esther's house and across the road to the dairy farm. Within a few minutes, he was knocking on a roughhewn wooden door to the farm's boardinghouse.

"Yeah, yeah, I'm awake," Chet's voice called from indoors.

"It's Joe—Joe Garrison."

"It's Sunday, ain't it? We don't work today," Chet called out to Joe.

"Yeah, it's Sunday. Can I talk to you for a minute?"

Joe could hear the man inside grunting as if getting dressed. The door opened, and a disheveled Chet stood on the other end. His hair was mussed, and sleep lined his features. He cleared his throat and waved Joe inside.

"Well, come on in. I guess I should get up anyway. Helping out with the milking today." He smiled over Joe's shoulder and turned to see who was there. Mrs. White was only several feet away. When Joe turned back around, Chet was tipping an imaginary hat toward the woman. "G'morning, Norma. Be out there in two shakes of a lamb's tail."

Mrs. White nodded. "Of course. And good morning, Joe."

"Good morning," Joe said with distraction. He was glad when she walked on.

"Walk with me toward the barn." Chet grabbed his hat from inside the door and stuffed it on his head. He closed the small boardinghouse door behind him and gestured for Joe to follow.

"Daisy has returned home to live—with me—probably from here on out."

"Is that right?" Chet paused for a few moments as if considering. "Well, I'm happy for you."

"I came to tell you because I thought that maybe you would move in with Esther. I think she is going to need you."

Chet's laugh turned into a deep cough.

"I kind of doubt that, son. You saw those letters. I don't see Esther forgetting about those soon. Even you told me to get outta town. Now you're changing your tune." He shook his head at Joe.

"I know. But things have changed, and I don't like the idea of Esther being alone."

A flash of memory pushed through the fog in his mind. Him, walking into his house after Irene died. He was alone—Daisy was with Irene's mother, Lucy. The silence built walls around him, trapping him. The aloneness had driven him to enlisting. When he'd come home from war and walked into the house, it was more like a coffin. He didn't want Esther to feel that pain.

"Will you at least think about it? After everything she's done, she shouldn't be alone."

Chet pursed his lips. The damp morning breeze picked up, and the scent from the barn filled his senses.

"Please?"

"Okay, okay," Chester nodded. "If she'll have me."

Esther

E sther's night was filled with memories, nightmares, and dreams that all blended together to the point that she couldn't remember what was real and what wasn't.

Crying until she fell asleep when her mother told her that her *dat* died in prison. Visions of Joe grieving the loss of Irene and the dead woman's ghost reappearing vividly enough to believe her death had never happened. Then the apparition whisked away into an unknown light. Daisy's head in her lap, sleeping as they sat on the backless benches during a wedding service joining two young people for life. Before the final vows were spoken, a casket appeared and Orpha sat up, humming a tune with a smile on her face. Joe entered the Amish house and shook Esther, telling her that she had to go home, saying that Daisy didn't need her. No one needed her. Her father was laughing at her and pointing at her with his missing finger. Then Joe's hands were on her waist and he was kissing her.

Esther sat up and found herself on Joe's sofa.

The morning had just dawned, and the sun cast light through the windows. An early birdsong's tune filtered into the house. A loud engine sounded, and she pulled the blanket up to her neck. Was Joe already here? She was wearing one of Irene's nightgowns, out of necessity; she didn't want him to see her in it despite its modesty. When the loud engine grew quieter, she realized it was just another automobile driving past. She moved the blanket from her and stood. After folding the blanket and putting it away, she pulled on Irene's bathrobe, cinching it extra tight at the waist, like she was used to with her belted dresses.

She stepped lightly across the wooden floor to Daisy's room and opened the door a crack. She was sound asleep, as she should be. According to the clock, it wasn't even six. After loosening the headscarf she'd used as a sleep covering, she pulled a comb and small handheld mirror from her purse. She set both on the table and began unpinning her hair. She hummed a tune as she combed her fingers through her curls, sinfully enjoying the way her hair felt down from the bun and the weight of it against her back.

While she'd never gone so far as watching something at the pictures or even on the television in Norma White's house, she'd seen plenty of photographs in Mrs. White's magazines. There were always women with shiny waves cascading down their shoulders with beautiful hair rolls at the top and sides. The look was almost always paired with red lips and sparkling big eyes. She had neither. Her lips were plain old pink, and her eyes, while large, didn't sparkle. Orpha often asked her what she was thinking about, saying that her eyes were thoughtful and inquisitive, though she'd never gone so far as to say they were pretty.

Suddenly the door opened. Esther gasped as Joe walked through the door and their eyes instantly connected. Esther stood still.

"Joe," Esther said, feeling vulnerable in her state. No man had ever seen her in anything but her dress, let alone with her hair down. All she could think of was the kiss they'd shared.

Why had she let him taste her so deeply, and why had she thirsted for him in return?

Joe looked at her from her unpinned hair down to the slippers on her feet. Suddenly even the pale blue color of the housecoat made her feel uncovered and bare. She was clothed completely modestly, but her appearance brought such a reaction to Joe's face, she was filled with vulnerability.

"I didn't think you'd be here so early." She breathed the words as they rushed out of her mouth. Her hands shook as she clasped them. "I'll go—I should—"

"Wait," Joe said. He closed the door behind him and walked toward her. "Don't go."

Esther froze in place, so taken with him. He was wearing the clothes he had left in the night before and his hair hadn't been combed. The memories of his boyish charm from years gone by were remarkably clear in her mind. Joe's eyes were on her so acutely that she was sure he could see right through to her soul. She'd never longed for a man before Joe. He had been her first taste of desire. The forbidden fruit frightened her.

"I can't, Joe," she said. The preacher's message from the previous week kidnapped her thoughts. *Rise up from the ground and stand against the wind of the world. It's a strong wind and it can push you or pull you, but you must be rooted deeply.* Ray was right, and she'd always believed in their Amish ways. But the wind had never smelled as sweet and never embraced her so warmly as it had now. The preacher's words had said that she couldn't have Joe and still remain loyal to the church, but even with that knowledge she did not move away from him.

"I've never seen you with your hair down." His smile was tender. His hand reached for a long tendril of her thick black hair and wound it around a finger.

The slight tension on her strand sent tingles through her scalp. As an adult, no one but Orpha had ever seen her with her hair down, let alone touched it. She only wished that in the intimacy of the moment, she could offer Joe the beauty a man like him deserved instead of a spinster's worn face and, worse, an inexperienced heart.

Esther's eyes trained on his hand, but she could feel his eyes on her. She took a small step back, and the lock of hair came loose from around his finger.

"What is it?" His hand fell to his side.

"Don't you feel her here?" Esther tried to force the words ahead of the lump growing in her throat. "She's everywhere, and for the first time in my life, it makes things harder."

"Her? Irene?" He tilted his head. "You're the one who told me that she wouldn't want me to be stuck in the past and that she's been gone for four years."

"I didn't say that for my sake, Joe. I said it for yours—for Daisy." Esther gestured toward Daisy's shut bedroom door. Was his attention toward her just to prove that he was moving on—moving past Irene? How was that different from any other widower who had shown interest in her over the years? None of them, however, had ever kissed her, touched her. None of them had ever gotten through the front door of her home more than once, for that matter. None of them had she desired. But she did desire Joe.

Joe blinked rapidly and stepped back. "But don't you—" He paused. Esther's eyes went to his throat, where his pulse rhythmically strummed beneath his tanned skin. Without thought, Joe reached for Esther's hand, a simple gesture that sent an electric shock through her entire body.

Joe was saved from finishing his thought when Daisy came out of her bedroom. Her eyes instantly went to their joined hands. Esther let go of Joe's hand, but he held on for another moment before releasing. His eyes lingered on Esther's before he exhaled and let go.

"Good morning," Joe said with a sign that was almost correct. Daisy giggled and waved him down to his knees. Joe obeyed and let Daisy correct his hand movements. Joe repeated. "Good morning, Daisy."

She signed it back and wrinkled her nose in a smile. Then she looked up at Esther and made quick steps over to her and hugged her around the middle. After a few moments she pulled back and signed.

Different clothes? Your hair is down.

Esther briefly signed to her the reason. Daisy pulled at the sleeve of the bathrobe and Esther knelt down. Daisy ran her hands down the side of Esther's hair. The smile on her face was like a sugar-dipped strawberry.

Daisy rotated the palm of her hand over her face and pulled outward. *Beautiful.*

"Even I know what Daisy's saying, and I agree with her," Joe said and stood to look Esther full in the face. "You're beautiful."

Esther, excusing herself, went upstairs to Joe's bedroom where she shed Irene's clothing. The warmth in the room came from more than the July heat on the other side of the thin glass windowpane. As she unfolded her own dress, she took in the scent of the room. His scent. This was where he slept. When she was dressed, she went to his bed and sat at the edge. She needed to strip it of its bedclothes but would have to wait until tomorrow, since today was the day of rest. She ran her hand across the white pillowcase. When she stood, she noticed a rope with a slipknot on one end that was tied to the foot of the bed. Why would this be here?

It was on her mind as she went back downstairs but she tried to make easy conversation with Joe. She wanted—needed—to move past their intimate moments together. They needed to stop.

"I'll wash the clothes I wore and bring them back," she said.

"Please, keep them," Joe said without hesitation.

"I can't," she said too quickly. Esther fingered the soft cotton. It was too light. Too fine. There was lace at the neck and buttons down the front. The housecoat had a pattern in its light blue flannel fabric, and she wanted to keep it. "It's not our way."

Esther stepped around them and started breakfast. Joe had bacon—which usually would be something to celebrate, but today reminded her again of what this house had and what she did not. Between thinking about the crude rope on the frame of the bed and watching Daisy look at her dad with stars in her eyes, Esther was distracted. Daisy attempted to teach him several signs by pointing at a series of objects, then sharing the sign. Joe's thick fingers and callused hands looked giant-like compared to Daisy's pixie-sized fingers.

"You'll have to teach me," Joe said as Esther cleaned up the breakfast dishes.

"Teach you?" she repeated.

"Sign language. I need your help." Their eyes joined with such force that it startled her. He searched hers, and she wanted to look away because she didn't want him to see how much she hurt and how stripped she was because of Daisy. She couldn't have him see her confusion over her feelings for him either. But he stood so near to her that she could've reached out to touch his tanned jaw that had remained unshaven since the day before. His breath smelled like coffee, and she could see the boyishness in his blue eyes. Then there was his smile. "Will you help me?"

Esther turned away and focused on the cast-iron skillet she was washing.

"I'll help you." The words barely made it out of her mouth and past her lips. She knew it was the right thing to do, but the last thing they needed was to be around each other alone. "We can start tomorrow."

A battle waged within Esther's mind. She wanted Daisy to

be happy with her new home, but she also wanted the little girl to hang on her arm and plead with her not to leave. She was as much a mother to the child as she'd ever had. For four years, she'd done everything for and with Daisy, and she loved her as her own. Since she had little chance of having a daughter of her own, she'd devoted herself to her cousin's child. But as she saw Daisy's gleaming eyes smiling up at Joe, Esther found pride in what she'd accomplished with the wild girl she'd been given charge of over four years earlier. She had barely left his side since she had woken except for changing back into her Amish clothing—she had nothing else to wear. Tomorrow Esther would give Joe the bag of dresses Mrs. White had given her for Daisy.

Joe was attempting to decipher Daisy's signs, asking him to push her on the swing. She hopped up and down and laughed when he tried to manipulate the same signs. Clearly reveling in the attentions of his daughter, he smiled at Esther. Esther smiled back, but with a kind of reluctance she wished didn't exist. As much as she knew that Daisy loved her, she also knew that the sand she stood on was shifting. Would the four years of impressions that Esther had made in her life be washed away to nothing?

"I'll see you both tomorrow," Esther said and signed. She smiled, hoping none of the fear and hurt seeped through her tone and put on her black bonnet over her *kapp*.

Daisy's brows knit together and cocked her head to one side. *Why are you going?*

"I don't live here, Daisy. You do—now." Esther swallowed so hard it hurt. She couldn't keep her hands from shaking as she formed the signs. Her heart harvested sadness from her soul and feasted on it, but she had to keep moving.

Joe pursed his lips, and his eyebrows were as rumpled as Daisy's. They looked like two of a kind.

"I should go now." Fresh tears burned Esther's eyes, and she pretended to rummage in her purse until she could blink them away. She went to the door and pulled it open.

"Don't go," Daisy yelled, more clearly than any other words she'd ever spoken.

Esther turned around, and as terrifying as it was, she let the tears stream down her cheeks. How she wanted for Joe to ask her to stay, even though she knew he and Daisy needed to have their own start. Their own life. Their new beginning.

She had turned to leave when she heard his voice: "We still need you, Esther." His voice came out as if it scraped against sandpaper. "I need you."

For a moment, she paused at those words, then pushed herself to take this first step toward her home without Daisy. If she didn't do it now, she might never want to leave the red clapboard house that had suddenly become a real home again.

The sun was warm as she walked home. It was almost pleasant but for the terrible ache in her chest that made it hard to breathe. Every footprint in the sandy ditch of the gravel road declared that she was walking away.

Esther

Esther sat on the back porch that evening. She felt less alone there. Wrapped tightly in her thoughts, she watched the stars burst forth above the lavender-pink horizon across the expanse of hay fields. It never ceased to amaze her how the spring and summer brought forth life where only months before there was none. Everything that was dead became new and alive again in the spring. How could something so dry and sad possibly begin its regrowth—and then submit to the cycle every year? Did the hay know that it would die? Was it as afraid as she was to start over again?

With all the death and loss Esther had experienced, she'd never become new again the way crops and nature did. She'd seen renewal bloom across Joe's face when they found Daisy. How she longed to see herself as more than the shell of a seed that never had the chance to bloom.

It wasn't that she was unhappy. She had experienced great joy—namely in Daisy. She had the security of her community and a child who loved her. The summer's evening chorus grew louder as the sun continued its descent. Daisy would never hear the chirp of a bird or the strumming of hundreds of katydids, but she had the love of a father Daisy could depend on. Her eyes closed, and Esther folded herself within the quiet sigh of the soil as it nourished the roots and breathed in the slow-moving wind that threaded through the trees.

"Bish en schlofa?" Chester's voice was softer than normal when he asked if she was asleep.

Startled, Esther's eyes opened. Her solitude had been her cross to bear, but now Chester was there. His presence pulled her away from her mourning and back to her reality. While it could be easy to pretend that Daisy was upstairs in her small cot sleeping and she was merely relishing the quiet of the evening, it wasn't the truth. Daisy was with Joe.

Chester, on the other hand, was with her. For the moment.

"Chester," she said quietly and sat straighter on the porch chair. She nodded her head toward the bench that had been retired from church use years ago, silently allowing him to sit.

Chester sat, leaving a gap between the two. He was cleaned up, and his upper lip appeared recently shaven.

They sat in silence for several minutes. It might have been longer; Esther wasn't sure. Chester leaned against the rough exterior of the house behind them, stretching his legs. All she could think about were the letters upstairs in her room.

"Why are you here?"

"Thought it was a good day for a visit. I'm not going to leave like you told me to. I'm going to stay."

There was a sense of relief in his surety.

Green velvety leaves brushed against each other in a gust of summer-scented wind. Mrs. White's dog's bark echoed over the field. The night seemed brighter than usual, in contrast to her mood. Chester began tapping his foot on a creaky slat on the porch.

"I heard—"

"Those letters prove that you lied to Willie and Ray. And to me."

Chester's knee stopped bouncing, and the very air stilled around them.

"You never went to the military prison, did you?"

"No, I didn't."

"Why did you lie? Why didn't you tell me the truth?" Esther wanted to look at him and let the disappointment in her eyes bore into his, but she couldn't. Her eyes instead went to the moon that was spotlighting the bouquet of trees in the horizon.

"Essie, let me—I mean. I didn't think anyone would understand the truth." The words spilled from Chester's mouth.

"*Fasteah?*" *Understand?* she questioned. How could anyone understand? She stood, forgetting the mug of tea she had on her lap, which spilled and then broke. Neither of them bothered to do anything about it. The warm temperature permeated her skin, but her heart was like ice and ready to break under the pressure.

"It's all right, Esther." Chester stood too close to her. "It's okay to be angry with me."

"I *am* angry. I am *so* angry," she was yelling now. Her voice reverberated against the porch ceiling and up to the man in the moon where her eyes went, refusing to look at Chester.

"That's right, Essie." Chester grabbed her by the arms and made her face him. His brows were knit, and his eyes as dark as her own. "You're angry with me. Tell me why."

Esther shook her head and pulled away from his grip.

"You left me when I needed you. *Mem* couldn't take care of me. Then she died." She pushed against his chest. Her eyes were squeezed shut.

"What else?" His sharp voice cut through her tolerances and through the history of her quiet and hidden life. Chester stepped closer, now within a few inches of her. She could smell his aftershave. "Keep going."

"You pretended to be dead, but *Mem* was the one who died. Why couldn't it have been you instead of her? She died because you broke her heart. And Norma said she lost a baby. I could've had a brother or sister." Her palms against his chest pushed him away again, but he wouldn't stay away and stepped back toward her. "I could've had someone to share all of this with and not always carry everything myself."

"Don't stop now, Esther. What else?"

"We were hungry—every day. We sold the fields, but it wasn't enough to keep us because of the back taxes and *Mammie*'s doctor bills. But we couldn't ask the church for help or they would've sent me away to relatives. I had to wear feed-sack dresses and had to leave school in the seventh grade so I could work because *Mammie* couldn't."

Even in her torment, she saw Chester's face flinch. But he moved closer to her even after she pushed him away.

"Did that make you angry?" His voice faltered.

"Yes." She'd never screamed so loud before. Her throat hurt. Her hands turned into fists and she pounded his chest.

"Is that everything, Essie?" He was almost out of breath. "Is that all you got?"

"I hate that nickname, and I hate you. A father is supposed to keep his promises and take care of his family. You didn't do any of that. You broke every promise you ever made. You're a coward." She pounded his chest again, but this time it didn't push him away.

"What was that? I didn't hear you." Chester's voice broke.

"You're a coward, and I hate you," she said louder and her words scratched against her throat.

"No, you don't," he countered.

"Yes, I do. I hate you!" She couldn't yell anymore and hammered her fist on his chest again, but had no strength to lift her hands back up before she crumbled into Chester's arms.

For the first time since she was a child, her father's arms were around her, holding and comforting her.

She wept painfully this time. Not the gentle weeping from the night before, when she'd broken down with Joe. These sobs came from the deepest part of her soul, from the darkness of her stomach, from her summer-worn feet.

"I had to grow up without parents." She sobbed. "I was so alone."

Her father's gentle shush calmed her, and within a few minutes, she moved away from his hold and looked at him. His eyes were red-rimmed. Sweat was dripping down his face, and his breathing was heavy.

"You're right. I am a coward. I'm sorry, Esther." His whisper was throaty and thick. "I was a coward and thought losing a finger would keep me out of the war, prison—everything. But when I learned that I would've been sent home because of a heart murmur and your *mem* had cut my finger off for nothing, something just snapped inside of me. I couldn't come back. I knew that everyone would know what we'd done, so I left. I did work with the Mennonites in relief work and all the places I said I'd been to—that was all true. But I never went to prison. I never put on a military uniform in return for being released from prison. I lied. You're right, I am a liar. I am a coward."

The nighttime sounds consumed several lengthy moments.

"Why are you telling me all of this now?" Esther couldn't say that she had learned anything new, except that she could hear in every word his regret and his self-loathing.

Chester released a heavy sigh and shook his head. "I think you were ready to hear it, and I was finally ready to tell you. And because I want to be the kind of father you deserve."

She whispered, "I don't know if I can forgive you," and shook her head.

He hung his head for a moment before looking back at her. "Can I come home?"

Esther didn't know how to respond at first.

"Joe told me about Daisy and that you're here alone now."

"What?"

"He came to see me early this morning. He's worried about you. I'm worried about you and want to help. Would you let me come home and try?"

Joe and Chester were both worried about her. Had anyone ever worried about her before?

"Yes."

Joe

Joe woke at dawn with his leg twisted awkwardly in the rope attached to his bed. He was lying on his wooden bedroom floor and his head ached. His solution of binding himself to the bed was working. He hadn't destroyed the house or hurt Daisy. But the problem was that even when he wore a sock, the rope gave him a bruise around his ankle and had started cutting into his skin. With Daisy sleeping in the house, however, he refused to take any chances. He didn't trust himself. Not with the faces of the lost in his sleeping mind. It didn't matter that he could've gotten another hour of sleep. He was awake, and the last thing he wanted was to have more time living in his nightmares.

The weather was already hot and sticky by the time Joe and Daisy got into the truck. Daisy's smile and presence pulled Joe from the mood he woke with. Reliving the same battle scene in the form of a recurring dream every night ratcheted his nerves. Esther was pale when she opened the door at his knock. But her eyes landed on him with a friendship that brought him peace.

"We hadn't talked about how this would work, so I just

brought her over," he stuttered. He was suddenly nervous. He pulled the cigarette out of his mouth and squished it under his work boot, leaving a small circle of soot on the wood porch. "It won't be much different from before."

When he looked back up at Esther, her face grew pinker as a smile spread across it.

"Good morning, Daisy-girl," she signed and spoke. A sparkle returned to her eyes. Daisy rushed over to Esther and threw her arms around her. They instantly started signing so fast Joe couldn't keep up. What he could sense was that they were happy signs by the look on Daisy's face. Esther turned back to Joe. "Come on in. My dad is almost ready."

"Your *dad*?" Joe's first surprise was hearing Esther call Chet *dad*. The second was that Chet had been able to move back so quickly and that Esther had allowed it.

Esther looked away and didn't answer Joe's question. Chet came from his first-floor bedroom and nodded at him.

"I have some hard-boiled eggs for you and some bread. I'm sorry I don't have more," she said to Chet.

"That's a right fine lunch, Esther," Chet said and smiled at her. She smiled back. He turned toward Joe and offered a hand. When Joe shook it, he had the sense that Chet had gone through as much of a change with Esther as he had with Daisy.

As the men began walking out of the house Esther spoke again.

"Joe?" Esther walked up to him and touched his arm. A surge of heat ran through his veins. "Thank you."

Her words energized him all day as he worked and every morning as he dropped off Daisy. Other than Daisy sleeping at Joe's home, everything else was generally the same. They ate many suppers together and worked like a family. More than ever before, he looked forward to any time he had with Esther and he knew that he needed her. It wasn't just her communication with Daisy. She had become an anchor to him, keeping him tethered to reality.

~⁓

After Daisy had lived with him a week, their routine became fluid and comfortable. He sensed that Esther struggled with it, but she did everything she could to keep Daisy happy. Esther smiled genuinely, and he could see she was pleased with Daisy's progress, but in the in-between moments that she thought went unnoticed, her somber gaze landed on blank spaces and bare walls. Joe could see the empty heart she tried to hide. Having Chet in the home with her had helped, he suspected, but it couldn't compare to losing the constant presence of Daisy.

"Do you really think I should go to Alvin and Dorothy's barn raising?" Joe asked as he sat at the kitchen table, waiting to have a lesson in sign language. "I have to admit, I wouldn't have been more surprised if President Truman had come for a visit than to see Alvin Bender standing on my front porch. But I'm nervous about Roy. He and I never got along."

Esther smiled and poured coffee into his mug. "Don't be afraid of Roy."

Joe rolled his eyes considering the heavy brow of his father-in-law. Joe was always respectful, but Roy had made it very clear that he would not forgive him or Irene for their marriage or her death.

"I think it would be a good way to show that you still care about the family." Esther poured her own mug and then walked back into the kitchen.

"And I know Daisy loves Lucy and her cousins," Joe called louder toward the kitchen. "And you'll be there?"

"I will." Esther finally sat down at the table with him and pulled open the sign language book.

"Then it's settled. I'll go." He tilted his head toward the book in front of Esther. "And how did you learn out of this book?" Joe flipped through the thick yellow-pages.

The heavy black cover looked old and the text inside was small and difficult to read. It was after supper and Chet had already gone home and Daisy was in bed, but Esther stayed to help Joe learn some more signs.

"You taught many students out of textbooks. How is this any different?"

He supposed she was right, only this felt foreign to him. He turned toward her where she sat next to him at the table and nudged his chair a little closer to hers.

"Let's do the alphabet again," she said. She took the book from him and closed it and said, "Let's see if you can do the signs without looking at the pictures."

"I don't think I can. All I can seem to remember is the letter *L* because it looks like an *L*. But how in the world does that look like a *G*?" He did his best to form the letter, but when Esther laughed, he looked at her and feigned hurt. "What?"

"Here, like this." She was still smiling when she adjusted his hand to fit the correct sign for the letter *G*. Then she did the sign as well. "See?"

The sensation of her touch lingered over his skin. He liked it and hoped she would touch his hand again. Perhaps if he continued to do the signs incorrectly, she would continue to fix his mistakes. He watched her as she explained each letter again. He didn't hear her voice as much as he watched the way her mouth moved. She had full pink lips, and her large dark eyes wildly expressed everything she signed. Her face was far more expressive than the common sober-faced Amish church member. He'd grown used to her usual appearance: a covering on her head, a dark dress, and shoes. There was no nuance with her clothing, but there had been on the morning he'd seen her with her hair down. Something in her countenance had shifted from the morning he'd found her unprepared. The memory of her standing there with the housecoat on and her hair down her back was imprinted on his mind. An expression of shame had crossed her eyes and he longed to tell her not to be ashamed of herself. She had no awareness of her beauty.

Looking past her Amish exterior had not been a problem for him. It had been no different from Irene in that way. It had been easy to see past the uniform-like dress Irene wore because she'd flirted with him with her sparkling eyes and gleaming smile. Esther, of course, didn't have any reason to intentionally entice him, but she did it without trying.

"Joe, have you been listening to anything I've said?" Esther took her eyes from the book and turned to him.

She was so close. He could see the flecks of blue in her dark eyes and the waves of her hair through her covering.

"You really have done an exceptional job with her." His arm was draped around the back of her chair as he leaned toward her. Her dark eyes connected with his and her lips pursed. Her chest rose and fell and he shifted to be closer again.

"You don't have to say that," Esther returned. "I love Daisy. I'd do anything to help her. You know that."

"Well, you're a great teacher."

"You're the teacher, Joe, not me." Esther sat straighter and waved off his compliment.

"Not anymore," he said. He pulled the book back over to his side using both hands and opened it up, hoping it would deflect the conversation. He didn't like talking about the life he'd left behind.

"Don't you miss teaching?"

He offered a subtle shrug. Yes. He missed it greatly. But he didn't respond. Instead his fingers deftly perused through the pages as he skimmed the descriptions of the signs.

"Will you return to teaching someday?"

Joe turned toward Esther. He decided he didn't want to answer and waved a hand in a circle around his face. Esther tilted her head at him as he signed and said, "Beautiful."

"Joe," she whispered and looked down. Her black eyelashes fluttered on her cheeks, and the delicate expression stilled Joe's heart for several moments.

When Joe gently lifted her chin with a finger, she didn't resist. His hand went around to the back of her neck, and her lips parted instinctively. He drew closer to her. The kiss was gentle, but kindled a spark through his center and then straight to his head. His hands roamed to her covering, and he deftly pulled the straight pins that held it in place and let them fall on the table. He took her covering off and wrapped a hand around the back of her neck with impatience and pulled her closer. Her hands gently rested against his chest. When the pulse of their kiss became more eager than their last she pulled away.

Esther's breathing was rapid and she didn't let go of Joe's gaze. Her eyes roamed from him to over his shoulder and toward the staircase. After several long moments, she squeezed her eyes together and shook her head. Joe stood and took her arms gently. She opened her eyes and looked up at him.

"Esther?" He brushed a finger over her cheek, then pulled her back into an embrace and their bodies heated the room.

"Can I ask you a question?" Her voice was shaky like she was nervous.

Joe tilted his head. His curiosity was piqued.

"Why is there a rope attached to your bed?" Her voice was a whisper.

What? She'd found the rope? What could he say? He couldn't explain that the memories of war and of his failures plagued his sleep. He couldn't tell her that when he closed his eyes, he saw his men's faces—dead—and that he could hear them fighting for their very lives.

"Joe?" Esther's voice echoed somewhere in the back of his mind. His ears picked up her words but couldn't register what she was saying. Her hand touched his face, and he returned.

"It's nothing," he lied.

"It's not nothing. Just tell me."

"I think you should leave," he said slowly and slid the book toward her.

He didn't have to look at her to know the hurt that cascaded from her eyes. The next thing he heard was the door closing behind her.

1944
Mariana Bay, Saipan

By the first light of dawn, the firing had stopped. Bodies were scattered all over the red-stained terrain. His jaw ached from being clenched. He was hotter than usual, and his sweat smelled sour.

"You're a poor excuse, Garrison. I just finally got relieved from the line and where've you been? Relaxing in the sun all day? Getting some grub?" Sergeant Barker yelled at Joe as he left the field kitchen unable to eat. "Didn't think a clumsy man like you would survive. Why don't you go pick up the ammo you dropped so that you get nailed instead of all the men the platoon lost yesterday? Their blood is on your hands."

As Barker continued to berate him in front of the other Marines, every muscle in Garrison's body tightened. He didn't want to let this hothead get to him. Garrison had never liked Barker as a squad leader because of the cruel way he treated his men.

"Hey, Garrison, I'm talking to you." Barker's spittle sprayed onto Joe's face. "All the gunfire make you deaf as well as dumb?"

That was all Garrison could take. He'd never mentioned that Esther Detweiler said that his own daughter was a deaf-mute, but the dig from Barker was too personal. He inhaled, and after his fist hit Barker in the temple, the man fell and Garrison kicked him in the gut. Before Barker could defend himself, their platoon sergeant came over.

"Garrison!" Jacobs's voice forced Garrison's second fist to pause in midair.

He knew instantly that he'd gone too far. They'd all given one another backhanded insults from time to time, but sucker punching crossed the line. "That's going to cost you a stripe."

Within twenty-four hours, Garrison's sergeant stripes went to Fielding. The young corporal had completed Garrison's ammo distribution in the midst of a firefight. Fielding's corporal stripes went to Garrison. His demotion cost him his rank and his squad. He was moved to a supply tent away from the line. He'd failed.

"You bought her a dress?" Esther looked at the smile Joe was sharing with Daisy. It was made from pretty red-and-white-checked fabric, with two blue buttons on the bodice and a wide ribbon waistline. The skirt flared out with the same blue ribbon tracing along the bottom hem. Daisy held it against her shoulders and did a twirl. Esther recalled that she'd done the same with her first Amish dress despite the fact that it had been brown and plain.

Esther had to pretend that his words to her the week earlier had not been all she could think about. Little else coursed through her mind but his asking her to leave his house and the stark contrast it was to the kiss they'd shared just before. She'd been reluctant to return, so she still made supper at Joe's house but left when he arrived, taking a plate of food for herself and her dad. The anger she let simmer was nothing compared to the hurt. He'd trusted her with so much—with his daughter—and yet he wouldn't let go of some secret.

"Wayne gave me a raise—made me a crew chief. The dresses Mrs. White gave her are nice, but I thought it was high time that Daisy get a new dress. I know it isn't what you are used to seeing. But do you like it?"

The hope in his voice was unmistakable. She could see in the intensity in his eyes that he wanted to make things right with her. She wouldn't let him until he was honest with her. If he expected them to work together to learn sign language and wanted Esther to be part of Daisy's life, he needed to be forthright with her. She wasn't a child. She wasn't Irene, who had always avoided the discomfort of conflict.

"It's pretty," Esther agreed, then turned around and grabbed a cucumber from the hanging basket. Joe had returned earlier than usual, throwing off Esther's new routine, and she hadn't finished preparing their dinner yet.

Esther sensed him looking at her. She could feel his desire for her to meet his eyes. But she couldn't. She didn't want him to see how much he'd hurt her. If their eyes met, she knew she would not be able to keep the hurt away.

"I'd like to take her to church with me this week. What do you think?"

"Church?" Her hands paused their work. Esther hadn't thought of it at all before now. Daisy had been attending services with her still, and Joe hadn't been attending at all.

Joe didn't say anything, but his blue eyes drilled into her. Of course he should return to church; of course he should take Daisy with him. She knew this was the right decision, but this change peeled away a painful layer.

"Of course, you should go. And Daisy should go with you." She cleared her throat. The thought of sitting in church without Daisy flipped her stomach inside out. She turned around and continued slicing the cucumber. Her eyes blurred, and suddenly a searing pain shot through her thumb. She gasped.

Joe came up from behind her and looked over her shoulder. "You're bleeding, Esther."

"It's not that bad," Esther said, but wasn't sure she believed herself.

"Here," Joe held a dish towel on her thumb and led her to a chair. "Sit down."

Joe ran a hand through his hair and paced the floor.

"It's not that bad," Esther said again. She opened up the towel to look. Joe looked at the wound as well.

"Not bad? You're really bleeding," he said and his breathing intensified.

"I always bleed badly. My grandma did too. Something about our blood, a doctor said once. But the cut isn't bad. Why are you pacing?"

Joe pushed the heels of his hands over his eyes. Why was he acting so strangely?

"Does the blood bother you that much?" Esther asked seriously.

Joe shook his head but kept his back to Esther. "It didn't used to, but . . ."

Did he mean because of the war? She was sure he'd seen far worse. Why would a small cut cause such a reaction?

"Do you think you can bandage it up for me?" Esther asked. "I'm not sure I can do it myself."

He turned back toward Esther, and she saw that his face was white and pasty. He nodded his head without saying anything, then left the kitchen.

What happened? Daisy questioned and dropped the dress onto the floor to look in on the activity.

Esther pointed toward the knife. Daisy leaned in closer to see and sympathized with Esther. Joe returned with a bandage and, with shaky hands, wrapped Esther's thumb. Daisy stood by and watched with admiration in her eyes.

"Daisy, get Esther water." While Joe signed only the word *water,* Esther was glad to see how smoothly he had done so.

Esther continued to watch as Joe insisted on preparing the rest of the small supper, even though it was only mashed potatoes with some hamburger gravy—light on the beef—along with most of a sliced cucumber. Joe communicated with Daisy without asking for help from Esther even once. Daisy set the table, pouring water into the glasses without a single spill. She helped stir the gravy so it wouldn't stick and reminded Joe to put a pot holder under the pan when setting it on the table. Even when Joe didn't have the right sign or had to make one up, Daisy giggled and somehow understood each time.

The two seemed to not even remember that Esther was there.

Joe offered to do the dishes, saying that she shouldn't get her bandage wet. Daisy charged herself with clearing the table and smiled at Esther in her independence.

~

Later, as Esther walked home, purple and orange streaks were crawling across the sky. As she reached the curve in the road where she could see her house, she noticed a shiny green car parked there.

Who was at her house? She saw her *dat* standing on the porch with a man in a dark suit. He threw his hands in the air, like he was upset. The man in the suit moved in closer to her dad and pointed a finger at his chest. It was just then that they noticed her. Her dad moved the suited man toward his car in a rush and gestured wildly. The stranger looked over at her and after he looked back at Chester for several moments, he turned and left.

Esther was almost in the drive when the car pulled out. She had to duck her head to shield herself from the gravel that the tires threw.

"Who was that?" Esther questioned.

"Oh, just a traveling salesman," her dad said and sniffed.

"A salesman?" Esther cocked her head as she spoke. It didn't make sense. "What was he selling?"

Chester looked down the road in the direction of the car for several beats before he spoke again.

"Nothing worth buying." Chester walked back into the house.

Esther

By the time Sunday came, Esther was drawn only to her black dress. She pulled out her navy dress instead. She was careless as she dressed and stuck herself with a pin twice. Her cut thumb had healed quickly, and she'd grown a callus over it, but there was no callus large enough or strong enough to keep the hurt from losing Daisy at bay.

Esther would be sitting alone at church today. Daisy wouldn't nudge her to roll her church hanky into babies. She wouldn't lean her head against Esther's arm and fall asleep in the last twenty minutes of the service.

"You're about as white as a new wife's *kapp*," Chester said when Esther came down to the kitchen. His Dutch was still broken sounding and his Texas twang noticeable. "Sorry, Essie, I didn't mean . . ."

He was probably right. Her stomach twisted around, and even her legs felt weak. For over four years, the little girl had been with her, and now she'd lost her. Daisy's going to Joe's church and wearing English clothing made the transition into Joe's home even more permanent.

Esther nearly spilled milk in her distracted frame of mind before Chester took the pitcher away.

"Sit," he ordered. Esther obeyed and looked at him. His beard had grown in well, and she'd pressed his suit the night before. It looked good on him. At this point no one would know that he'd returned only two months ago. He finished pouring the milk, then handed it to her. "Here."

"*Dangeh*," she thanked him.

"*Oiyah?*" He held up a few eggs to her, and his own concerned eyebrows rose in question.

Esther shook her head. "I don't think I can eat eggs—or anything. I don't even think I can finish this." She put the glass of milk down after only one swallow. She briefly closed her eyes and rubbed her forehead. When she opened her eyes, Chester was watching her, as if he was analyzing her.

"I remember that the night before you left, you played 'His Eye Is on the Sparrow,'" she said. Her voice was breathy and filled with nervousness. Her eyes landed on the harmonica that sat on the window's ledge. She could still hear the vibration and reedy chords that he'd played nearly every night of her young years. She was on her way to forgiving him but she was still suspicious about the suited man with the green car, but in this quiet moment, all she wanted was the security that only a parent could give.

Chester looked at Esther, his forehead lined with their history. He swallowed and stuttered as he spoke. "I remember, sweetheart."

For the first time in two months Esther found herself appreciating Chester's Englisher ways. She overlooked her frustrations with him for the moment because she'd never been anyone's sweetheart. In Esther's thirty-four years, she'd rarely heard Amish men refer to their children in such affectionate terms. It wasn't for lack of love; it just wasn't their way. There were occasions, however, when she'd heard a child or wife given a pet name, and she secretly coveted the endearment. She'd often heard Mrs. White call her daughters *honey* or *darling*.

"Will you play for me now?" Esther asked. She didn't want to fight with him. She was so exhausted from the fight she'd had to keep up for nearly thirty years. Her heart hadn't calmed since the morning she questioned her *detteh's* bloody hand. The confusion of those few minutes set the course for the next three decades. But she was tired and exhausted of it all. His harmonica playing had been one of the sweetest memories of her childhood and might be the balm she needed now.

"I'd be happy to." He didn't waste a moment and picked up the instrument. When the music began, she sensed the words— *Why should I feel discouraged, why should the shadows come?* She'd had the same question for most of her life. When the strains played that reminded her that Jesus was her constant friend, she knew that this was where her problem had been. She hadn't let her Savior be her companion.

The melody continued to fill every space of the old home and filled the breadth of Esther's spirit, and for the next few minutes she grew into childhood again.

Joe

The morning had gone well so far. Joe looked over at his daughter, who sat in the truck with him. She tilted her head to see the white steeple that pointed high into the sky. It wasn't a large church, but all she knew of church was sitting together in an Amish farmhouse. Did Daisy remember her mother holding her hand as they walked into the country church together years ago? Could she remember that her mother's funeral had been here? Surely she didn't remember that by the time the funeral director closed her mother's casket, she'd become so wild it had taken two churchwomen to hold her down so that she could be sedated.

Neither of them had been back to the church since then.

Joe reached over and tapped her on the shoulder. Daisy looked over at him with a bright smile stretched across her face. Her eyes were so blue. Had Irene's been that blue? Why couldn't he pull together an image of Irene and her beauty anymore? Instead, Esther's dark eyes came to his mind. He missed her, and more than he wanted to admit. But she couldn't find out about his nightmares. They weren't happening every night now. Some nights he even slept soundly.

"Ready?" he asked, pointing to the church.

Daisy nodded and signed while attempting to verbalize. Her sounds were always round and textured with song.

"Slow down." He laughed as he spoke. He used a simple sign he'd learned quickly since asking her to slow down was something he did often.

She giggled then signed more slowly.

Not like Esther's church. She did one sign at a time and he understood exactly what she was saying.

"Yes." His fist bobbed up and down. "Okay?" He signed the letters *O* and *K* that he'd also learned quickly.

Daisy's expression shifted, and she looked back at the large white building. The bells were chiming now, and he opened his mouth to comment on how the bell was telling them it was time for Sunday school when he remembered that she would never hear church bells.

Yes, she signed simply.

They walked hand in hand through the gravel parking lot and through the double doors. A man in a suit stood in the front and shook Joe's hand. He introduced himself as Lou Jefferson. Joe introduced himself and Daisy.

Lou looked over Joe's shoulder. "Is your wife here?" The words scraped over Joe's nerves. They had too much history with the church for these questions, and he didn't feel like explaining everything to a too-cheerful stranger.

"No, she passed away," Joe mumbled and cleared his throat, "a few years ago."

"Well, there's hope in the Lord." Sympathy ran the length of the man's face. A moment later, his joy returned and he bent down to Daisy's level. "Hi there, Daisy. Are you ready to go learn about Jesus?"

Daisy's head tilted and then she looked up at her father.

"She's deaf," Joe said. He hadn't taken her in public himself since his return, and this was the first time he had to explain her deafness.

"Is that so?" The man looked up at Joe, then at Daisy, and spoke louder. "Are you ready to learn about Jesus in Sunday School?"

"She's deaf—she can't hear." Maybe he needed to clarify.

"That's why I talked real loud." Lou stood. "I'm sure if you asked her if she wanted a piece of candy, she wouldn't be deaf."

Then Lou's elbow shot into Joe's ribs. It was all he could do not to give the man a fist in return. Is this what Esther had had to deal with for the four years he was away? People simply assuming that she was exaggerating or wrong? Hadn't he even believed that she was wrong and that Daisy was merely simpleminded? Hadn't Joe even told her not to take Daisy to a doctor?

"She can't hear anything you say," Joe said steadily.

"Oh, really?" The man's face declared confusion. "Then how will she hear about Jesus?"

Was he serious?

Joe looked down at Daisy and signed.

"Go to Sunday School with other kids?" Joe's signs were broken, like he was stuttering through his speech. Lou's eyes were on them both.

Alone? she asked, eyebrows up, eyes wide. *Who will sign for me?*

"Not alone," he started. "You will be with the other kids. Fun?"

She slowly nodded her head and offered a weak smile. He wanted her to see that his church also had fun children, just like her Amish friends.

"Where do I take her?" Joe asked Lou.

"Down the hall," Lou said with a shocked expression.

The hall was filled with the noise of the other children. A

woman's voice, like a teeter-totter on the playground, moved up and down as she tried to get them settled.

Joe put an arm around Daisy's shoulders as they stood in the doorway.

"Oh, lookie here," the woman said as she trotted over. The other children all became silent and stared. "I'm Mrs. Underhill. And you are?" She spoke entirely in falsetto.

Mrs. Underhill leaned an ear toward Joe and Daisy, her eyes twinkling. The older woman had her gray hair rolled in a bun and wore a floral dress over her buxom frame.

"I'm Joe Garrison and this is my daughter, Daisy." Joe patted Daisy's shoulder. "Daisy is—"

"Welcome, Daisy," Mrs. Underhill interrupted. "Why don't you go have a seat over there next to Lucille. Lucille, wave to Daisy."

Daisy smiled at her and looked over at a little girl with bobbing pigtails who was waving at her. Daisy raised her hand and waved back.

"Daisy is deaf." Joe leaned toward Mrs. Underhill.

"What?" Mrs. Underhill put a hand to her chest as if Joe may have said that Daisy ate stray cats for breakfast. "She's what?"

"Deaf." He pointed at his ears. "She can't hear."

"Now, surely . . ." The gray-haired woman waved a hand at Joe and tsk'd at him. She bent at the waist to get close to Daisy's face. "Daisy. You. Go. Sit. Over. There."

Mrs. Underhill spoke loudly. Clearly. And pointed at Lucille, who waved again.

"She can't hear you," Joe reassured her.

"Then why is she here?" The woman tucked her chin and raised an eyebrow. "What could she get out of church if she can't hear? Aren't there *places* for people like her? The deaf and dumb?"

"Don't call her that," Joe barked. He was sweating. He clenched his teeth and cleared his throat to keep his cool.

"Well," she huffed and put a hand to her chest. Her mouth agape.

"Daisy would like to spend some time with the children. She's a good girl and will sit still." He felt pride surge through his veins with how well behaved Daisy was—even with her deafness. Joe would not let this woman take away his daughter's chance to attend church.

"In here? With my class?"

"Sure. She loves other children and she will gain some sense of what you talk about through pictures and any gestures you use."

"I'm sorry, Mr. . . ." She squinted an eye at Joe.

"Garrison," Joe finished.

"Garrison, yes. I'm sorry, but I don't see how it could work."

"Can you just—" Joe interrupted himself with a deep breath. "Can you just give her a chance?"

The woman sighed and raised an eyebrow as she looked Daisy up and down. Daisy looked from the teacher to Joe and back again, then took a step back and tucked herself a little closer into Joe's side.

"All right," Mrs. Underhill finally said.

Joe turned Daisy toward him and he squatted down. "Daisy, this is your teacher."

Daisy looked up toward the woman, then back at Joe.

"Sit quietly. I'll get you in one hour." He did the best he could with his memory of these signs and made up his own that he hoped would get the point across.

"And she knows what you mean?"

"Sure," Joe said. She did, right? He pointed over Daisy's shoulder and reminded her where she could sit. Daisy hugged Joe around his middle before she bounded over to sit next to Lucille. The difference between the girls' appearances were minor—Daisy's hair was combed with a small ribbon holding it back, while Lucille had bouncing curly pigtails. Their dresses were similarly nice. But Lucille could speak and hear—she was *normal.*

"Off with you now." Mrs. Underhill waved him away and closed the door behind her.

Joe watched as an usher seated Mrs. White. He was sure she saw him, but she did not give him even a second glance. Joe sat near the back with Angelica and her family and was restless throughout the service. He checked his watch every five minutes, and after he'd been sitting for almost thirty minutes, he leaned over and whispered to his sister, "Why don't your girls go to Sunday school? Daisy would've loved to have her cousins with her."

"With that Underhill woman?" Angelica whispered back. "She tried to whip Jonna and pulled Paulina's ear. I haven't cared to send them since. I should've told you not to bother."

Joe nodded and leaned back. Yes, he wished she had told him. A wave of discomfort journeyed from his mind down to his heart and into his stomach and sat there like a rock. Daisy would've been perfectly happy with him since she was used to sitting quietly through the long-winded Amish sermons. His feet bounced up and down. He wanted to go and get her. No. Everything would be fine. She would sit there quietly and enjoy the activity of the children and of the Bible story.

A heavy tap came to his right shoulder and he turned to find a girl of eleven or twelve with panic written across her face.

"Mrs. Underhill wanted me to come and get you," the girl said.

Joe closed his Bible and didn't even care if he was disruptive. Obviously his bad feeling had been warranted. He rushed through the back of the sanctuary and then down the hallway. He heard yowling that could've been only from Mrs. Underhill. When he stood in the doorway, the older woman caught his gaze and snarled at him. "Get that animal out of here, Mr. Garrison. She ought not to be allowed in public." She wailed as she held her hand up. From across the room, he could see nothing wrong with her hand until she walked over and showed him the teeth marks around the heel of her hand. "She bit me. Do you hear me? Your daughter bit me."

Every inch of Joe's skin tightened. This was provoked.

"Where is she?" he yelled. "Where's Daisy?"

He looked in every corner and behind the door and couldn't find her. The children around him were laughing with one another, running in circles around the tables, or watching the exchange in horror. But where was Daisy? He looked at Lucille, who had eyes the size of half-dollars.

"Lucille, right? Where did Daisy go?" Lucille didn't say anything but simply pointed toward a closed door.

Joe rushed several steps forward and opened it. It was a small closet with a broom and mop in it. Daisy was in the corner with her head curled around her knees. Her whimpering came in loud gasps, and she was so deeply tucked into the corner she hadn't even flinched at the light that shone through the open door. He shoved the broom and mop out of the way and squatted down. When he touched her, she didn't move or even look his way.

"It's me," he said and gently took her arms. Her eyes finally found his, but there was no recognition in them. "Daisy, it's Daddy. Come here."

He opened his arms, and she just continued to stare, her eyes not meeting his. His heart throbbed hard against his chest, and his breathing quickened. She didn't know him. Where was Daisy? He gathered her in his arms, and her touch in return was unresponsive and impersonal.

Joe looked at Mrs. Underhill. "Did you put her in there?" When she didn't answer, he said it again, but this time his voice reverberated against the four walls and the ceiling. "Did you put her in there?"

"She bit me," she said, showing him her hand. "She needed to be restrained—or hog-tied. Mr. Garrison, if you can't take care of your own daughter and control her behavior, she should be with someone who can. Or an institution!"

"Well, we won't ever return to *this* institution," he said through clenched teeth.

"Well, I never."

Her words did not offend him nearly as much as he offended himself. He had failed Daisy. He never should have left her without a familiar face. What had he been thinking? For four years, she had been encompassed in the protection of Esther's simple lifestyle. The consistency of her church had offered Daisy exactly what she needed, and throwing her into such a different situation had been too much for her. Just as he'd been confirmed to be a failure as a sergeant, he was not a good father.

Esther

Esther couldn't help but roll and reroll Daisy's church hanky into babies over and over. Alberta touched her arm and patted it lightly. Their eyes met. The older woman leaned over and whispered.

"I know you miss her," Alberta said, and then silently sighed as she looked toward the preacher and then back to Esther. "I miss her too."

When Alberta's hand returned to her own lap, her eyes forward, Esther couldn't help but see her lips purse and a few quick blinks pushing away tears. Alberta had sat next to Daisy for the last six months since her husband passed. Her missing Daisy seemed to be a way of saying how lonely she was for her own loved one.

"Jesus said that those who do God's will, they will be brothers and sisters. So woe to those who don't do the *Got sah villa. Sie sint net unser bruders. Sie sint net unser schvester.* Turn your back on those who go toward the world like Lot went toward Sodom. Be like Abraham and stay on the side of God and the church."

Esther considered his words: *Those who don't do God's will are neither their sisters nor their brothers.*

Irene had turned her back on the church. Had loving Joe directed her life toward Sodom? Was Daisy's deafness the result of sin? Irene and the baby's death? Esther had done exactly what the church had called for all her life, but she'd never experienced the beauty of joy that her shunned cousin had. How fortunate for Esther that she had had the chance to see Irene's happiness before her too-soon death. No, Esther thought. Irene had not stepped toward Sodom by leaving the church to marry Joe.

Often when someone was shunned, the community simply didn't see them anymore. It was truly as if they had never existed. No one spoke of them. Or, if they did, it was behind the cover of a thick wooden door and sounded like tears. She had never wanted that for her and Irene, and looking back, she knew she'd kept her promise of friendship. Esther had no regrets about how she'd responded to Irene. How many around her could say that about a shunned family member or friend? Could she say the same about her *dat*?

She couldn't see her father through the sea of white and black coverings. With the preacher talking about devotion to God and church, she wondered what he was thinking. He was almost a month into his own *bann* and still had several to go. Then there had been the suited man at the door—though she'd chosen to ignore her suspicions for the time being since she was beginning to appreciate Chet's companionship. While he'd said that the stranger was only a salesman, Esther knew he was lying. She battled between keeping her eye on him to look for the truth or to just simply forget it ever happened for the chance to rekindle a relationship with him.

Esther let her mind wander, and before she knew it, she was on her knees in prayer at the end of the service. Where had the morning gone? The bigger question was: How was Daisy? She moved from the barn where church was held into the kitchen to set up a serving line for food. Usually she could ask Daisy to pour cold water into the cups, but today she asked another child. She cut the pies and cakes, then stood behind the table to serve.

"Esther?" A man's silky voice spoke her name.

"*Ya?*" She looked up into the eyes of a former classmate. She didn't know him well; he was older than her. He was as black-haired as she was, with strong features in his face.

"I'm Harvey Miller, Marty's son. Remember me?"

She remembered that he was recently widowed.

"I remember," she said it blandly, so not to give the impression that there was any hint of interest. "I didn't know you were still here."

"Coming back to stay. *Mem* is going to help me out with my *kinnah* until—well . . ." Harvey suddenly looked uncomfortable as he shifted his eyes.

Esther was sure that his mother would be helpful with his children and even more help in finding him a new wife.

He leaned forward. "*Mem* told me that you're known for your baking. Which pie is yours?"

So Marty had talked to him about her? She shook her head no and diverted her eyes. "I only brought some butter today."

"No shame in that." He showed her his plate and whispered across the table when he saw a line of men forming behind him, "I love butter."

"Why don't you try this coconut cake," Esther suggested, holding up a large square—it was made by another unmarried woman who had been jilted by a young man only a few months ago when he ran off to marry an Iowa girl. She was already twenty-six and had no other prospects. "It was made by Ruthie Lee right over there. That's Marvin Lee's girl."

Esther pointed at the pretty red-haired woman serving potatoes. By relating who she was with her father instead of her husband, she was hoping he would understand that she was unmarried. Harvey's eyebrows raised and he offered his plate.

She put the piece of cake on his plate, and he walked away as she continued to serve the rest of the men in line. She had to admit that Harvey was handsome, though she had never found such dark features as enticing as a man with light hair and eyes. She didn't usually play matchmaker, but she was in no mood to entertain the ideas of a widowed man. Though, wasn't that what she'd been doing with Joe? Why was that any different? Maybe she should've given Harvey some consideration to persuade her feelings away from Joe.

Her thoughts danced over the words she'd just spoken to herself and realized she'd admitted she had feelings for Joe.

Joe

As Joe drove away from the church and toward home, Daisy didn't move; in fact, she barely blinked. How could he have trusted a stranger with his daughter? Had she really tried to bite the woman? If so, how could he ever know how to help her control that kind of rage? How could he parent a child he didn't understand?

As he left town and the rural countryside began to fly by, he caught sight of Dr. Sherman's grand house in the distance on a hill. Some would say that a house *sat* on a hill, but this house didn't. It *stood* there. Tall and stately with gables in every corner, it was the yellow color Irene would've called buttermilk, and it made him hate the house because it had been her favorite color. As he got closer, he slowed. The good doctor and his wife, in their Sunday best, had just arrived home themselves and were climbing out of their red Buick that easily could've cost over a thousand dollars. As he drove past, both Dr. and Mrs. Sherman waved.

In a moment of desperation, he spun around in the middle of the road, drove back to the doctor's house, and pulled into the drive. Dr. Sherman had been at Joe's house when Irene died.

Before that day, he'd liked the man, but ever since, he was sure that the good doctor hadn't done enough—that he could've done more. But what choice did he have in the moment? He needed help.

Dr. Sherman and his wife were still walking into their house when they paused on the porch steps, watching him. Gravel flew from his tires, and the truck stopped abruptly. The tall doctor patted his wife's shoulder, and she went into the house, but not without giving Joe another glance up and down. He looked down at himself and wondered what was so distasteful. He was wearing a buttoned shirt and pants—but his shirt tails hung out, his hair flopped down on his forehead, and he had a cigarette in his mouth. He hadn't even remembered lighting it.

"Doc, I need to talk to you," he yelled up toward the porch.

"Now, son, this is the Lord's Day. My office isn't—" the doctor started saying.

Joe walked briskly. The gravel crunched beneath his feet, the sound grating on his nerves. His stomach pulsed and his heart felt empty. Nothing was right. Nothing felt right.

"I don't care about your office hours," Joe said. "My Irene died on a Sunday afternoon a lot like this one and you came. Are you telling me that you didn't work that day because it was the Lord's Day? You didn't do anything to save her, so maybe you didn't."

The doctor let out a heavy sigh and waved Joe to the porch bench. It was too pretty to sit on, so he stood.

"Listen, Joe, your Irene was too far gone. You saw how much blood she lost." The doctor had his arm around Joe now and it was so heavy on his shoulders that he couldn't shrug it off. "Why are you here, son?"

Joe felt sobs push up through his stomach, then his heart, and filled his mouth as he spoke.

"It's my little girl, Doc. I don't know what to do." He pulled away from the doctor and walked back to his truck. Daisy still sat there as blankly as before. He gathered her into his arms and walked back toward the doctor. "It's Daisy. She needs your help—I need your help."

Dr. Sherman eyed the girl in Joe's arms and led them into the house rather than the clinic. Joe followed. He then told the doctor the whole story as Daisy sat motionless on the parlor couch.

"I saw your little girl once. That Amish woman was doing real good with her. What happened, son?" The doctor's voice was the complete opposite of the doctors out in the field. When there's blood everywhere and limbs lost, you don't get words like *son* or the inflection of a gentleman.

What happened? The man asked what happened? Joe had happened. Joe hadn't died in Saipan but had lived to tell the tale of what hell was like. He squeezed his eyes shut when he heard a mortar round, yelling, gunfire—everything was red. He told the doctor the story of their morning.

"You've gotta help her. I don't know what to do. I'm no good at being a dad now that Irene's gone, and even when I try really hard, I just mess everything up."

Mrs. Sherman came into the parlor and handed each of them a tall glass of lemonade. When Daisy didn't respond, she sat the glass on a coaster on the coffee table in front of her. The lack of enthusiasm—or any emotion—made Joe put the ice-cold glass against his face to cool him. The woman smiled so nicely at him too. He didn't deserve her smile.

"Thank you, ma'am."

She nodded back at him, then quickly brought the doctor's black medical bag.

Dr. Sherman moved to sit next to Daisy and waved a hand in front of her eyes without response. He examined her eyes with a small light. When he lifted her arm and released it, it flopped down onto her lap without any resistance. He rubbed his jaw before patting Daisy's knee then returned to his chair.

"I believe, given what you said she just experienced this morning, that Daisy is in a state of catatonia." Dr. Sherman leaned back into his chair and pulled a leg up onto his knee.

"What does that mean? Can you cure her?" Joe scooted to the edge of the couch and instinctively took Daisy's hand, finding it limp in his own.

"From what you're telling me, she's been accustomed to a very different life. Her life has been very protected and comfortable with this Amish woman. She's taught her how to manage in the world around her, but this morning she was in what to her was a vastly different situation. And for her to be put into a closet—dark and with the door shut—that may have been enough to push her into this state." He paused and studied the little girl from across the room for several moments. "Her deaf and dumbness is a condition that the medical world has come to understand a great deal about, and there have been advancements made—though I'm far from an expert—but there are still things we cannot understand. Imagine not being able to communicate and that the world around you lacks any empathy toward you. It continues to move at a pace you cannot keep up with. Eventually what response would you have? I would venture to say that among the deaf and blind, this is common with exposure to something new."

"So, what can you do for her? Is there a medicine you can give her?"

"I'm sorry, Joe, but there's not."

"But what am I going to do?" Joe gestured toward Daisy. "Look at her. Look! You can't leave her like this."

"Here's what I suggest." The doctor leaned toward Joe. "Now, I'm no expert in something like this, but I have a few thoughts. First, I'd get her back into a situation that she's familiar and comfortable with. I'm not sure exactly what that is for her, but I'm guessing you might know. She has experienced some trauma, but I think she'll pull through with a little time. Familiar, comfortable, with no stress. That'll be a good start."

"Okay." Joe took it all in and nodded his head. Just as he'd suspected, he was the problem.

"But that isn't going to work forever."

"What do you mean? This is going to keep happening?"

"Now, now. Keep your shirt on, son. Let me finish." He raised his eyebrows at Joe as if questioning whether he wanted to hear anything further.

Joe sighed.

"I think she'll come back around, but in the long term, I think you should consider a deaf school."

Joe stood and brushed away the doctor's words with his hands.

"I'm not sending her away to some institution. My mother did that with my brother, and he was dead in a few years."

The doctor stood as well.

"Your mother sent Jason to an asylum. I'm talking about a real school. Now, Joe, I've known you most of your life, and I know that where your brother was sent is not what I'm proposing. These are schools that help deaf children learn to get on in life, read—speak even."

"Speak?" He wanted to shake his head at what he was hearing.

While there was something to what the doctor was saying, Joe would never send her away. Esther would never forgive him and he would never forgive himself.

"I'm not sending her away." The darkness in his voice cast a shadow over the room.

"You might not have to, Joe. But you do have to do something if you want more for her life than this." He paused for a few moments. "Come to think of it, I might have a pamphlet about a school." The doctor excused himself.

As Joe waited, he began imagining how it would be to hear Daisy speak clearly. It would almost be as if she wasn't deaf at all. Right?

"Here you go." The doctor handed him a pamphlet. "Esther's done right fine for her—more than anyone would've ever expected—but she's probably taken Daisy as far as she can at this point. These schools, however, have trained teachers who could take her the rest of the way through her education—and into life."

Joe took the brochure and opened it up like an accordion. There were pictures of children smiling at their teachers. A schoolroom filled with children who were apparently deaf, and it looked nicer than the school he had taught in years earlier.

"This says the school is for residents of Alabama." Joe pointed at the small print.

"The tuition for students from Alabama is covered by the state's funding. Daisy would have to pay tuition, but I'm sure there are grants or scholarships available." He paused. "I'm sure something could be worked out."

Joe left the doctor's house after much apology and thanks. Joe cradled Daisy again and took her back to the truck. After sitting in the truck for several minutes, Joe knew what he needed to do.

Esther

The room was filled with men eating after church; she'd served them all desserts without having really seen any of them aside from Harvey.

"Esther?" Her father stood in front of her sometime later. "You sure are lost in your thoughts."

She gave him a weak smile, then looked confused. "Where's your plate?"

"Oh, I ate a little." He threw a thumb over his shoulder to the corner of the room where he ate, not sharing a table with anyone because of his *bann*. "Were you expecting Daisy? Looks like Joe just dropped her off."

"What?"

Esther looked out the window where her father had pointed. Sure enough, Daisy stood there. Even at a distance, Esther could see that her face was sullen and—somehow different. Esther left the table quickly and ran out to the little girl.

"Where's your dad?" Esther signed and looked around.

Daisy's blank eyes didn't find Esther's. She looked past the little girl and could see tire marks. This didn't sound like Joe. His commitment to Daisy had seemed secure. Something had to have gone terribly wrong. Here she was again with a little English girl with a crowd of eyes on her. She'd been here before. The weight of the unknown pushed down on her.

"How about we just go home?" her father suggested, coming up behind them.

Esther looked at him and saw two plates of food in his hands—one for her and one for Daisy.

"You can bring the plates back later," he whispered. "And I gave you an extra serving of tapioca. You always loved tapioca when you were little."

The most unlikely person had just become Esther's rescuer.

Joe

What had he just done? Had he just left his daughter with Esther again? But this time he hadn't even offered an explanation. Parenting her alone had just turned into a disaster. The doctor had suggested surrounding her with what was familiar and comfortable. That would be Esther. Not him.

He walked up to Esther's house that evening, and hadn't even made it up the porch when Esther came flying out. She wasn't wearing her head covering as usual, and she was barefoot, as when he left Daisy with her and she was working in the garden. Her eyes were on fire and her skin was as fair and soft as the peach sunset. He was taken with her for the moment.

"What have you done?" she said to him and got within inches from him. She was several inches shorter than he, but her pride and strength grew her easily to his six-foot height. "I have a little girl in there who won't talk, won't eat, and won't even cry. Her dad ran out on her for the second time."

By this point, she had her hand pushing against his chest. It was warm, and suddenly he had the urge to grab her by the waist and pull her close to kiss her. He looked down into her face and she was breathing heavily—angrily.

Their eyes locked for the moment, and he did what his instincts told him to do. In a wave of desire, his mouth was on hers.

Esther

Esther wasn't sure what had gotten into Joe when suddenly his lips were on hers and his hands held her tightly against his body—right in front of her home for all to see. What had gotten into her for kissing him back after everything that had happened? Had any buggies passed by and witnessed the intimacy?

This kiss was different from the few others they'd shared. Joe's salty lips were eager, and his hands moved from her waist to the small of her back, pressing her into him. She wrapped her fist in his half-unbuttoned shirt while her other hand found his warm chest. Her passion grew and an unknown stirring turned in circles and wrapped around every inch of her insides. She was full and empty. Satisfied and hungry. It was thrilling and frightening all at once and unlike anything she'd ever experienced. Every time they kissed she found her connection to him deepen—that she saw his fears, his humor, and his thoughts all the more clearly. But this was not right.

Esther pushed away from him—far enough to break their connection but close enough that when the palm of her hand flew to his cheek, it stung her skin and her heart. She'd never slapped anyone before, and in the moment that she hit Joe, she knew that there was a fine line between desire and malice. In all ways that she imagined, Joe pushed her past her limitations.

"Why did you do that?" He was out of breath.

"Why did *you* do that?" Their breathing mirrored the other.

Joe didn't answer. He didn't even touch the cheek that she'd slapped. In the dim light of the sunset, Esther could see her handprint's red imprint on his tanned skin. Then there he was—Joe Garrison, the Joe whom Irene had fallen in love with, had swept her cousin off her feet. But there was something still changed about him. It was more than the experiences of war and more than Daisy. His eyes weren't filled with the memory of a love affair and marriage to a naive Amish girl, but a deep cascading desire. But desire for *what*?

"Why did you do that?" she asked again, this time in a whisper. She wanted an answer, didn't she? What if he'd done it only out of misplaced passion? Or did he desire her? Had he gone from tolerating her at the train station to caring about her now? To what extent did he care? Or was she just a plaything to him?

With these thoughts running through her mind, her soul told her that she was talking about herself, not him. Were these her feelings? She desired him. As the days and weeks went on, the shared time had turned into her own attachment to him. Was it the way he had fought for Daisy and how hard he was trying to learn sign language? Or the way he'd let her stay the night on Daisy's first night home? Or the way he'd looked at her when he'd returned early the next morning? The way he'd kissed her. She'd had to fight the shame of being in Irene's nightgown, but his blue eyes hadn't looked at her accusingly or even regretfully when he saw his dead wife's clothes on another woman. There was something else there. But what? She didn't know.

"I don't know why," Joe finally answered. He stepped back and ran a hand through his waves. His hands hung loosely on his hips and he looked at Esther. "I don't know." His repeated words danced on the dusky breeze.

Their eyes locked for what seemed like the length of the sunset. By that time, Esther noticed, the peach, pink, and purple had been covered with a blanket of black. All she could think of was the kiss. Her body was still reacting to their mingled passions, though they were so far beneath her Amish clothing. Was her body stirring, or was her imagination? But right now she needed to be Daisy's guardian and get answers.

"What happened with Daisy?"

Her eyes roamed his. He looked beyond her into the face of the moon. His tanned skin had made his eyes appear lighter even in the drape of night they stood in. He bit his lip—the same lips that had been on hers.

"Joe, talk to me," she ordered.

"It was awful, okay?" He splayed his arms and hands out toward her, his eyes desperate. "No one at church understood anything about her and even wondered why I brought her. Since she couldn't hear the *Good News* of Jesus, why does she have to be there at all, right? Then Mrs. Underhill."

He hung his head and a mixed sigh and groan escaped his mouth.

"You wouldn't understand. You're so good with her. I'm not like you, Esther. I'm not perfect. I'm not patient."

"I wouldn't understand?" Esther had barely heard the rest of what he said. "What do you mean by that?"

"You should've seen the way they looked at her—at me." He tapped his own chest. "They made it out like I was lying about her deafness. They acted like she was second-rate and didn't deserve to be there with the rest of the kids—who were little devils."

"Don't you remember what you said in your letter to me when I told you that she was deaf? Don't you remember that at the train station only a few months ago you talked extra loud to her, thinking she would hear you? You didn't believe me, Joe. You treated her second-rate because you didn't understand. I saw the shame in your eyes at the train station when people stopped to stare at her." Esther's throat throbbed in pain. Her voice had to push past the emotional knot that was lodged there. "You wouldn't let me take her to the doctor who might have had some idea of how to help, so instead I had to figure it out on my own. You have no idea how difficult it was for us. You're the one who doesn't understand."

"Well, I messed up again," he yelled. "Now look at her. She's—she's—not Daisy anymore. The doctor called it catatonia and said that she should be in a familiar and comfortable setting."

"What?"

Joe went on to tell Esther everything that had happened that morning and what the doctor had told him. Part of her wanted to scold him for leaving her with the Sunday school teacher at all. What was he thinking? She could only imagine the panic Daisy experienced when no one could communicate with her.

With everything that Joe was saying, the color in his face drained by degrees. He kicked the dirt and picked up a rock and with a loud yell threw it in the field.

"After all of this, it's finally clear to me that you've been right all along. I'm no good for her." His voice warbled now and his eyes sparked with emotion. "She's better off with you. I failed, Esther. I failed."

Esther could think of nothing to say. After too many uncomfortable moments, Joe turned and left.

Joe

Joe sounded the horn when he drove into Esther's drive at six the next morning to let Chet know he was there. He hadn't slept well and had been up since four. He'd finished all the coffee in the house and hadn't eaten much of a breakfast. This routine would have to do. The last thing he wanted to do was see Esther or Daisy. The shame that weighed on his shoulders was too great.

Many things grieved him—his irresponsibility with Daisy, his argument with Esther, and the kiss. It hadn't been the right time to kiss her, but he'd followed his instinct. That woman needed to be kissed, and by the reaction he got, she knew it. Their closeness always felt like more than a kiss but an exchange of passions, devotions, and thoughts. It made him want to keep learning about Esther—and to kiss her again.

This was where his thoughts became muddled. The draw he had to her was too unexpected. During his time at war, he rarely thought of coming home, remarrying, and settling down again. He'd filled his mind with happy memories of Irene and Daisy and tried to forget that it was all just a fantasy.

His thoughts toward Esther trespassed the boundaries he'd

set for himself. Esther was more than a temptation of a deprived man, but he'd sent her away when she asked questions he didn't like. He wasn't sure he could ever be the kind of man who could be vulnerable enough to keep a wife. Irene had made it easy to be himself, but that man didn't exist anymore. When things had just begun to make sense, everything changed again, and he missed his daughter.

The tension and changes caused his night terrors to be more active than ever before. They had slowed down with Daisy at home. He would wake up in a cold sweat every few nights and had once found himself under the bed, taking refuge in what he thought was a foxhole, and breathing quickly through his teeth as if preparing to fight the enemy.

This week he hadn't bothered to tether himself to his bed, partly as penance for his mistakes. During a night terror, he found himself standing in Daisy's room, her clothes pulled out from her bureau and tossed everywhere. Another time, he woke in the middle of the road, facing in the direction of Esther's house. Was his subconscious telling him to go to his daughter? To Esther? These night terrors weren't like the ones from before. Instead of hearing gunshots, his squad leader yelling orders, men screaming, and bombs exploding, he simply heard nothing. It wasn't just quiet; it was complete silence. Visions of Daisy's tied hands would cut into his mind, and when he would go to rescue her, he found that his own were tied as well.

"Garrison." The gruff voice right behind him made Joe jump.

"Yes, sir," Joe said, raising his hand to salute.

"Now, now, don't you go and salute me. Those days are over for me—but," Wayne winced a little, "I wanted to talk to you about something. Let's go in my trailer for a smoke."

Joe was intrigued by his boss's comment and wasn't going to turn down a cigarette. He'd run out two days ago and hadn't been anywhere to buy more. Wayne's trailer was cooler than the heat of the sun outside, and it was cared for meticulously. As it appeared to Joe, nothing was out of place.

"Sit down," Wayne said and gestured to the chair on the other side of the small table that was used as a desk. Wayne pushed a cigarette package across the table and a matchbook behind it. "I've got a proposition for you."

A proposition?

"Maybe we can call it a mission." Wayne winked.

Something about this conversation didn't sound right to Joe but he would hear him out.

"I'm taking a crew over to God-forsaken Poland to help with reconstruction. We'll be gone for maybe six months or maybe longer."

We?

"I don't want to go over with a bunch of jokesters, but some fellows ready to get the job done. Wage would go up, not as high as it was when you were serving, but better than what you're making now." Wayne paused to take a pull from his cigarette. "I'd like you to come as my right-hand man. What do you say?"

"Go over there? To Poland?"

Wayne chuckled and leaned back in his chair.

"I know you were in the islands, but I'm sure it ain't looking much better. Those countries are torn up. And we can make some good money and do a lot of good, of course."

"What about your wife?" Joe asked.

Wayne waved a hand at him and mumbled something under his breath. "At least you don't have to worry about a wife." He sat up in his chair and stretched as he stood.

No. He didn't have a wife. He had Daisy. And then there was Esther. But would it matter? For nearly a week, they'd been living separate lives, and he didn't know if that would ever change.

"Well? Can I count on you?" He pointed a finger at him, reminding him of the Uncle Sam posters saying *I want you.*

"I'll need to think about it," Joe said. He'd just told Esther that he wasn't any good at parenting. Daisy would ultimately be happier with Esther anyway—if she was ever herself again anyway. She could go back to the world that had begun to accept her for who she was and never be put through Joe's poor decision making. Esther could be her mother—he'd never asked, but wasn't that what she wanted? Irene would approve of that much anyway, though she would hardly approve of anything else.

"I need an answer by the end of the week. We ship off next month." Wayne opened the door to the small trailer. "What about Chet? I was thinking of asking him."

"I thought you said he was a good-for-nothing?"

Wayne shrugged. "He's not so bad. He's really proven himself over the last few months. Done pretty good work lately, and the guys all like him. He might be good for morale." Wayne walked out and was calling out orders before the door slammed shut, leaving Joe alone.

"He asked you, didn't he?" Chet asked him as they drove home a few hours later. "To go to Poland."

Joe looked over at the older man. This was the first time in all their weeks of working together that Chet hadn't fallen asleep by this point on their way home. He really had cleaned up his act at work also. Joe had to agree with Wayne.

"Did he ask you?" Joe questioned.

"Sure did." Chet nodded his head dramatically. "That was an easy decision. I ain't going."

Joe shrugged, keeping his eyes straight ahead. "You're not even going to think about it?"

"What's there to think about? I returned to Sunrise to get away from that life. I'm settling down."

"It's just six months or so. It's not forever."

"That's how it starts. But it's never over, Joe. Six months in Poland, and then something else will come up or it'll get extended to a year. Then with one thing or another, it'll be years before you return and your girl won't even know you—again."

"Are we talking about you or me?" Daisy wouldn't forget him. She was older now. And it wouldn't be the way he made it out to be. It would be six months, and then he'd be home. Maybe a little while away would do them both some good. He could come back and they could have a fresh start.

"Both of us. You know that. We both went running off, away from our demons, for one reason or another, and we missed out. You and me, we ain't much different."

Joe laughed, getting angry. "You and me? You left your family and made everyone believe you were dead. You were away for almost thirty years."

Joe turned into Esther's drive roughly, spinning gravel. Chet had no right to talk to him that way.

"I don't deny it. It's the worst decision I ever made. I seem to remember you leaving behind a particular little girl. You might have had different demons chasing you, but they were there and maybe they still are." Chet opened the truck door. He grimaced in frustration. He'd never shown so much passion in anything before. "You think on it long and hard, son. There's a little girl in there who can barely eat for grieving over her daddy. And there's a woman in there who I think might love you and I think you love her right back. You ready to walk away from that?"

Joe waved his words off.

"I just don't think I can stay here. It's just too hard. Daisy's better off."

"Listen, I told myself that for years—for decades. But what it came down to was this. Who do you love more? Daisy and Esther—or yourself?"

"Don't you preach to me. I know I'm a terrible dad, Chet. And I think you know all about that." He threw the low blow hard enough to hit the older man deep in the gut.

Chet shook his head. "Well, I'm going to keep trying with my girl. Someday it'll be too late, but it's not too late right now."

~

The next morning Joe woke up sitting on the couch with his shotgun on his lap. Loaded and ready. What if he'd taken the shotgun to Esther's house in his sleep? He would have to tie himself up again—leash himself to the bed like an animal before he hurt someone, or worse. And then he would have to leave. He was too dangerous to be around the two people he loved most—Daisy and Esther.

He knocked hard on Esther's wooden door. It was barely five o'clock, and Esther was in her nightgown when she opened the door. Her face was pale, as if she'd just woken up, which she probably had. Her hair was in a long braid that cascaded down the front of her shoulder. She was striking even in the early morning. Esther's Amish dresses were always so cinched at the waist that having the billowing thin fabric hanging loosely around her body made his mind wander. He looked away—she was too distracting.

"Joe?" She widened the door and looked around at the quiet road before she walked out onto the front porch.

She rubbed her face and Joe realized how tired she looked.

"I just couldn't wait any longer to have this conversation." He began pacing the creaky porch.

"Conversation?" Esther touched his arm and looked at him in the eyes. "Have you slept at all?"

Joe pulled his arm from her warm touch.

"I could say the same thing about you."

"Daisy's not sleeping." Esther stated it so simply, there was no hint of condemnation in her tone. "She's much improved from Sunday, but she's—"

"I'm leaving," Joe interrupted. "And I want you to keep Daisy."

She would grow accustomed to the new arrangement. She had once before, and she would again. She loved Esther. Esther loved Daisy. They were good together.

Esther hung her head and shook it back and forth. She leaned against the rail of the porch. "Oh, Joe. What are you talking about?"

"My boss wants me to go to Poland with him to help with reconstruction. It's a great opportunity, and you and Daisy will want for nothing. I'll send you most of my check. I won't go through Angelica this time." He spoke everything fast to get it all out, afraid he might take it all back if spoken slowly. "Maybe when I get back . . ."

His voice faded.

"What?" Esther stood straighter. Her voice was barely audible. Her large dark eyes blinked and her tears fell. He wasn't sure she'd ever looked so pretty. Large teardrops, glimmering in the sunrise, trailed down her cheeks.

Joe looked away and stared at the sunrise until his eyes burned.

"I can't stay." Joe's heart shrunk into itself and beat only half beats at a time now. Pain. But he had made too many mistakes with her already and with his night terrors—he couldn't bring her home. "I'm no good for her. I'm no good for you."

Esther

Esther had a mix of emotions about having Daisy living with her again. When she'd arrived years earlier, she'd been wild and uncontrollable, but this time she was so quiet, she nearly blended into the wall.

The morning after Esther got her back, Daisy woke with her eyes focusing again and signing ferociously about wanting to see her daddy. After she realized she'd been dropped off again, she wouldn't leave Esther's side. During the first week, she would sleep soundly for only an hour at a time; then it took another hour to calm her out of her terrors. As much as Esther loved Daisy and would sacrifice her very life for her, it was clear that at this point, the little girl was more than she knew what to do with. Convincing Joe to stay and nurture that relationship a second time might work, but being bounced back and forth between the two of them was not the answer.

Joe had avoided Esther for more than a week. She had tried to talk to him in the short period that Daisy was asleep, but he wouldn't answer his door. When he came to pick up her dad for work, he wouldn't get out the truck.

"Give him a little more time, sweetheart," her dad told her. "I'm working on him."

But after nearly two weeks, Esther had exhausted her efforts and wasn't sleeping well herself. She woke in the middle of the night, feeling as if she'd been tapped on the shoulder by some unseen being. An owl was surprisingly loud right outside her window. Calling her. Blue moonlight filtered through the window and created a path to the open bedroom door.

Why was it open?

Esther's head snapped over to Daisy's cot. She wasn't there. Esther was at the bedside in half a breath. The small afghan that Esther had finally finished crocheting for Daisy was unraveled and in a heap on top of the cot. Esther ran her hands through the tangled mess. Panic stirred in Esther's middle, and her insides began to tremble.

She nearly tripped over her own feet as she ran down the closed staircase. The front door was open. The grass was damp and the moon was high in the sky. It was round and silvery and she silently thanked God for the light it yielded. She ran the entire way to Joe's house. Her breath was ragged as she turned into the drive. A loud, anguished yell came through the open front door and windows. But it wasn't Daisy. It was Joe.

Esther picked up her pace and slipped on the dewy grass. Her heart was beating so wildly and her breathing had turned to sobbing.

As soon as she got through the front door, she stood there and took in her surroundings as she caught her breath. An August breeze picked up her nightgown and made it billow up around her. The warm breath of summer was cool against her skin. Nothing looked unusual. Esther walked into the house and turned into Daisy's room. Tears poured from her eyes when she found the little girl curled up in her bed, sleeping soundly.

Esther went to her and knelt by the bed. She touched the little girl, as if trying to confirm that she was not just a figment of her imagination. The little girl was real. She was there. Her chest rose and fell, and a soft sigh escaped Daisy's mouth.

As her heart settled down, she remembered that she'd rushed into the house after hearing Joe yell. As if on cue, more yelling sounded from upstairs.

"No! No!"

As Esther left Daisy and closed her door, she bounded up the stairs. Everything else she heard was garbled. Joe's door was closed. She heard something pounding on the floor. Scratching. Yelling. Crying. She knew she should not go in. Entering a man's room while he was inside was something she'd never done. Joe was probably not fully dressed.

The metal doorknob squealed as she turned it. She pushed the door open and the whine that came from the hinges was deafening in the sudden silence. She looked at Joe's bed and it was empty. She stepped inside the room slowly and walked around to the other side of the bed to find Joe hunkered in the fetal position on the floor. The sight of him and how quiet he was confused her, and she went to his side. He was wearing only pajama bottoms. His chest was bare and his muscles were flexed. Esther had never seen a man in this state of undress. When her hand went to his arm, his skin was warm. His head gently lolled next to her on the floor. He was so peaceful at the moment. Why had he been yelling, and why was he on the floor? Perhaps he'd just fallen off his bed in the midst of a dream.

It was dark in the room, but a little of the moon's glow filtered through the window. She moved her hands down the side of his body, inspecting him. His muscles were tense, but he remained asleep. When she got to his ankles, she saw the rope she'd found weeks ago around one. His sock was mostly off, and the rope was twisted tightly like a tourniquet. He was too big and heavy for her to uncoil it; she should wake him up anyway to explain that Daisy was downstairs. She would also insist that he explain to her why he was tied to his bed.

Suddenly Joe grabbed her arm and gripped her tightly. He

pulled her toward him so roughly her neck cracked. He pushed her down onto the floor and was on top of her before she was able to make a single sound. The bed shifted with his movement. His teeth were bared, and his eyes were open as he hovered over her. His hands were on either side of her shoulders, but he was so heavy she couldn't move.

"No." He yelled into her face.

"Joe," she cried and put her hands on his face. His eyes were on her, but he didn't see her. Where was he? "Joe, it's me—Esther."

She spoke with as much force as she could, but no matter how loud she screamed, he didn't hear her. He didn't *wake up*. He punched the floorboard next to her head. Panic surfaced, and with all her strength, she slapped Joe across the face. She did it again. After the third time, the hit startled him. She did it again. And she saw his eyes turning from terror to recognition.

"Esther?" He was out of breath and his voice was hoarse. "Esther?"

Esther couldn't answer but wept from the fear and relief. He instantly moved off her and leaned against the bed, holding his head in his hands. Her muscles twitched from the sudden release of tension. She looked into Joe's eyes, and the gentleness in them was in such contrast to the sandpaper gaze from only moments before. Had they really come from the same man? Neither of them moved. Only Esther's quiet weeping filled the room.

Joe's blond waves fell between his fingers. He was still catching his breath. Esther scooted away from him but didn't have the energy to get up from the floor.

"Did I hurt you?" Joe's words fell into gaps between half sobs, as he didn't raise his head to speak.

Esther closed her eyes and took several deep breaths before she pushed herself up from the floor.

"No," was all she could say.

"Did I hurt you?" He spoke louder and with more force and raised his eyes to look at her.

"No." She matched his intensity.

Esther tried to stifle the cry that continued to grow in her throat. She wanted to stop weeping but couldn't. The intensity of the moments when Joe was enraged was too alarming.

"Why didn't you tell me?" she asked.

"Why are you here?" He didn't answer her question. He stared out the window. The small bit of light that traveled in caught his eyes. Sadness bloomed and broke her heart.

Esther couldn't answer, and the two remained silent for what seemed like an hour. When she found that she was breathing normally again, she spoke. "I woke and Daisy was gone."

"Is she all right?" Joe's eyes sharpened.

"Yes. She's downstairs in her room sleeping." She spoke only above a whisper. "She walked here in her sleep."

Joe hung his head.

"It's because of me." His soft voice broke. "It's my fault."

Esther gathered her strength and moved toward Joe. She moved her hand out toward him and then pulled it back; then she reached for him again and gently caressed his hair. He startled at her touch at first, then leaned into her touch. Esther had never touched a man so intimately. His flaxen hair fell like fine corn silk between her fingers. It had grown long since he'd come home and fell over his ears, making him look younger. The muscles in his shoulders were tense, and his skin gleamed with sweat.

Joe suddenly jumped up and pulled his leg to rid it of the rope. But it was tighter than ever, and the bed skidded. He yelled as he continued to pull. Esther backed away before she stood. She went to Joe's side and her hand stuttered forward before she finally took his arms, holding both of them gently to calm him.

"Let me," she said. She went down the stairs on wobbly legs and went to the kitchen for a serrated knife. Joe was standing in the same position when she returned. It took great effort to saw through the rope, but when she did, it untwisted and released. She moved over on the wooden floor and took Joe's calf in one hand and with a gentle lift carefully took the rope from his ankle. He winced.

"I'm sorry," she said, looking at him.

"Don't apologize to me. I'm getting what I deserve."

Joe

Joe let Esther tend to his wound. Her touch was healing, and her very presence was a salve to his soul. Though with that came shame, deeper than perhaps he'd ever experienced before. It was different from Saipan.

Esther broke the silence. "Why didn't you tell me?"

"Would you have wanted Daisy living here if you knew this? The rope was working." He flinched as she cleaned his wound.

"How can you say it was working? Look at your ankle."

"I'm not worried about myself. I'm worried about not hurting my daughter and destroying my home." Joe knew she wouldn't understand. How could she?

Esther finished bandaging his wound, and he suddenly realized he was shirtless. Neither of them was in the state of dress they were used to. She was wearing a simple nightgown, and while it swelled around her and hid the curves, it was thin and almost revealing. Her hair was held back in a thin white cotton bonnet, neatly tied under her chin. He wanted to take the covering off her and pull the pins from her bun so he could see her once again with her hair cascading down her back.

"When did the nightmares start?" she asked gently.

He bit his lip. Should he tell her the whole story? Did he really want to relive it again?

Esther sat with his ankle in her lap. He relinquished himself to her touch. She looked up at him and kept her eyes on him. Her face was pure and breathtaking. He remembered the way she'd put her hand through his hair and touched his bare skin and shivered at the thought of it.

With deep breaths and with slow and careful words, he told her about his time in Saipan and the night that he let his squad down.

"So you left your squad?" Esther asked. "I don't understand everything in the military, but I know it wasn't your fault that so many men were killed."

"Yes, it was," he insisted.

He told her about losing his temper the following morning and hitting Sergeant Barker, and about the humiliation of being transferred and losing a stripe.

"It was only a few weeks later that we got word that my entire platoon was annihilated."

"What?"

"Almost all of them were killed. The few who weren't lost limbs or may as well be dead."

"And this causes your nightmares?"

Caused them. Tormented him. It was like the rope on the bed. The memories of that night tied him forever to the belief that he'd failed and that he should've died along with his men.

"I shouldn't be here. I should've died with my men. I never should've come home."

Esther shook her head. "You're wrong, Joe."

"I'm not wrong. And look at what it's caused." He threw his hands up in the air. "I could've really hurt you. I could've killed you."

"Joe, listen to me." Esther moved his ankle gently onto the

floor and knelt next to him, taking his hands. "God spared you. Believe *that* instead of believing that you're going to hurt me or Daisy."

Joe shook his head. "You don't know that."

"But I do. We have both had a lot of loss. I have had to believe that God has a plan in all the hurt and pain. How else could I have gone on?"

Joe looked at her and put his hand on her cheek. Tears welled up in her eyes. She believed what she said. She believed that God had a plan for all of his heartache.

"But were you happy?"

Esther furrowed her brow and her lips pursed into a small frown. He wanted to kiss away the pain that he could see sewn through her face. His thumb caressed her beneath her eye, wiping tears away.

"I don't think I knew real happiness—until Daisy." As she spoke, her face twitched with anguish and honesty. She inhaled several times and looked down. He lifted her chin, forcing her to look at him. "And, now you've made me feel things that . . ."

"Esther." His voice brushed smoothly against his throat. He didn't know how to say what he was feeling. He didn't know how to tell her that he wasn't the same person who had loved Irene. He was a different man now—because of losing his wife, the war, Daisy's deafness—because of Esther. She was the one he thought about when he woke and when he fell asleep. He wasn't sure when it had begun, but he knew it would never end.

There was silence for several minutes. Then the clock on the wall chimed four o'clock.

Esther broke the silence. "You should get some rest."

Joe smiled at her words. She was always taking care of everyone around her, even him.

"I can't unless I know you and Daisy are safe at your house, and I can't ask you to leave in the middle of the night like this.

It's not safe for you both to be here. I'll go—somewhere—so can you sleep here."

Esther shook her head. "No."

"But I might hurt you. I will. I know it. The rope is too small to tie again."

"I'm not going anywhere, and neither are you." Esther's eyes were velvety soft as she gazed into his. She gently pushed him to lie on the bed, but he didn't stay down.

What was she doing? She pulled the rest of the rope off of the bed and threw it on the floor.

"You don't need this anymore."

"I don't understand, Esther."

"You're not dangerous, Joe, and I'm going to prove it to you." She moved next to the bed on the floor and put her head on the mattress, next to his pillow.

"No, Esther." His face twitched. "I could hurt you. I could really hurt you. And this isn't right. I don't want to put you in this type of position. What if someone finds out you stayed here alone with me?"

"This is between me and you, not the church."

He couldn't believe she'd just said that.

"I'm not afraid of you. You are not dangerous. I'm staying right here. You don't even need to touch me." Esther nestled in.

Didn't she know how much he wanted to touch her? How much he wanted to kiss her? How having her that close in the quiet of the night made him want all of her? Didn't she understand what she did to him?

"I can't, Esther. You don't understand—"

"I trust you." She patted his space on the bed. She yawned and repeated her words in a whisper. "I trust you."

Her eyes fluttered, and her even breathing told him that she was falling asleep. What if she wasn't right? What if he had another fit and he hurt her? He'd told her why he was tormented.

She believed in him. She trusted him by putting herself in a position that could go wrong in so many ways for them both.

He sat for a long time and watched her sleep. Her eyelashes rested gently on her fair cheeks. Her pink lips full and perfect. A quiet sigh escaped her mouth. He leaned forward and kissed her forehead, as light as a feather. A light smile played over her lips for a split second.

"I love you," he whispered, and he meant it.

Then he put his head down on the pillow next to Esther and let himself fall asleep.

Esther

Esther woke squinting her eyes as the sunrise cast its light on her. A heaviness lay across her, and she smiled when she saw that it was Joe's arm hanging off the bed around her. His tousled hair glowed in the light. He'd finally let himself sleep. She was right. He hadn't hurt her. He'd slept soundly.

Her body was stiff, and she readjusted gently so not to wake Joe. She wanted him to keep sleeping—and she wanted to keep watching him.

In a few hours, they would be at Alvin and Dorothy's barn raising. While she was glad he was going, she was sure that everyone would know of what had occurred between them and her feelings for him. Wasn't it all written across her brow for everyone to see?

For the first time, she understood why Irene left all she knew—her family, her church, her life—for Joe. She could imagine waking to his eyes and touch every morning. His voice would be the last she would hear at night. To know that she would forever be Daisy's mother. Did it cheapen Irene's death by imagining a life with Joe? She couldn't avoid letting her imagination take her to this place though she knew it wouldn't be right for her.

She couldn't grasp life away from the Amish. She'd gained such security and constancy from the church. She was loyal to the community and to the faithfulness of serving God. Anything other than her life as it was with the church was completely unfamiliar, even peculiar.

She ignored the push-pull for the moment and let her eyes graze over his tanned face; she longed to see his eyes open so that she could sink into their blueness. She'd never imagined feeling this way about a man. Before now, she wasn't sure she'd believed in real love. But Joe wasn't any man, he was the forbidden fruit. Had he really said that he loved her the night before? In the light of day, she wasn't sure if she'd heard it or dreamed it. But he was leaving for Poland in a few weeks. The idea of watching him walk away again, this time with her heart in his hands, started a fire inside her.

"Don't leave me," she whispered as she ran a finger over the side of his face.

When Joe's eyes opened, Esther realized how close his face was to hers. They looked at each other for several long moments.

"Daisy needs you. Don't go away again."

All that could be heard was the sizzle of the large red sun lifting from its cradle in the far horizon. The scent of heat was in the air, but a chill ran down Esther's back.

"I need you," she finally admitted in a whisper. "Please, don't leave."

Joe

Though Alvin and Dorothy Bender's house was only a short walk up Sunrise Valley Road, Joe drove so he could bring his tools. He had never been to a barn raising, but since he'd been invited, he wanted to be useful. When he drove up, he moved slowly behind a line of buggies, his truck engine loud against the quiet sounds of hooves against the gravel.

Several families walked by the truck, and Daisy waved. The children waved back signing the word *play*. She'd woken up disoriented and confused, but Esther explained to her that if she wanted, she was allowed to stay with Joe and meet her at the barn raising. Daisy's smile returned within moments; she eyed Joe with suspicion, but decided to stay.

Joe parked on the side of the road and suddenly wished he'd taken up Irene's offer to learn Pennsylvania Dutch. The Amish children waved at them, but the women in their bonnets didn't look over. Joe hadn't been around his Amish in-laws since his return to Sunrise, never having had a comfortable relationship with them. His mother-in-law, Lucy, was a friendly woman, but his father-in-law, Roy, had discouraged any fraternizing with him. Why had Joe decided to attend?

His defenses had fallen because of Daisy's complete immersion into the Amish lifestyle. Or maybe it was because Esther had shown him a different side of the Amish that he hadn't seen before, not even from Irene, and it had changed his views on who these people might be. Esther had shown him that the Amish weren't so different from himself. They looked different, but they wanted the same things out of life. What Esther had done last night to prove that he wasn't dangerous was more than he imagined any woman, English or Amish, would ever do for him. Maybe he wasn't cured from his night terrors for good, but he finally had hope that it could happen.

"Good morning, Daisy-*maetleh*," his mother-in-law, Lucy Bender, said. As the older woman made a sign to Daisy, Joe recognized the signs for *sweet* and *eat*. "There are cinnamon rolls on the porch."

Daisy looked up at Joe, and his nod sent her running with several other children to the porch, ready to take her fill of the traditional Amish pastry. Daisy's long ponytails flew back behind her. He'd chosen a plainer dress for her out of the stock of clothing Mrs. White had given her so she wouldn't feel too out of place. He watched as she took a roll and was glad to see the glimmer in her eyes return.

"Joe," Lucy said and pinned her hands behind her back. Still, her wide smile provided some comfort to Joe. He could see Irene in the old woman's eyes. The eye shape was the same, and her voice had the same timbre as Irene's. Soft and sweet. Easy on the ears. "I'm surprised I haven't seen you since you came home."

Here was where the similarities ceased. Irene had never been very direct. She preferred easy conversations to anything that might bring along any discomfort. Irene had strived for peace between her and her family even after she'd been shunned, though several brothers refused to even look at her when they passed by each other. Her wishes had never been met.

"I wasn't sure I should visit," he admitted.

"It's been a long time," they both said together. Then they chuckled.

"Well, I think it's good you're here. And Daisy too. I hear you're a carpenter now—Alvin and Dorothy will be beholden. Maybe a little bit of our Irene's Amish ways rubbed off on you, after all."

The older woman winked at him, and he smiled. Then she became serious as she moved close to him.

"You took Irene from us, and I came to forgive you—even when she died." Lucy's voice quavered. "Leave Esther alone."

"But I—I'm not—" He was flustered. Her face was so tense, and he did not see the same laughter that had been there only a minute earlier.

"Isn't taking one Amish girl enough?" Lucy whispered, and then walked away.

Despite Lucy's words, all he could think about was finding Esther. Joe's eyes moved over the crowd ahead and saw how much he stood out from the Amish men. He didn't have a straw hat—or any hat for that matter—no suspenders, no beard, and no wife. The only resemblance was that all their faces had been tanned from the sun in their hours and days outside.

Where was Esther?

He turned to look down the road. Several more buggies were making their way toward the already crowded property. Children were running, playing kick the can, and the young women were whispering between parked buggies while pointing at the young men who were congregating near the site of the barn.

Where was Esther?

Then the sun forced its rays through the morning clouds and beamed down on her like a spotlight. She was leaning toward Chet as they walked down the sloped gravel drive. She hadn't noticed him yet. Chet responded to her and she elbowed him, giggling behind her free hand. Chet waved a hand at someone ahead and jogged off.

Around one of her elbows, Esther carried a basket covered with a white cheesecloth. The vision of waking up with her lying her head on his bed made his heart skip a beat and he cleared his throat. She looked over right at that moment and found his eyes.

Her smile gleamed in the sea of Amish faces. She had a sunkissed glow from her outdoor garden work that he hadn't noticed until now. Seeing her made it possible for him to stay and help with the building. Without her, he would leave. There was a crowd of ladies around her, preparing food, but her eyes continued to find his.

No one would know that she had been awake with him for hours during the night. Warmth filled his body and senses as he let his smile rest on her eyes. He didn't want to look away. Had they been alone, he would've kissed her again. When he saw his brother-in-law, Alvin, come into view, it was like a cold rush of air, reminding him that Esther was Irene's cousin. Esther was Amish. This was her world. Not his. Joe pulled himself from his dangerous thoughts.

Once everyone was gathered, Alvin spoke to the crowd, first in their dialect and then, when Alvin caught sight of Joe toward the back, in English. Half of the men standing before him turned to see what had caused the change in Alvin's speech and a quiet murmur ran through the crowd. Alvin didn't seem to care and continued. After Alvin thanked everyone, the men instinctively broke off into groups, adding to Joe's intimidation.

"Howdy, Joe," said Alvin as he ambled up to him. "Glad you could make it. Sure 'preciate the help."

Joe shook Alvin's offered hand. The tight grip from the Amish man and the way he looked directly into his eyes lessened Joe's discomfort. Alvin had grieved greatly over Irene's death.

Their family was so large and she was the only girl until she'd turned eighteen, so she had cared for many of her brothers like a mother while her mother cared for a newborn.

"Glad to be here," Joe said as both men released their hands and folded their arms in front of their chests. Irene's ghost stood alongside them.

"I heard you're a good carpenter, so just jump in where you can. Cold water is over there. We'll have a meal around noon and break again for supper."

Chet walked up to the two and clapped Joe on the back and shook Alvin's hand. The young Amish man was a little less warm and friendly to the older man, but it didn't diminish the smile on Chet's face. He looked so much like the other men now. His salt-and-pepper beard had grown faster than Joe had expected, and his clothing no longer looked newly sewn. His Texas twang was still present, however.

"Where do you want me?" Chester asked.

Alvin rubbed his brown beard several times as he surveyed the groups of men beginning to work. Roy Bender, Irene and Alvin's father, sidled up closely to impish Alvin. Roy was an imposing man at over six foot and had a booming voice. He crossed his arms over his inflated chest.

"I think we've got all the help we need there, Chester. Maybe you can make sure the horses have enough water." The father led his grown son away and left the Englisher and the outcast to stand alone.

"Water for the horses," Chester said in English to Joe. "Now that's what I call horse—"

"Don't, Chet," Joe stopped him, knowing exactly what he was about to say.

The older man walked off in a huff.

Joe took Alvin's advice and jumped right in. The foundation was already laid, and they quickly began to frame the walls and get them into place. It wouldn't be a large barn, since Alvin's farm was small. He would need enough space for their buggy and several horses that he trained. Joe worked on some of the interior walls. After some time, he could feel good-natured competition among the other men and joined in—which team could frame faster than the next or who could carry the most lumber. While he wasn't sure he cared to prove that he was as fast and good as any Amish man, deep in his mind, he wanted to prove to himself that he was good enough for the love of an Amish woman.

Esther

I t never ceased to amaze Esther how fast a barn could be built. When the building stopped around lunch, the barn was already completely framed. The efforts of so many people always proved to her the blessings of Amish life—a community of people who came together to serve, feed, build, even financially support one another. The warmth in her heart for her people was bested only by the sun's heat.

As she began to set up the food in the buffet line while the younger girls put up tables and their church benches for lunch, she saw Joe pour a ladle of cool water over his head. He shook off the excess and wiped a hanky down his face before stuffing it into the back pocket of his pants.

Without a moment's break, he spun his hammer in the air and caught the handle. The little boys made a bit of a racket over it, and he did it again, making them *ooh* and *ah*. As if he could feel her eyes on him, he turned and found her standing on the open lawn at the buffet table, watching him. After he held her gaze for several heated moments, he returned to his work, and she found that she'd held her breath through it. She had touched the skin beneath the shirt he wore. The fine waves of blond hair had moved through her fingers.

"Be careful, Esther," Dorothy warned. "If I can see who you're watching, I'm wondering who else can."

"Nah, Dorothy." Esther narrowed her eyes. The thought that Dorothy noticed her staring at Joe had made her face grow hot. "What are you suggesting?"

"I was hoping you'd tell me." Dorothy leaned toward Esther. "I'll keep your secret, but I know you're there late in the evening. I just want you to be careful because I think Lucy knows. I feel like I should tell you about what is being said, Esther."

Esther inhaled. "Tell me what?"

"Rumors about you and Joe. Your *dat*'s reputation shouldn't make a difference, but you know it does. I think, with how close you are to Daisy and Joe, people are waiting for the next Detweiler scandal."

"Look at Chester," someone said behind her with a laugh.

Esther's face burned. She recognized the voice as belonging to Nancy, a cousin's wife who was visiting Sunrise from Lancaster. Nancy was a woman who thought very highly of herself and enjoyed her fancy *kapp* and sleeves. Esther's *dat* was carrying buckets of water and spilled one when he wasn't able to lift it high enough to put in the horse trough. The water went everywhere. Why was he watering the horses to start with? This chore was usually left to the boys to keep them out of trouble.

"Leave it alone," Dorothy said.

"I'll be right back," Esther said to Dorothy and to Aunt Lucy, who had just walked up to start directing the traffic of women carrying food.

Esther jogged over to Chester. He pulled out a hanky from his back pocket and dipped it into the trough water and then wrapped it around his head before smashing his hat back on.

"*Dat*, what are you doing?"

"What's it look like?" he answered her in English words laced in bitterness.

"This is usually a boy's job," Esther answered him back in English, surprising even herself. She reverted to their dialect as she continued. "You're a great carpenter and could oversee this whole project."

"But I'm in the *bann*, Essie," he spoke in dialect more calmly. "I can't say much against it now, can I? That Roy, now he's a piece of work."

Esther furrowed her brow. She hurt for him. She looked back at the bustling women going in and out of the house.

"Don't you worry about me." Chester patted her arm. "I'll be all right. I suppose I deserve the humiliation after everything."

Chester walked away.

Esther returned to the house and helped serve all the men, then children, and then the women. By the time she ate, all that was left was scraped-from-the-bottom potatoes and cold gravy. She wasn't the only one either. Once the women finished their small meals, they gathered it up, washed everything, and started over for supper. The barn would get done, but only if another meal could be served.

"Caught these two fiddling with matches in the shed," Chester said to Esther as he pulled two boys by their ears.

"Marvin?" Esther questioned. Marvin was one of Aunt Lucy's many grandchildren. He was six and knew better than to play with matches. Along with him was Alvin's little Junior, who was only four. He'd been caught with matches before and knew better too.

Marvin looked up at Chester, yanked his ear from the old man's grip, and stomped off. Junior, looking frightened, dared not follow his big cousin.

"I'll take him," Esther said and marched him off to his mother, Dorothy. He received a spanking and was sent to his room.

Esther heard a car engine outside and ran out to check.

The man she'd seen several weeks earlier with the shiny

green car was standing in the drive. Her *dat* had told her that the stranger had been a salesman. Why, then, would he return? As Esther walked closer, she saw that the man had a pointy beard and a small mustache. His suit was sharp and crisp. He was maybe in his fifties and handsome. She'd ignored her earlier suspicions and over time thought that she might have been wrong, but this second visit confirmed that Chester was in fact keeping secrets.

"I'm looking for Chester Detweiler. I was told he might be here." The man's voice was booming.

Like the Red Sea, the crowd of women and children parted. Chester jogged through and as soon as he got to the man, pulled his arm and walked him back to the green car. Esther was relieved when most of the onlookers returned to their work and play, but she continued to watch.

Her *dat* was red-faced—and not from the sun. His gestures showed that he wasn't happy about the man showing up. Who was this man, and what did he have to do with her *dat*? He held up a single finger in Chet's face before he calmly returned to his car and drove off. Chester's shoulders slumped, and he wiped a hand over his face.

Esther jumped off the porch and jogged over to her dad. She wasn't sure what she would say. He'd lied to her again, hadn't he? If that man was not a salesman, then who was he?

"Who was that?" Esther asked hesitantly.

"No one. He's no one," he barked at her. Her *dat* didn't meet her eyes but kicked the gravel under their feet and cursed quietly. Sweat dripped from his temples, and he bit his lip. She hadn't seen him acting like this since the day the church leaders came to their home. The day he'd lied to them all.

"You told me that he was a salesman. Is he a—he's not a salesman, is he?" Esther's chest tightened, and she felt too hot for the mild August afternoon. Out of desperation for a new start and being too exhausted to fight, she'd chosen to ignore her suspicions. How could she have let the man who had abandoned her, and lied about it, come back only to hurt her again? Why had she given him any portion of her trust? She hadn't even told the preachers that he'd lied to them, which made her as bad as him. She'd overlooked all of that in an attempt to finally have a father. She had been a fool.

"No, he's not a salesman." The intensity in his eyes made Esther step away from him. They looked at each other for several long moments before he started speaking again. "I'm a coward, Esther. A coward. You know I am. My car is sitting in Joe's barn, and now I have to sell it and the house in order to pay back my debt."

"The car? The house?" Had her father just said he was going to sell the house?

"Careful, Chet." Joe's thick chest was between Esther and Chet a moment later. "Don't say anything that you'll regret."

"Joe?" At Esther's voice, Joe turned. Their eyes met. In the lines of his brow was written the truth. He had known. He had even been a part of the secret.

"You knew," Esther whispered. "I trusted you."

Her wide eyes filled with tears, but she blinked them away and swallowed as she stepped back.

"I trusted you, and you lied to me." The words were barely spoken aloud. "You knew this whole time that he had more secrets—that he had this debt to pay off—and you didn't tell me?"

Both men carried the burden of their lies. Chet wiped a hand down his face, his missing finger taunting her. Joe reached for her, and she backed away again. After everything she'd done for him. After everything he meant to her. He'd helped Chet lie to her?

Esther didn't look around, but felt the eyes of her community on her. Her basket, bonnet, and purse were inside Dorothy's house, but she didn't care. She had to leave. The gravel beneath her feet slid as she walked up the drive and out onto the dirt road. A roll of thunder barreled across the sky. She looked up and saw that the white clouds were gone. All she could see was gray.

Joe

Joe wanted to tell Esther that he wasn't going to Poland—and apologize. But she refused to see him. After sharing such intimate moments together, he didn't just miss her; he longed for her. He desired her. He had assumed his role in Daisy's life again, which proved quickly to be right for Daisy, and he dropped Daisy at Esther's every morning. Esther avoided eye contact with him. Chet was still living with Esther, but Joe wondered how long that would last. He admitted he'd gone about everything the wrong way, and while he was less concerned about the church's discipline toward him, he was afraid he'd never win any of Esther's trust back.

A knock at Joe's door late one evening came as a surprise. He and Daisy were looking through a book together. Joe was learning signs by pointing at pictures, and he was in turn showing her how to read the word. He would have to find a way to teach his daughter. He signed that there was someone at the door and left her on the couch.

A familiar black Cadillac sat in the drive.

"Doc?" Joe said as he opened the door.

Dr. Sherman was standing on his porch wearing a dark suit

and a black hat on top his balding head. Even when the doctor
was treating patients in overalls, he had the same regal and
proud stance.

"May I come in?"

Joe stepped aside and let the man through. He offered him
water, which he declined. He looked over at Daisy, who was
sitting on the couch with the book in her lap. She was flipping
through the pages when the doctor bent down and tapped her
shoulder.

"Hello, Daisy," the doctor said as he waved.

Daisy waved back and gave him a smile.

Dr. Sherman pulled a peppermint from his coat pocket
and offered it to Daisy with an eye toward Joe. Joe nodded his
approval and the little girl snatched up the sweet treat in a blink
of an eye.

"Looks like she's much improved from the last time I saw
her."

"She is. Thanks to Esther." When he said her name, his skin
became warm everywhere. He cleared his throat. "What can I
do for you, Doc?"

"I'll not beat about the bush, Joe, as to why I've come." He
cleared his throat and then pulled out a letter from his inside
suit coat pocket. "I took it upon myself, as a doctor who loves
the people in this community, to see what I could do for your
daughter. Deafness is not something I know much about. I can
say that I am certain of two things. Her hearing won't improve
outside of a miracle from a greater physician than me. The
second thing I am certain of is that you are not equipped, nor
is Esther, to give her the education she needs to truly make it
in this life."

Joe's heart went from feather to stone, making him feel
dizzy. He pushed the feeling aside in order to confront the
doc's words. Daisy would always be deaf—this he had also been

certain of. He was not enough for her, and neither was Esther. This was where he faltered. He was her parent, and Esther had worked magic with the girl. This was still not enough.

"Do you want her to someday have real schooling, college even—get married, be a wife and mother? And what will happen to her when you die? And don't say that the Amish woman could take her. She might be dead by then also, or at least too old to handle a grown deaf woman incapable of taking care of herself."

"What are you saying, Doc?"

"I made a phone call on your behalf and Daisy's to learn more about the school in Alabama. It is a good school. She would be educated not just in the typical academics, but she would learn to become oral. This is the best way for the deaf community to become part of society and be self-sufficient."

Joe's heart pulsed in his ears. His mind turned over like his stomach. Nothing seemed normal or as it should be.

"They said they'd take her starting in September." The doctor handed Joe the letter.

Joe scanned it and looked up at the doctor.

"You want me to send my daughter away in just a few weeks?" Joe pushed the letter back into the chest of the doctor, but when the doctor didn't take it back, it fell on the floor between them.

"No. Don't send her away—go with her. Call the number listed and get the information for yourself. I think you'll be more than satisfied." The doctor became intense. "Listen, I know everything that's happened to you, Joe. This could be a new start for you both. There are jobs down there for you, and don't you think that's what Daisy deserves? What you both deserve?"

The doctor raised an eyebrow and walked out of the house.

After the doctor left the house, Joe, stunned, sat on the couch. He finally retrieved the pamphlet he'd stuffed into a drawer and read it over and over, along with the letter that told him that Daisy would be given the best education possible with a trained group of nurturing teachers.

Joe got Daisy's attention.

"Do you want to learn to read books?" he asked with broken signs.

She signed, *Just like you and Mama Esther?* Her eyes were bright.

"Yes." His fist bobbed up and down. "Do you want to go to school to learn?"

She tilted her head and her unlined brow wrinkled, confused. *You and Mama Esther can teach me,* she signed.

"No, we can't."

Yes. Her fist bobbed up and down and her face grew grim. *Mama Esther can.*

"What about going to a school where the other pupils are like you? Deaf." Joe hadn't signed every word but he'd made sure his thought had come across.

Her grim frustration turned into curiosity. *There are other children like me?*

"Yes."

I want to meet other children like me. And learn to read. Her signs were clear, as were her expressions that always mirrored her emotions so well.

~

The next day, Joe asked Wayne Good if he could use his phone during his lunch and take the charge for it from his paycheck. Even though Wayne was a bit disgruntled over Joe's backing out of going to Poland, he'd only grumbled a bit more and then made Joe the manager for the site once the Poland crew left. When Joe heard the telephone operator make the connection to the deaf school, his heart beat double time.

"Hello. Alabama School for the Deaf and Blind," a woman said on the other end. Her voice was friendly, with a significant regional drawl, which he recognized from several fellow Marines.

"Hi, my name is Joe Garrison," he said, stuttering over his words. He quickly explained to the woman about Dr. Sherman and Daisy. "I wish I knew more about the school and what to expect. I live in Delaware."

"I recognize your name, Mr. Garrison. It appears that your daughter has received a scholarship from one of our benefactors that will cover her tuition." The woman paused for a few moments. "I have your daughter's paperwork in front of me. It looks like I'll need a few more pieces of information."

"But I don't even know if I'm going to enroll her," Joe protested, though curious whether Dr. Sherman himself was Daisy's benefactor. "She's never gone to school, and we aren't sure what to expect. And I don't want to send her alone. I'd like to come with her."

"I understand." The woman paused. "Let me learn a little more about Daisy. It says here that she's deaf. Is that all?"

"What do you mean *is that all?*" Joe chuckled. "Isn't that enough?"

"We have many students who are both blind and deaf. Some who have other handicaps as well."

"Oh. Yes, Daisy is just deaf." Thank God she was *only* deaf.

"Well, that simplifies a lot for us. She'll be easy to work with." Her voice was light-hearted and encouraging. There was a short pause. "Is she oral?"

"She tries to speak. Sometimes I understand her. But she mostly uses sign language. And she can read a handful of words for the purpose of finger spelling."

"Sounds like she's ahead, especially for her age. At this pace, she'll be talking the freckles off a skunk by Christmas."

Joe had never heard that phrase before but caught the intent
and stifled a chuckle. This woman was so calm about it all.
Maybe she didn't work with any deaf children and only answered phones. She didn't seem to understand the enormity of
working with a deaf child.

"She has outbursts sometimes when she gets frustrated," Joe
challenged.

"How common are they? Daily? Hourly?"

"Oh, no. Nothing like that."

"Mr. Garrison, I can hear the concern in your voice. Daisy
sounds like a lovely little girl—and what a pretty name. I
believe she'll have a great time here while learning to be
self-sufficient. We have seen that the more deaf children
become independent and strong academically, their fits and
frustrations decrease substantially. We have several little girls
her age, and she will be very accepted here. Nothing about her
paperwork or our conversation sounds unusual or worrisome
for me or our teachers."

She paused for a moment, and Joe could hear papers moving
in the background.

"I see that Dr. Sherman has provided us with all of her medical information, and I can't see any reason she wouldn't be an
excellent student."

"Do you work with the students?"

"I help my mother a few times a week. She's one of the
teachers, and she's also deaf."

Joe wasn't sure how to respond to that. "Your mother is
deaf?"

"So is my daddy, but he didn't want to teach, so he went
to college to become an engineer." Her southern tone was so
cheerful Joe found himself smiling.

"Both of your parents are deaf?" He knew he spoke in disbelief, but the woman merely laughed gently in return. The

sound was a gentle balm to Joe's spirit. *What could Daisy grow up to be? What were the possibilities?*

"Mr. Garrison, with everything in her paperwork and from what you're telling me, it sounds like there is nothing abnormal or remarkable about your daughter. She will fit in nicely here."

The woman talked with him about housing and jobs. With every minute that passed, he stopped imagining the charge against his wage but added hope and real answers instead.

For the rest of the day, those words rang through his mind. There was nothing remarkable or abnormal about Daisy. Going to a school like that, Daisy would be one of many, and with teachers who didn't just understand her but were like her. Even after he tucked Daisy in for the night, his mind still raced with the possibilities, and his new prayers were fortified with thanksgiving to God.

Joe knew he could not provide this type of education to Daisy, and certainly not the atmosphere of such acceptance. From his perspective, reading was one of the most basic skills, and he hadn't been sure how she would advance further from where she was already. Esther had learned and taught her sign language but had to forgo teaching Daisy to be oral because it took training. It would seem negligent to not at least try.

He needed to see Esther. It was late. Daisy was sleeping soundly in her room. Esther might be in bed as well. But he needed to try. The option of this school was far too great to wait even another day. He walked out the back door, and as he walked down the overgrown trail, he remembered the first time he'd walked this path with Esther and the moments they'd shared. And now she wasn't even speaking to him.

Standing a short distance from the Detweiler house, he could see Esther sitting on the steps of the back porch. He rested his eyes on her face, pale in the moonlight. He took several more steps and his movement caused her to turn. She was wearing her nightclothes, and to his surprise, her damp hair cascaded down her back. The weight of her gaze caught his breath, and in that moment he knew that he loved her.

Her jaw tightened when she saw him and she turned her back to him. At least she didn't leave. This was an improvement over the last few days. Something in his stomach spun, and he had to swallow back his instinct to pull her into his arms.

"I had to come see you," he said.

She didn't respond.

He went to the porch and sat next to her. Her feet were bare and green grass pushed between her toes. At first he left a respectful gap between them, but the magnetic pull she had brought him closer. He put his hand on her shoulder and tried to gently unfold her toward him. His touch was met with firmness and he winced, closing his eyes.

"I need you to hear me."

"You lied to me." Esther's whisper was raspy. She pulled her damp hair around to her shoulder away from him. "Why should I listen to you?"

Joe sighed. How could he get her attention so she would listen to him? He'd tried to apologize to her for several days after the barn raising, but she'd been unwilling to hear him out.

"I didn't say no to Poland just because of Daisy. I stayed because of you, Esther. I love you."

Esther

Esther's head snapped over to him. Her chest rose and fell, and her breathing quickened. Joe's brow was that of an old man's; it no longer had the youthfulness that Esther had grown accustomed to. His eyes held deep winter instead of the newness of spring. Did this declaration come at such a weighty price that his face bore the burden?

She couldn't say anything. The shock of his words on her heart made her speechless.

"Why did *you* want me to stay?" he asked. He took her hand and every inch of her skin tingled.

The cigarette in his mouth bobbed up and down as he spoke, as if he had no cares, but Esther learned that this was his facade. He wore the smokes like a mask. But with his eyes on hers, his touch on her skin, and his lips kissing her—somehow, without trying to or realizing it, she had fallen for him. Admitting that she loved him was dangerous, but it was the truth. She loved Joe.

"*Why?*" How much should she divulge? "Daisy needs you."

"But you raised her on your own for four years." He snuffed out his cigarette as he searched her eyes, and she was sure he could see her weakness for him.

"A girl should have a father. I didn't have one until a few months ago, and I know how difficult it can be."

"And what about a mother? Should she have a mother?" His voice was as soft as the sound of the leaves brushed by the breeze. He ran his thumb over her hand.

"Yes," she whispered. She suddenly sensed what he was insinuating.

"Then should I remarry?"

When had Joe begun holding her so tightly? How had she let him pull her back in even after he'd hidden a lie for Chester?

"Should I remarry, Esther?" Joe's voice was husky.

She didn't answer but instead closed the physical gap. All she could think about in the moment was that he was so close she could smell the saltiness of sweat that had dried against his chest and back. She could see the fine bright blond streaks that ran through his waves and that he hadn't shaved in several days. She could see his eyes go from winter to spring. For the first time she imagined growing old with a man she loved. She'd never let her imagination take her there before.

When her fingers touched his arm, the heat of his skin sent a current of electricity through her. A jolting heat. His arms encircled her and she lifted her face—her chin—her lips—to meet his. His stubble rubbed against the smoothness of her skin, making the kiss more real and memorable. His hands were eager and held her closer, and she didn't fight the sensations it aroused.

Irene.

The thought came to Esther like a rush of wind across a still pond, a blizzard on a summer's day, a scream during the sweetest of dreams. She pulled away from the kiss but not from his hold. Their eyes were close.

"Irene," she whispered.

"She's gone, Esther." He cradled her face. "You loved her.

I loved her. We'll always love her memory for the woman she was."

"But what are we doing? Why are we doing this?" Esther couldn't keep herself from him, but she also couldn't keep doing this every time they were alone together. She squeezed her toes in the tall grass and it was warm against her feet.

Joe released one hand and pulled something out of his back pocket. He handed it to her, and they parted. She looked down in her hands at what he'd given her.

Esther tucked her hair behind her ears. It was a pamphlet. The photo in the front showed four rows of children standing, with several adults standing next to and behind them. The brochure read *Alabama School for the Deaf and Blind*. Without reading all the smaller print, she flipped the paper over and saw another photo, this of a woman staring with blank eyes near where the camera had shot. Her smile was real, however. The name below it identified her as Helen Keller.

She set the brochure in her lap and read the typed letter. It indicated that Daisy had qualified for a scholarship to the school and they wanted her to be at the school by the first full week of September.

A deaf school? He was sending Daisy off to a deaf school?

She looked back and forth between the paper and Joe. "What do you mean by this?" Her heart's pulse became like a train and filled her ears. She couldn't wait a few seconds for the answer, so she stood and faced him. "You're sending her away?"

"No, I'm not sending her away."

"Then what's this?" Esther wanted to throw the papers at him but resisted.

"I'm going to go with her." He spoke quickly with a breathless voice. "We are going to start over."

"But you can't." Esther took a step away.

Joe stood with her.

"But you can come with us. I want you to come with us." He took her hands, but she dropped them and the pamphlet and letter.

"Go with you?" Esther shook her head. Her ears began to ring. "Joe. No. No. I can't leave my home, my church."

"But what's here for you? You've hinted to me that you don't really belong, that you're alone here. You're not one of the married women with a brood of children. You're not a widow or young enough for those Sunday night singings. And you're losing your home. Chet's going to sell it."

As she started to leave, Joe gently took her by the shoulders. She didn't resist further. She knew she couldn't run away from this.

"You can't do this. You can't just leave." Her throat was pained with emotion.

"We can't teach Daisy what she needs to learn. What happens to her when we're gone? What about reading? Or taking care of herself—really taking care of herself." He paused for a moment. "You should've heard what the woman on the phone said. Her mom is deaf and she's a teacher. Her dad is also deaf and he's an engineer. I want those things for Daisy. Don't you?"

His questions were all running together. They raced around inside her head and spun like a dirt devil over a gravel road. She'd taught Daisy to sign and crochet. She'd taught her to fry eggs, bake bread, and make applesauce. She taught her the alphabet and at least a hundred finger-spelled words and hundreds of other signs.

"She'll be so confused. What if she goes back into shock like after the incident at your church?" Esther argued. She knew in her heart that the situation at the church had been exceptional. The school in the brochure was trained to care for the deaf.

Even if she'd had the chance to raise Daisy as her own child, she would get only an eighth-grade education at best—and with her deafness, maybe not even that. She didn't want that for her. She wanted Daisy to have more than she had had.

"Can you teach her what this school is offering?"

It wasn't that she didn't have an answer to Joe's question. It was more as if her very voice had left her body. There was nothing she could say. She wasn't sure how to teach a deaf child more than what she'd already taught. She shook her head at Joe. Daisy belonged with Joe and, it seemed, also at this school. But was he really going to do this—take her so far away? This also meant that he would be gone as well.

"Esther," Joe said and moved close to her without touching her. "Don't you see? Irene had the boy that I was—but you have the man that I am. Marry me. Be my wife. Be a mother to our girl. We both need you."

What broke her heart more than him taking Daisy far away was knowing that she could never answer his question the way he wanted. She couldn't marry him.

Joe's proposal had come as a shock. It hadn't been her first, but it had been the most surprising. Several years ago, Andy Miller had asked her to marry him so he would have a mother for his children, and before him—years earlier—so had Davey Schrock. Neither were men she wanted to marry, so telling them no had come at no loss to her personally.

But, Joe.

Joe.

She knew he didn't just want her as a mother for Daisy. There was much more. Hadn't she already imagined what it would be like to live a life with Joe? To live together with Daisy as a family? How often had she fought to see the sin in Irene's choice to marry outside the church? But she had found none, and more than that, she understood why Irene had done it. Hadn't she secretly agreed with Joe when he suggested that going against the *Ordnung* and sinning were two different things? But where was her courage now? She couldn't do this. She was too afraid.

Her life was in Sunrise with the Amish. These were her people. She knew no other life. Wouldn't leaving be disloyal and prove once again that the Detweilers were cursed? Wouldn't it make her no better than her *dat*?

Joe

O nly a week passed before Joe found himself with train tickets in hand and their suitcases packed. He'd worked a few more days for Wayne's benefit. Chet, with no way to get to the job site, was welcomed back to the dairy and, for the season, picking peaches at the orchard neighboring Alvin and Dorothy's house. Joe had made a call to the school for the deaf, and they said there was a neighborhood of small houses near the school that many other families rented. They could get settled there quickly.

After another several conversations with a school administrator, he had a job working as a janitor until the local school could interview him for a teaching job. His desire to return to teaching brought the pain and pleasure he'd expected. Their new start, however, brought him the hope that he could teach again.

He'd offered his house to Angelica. She cried out at his announcement that he was leaving, but she was thrilled that they would have a new home. It didn't matter that the red clapboard house was smaller than their own farmhouse; it was well maintained, and with it came a new start for them as well.

Mrs. White bought the Blunts' house and land to expand her farm. With that, the Blunts would have some additional money to live on.

Joe stood in his bedroom and looked around. He'd taken Irene's quilt and packed it away in one of their trunks, along with photos of her and her wedding band—Daisy would want them someday. All of Irene's clothing belonged to Angelica and her girls now. He'd packed his books, his old toys that Daisy loved, and the comforter Irene made for Daisy from her dresses. Everything else would stay. Their new house would be simply furnished, and they really didn't need much.

Daisy sat on the edge of the couch looking straight ahead. At first she'd shown great excitement at learning that she would be attending the deaf school. But when she realized that Esther would not be moving with them, she refused to even see her.

He tapped her on the shoulder. She looked up at him and her lips were thinly pressed together. Her eyes red. She wore a deep blue beret and a matching cape for traveling. He'd found it on a mannequin in a department store and thought it would be the perfect traveling outfit. With her hair pulled back and her emotions contained, he could see her growing up before his eyes. If he didn't believe that Daisy was in part excited for their journey, he would feel far more guilt at taking her away from Esther.

"Ready?" The sign for *ready* included the sign for *finished*, which reminded him of brushing away a desk full of papers. It seemed too frivolous in nature for what they were about to do.

Daisy looked straight ahead again and shook her head *no*. But still she stood and took Joe's hand, waiting to walk away from the red clapboard house on Sunrise View Road.

Joe loaded Daisy and their luggage into the truck, and Angelica drove them to the train station. She chattered in her nervousness, but he couldn't hear her. He settled into the silence of his mind as they passed all of the haunts they would never forget. When they passed Esther's home, Daisy began weeping quietly.

Joe may have been as anxious as Daisy. He was leaving his only real home, the home of his childhood. He could almost hear his parents bickering over things like whether Angelica could crimp her hair or Joe read anything other than the Bible. It was where he and Jason had played and where he'd last seen him before he was taken away. The home his children had been born in and one had died. It was where he fell in love with Irene and proposed to her, and where he watched her soul slip from her body. It was also where he'd seen Esther as his future. But he knew now that that would never happen. Esther hadn't spoken to or even looked at him since she declined his proposal.

He wasn't sure what he'd expected her to say. He loved her, but apparently she didn't love him. There was something so uniquely special about Esther that he hadn't been prepared for. She was the perfect mother for Daisy. Even though Irene was Daisy's birth mother, he knew in his heart that Irene never would have gone to the lengths that Esther had with sign language. Irene would've made the best of what she was given and loved Daisy no matter what. But Esther was different. It wasn't about her being Amish and not English but that she was unlike any other woman he'd ever known. Her entire life had been painted with broad strokes of abandonment, being forced to become an adult when she was only a child, and loss. The only woman she reminded him of was Rosie the Riveter. A woman who could handle anything that came her way with strength and dignity. All the things he'd witnessed in her over the last several months had brought him to the point of loving her more than his own life. Her rejection was like another death to him.

They made it to the train station and said a final good-bye to his sister. They had plenty of time to prepare for their trip. He hadn't made a lunch for them, so he bought some fruit, bread, and cheese at the small stand in the train station. When he turned, Daisy was gone.

Esther

E sther had cried all the tears she owned and some that were borrowed. It was all happening too quickly. The sun still rose in the morning and set in the evening. The stars still twinkled, and even though she hadn't spoken to her *dat*, he still spoke more English with his Texas twang than Pennsylvania Dutch. He had apologized and tried to explain what happened, but she hadn't forgiven him. He'd absolved Joe from his part as well, leaving her more confused than ever.

As if she didn't have enough to be burdened over. All she could think about was Joe and Daisy leaving Sunrise—and refusing his proposal. Had she made the right choice? She couldn't say yes—could she? She stopped imagining a life with Joe. She could never leave the Amish. She could never be like her *dat* and abandon her life.

"Esther?" Her father walked into the kitchen. "I thought you'd at least go to the train station."

Esther shook her head and pretended to be busy. Her hands shook and she dropped an egg. She leaned against the countertop and wished she could cry even more, but nothing came.

"You need to at least say good-bye, Essie." He put an arm

around her and squeezed her shoulder. "Think of that little girl."

"I can't. I don't think I can say good-bye." Esther turned to face her father. She shook her head. "I just can't, I—"

He took her by the arms and shook her.

"Essie," he barked, "you can and you will. You're the strongest woman I know. Better than anyone I've ever met. You can do anything."

His words settled on her heart like a blanket in winter. She looked into his eyes and saw herself in them—she saw what he saw. Her head fell on his shoulder and she wrapped her arms around him. He held her for only a moment, then pulled her to the door.

"Come on," he said.

"Where are we going?"

"To Joe's barn. My Ford is still there."

Esther inhaled. They could both get in trouble with the church, though Chet had far more to lose at this point than she did.

"Don't think about it, Esther." Chester shook his head. "Let's just do it."

He was right.

They ran the entire way to Joe's red clapboard house and down the drive. They were both winded by the time Chester opened the sliding door. He rubbed the palms of his hands together before clapping them loudly and laughing. He patted the off-white hood like a pet.

"I've missed driving my girl," he said, smiling. "Hope she'll start up all right."

He opened the passenger-side door and pretended to be a gentleman and bowed. "Ma'am, your carriage awaits."

Esther stood several paces away. Not only was it wrong for Chester to own or drive a car, but it was also wrong for her to ride with him. She closed her eyes and heard Joe's voice in her head. *Just because it's against your* Ordnung *doesn't make it a sin.* Was he right?

She didn't know if he was right or wrong, but she did know that she couldn't let Joe and Daisy leave without going to the train station. She opened her eyes and found her *dat* looking at her.

"It'll be okay, Essie," he said soberly.

She climbed in.

When the train station came into view, she nearly opened the car door while they were still moving. Chester took her to the front sidewalk and said he would park. She scrambled out, and as she looked for Joe and Daisy, she fixed her covering, tucked her stray curls back, and wished she'd worn something nicer than her gray work dress.

She walked into the station and looked around. She didn't see them and walked back out toward the platform when she was nearly bowled over by Daisy running and hugging her from behind. Esther turned and wrapped her arms around the little girl, likely the only daughter figure she would ever have. Was this the last time she would hold her? The last time she would see her blue eyes? The last time she would use sign language?

"Come. Come," Daisy begged, her words coming out ragged and loudly.

Esther caressed the little girl's face but couldn't speak. She swallowed, and all the words she meant to say were gone. With her arms around the girl, her heart was filling again, but for how long? Would she be gone in ten minutes? An hour?

"Esther?" Joe's voice brought back too many sensations and reminded her of all that she was losing. The last time they had been at the train station, they'd been curt with each other. She'd wished he hadn't existed, because she wanted to keep Daisy to herself. But now, there he stood, and all she could think of was that she'd fallen in love with him.

She loved Joe. Not just because of Daisy, but because of him.

She pressed her palms against the little girl's cheeks before standing up and facing Joe. He looked so handsome in his three-piece suit. She'd never seen him so dressed up. His hair was slicked, though a stray curl fell down on the side of his forehead. They were close enough for her to catch the scent of him when the breeze picked up his aftershave.

When she took several steps toward him, she wasn't sure what she'd planned on doing, but with his arms around her and his lips on hers, nothing felt more natural. Her kiss was aggressive and hungry. She wanted to say hello but knew it was good-bye. He held her gently, and the warmth under his fingertips energized her. But as quickly as she kissed him, he pulled her away. She was startled.

"I can't," he whispered, dropping his chin. "If you're not coming with us, I can't do this, Esther. It's—too confusing."

Esther stepped back. The hurt was too great. He was right. She shouldn't taunt him with a stolen kiss. He was determined, and he wasn't going to stay. This was it. He was doing this for Daisy's best interest and she wouldn't see him again. She turned away from him and walked Daisy over to a nearby bench. She didn't speak aloud as she signed. She and Daisy had the luxury of having a near-private conversation, since Joe wasn't fluent yet.

I love you and I will think of you every day. When her hand in the letter *A* brushed against the side of her face to sign *every day*, her lips pursed, not wanting to release any additional emotion.

I'm still Mama Esther's girl? The little girl's lips turned down.

Esther spun a finger in a circle several times. *Always.*

They embraced and then behind her, she heard the dreaded words. *All aboard.* Her eyes looked up at Joe, who looked away. She gave Daisy an extra squeeze before releasing her. Esther signed carefully.

Time to go. Your dad can write letters for you.

Daisy nodded and curled her lips in. Joe's hand was on his daughter's shoulder, and she took it with her hand and stood. They walked toward the train, and Daisy looked toward Esther, a path of tears trailing down her milky skin. Then she waved timidly as she climbed the train steps.

Esther stood and took a step forward. Would he look back at her once more? Would he try to convince her to come with him with another declaration of his love? If he asked her once more, she might have the courage to say yes.

No.

He didn't look back.

Joe was gone.

Esther

Dorothy waved at Esther as she pulled the buggy up to the house. Esther wrapped her reins around the hook in the open buggy and hopped out. Her Friday visits were still the hardest days for her. Daisy had loved their visiting. She'd lost Orpha in June and Daisy in August. So much had changed since then.

Esther waved at Junior and Rebekah, who were playing with their older cousins, Marvin and Martha.

"You have Rudy's twins?" Esther asked as they walked into the house. A chill had settled by September, and without an Indian summer, October was colder than usual.

"Lissy is with IdaRose today." Dorothy met Esther's eyes and pursed her lips. IdaRose was Lissy's mother, who had begun failing weeks ago and was fading quickly.

"I heard she was still eating," Esther said, trying to offer hope.

"Not for a few days now." Dorothy shook her head.

Sadness brought Daisy's ghost to haunt Esther, missing the little girl's companionship. At first people had asked about her and how she was doing at the newfangled deaf school. Many had never heard of such a thing and were curious to hear more. Esther hadn't been very forthright in conversation, hoping that people would stop asking.

Joe wrote letters for Daisy, the highlight of Esther's week. None of it was very personal about Joe, only about how school was going, what Daisy was learning, and what their house looked like.

Esther showed Dorothy several jars of peaches in her basket.

"The orchard sells the extra peaches to their workers for almost nothing. So I've been busy canning." Esther smiled at how Chester had yelled *yee-haw* when she'd made peach cobbler the night before. He'd made her laugh, and it had felt good. He was good at bringing laughter back to their home now that Daisy wasn't there.

Esther and her *dat* had rekindled their relationship with Joe gone. Most of that had come out of desperation. She couldn't handle any more tragedy and division. *Dat* had assured her that he was paying installments on his debt, and it kept the bank at bay for now. The church had not caught up with them about the drive to the train station yet, though Esther knew it could come any time if they learned of it. The remarkable thing was that she had no guilt over her transgression. It hadn't been sinful; her heart knew this.

All she regretted was losing Joe and Daisy. But Joe had given her an impossible decision. In the months that she'd been without them, she was losing pieces of herself. She put her mind back on the canned peaches. "I brought you some, and thought maybe I could swap with you for some peas?"

"Sure." Dorothy peeked into the bag of goods.

"I also have kerosene oil today." Esther pulled it out of the bag. "Mrs. White said that since the sun sets so early, it's good to have more oil for our lamps."

"I'm so low on kerosene," Dorothy said. She pointed at the

lamp in the center of the table. "This one hasn't been filled in a week."

Dorothy poured some oil in a smaller lamp and lit it, then waved at Esther to follow her down to the basement to swap their canned goods. They crawled through a small square door in the kitchen floor with Dorothy leading with the small glow from the lamp.

After several minutes trading goods, the door in the ceiling was slammed shut, and Esther could hear Marvin cackling with laughter.

"Dorothy, please tell me Alvin fixed that latch," Esther said.

Dorothy shook her head *no*.

"Marvin Bender, you open this door right now," Esther yelled at the boy.

"Na-na-na-na," the little boy taunted.

Esther looked around to see what could be used. When she didn't see anything, she went up the stairs to the door and pushed against it. It didn't budge. She held an ear up to the door. It was silent except for a distant rustling. She knocked on the door. It sounded as if someone was up there. She could hear the screen door slapping shut several times.

"Junior," Esther yelled. Then she waited for several long moments. She could hear something scrape above them, maybe a chair against the wooden floorboards. There was more movement, then footsteps and muffled voices.

"*Kinnah!* Open the cellar door!" Esther banged on the door after she yelled and waited again. She looked down at Dorothy. "The *kinnah* are up there. I can hear them running around. Why can't they hear me?"

"Try again," Dorothy encouraged. "The door is pretty thick."

Esther opened her mouth to yell when she heard one of the children start screaming.

"*Fiyah! Fiyah!*" Esther heard from one of the boys. "*Fire!*"

"What did he say?" Dorothy asked in a ragged voice.

"He said fire," Esther said breathlessly, then started banging on the door. "Marvin! Junior!"

She banged on the door, scraping her knuckles hard against the wood, yelling for Marvin to open the door. *"Mahs ouh! Mahs ouh!"*

"What's happening?" Dorothy asked as she began to pace. "It's just a joke. They are always crying wolf and Marvin's the worst of them."

Esther came down the few steps and took the small oil lamp to look in the dark corners for anything that could help them open the door.

Esther had found a hammer and banged against the cellar door above her head, but it would only rattle against the lock and the old iron hinges but nothing came loose.

"We're stuck, Dorothy. Please tell me—" Esther paused when she saw smoke coming through the cracks along the side of the door. Both women went silent, and she could hear the crackling of the fire. "Dorothy, there really is a fire up there."

She began frantically banging on the door with the hammer, to no avail. She found a small window that was nearly below the ground and opened that, but it was so small it didn't bring in much fresh air. "Is there any other way out?"

Dorothy's eyes were large and she shook her head. "That's it. That's the only way out."

"What about Alvin?" Esther knew that he worked in their pasture most days with the horses he trained.

"He had to go look at a horse." Dorothy wiped away the tears that had begun to fall.

Esther continued to yell and bang the hammer against the door. The crackling above her was getting louder, and enough smoke was coming through now that she had to get down from the stairs. The house was on fire, and they were trapped. Dorothy began crying and coughing.

"Marvin! Junior!" Esther yelled the names over and over again. Of course, there was no answer. Why would they have stayed inside a burning house? Everyone, even naughty little boys, knew better than that. But what could they do? Smoke hovered above their heads. Breathing it in made them cough, and it was going to get worse.

"Do you have any water down here?" Esther asked.

Dorothy was only able to shake her head as she worked through a fit of coughs. How much longer would they be able to breathe? Dorothy was doubled over and rocking back and forth. Her eyes were closed, and Esther could hear her whispering the Lord's Prayer. Was she preparing to die?

"Dorothy, we're not going to die," she yelled. "Stop doing that."

"There's no way out. I don't even know if my children are safe. If they aren't safe, I'd rather die. I don't want to live if they die."

"You can't talk like that." Esther looked up to the ceiling as if she could see the fire in a blaze above them. "They didn't stay in the house. We would hear them. The boys would know to go for help, right?"

"I don't know, Esther. If they die, I don't want to live." Dorothy sobbed loudly. The fire above them was growing louder, and they could hear things falling and dropping on the floor above them. "You don't have children. If you did, you would know that life isn't worth living if they die."

"You listen to me," Esther growled her words and took the younger woman by the arms. She shook her and clenched her jaw tightly. "Life is *always* worth living. I don't have the family you have, but I've lost everything more than once and I've kept going. You can't stop. We are not going to die."

"Okay. Okay." Dorothy kept repeating it.

"Someone will come. Someone has to come." Esther went into a fit of coughing and let go of the young mother's arms.

"Someone will come." Dorothy nodded her head as tears trailed down her cheek. By the time they dripped from her jaw, the tears were gray.

The smoke was at Esther's eye level now, and her lungs couldn't find any clean air. She could only vaguely see the door at the top of the wooden stairs. The canned goods were fading away into the walls. Coughing racked her body. Her throat and eyes burned. Her heart felt as hot as fire itself. She couldn't speak anymore. She stumbled up the steps. She leaned her hand against the concrete blocks to steady herself, but the smoke was too thick. Her lungs were full of smoke. All she could do was hear the fire blazing above her, Dorothy's crying, and her own thoughts. She walked back down to the dirt floor of the basement, and the coolness of it invited her to rest.

"Esther!" The voice seared her ears.

Their only hope was that the fire would burn the door away but still somehow provide a path for their escape. The fire was so loud now that her ears were consumed with the rage and crackle of the flames.

"Esther! *Sis detteh! Sis detteh!*"

She heard his voice; the voice of her father, her *detteh*, speaking her name and calling to her.

"*Detteh! Detteh!*" she yelled back. The smoke burned her throat.

A dark image came down the stairs. She looked over at Dorothy, who was lying near her with her eyes closed. Everything moved in slow motion, and she realized she was also lying on the sandy floor. Hadn't she just been standing? As her *dat* helped her up, she put her hand in his, and she was five years old again and knew that he wasn't going to let anything bad happen to her.

But there was so much heat. The sound of the fire was deafening. It took several moments before Esther's mind could catch up with what was happening. How had he gotten there to them?

"Wait for me by the stairs," her *dat*'s voice boomed in her ears and he pointed toward the stairs.

"How did you know?" she yelled and watched as he tried to rouse Dorothy but she kept crumpling down in a heap.

"We saw smoke. The boys were halfway to the dairy when we started running. It doesn't matter right now. Just go!" He lifted Dorothy up all the way to her feet and she opened her eyes. He slapped her gently, but hard enough to get her attention. Then he yelled for Esther to carefully begin going up the stairs.

With her *dat* keeping Dorothy upright, they moved slowly. Fire dripped from above them as they reached the first floor. Esther was disoriented. She looked back at Chester, and his breathing was ragged as he gestured for her to continue. She hunched and ducked as she took several more steps. Her foot got caught and she fell forward. Her hands seared painfully and she heard her *dat* yell behind her.

"Essie!"

She pushed against the burn of her hands and stood again. Her lungs burned with every breath and she couldn't stop coughing. Esther spun around to face him. He was waving for her to turn and to continue but she couldn't hear him anymore.

She did as she was told, but there was so much fire around them that every movement had to be steady and deliberate. A sea of fire covered the ceiling. The window to the right was blown out. The table in front of her, where the kerosene oil had been sitting, was orange and hot. She could taste the ash in her mouth.

She would have to go around the table, and then she would be only a few steps from the front door. As she took several more steps she could see shadows of another dairy farmhand waving to her, and his mouth yelled words she couldn't hear. He looked up and then with more eagerness waved for her with both arms to come now. He began moving toward her himself.

"Esther," her *dat* called. She could hear his voice again. "Don't be afraid—keep going."

She turned to find the man pulling her arm and forcing the rest of her steps at a quick pace. There was a sudden cracking sound above them when they were only steps away from the door. She turned around as her *dat* pushed Dorothy away from him. Esther found his eyes for a brief moment before she saw him fall through the floor.

"No! *Detteh!*" The scrape of her voice rubbed like gravel against her throat.

She continued yelling and crying when the farmhand pulled her and Dorothy the rest of the way out. She heard the fire truck arriving and men in heavy coats began spraying the water on the house.

"My dad is inside!" She found the strength to pull at one of the fireman's coats. "Someone needs to get him." She yelled for him, calling to him, expecting him at any moment to run out of the door toward her.

A thundering forced Esther to her knees, and the last thing she remembered before she blacked out was the roof collapsing.

Esther

"E sther," a woman's voice said gently. "Esther."

Esther blinked rapidly before opening her eyes fully. She inhaled and exhaled rapidly before she took in her surroundings and realized that she was in her own upstairs bedroom.

"The nurse has come to look at your burns," Lucy said. Her eyes were kind, and she gently patted Esther's shoulder.

Esther tried to speak, but her voice was hoarse and unintelligible.

"Don't try to speak," Lucy said. "Remember what Dr. Sherman said about the smoke damage to your throat. Give it another week, he said."

Esther looked at the woman behind her aunt. She lifted her hand and tried to sign the word *who* before she remembered she couldn't—both her hands were bandaged because of the burns.

She couldn't speak. She couldn't sign.

"This here is Christine Brenneman." Lucy stepped aside and waved at the woman to step forward. She was a young Amish woman with bright eyes and a rounded belly. "She helps Dr. Sherman with house calls. Okay?"

Esther looked at the woman and then at Lucy and nodded.

She'd heard of Christine before. At the moment, she was wearing a deep plum dress. The style looked more like the girls from Ohio rather than Delaware. She had golden hair and kind brown eyes. Lucy walked away, leaving the woman with Esther. Christine pulled a chair up to the side of the bed and set a large black bag on the bed.

"Hello, Esther. I'm glad to come help, only I'm very sorry for everything that's happened," Christine said and put a warm hand on Esther's arm. Esther was surprised how good her Pennsylvania Dutch was. It was only a little broken and awkward, which was impressive since Christine been raised as an Englisher and joined the Amish church only as an adult. "I'm sorry to hear about your *dat*."

Yes. Her *dat*. He had come home after being dead for nearly thirty years. Maybe he would return from the dead again.

Esther nodded in response and winced when she swallowed.

Water, Esther thought. She mouthed it and pointed with a bandaged hand toward the glass on the bedside table.

"You want water." Christine helped her drink.

The cool refreshment tasted good. She drank her fill and licked her dry, chapped lips.

"More?"

"No." Esther spoke the word quietly, surprised at her own voice.

"You're not supposed to speak." Christine spoke in English without warning. Then covered her mouth, as if realizing her mistake. "Old habits."

Christine's *old habits* were endearing since they reminded her of her *dat*. The Amish nurse unwrapped the right hand first and gently inspected it before rewrapping it.

"You're healing very nicely." She moved on to the left.

Esther watched as the woman worked. She knew her story

from the gossip circles. Christine looked happy and was expecting another child. Her new life in the Amish community, from what Esther could see, was going well. How had this woman made such a decision? She'd left her English life behind her to be with the man she loved within the Amish church. The one big difference was that Christine wasn't shunned by her family and friends from her English life.

"I will tell Dr. Sherman that you're healing nicely—you only need a few bandages now. He will be glad to hear that. He told me to tell you to keep drinking water to help your throat heal, and besides the use of your hands, you can be up and around as you feel able. But when you get tired, you need to get back to bed." She raised an eyebrow at Esther. "One of us will be back in another few days, and we'll see how your throat is feeling."

Esther nodded. "Dorothy?" Her voice was raspy.

"She's healing well. Her burns were worse, unfortunately, but she'll be up and around in a few weeks."

Esther nodded and smiled. She was glad to hear that.

Christine packed her bag again and stood. She smiled at Esther and walked toward the door.

"Wait." Esther spoke and was glad that the pain was only slight.

"Yes?" Christine turned.

She had her attention now. What would she ask?

"What is it?" Christine walked back several steps. "Do you need something?"

"Are you happy?" Every word was spoken with deliberation.

"Very happy, Esther," Christine said.

Esther opened her mouth to ask if she was afraid, but Christine held her hand up toward her.

"Don't speak. Doctor's orders," she reminded her. She squared her shoulders to Esther and held a hand down her rounded abdomen. She smiled. "Don't look for your answers;

just wait for them. Now rest." She smiled sweetly, then left Esther alone.

Esther nestled down again and her eyes landed on the cot across the small room. Daisy's cot. It was empty. Everything in the house was so empty. She was completely alone.

⁓

Another week passed, and Esther's hands were almost completely healed. The community continued to gather around her and serve her every need. Even Angelica Blunt brought over a freshly baked loaf of bread and, even more important, gave freely the warmth of an embrace—and honored Esther's request not to write or call Joe about what had happened. Lucy agreed to this as well. Esther wanted to write Joe herself. Or call him from Norma's. It would be nice to hear his voice.

Norma had offered a raise to her wage and gave her new fabric to replace the dress that had been destroyed in the fire. Every visitor was filled with pity and sympathy, but she hadn't been back to church yet. The idea of sitting through a service felt somehow foreign to her. It had been all she'd known her whole life, but it was the last place she wanted to be. Everything around her reminded her of all she'd lost. It had been three weeks since the fire, but Esther relived it every night.

The first snow of the season came in early November. Esther squinted against the white sky. Flakes like powdered sugar covered most of the ground around her, but it didn't stop her from making her visit. She tied the reins together and used her hands carefully as she gripped the side of the buggy to get down. She pretended not to notice a passing buggy with children waving at her. She already knew that every woman in her dark bonnet and cape looked at her with mournful eyes and the men just simply avoided eye contact altogether.

She walked up the snowy graveyard path and became winded after having no exercise for these three weeks. She shivered as she walked through the yard now dotted with snow. Small white hills grew on the tops of the stone grave markers. She moved to the end of the third row.

Leah Detweiler.

Orpha Detweiler.

Chester Detweiler.

Most of her life she'd mourned a grave marker that held no body, only a few items her mother had buried in his memory. Now, she knelt next to her father's grave, knowing that he lay underneath the soil. Chester Detweiler, the deserter and coward, had died a hero.

He'd become a man she'd finally grown to love, and he had given his life with bravery. She could hardly believe it was true.

"I got a letter from the bank yesterday," Esther said, looking down at the earth over the grave. She'd never talked to a grave before, not her *mem* or *mammie's* graves, but talking to Chester's grave comforted her. She had so much left to say. So much to tell him. "The house is being sold to pay the debt."

The wind whistled through the trees that surrounded the small plot of land. Dark snow clouds were visible in the distance.

"I'm not angry," Esther said, then sat in the snow and grass, not caring what her dress would look like when she stood or how cold she might get. She could warm up later. For now, she just wanted to talk with her *dat*. "It's really better this way. The house has so many . . . It doesn't feel right anymore."

She cleared her throat.

"I'm sorry I didn't come to your funeral. I just wasn't up for it," she paused for a moment. "I was at your first one, though."

She smiled, knowing that he would have laughed at her attempted joke.

"The buggy wheel broke this morning. I had to ask one of Norma's farmhands to help me since my hands aren't quite strong enough for man's work yet." The sound of her laugh died in the dense air. "It made me think about you saying that when it rains, it pours. It's definitely been pouring lately." Her voice faded away into the flurry of snowflakes.

"You're the only one I've really spoken to. Everyone still thinks that my throat hasn't healed yet. I just don't want to talk about what happened to every visitor who comes by, so I just stay quiet. When I talk about it—the fire—it takes me back into Dorothy's house that day—so I just let them believe that my throat isn't healed." Why would she ever want to talk about the fire? "I made Angelica and Aunt Lucy promise not to tell Joe. I'll write him when I'm ready."

She paused as if she was waiting for a response from her *dat* even though she knew it would never come.

"What am I supposed to do now?" Esther's tears were warm on her cheeks. "I wish we could have one more conversation."

She had gathered the last of the autumn-blooming flowers that were now covered from the early snowfall for Orpha's grave. She tucked them carefully next to the rustic stone marker. She finally had her son back.

Esther

*T*he winter snow was prettier than she'd ever seen. Like powder. The sun was wrapped in a blanket of clouds, and the field where she stood was peaceful and quiet. Every branch was so covered in white that the horizon couldn't be seen even though she knew it was there.

"Sis soh sheah." *Her dat's voice was serene and collected.*

"Ya," *Esther said, agreeing that the view was pretty. She turned to find the gentle greeting of her dat's eyes. He smiled at her, and as they began walking together, Esther took his hand in hers.*

"Let's go sledding," *she said and heard the voice of a child, suddenly realizing it was her own. All the innocence of her five-year-old self braided together with her adult wisdom. The thought brought a giggle and a skip to her step.*

"I brought it."

Esther turned to see he held a string of twine with his other hand and the rails of the sled began making two long lines behind them. She hadn't noticed it before.

"There's a hill up here." *Detteh pointed.*

The walk seemed long, but she didn't tire. When they got to the hill, she sat on the sled and scooted up to the front. She patted the space behind her with a small mittened hand and invited him to come and sit down.

"Kumm, hoak annah?"

Her dat squatted down at her level. His nose was red with cold, and his eyes were bright and happy.

"It's your turn to ride," he said. "Are you ready?"

"No, I'm not. Why can't you come too? I'm too scared to go by myself."

"Look at the bottom of the hill." He pointed.

Esther looked and was confused at what she saw. Was that the train station at the bottom of the hill? Joe and Daisy were there— waving at her. But why were they there?

"But I'm supposed to be here with you. You just got home." She was an adult again and felt stripped away from the childlike innocence, like a bandage pulled off too quickly.

"You're ready to go, Essie." He smiled at her.

"Why do you want me to leave you? I'm supposed to take care of you." She looked down toward the train station, and the snow made it difficult to see.

"It's time for you to go," Dat said. "All you need is just a little push."

"But I'm afraid." She grabbed his arm. "I'm too afraid."

"Don't be afraid, Essie."

She turned once more to look at her dat and saw Orpha and her mem standing near him. They smiled and waved at her.

The push was gentle but deliberate, and as it built momentum, she gripped the twine in her hands. When the speed frightened her, she pulled back, but it didn't slow her down. She turned around and her dat was still waving.

Esther startled awake, and the silence in the house was deafening. Since the day she'd heard her dat's voice through the thick wooden door and the day he passed from this life to the next, her ears seemed to hear as never before. For weeks her hands were wrapped in bandages, and her throat raw. All she could do was listen. And for the first time in her life, she heard God speak. In those weeks she'd stared at the embroidered verse across from her bed. *Wait in silence.*

She'd grown comfortable in silence, but it was a different kind than had consumed Daisy in her deafness. The little girl's silence meant she couldn't hear. Esther's meant that she could do nothing but hear. But now that she had her hands and her voice back she didn't want to stop hearing everything around her.

Don't be afraid, Essie. Chester's words had been given to her in a dream, but in this moment she heard it in her heart, she knew it was from her other Father. The Father who had neither abandoned nor neglected her. She'd belonged to him all this time and only now could she see it.

It was time to write to Joe.

Esther

The sun had set in Sunrise, and it was Esther's last day in her house. The bank notice would be posted today. She wanted to be there when it happened. When her home became just a house again. When it was no longer hers. It had never really been hers, though, had it?

She sat in the rickety chair next to the table. She'd gathered up all the things that were truly important in her mother's small trunk. She'd taken the few dishes that her mother had loved. The doilies her *mammie* had crocheted. The embroidered wall hanging from her upstairs room: *For God alone, O my soul, wait in silence, for my hope is from Him.* There were some letters and the blanket she'd never fixed after Daisy unraveled it. She kept her *dat*'s hankies and his harmonica. How she wished she'd had his hat and boots, but he'd been wearing them when he ran into the burning house.

Ever since the dream she'd had of her *dat*, she often found him in her sleep. Sometimes she only heard his laughter or saw his smile. Then there was the dream in the snow and him telling her she didn't need to be afraid.

Was it a message from the other side of heaven? Or just a

dream? She would never know but it had given her the comfort she'd desired and had offered her one more push to return to her life.

Everything was in the trunk that sat outside, ready to be moved to Alvin's house. Her cousin had asked her if she'd help him with the children while Dorothy fully recovered. Esther wasn't sure she wanted to return to where her *dat* had died, but she knew her place was to serve and help where she was needed without complaining. The house had been a complete loss, and another had been built in its place. It wasn't completely finished, but it was livable. Living there was only temporary, Esther knew. What came after, she wasn't sure.

It had taken her days to find the right words in a letter to Joe. She hadn't even sent it yet. She didn't want to hand Joe and Daisy her grief now that they were doing so well. Joe was teaching again at a local high school. Literature, he'd said. Daisy was thriving. Her oral skills were far better than Joe had imagined they could be, and she was beginning to learn to read properly. The best part was that she had a classroom filled with friends who were all just like her.

Three knocks came to the door now.

She was surprised that the banker would knock. Or maybe that was him nailing the notice on the front door of her home— the house.

Esther's sigh filled the small kitchen, and suddenly she couldn't stand. Would she make a fool of herself in front of a stranger who didn't care? She closed her eyes. Her mind filled with the memories and voices and sounds.

Esther, Daddy's going to take you fishing. Get your coat.

Merry Christmas! The brown paper tearing, revealing a rag doll her mother had made.

I got the job! Her dad's heavy steps walking across the kitchen.

Esther squealed with delight when he twirled her around. The harmonica playing a tune to lull her to sleep.

Her childhood hadn't always been grim. It had been happy once. This house had been happy once too.

It had become happy again with Daisy's giggle. Her *dat*'s jokes. Joe.

"Esther?"

Her eyes opened. Was this a vision, or was Joe actually standing there in front of her? His hair was a little shorter than in her memory, and it was perfectly groomed. His eyes were bluer and clearer. He wore a tweed suit and a black overcoat and held a black felt hat in his hands.

And here she was, wearing one of her day dresses, the old brown one. And how thin she'd gotten in the last weeks. She must look terrible to him. And the house. It was even emptier than normal, since she had given away everything but the large pieces of furniture, which would stay.

"Joe?"

Joe stepped toward her and knelt down. Her hands were warm in his. He was real.

"You're here?" Esther whispered. She took his face in her hands and touched the curves of his ears and jaw, then returned her hands to his. He was there. Why was he there? "Is everything okay? Where's Daisy?"

Esther looked around him, then back to him.

"I'm fine. Daisy's fine. She's happy but misses you." His eyes roamed her face, and Esther found a thrill of pleasure in his gaze and closeness. "I haven't heard from you in weeks. I was worried so I called Angelica, and she just said that something terrible happened and that I should come."

"Did she tell you what happened?"

"I made her, even though she told me that you wanted to tell me yourself," Joe said. "My darling, why didn't you call me sooner? I would've come right away."

Before Esther could speak she replayed his endearment in her ears. *My darling.*

"I didn't want you to come to pity me," Esther admitted and stifled only part of the sob that rose in her throat.

"You lost your father, my dear. It's tragic, and I'm so sad for you," he said and caressed her face. "I wish I could take all the pain away."

Joe stood and gently brought her to stand with him and then kissed her. His love and touch filled all the empty spaces inside of her. Their lips together were warm and soft, and she let her body melt into his.

When he pulled away, he continued to hold her closely.

"I love you, Esther. I want to take you away from all of this and give you a new life." His voice was hoarse.

Esther couldn't find her voice. Could she say yes this time? Hadn't she written the letter telling Joe that she was ready to begin anew if he still wanted her?

She looked around the house and realized it didn't matter that it was no longer hers. The scene through the window was frozen and cold. The only warmth and heat that she could find was standing in front of her. And he loved her.

"I've lost too much. I even lost you, and I can't lose you again." He shook his head as if trying to find the right words. "But, Esther, do you love me?"

Joe looked into her eyes and searched them for her answer.

"Yes, I love you," she said with a mixture of laughter and tears.

"And you'll marry me? Be my wife?"

Esther smiled and pulled Joe closer. She offered her answer in a kiss. She drank it in and gave herself to the pure pleasure of his touch. Joe's hands pressed against her back and held her so close, and yet it still wasn't close enough.

When they parted, Joe curled Esther's hand around his arm and led her out of the house.

Esther didn't look back as they left that day, but in her heart, strains of a melody that brought the kind of peace that only came from the Promise Keeper:

I sing because I'm happy, I sing because I'm free.
For His eye is on the sparrow, and I know He watches me.

Acknowledgments

In closing this series there are so many people that come to mind. *Promise to Keep* was a bittersweet story for me. My time in Sunrise, Delaware, has been something out of my dreams. I'll miss Sunrise and my friends there. I learned a lot about my heritage and my family. I am so proud of their bravery and the legacy they have given me and the generations to come.

For my thank-yous . . .

—to the reader, I'm honored that you've picked up this book. I appreciate you. It truly is for you that I write.

—to Davis, you rock so much. Seriously. No one compares to you.

—to Felicity and Mercy, you earned a lot of plastic coins in the writing of this novel. XOXO

—to Natasha, my amazing literary agent, you gave me the confidence I needed to get through these edits. I'm so thankful for your belief in me!

—to Beth Adams, I simply couldn't ask for a better editor. You know my voice. You get me. You're amazing.

—to the team at Howard Books who have put such an effort into this book and my series: Amanda Demastus, Bruce Gore, the marketing staff, and the copyeditors and line editors who fix all my misplaced commas and keep me on track.

—to my amazing extended family who respond like normal people when I text like a lunatic during deadline weeks.

—to so many friends who lovingly support me with such encouragement. I wish I could thank you all by name. I would be remiss to not mention several who were especially supportive in this process. *Kelly Long*, our weekly meetings keep me sane. You're such a *Charlotte* in my life. *Carla Laureano*, are we twins? To quote a very wise phone case: God made us friends because no mom could handle us as sisters. *Alicia Vaca*, you have fed me so much that one of these days you may find that I've moved into your house.

—to my parents. I dedicate this book to you, Mom and Dad—the real Esther and Joe. While *Promise to Keep* is a work of fiction, I know that without you both, this story would not exist.

—to my influencer team, you bring me such encouragement. Your cheering me on is humbling. I am so blessed by each of you. Jennifer Naybr gets a very special shout-out. Thank you for all you do.

—to God. It seems cliché to leave my final acknowledgment to God. But I just don't know how not to do that with the completion of this series. Through writing The Promise of Sunrise series He has shaped me like a piece of clay. It wasn't easy and it wasn't always fun, but it was always with purpose. I'm so thankful I have a God who knows me so well.